César Cas

Jules Gabriel Verne

Volume 35 of 54 in the

"Voyages Extraordinaires"

First published in 1890.

2013 Reprint by Kassock Bros. Publishing Co.

Printed in the United States Of America

Cover Illustration By Isaac M. Kassock

ISBN: 1482584077
ISBN-13: 978-1482584073

Jules Gabriel Verne (1828-1905)

The Extraordinary Voyages
of
Jules Verne
~

Table of Contents

CÉSAR CASCABEL

Jules Verne

PART ONE

CHAPTER I - A FORTUNE REALIZED

"HAS nobody got any more coppers to give me? Come, children, search your pockets!"

"Here you are, father!" replied the little girl.

And she drew out of her pocket a square-cut piece of greenish paper, all crumpled and greasy.

This paper bore the almost illegible inscription "United States Fractional Currency," encircling the respectable-looking head of a gentleman in a frock-coat, and likewise the figure 10 repeated six times,—which represented ten cents, say about ten French sous.

"How did you come by that?" inquired the mother.

"It's the remnant of the takings at the last performance," answered Napoleona.

"Gave me everything, Sander?"

"Yes, father."

"Nothing left, John?"

"Nothing."

"Why, how much more do you want, César?" asked Cornelia of her husband.

"Two cents is all we want to make up a round sum," replied Cascabel.

"Here they are, boss," said Clovy, jerking up a small copper coin that he had just worked out from the depths of his waistcoat pocket.

"Well done, Clovy!" exclaimed the little girl.

"That's right! now we're all square," cried Mr. Cascabel.

And they were indeed "all square," to use the words of the honest showman. The total in hands amounted to nearly two thousand dollars, say ten thousand francs. Ten thousand francs! Is not such a sum a fortune, when it has been earned out of the public through one's own talents only?

Cornelia put her arms around her husband's neck; the children embraced him in their turn.

"Now," said Mr. Cascabel, "the question is to buy a chest, a beautiful chest with secret contrivances, to lock up our fortune in it."

"Can't we really do without it?" suggested Mrs. Cascabel, somewhat alarmed at this expenditure.

"Cornelia, we cannot!"

"Perhaps a little box might do us?—"

"That's woman all over!" sneered Mr. Cascabel. "A little box is meant for jewels! A chest, or at least a safe, that's the thing for money! And as we have a long way to go with our ten thousand francs—"

"Well then, go and buy your safe, but take care you get a good bargain," interrupted Cornelia.

The "boss of the show" opened the door of that "superb and consequential" wagon, his itinerant dwelling-house; he went down the iron step fastened to the shaft, and made for the streets that converge toward the center of Sacramento.

February is a cold month in California, although this State lies in the same latitude as Spain. Still, wrapped up in his warm overcoat lined with imitation sable, and with his fur cap drawn down to his ears, Mr. Cascabel little cared about the weather, and tripped it lightly. A safe! being the owner of a safe had been his life-long dream; that dream was on the point of being realized at last!

Nineteen years before, the land now occupied by the town of Sacramento was but a vast barren plain. In the middle stood a small fort, a kind of block-house erected by the early settlers, the first traders, with a view to protect their encampments against the attacks of the Far West Indians. But since that time, after the Americans had taken California from the Mexicans, who were incapable of defending it, the aspect of the country had undergone a singular transformation. The small fort had made way for a town,—one of the most important in the United States, although fire and flood had, more than once, destroyed the rising city.

Now, in this year 1867, Mr. Cascabel had no longer to dread the raids of Indian tribes, or even the attacks of that lawless mob of cosmopolitan banditti who invaded the province in 1849 on the discovery of the gold mines which lay a little farther to the northeast, on the Grass Valley plateau, and of the famous Allison ranch mine, the quartz of which yielded twenty cents' worth of the precious metal for every two pound weight.

Yes, those days of unheard-of strokes of fortune, of unspeakable reverses, of nameless sorrows, were over. No more gold-seekers, not even in that portion of British Columbia, the Cariboo, to which thousands of miners flocked, about 1863. No longer was Mr. Cascabel exposed, on his travels, to being robbed of that little fortune which he had earned, well might it be said, in the sweat of his body, and that he carried in the pocket of his overcoat. In truth, the purchase of a safe was not so indispensable to the security of his fortune as he claimed it to be; if he was so desirous to get one, it was with an eye to a long journey through certain Far West territories that were less safe than California,—his journey homeward toward Europe.

Thus easy in his mind, Mr. Cascabel wended his way through the wide, clean streets of the town. Here and there were splendid squares, overhung with beautiful, though still leafless, trees, hotels and private dwellings built with much elegance and comfort, public edifices in the Anglo-Saxon style of architecture, a number of monumental churches, all giving an air of grandeur to this, the capital town of California. On all sides bustled busy looking men, merchants, ship-owners, manufacturers, some awaiting the arrival of vessels that sailed up and down the river whose waters flow to the Pacific, others besieging Folsom depot, from which numerous trains steamed away to the interior of the Confederacy.

It was toward High Street that Mr. Cascabel directed his steps, whistling a French march as he went along. In this street he had already noticed the store of a rival of Fichet & Huret, the celebrated Parisian safe-makers. There did William J. Morlan sell "good and cheap,"—at least, relatively so,— considering the excessive price that is charged for everything in the United States of America.

William J. Morlan was in his store when Mr. Cascabel came in.

"Mr. Morlan," said the latter, "your humble servant. I'd like to buy a safe."

William J. Morlan knew Cæser Cascabel: was there a man in Sacramento who did not? Had he not been, for three weeks past, the delight of the population? So, the worthy manufacturer made answer:

"A safe, Mr. Cascabel?—Pray accept all my congratulations—"

"What for?"

"Because buying a safe is a sure sign that a man has a few sackfuls of dollars to make safe in it."

"Right you are, Mr. Morlan."

"Well, take this one;" and the merchant's finger pointed to a huge safe, worthy of a site in the offices of Rothschild Brothers or other such bankers, people who have enough and to spare.

"Come—not so fast!" said Mr. Cascabel. "I could take lodging's in there for myself and family!—A real gem, to be sure; but for the time being, I've got something else to lodge in it!—Say, Mr. Morlan, how much money could be stored inside that monster?"

"Several millions in gold."

6

"Several millions?—Well then—I'll call again—some other day, when I have them! No, sir, what I want is a really strong little chest that I can carry under my arm and hide away down in my wagon when I am on the road."

"I have just the thing, Mr. Cascabel."

And the manufacturer exhibited a small coffer supplied with a safety lock. It was not over twenty pounds in weight, and had compartments inside, after the manner of the cash or deed boxes used in banking-houses.

"This, moreover, is fireproof," added he, "and I warrant it as such on the receipt I give you."

"Very good!—can't be better!" answered Mr. Cascabel. "That will do me, so long as you guarantee the lock is all right."

"It is a combination lock," interrupted William J. Morlan. "Four letters—a word of four letters, to be made out of four alphabets, which gives you well-nigh four hundred thousand combinations. During the time it would take a thief to guess them, you might hang him a million times at your ease!"

"A million times, Mr. Morlan? That's wonderful indeed! And what about the price? You'll understand, a safe is too dear when it costs more than a man has to put in it!"

"Quite so, Mr. Cascabel. And all I'll ask you for this one is six and a half."

"Six and a half dollars?" rejoined Cascabel. "I don't care for that 'six and a half.' Come, Mr. Morlan, we must knock the corners off that sum! Is it a bargain at five dollars straight?"

"I don't mind, because it is you, Mr. Cascabel."

The purchase was made, the money was paid down, and W. J. Morlan offered to the showman to have his safe brought home for him, so as not to trouble him with such a burden.

"Come, come, Mr. Morlan! A man like your humble servant who juggles with forty-pounders!"

"Say—what is the exact weight of your forty-pounders, eh?" inquired Mr. Morlan with a laugh.

"Just fifteen pounds, but—mum's the word!"

Thereupon William J. Morlan and his customer parted, delighted with each other.

Half an hour later, the happy possessor of the safe reached Circus Place where his wagon stood, and laid down, not without a feeling of complacency, "the safe of the Cascabel firm."

7

Ah! how admired was that safe in its little world! What joy and pride all felt at having it! And how the hinges were worked with the opening and the shutting of it! Young Sander would have dearly liked to dislocate himself into it—just for fun. But that was not to be thought of; it was too small for young Sander!

As to Clovy, never had he seen anything so beautiful, even in dreamland.

"I guess, that lock's no easy job to open," exclaimed he, "unless it's mighty easy if it doesn't shut right!"

"Never a truer word did you speak," answered Mr. Cascabel.

Then, in that authoritative tone of voice that brooks no arguing, and with one of those significant gestures which forbid of any delaying:

"Now, children, off you go, the shortest cut," said he, "and fetch us a breakfast—Ah! Here is a dollar you can spend as you like—It's I will stand the treat to-day!"

Good soul! As though it were not he who "stood the treat" every day! But he was fond of this kind of joking, which he indulged in with a good genial chuckle.

In a trice, John, Sander, and Napoleona were off, accompanied by Clovy, who carried on his arm a large straw basket for the provisions.

"And now we are alone, Cornelia, let us have a few words," said the boss.

"What about, César?"

"What about? Why, about the word we are going to choose for the lock of our safe. It is not that I don't trust the children—Good Lord! They are angels! —or that poor fellow Clovy, who is honesty itself! None the less, that must be kept a secret."

"Take what word you like," answered the wife; "I'll agree to anything you say."

"You have no choice?"

"I haven't."

"Well, I should like it to be a proper name."

"Yes!—I got it—your own name, César."

"That can't be! Mine is too long! It must be a word of four letters only."

"Well then, take one letter off! Surely you can spell Cæser without an r! We are free to do as we like, I dare say!"

"Bravo, Cornelia! That's an idea!—One of those ideas you often hit on, wifie! But if we decide on cutting one letter out of a name, I'd rather cut out four, and let it be out of yours!"

"Out of my name?"

"Yes! And we'd keep the end of it—e l i a. Indeed, I rather think it would be more select that way; so, it will be just the thing!"

"Ah! César!"

"It will please you, wont it, to have your name on the lock of our safe?"

"It will, since it is in your heart already!" answered Cornelia, with loving emphasis.

Then, her face beaming with pleasure, she gave a hearty kiss to her good-natured husband.

And that is how, in consequence of this arrangement, any one, unacquainted with the name Elia, would be baffled in his attempts to open the safe of the Cascabel family.

Half an hour after, the children were back with the provisions, ham and salt beef, cut in appetizing slices, not forgetting a few of those wonderful outgrowths of Californian vegetation, heads of cabbage grown on tree-like stalks, potatoes as large as melons, carrots half a yard long and "equaled only," Mr. Cascabel was fond of saying, "by those leeks that you make people swallow, without having the trouble of growing them?" As to drink, the only puzzle was which to choose among the varieties that nature and art offer to American thirsty lips. On this occasion, not to mention a jugful of beer with a head on it, each one was to have his share of a good bottle of sherry, at dessert.

In the twinkling of an eye, Cornelia, aided by Clovy, her usual help, had prepared breakfast. The table was laid in the second compartment of the van, styled the family parlor, where the temperature was maintained at the right degree by the cooking-stove set up in the next room. If, on that day,—as on every day indeed,—father, mother, and children ate with remarkably keen appetite, the fact was but too easily accounted for by the circumstances.

Breakfast over, Mr. Cascabel, assuming the solemn tone that he gave to his utterances when he spoke to the public, expressed himself as follows:

"To-morrow, children, we shall have bidden farewell to this noble town of Sacramento, and to its noble citizens, with all of whom we have every reason to be satisfied, whatever be their complexion, red, black or white. But, Sacramento is in California, and California is in America, and America is not in Europe. Now, home is home, and Europe is France; and it is not a day too

9

soon, that France should see us once more 'within its walls,' after a prolonged absence of many a year. Have we made a fortune? Properly speaking, we have not. Still, we have in hands a certain quantity of dollars that will look uncommonly well in our safe, when we have changed them into French gold or silver. A portion of this sum will enable us to cross the Atlantic Ocean on one of those swift vessels that fly the three-colored flag once borne by Napoleon from capital to capital.—Your health, Cornelia!"

Mrs. Cascabel acknowledged with a bow this token of good feeling which her husband often gave her, as though he meant to thank her for having presented him with Alcides and Hercules in the persons of his children.

Then, the speaker proceeded:

"I likewise drink 'safe home' to us all! May favorable winds swell our sails!"

He paused to pour to each one a last glass of his excellent sherry.

"But then,—Clovy may say to me, perhaps,—once our passage-money paid, there will be nothing left in the safe?"

"No such thing, boss,—unless the passage-money added on to the railway fares—"

"Railways, railroads, as the Yankees say!" cried Mr. Cascabel. "Why, you simpleton, you thoughtless fellow, we shan't use them! I quite intend saving the traveling expenses from Sacramento to New York by covering the distance on our own wheels! A few hundred leagues! I guess it would take more than that to frighten the Cascabel family, accustomed as it is to disport itself from one world's end to the other!"

"Of course!" John chimed in.

"And how glad we shall be to see France again!" exclaimed Mrs. Cascabel.

"Our old France that you don't know, my children," continued Mr. Cascabel, "since you were born in America, our beautiful France that you shall know at last. Ah, Cornelia, what pleasure it will be for you, a child of Provence, and for me, a son of Normandy, after twenty years' absence!"

"It will, Cæser, it will!"

"Do you know, Cornelia? If I were to be offered an engagement now, even at Barnum's theater, I should say no! Putting off our journey home, never! I'd rather go on all fours!—It's homesick we are, and what's needed for that ailment is a trip home!—I know of no other cure!"

10

César Cascabel spoke truly. His wife and he no longer cherished but one thought: returning to France; and what bliss it was to be able to do so, now that there was no lack of money!

"So then, we start to-morrow!" said Mr. Cascabel.

"And it may be our last trip!" remarked Cornelia.

"Cornelia," her husband said with dignity, "the only last trip I know of is the one for which God issues no return ticket!"

"Just so, César, but before that one, shan't we have a rest, when we have made our fortune?"

"A rest, Cornelia? Never! I don't want any of your fortune, if fortune means doing nothing! Do you think you have a right to lay those talents idly by, that nature has so freely lavished on you? Do you imagine I could live with folded arms and run the risk of letting my joints grow stiff? Do you see John giving up his work as an equilibrist, Napoleona ceasing to dance on the tight rope with or without a pole, Sander standing no more on top of the human pyramid, and Clovy himself no longer receiving his half-dozen dozen slaps on his cheeks per minute, to the great gratification of the public? No, Cornelia! Tell me that the sun's light will be put out by the rain, that the sea will be drunk by the fishes, but do not tell me that the hour of rest will ever strike for the Cascabel family!"

And now, there was nothing more to do but to make the final arrangements for setting out, next morning, as soon as the sun would peep over the horizon of Sacramento.

This was done in the course of the afternoon.

Needless to say the safe was placed out of the way, in the furthest compartment of the wagon.

"In this room," said Mr. Cascabel, "we shall be able to watch it night and day!"

"Really, César, I think that was a good idea of yours," remarked Cornelia, "and I don't begrudge the money we spent on the safe."

"It may be rather small, perhaps, wifie, but we shall buy a bigger one, if our treasure takes larger proportions!"

CHAPTER II - THE CASCABEL FAMILY

CASCABEL!—A name, you might say, "pealed and chimed on all the tongues of fame," throughout the five parts of the globe, and "other localities," proudly added the man who bore that patronymic so honorably.

César Cascabel, a native of Pontorson, right in the heart of Normandy, was a master in all the dodges, knacks, and trickeries of Norman folks. But, sharp and knowing as he was, he had remained an honest man, and it were not right to confound him with the too often suspicious members of the juggling confraternity; in him, humbleness of birth and professional irregularities were fully redeemed by the private virtues of the head of the family circle.

At this period, Mr. Cascabel looked his age, forty-five, not a day more or less. A child of the road in the full acceptation of the word, his only cradle had been the pack that his father shouldered as he tramped along from fairs to markets throughout Normandy. His mother having died shortly after his coming into the world, he had been very opportunely adopted by a traveling troupe on the death of his father, a few years after. With them he spent his youth in tumbles, contortions and somersaults, his head down and his feet in the air. Then he became in turn a clown, a gymnast, an acrobat, a Hercules at country fairs,—until the time when, the father of three children, he appointed himself manager of the little family he had brought out conjointly with Mrs. Cascabel, nee Cornelia Vadarasse, all the way from Martigues in Provence (France).

An intelligent and ingenious man, if on the one hand his muscle and his skill were above the common, his moral worth was in no way inferior to his physical abilities. True, a rolling stone gathers no moss; but, at least, it rubs against the rough knobs on the road, it gets polished, its angles are smoothed off, it grows round and shiny. Even so, in the course of the twenty-five years that he had been rolling along, Cæser Cascabel had rubbed so hard, had got so thoroughly polished and rounded off, that he knew about all that can be known of life, felt surprised at nothing, wondered at nothing. By dint of roughing it through Europe from fair to fair, and acclimatizing himself quite as readily in America as in the Dutch or the Spanish Colonies, he wellnigh understood all languages, and spoke them more or less accurately, "even those he did not know," as he used to say, for it was no trouble to him to express his meaning by gestures whenever his power of speech failed him.

Cæser Cascabel was a trifle above the middle height; his body was muscular; his limbs were "well oiled"; his lower jaw, somewhat protruding, indicated energy; his head was large, and shagged over with bushy hair, his skin marbled by the sun of every clime, tanned by the squalls of every sea; he wore a mustache cut short at the ends, and half-length whiskers shaded his ruddy cheeks; his nose was rather full; he had blue eyes glowing with life and very keen, with a look of kindness in them; his mouth would have boasted thirty-three teeth still, had he got one put in, Before the public, he was a real Frederic Lemaitre, a tragedian with grand gestures, affected poses, and oratorical sentences, but in private, a very simple, very natural man, who doted on his wife and children.

Blessed with a constitution that could stand anything, although his advancing years now forbade him all acrobatic performances, he was still wonderful in those displays of strength that "require biceps." He was possessed, moreover, of extraordinary talent in that branch of the showman's profession, the science of the engastrimuth or ventriloquism, a science which goes back a good many centuries if, as Bishop Eustachius asserts, the pythoness of Edon was nothing more than a ventriloquist. At his will his vocal apparatus slipped down from his throat to his stomach. You wonder if he could have sung a duet, all by himself? Well, you had better not have challenged him to!

To give one last stroke to this picture, let us notice that Cæser Cascabel had a weakness for the great conquerors of history in general, and for Napoleon in particular. Yes! He did love the hero of the first Empire just as much as he hated his "tormentors," those sons of Hudson Lowe, those abominable John Bulls. Napoleon! That was "the man for him!" Wherefore he had never consented to perform before the Queen of England, "although she had requested him to do so through her first Steward of the Household," a statement he had made so earnestly and so repeatedly that he had eventually acquired a belief in it, himself.

And still, Mr. Cascabel was no circus manager; no Franconi was he with a troupe of horsemen and women, of clowns and jugglers. By no means. He was merely a showman, performing on the public commons in the open air when the weather was fine, and under a tent when it rained. At this business, of which he had known the ups and downs for a quarter of a century, he had earned, as we know, the goodly lump sum just now put away in the safe with the combination lock.

What labor, what toils, what misery at times, had gone to the making up of this sum! The hardest was now over. The Cascabels were preparing to return to Europe. After they had crossed the United States, they would take passage on a French or an American vessel,—an English one—no, never!

As to that, Cæser Cascabel never let himself be beaten by anything. Obstacles were a myth for him. Difficulties, at most, did turn up on his path; but, extricating, disentangling himself through life was his speciality. He had gladly repeated the words of the Duke of Dantzic, one of the marshals of his great man:

"You make a hole for me, and I'll make my way through it."

13

And many indeed were the holes he had wriggled through!

"Mrs. Cascabel, née Cornelia Vadarasse, a genuine native of Provence, the unequaled clairvoyant of things to come, the queen of electrical women, adorned with all the charms of her sex, graced with all the virtues that are a mother's pride, the champion of the great female tournaments to which Chicago challenged the 'first athletes of the universe.'"

Such were the terms in which Mr. Cascabel usually introduced his wife to the public. Twenty years before, he had married her in New York. Had he taken his father's advice in the matter? He had not! Firstly, he said, because his father had not consulted him in reference to his own wedding, and, secondly, because the worthy man was no longer on this planet. And the thing had been done in a very simple way, I can tell you, and without any of those preliminary formalities which, in Europe, prove such drawbacks to the speedy union of two beings predestined for one another.

One evening, at Barnum's theater in Broadway, where he was one of the spectators, César Cascabel was dazzled by the charms, the agility and the strength shown in horizontal bar exercises by a young French acrobat, Mlle. Cornelia Vadarasse.

Associating his own talents with those of this graceful performer, of their two lives making but one, foreseeing yonder in the future a family of little Cascabels worthy of their father and mother, all this appeared as if mapped out before the honest showman's eye. Rushing behind the scenes between two acts, introducing himself to Cornelia Vadarasse with the fairest proposals in view of the wedding of a Frenchman and a Frenchwoman; then, eyeing a respectable clergyman in the audience, hauling him off to the green-room and asking him to bless the union of so well-matched a couple, that is all that was needed in that happy land of the United States of America. Do those life-contracts, sealed with full steam on, turn out the worse for it? Be the answer what it may, the union of Cascabel and Cornelia Vadarasse was to be one of the happiest ever celebrated in this nether world.

At the time when our story begins, Mrs. Cascabel was forty years old. She had a fine figure, rather stoutish perhaps, dark hair, dark eyes, a smiling mouth, and, like her husband, a good show of teeth. As to her uncommon muscular strength, she had proved it in those memorable Chicago encounters, where she had won a "Chignon of honor" as a prize. Let us add that Cornelia still loved her husband as she did on the first day, feeling as she did an unshakable trust, an absolute faith in the genius of this extraordinary man, one of the most remarkable beings ever produced by Normandy.

The first-born of our itinerant performers was a boy, John, now nineteen years old. If he did not take after his parents with regard to muscle or to the performances of a gymnast, an acrobat or a clown, he showed his true blood by a wonderfully dexterous hand and an eye ever sure of its aim, two gifts that made him a graceful, elegant juggler. Nor was his success marred with self-conscious pride. He was a gentle, thoughtful youth with blue eyes, and dark-complexioned like his mother. Studious and reserved, he sought to improve himself wherever and whenever he could. Though not ashamed of his parents' profession, he felt there was something better to do than performing in public, and he looked forward to giving up the craft as soon as he would be in France. At the same time his genuine love for his father and his mother prompted him to keep extremely reserved on this subject; indeed, besides, what prospects had he of making another position for himself in the world?

Then, there was the second boy, the last but one of the children, the contortionist of the troupe. He was really the logical joint-product of the Cascabel couple. Twelve years old, as nimble as a cat, as handy as a monkey, as lively as an eel, a little three-foot-six clown who had tumbled into this world heels over head, so his father said, a real gamin as ready-witted as full of fun and frolic, and a good heart withal, sometimes deserving of a thump on his head, but taking it with a grin, for it was never a very hard one.

It was stated above that the eldest scion of the Cascabels was called John. Whence came this name? The mother had insisted upon it in memory of one of her grand-uncles, Jean Vadarasse, a sailor from Marseilles, who had been eaten by the Caribbean islanders, an exploit she was proud of. To be sure, the father who had the good luck to have been christened Cæser, would have preferred another name, one better known in history and more in accordance with his secret admiration for warriors. But he was unwilling to thwart his wife's wishes on the advent of their first-born, and he had accepted the name John, promising himself to make up for it, should a second heir be born to him.

This event came to pass, and the second son was called Alexander, after having a narrow escape of being named Hamilcar, Attila, or Hannibal. For shortness sake, however, he was familiarly known as Sander.

After the first and the second boy, the family circle was joined by a little girl who received the name of Napoleona, in honor of the martyr at St. Helena, although Mrs. Cascabel would have loved to call her Hersilla.

Napoleona was now eight years old. She was a pretty child, with every promise of growing to be a handsome girl, and a handsome girl she did become. Fair and rosy, with a bright, animated countenance, graceful and clever, she had mastered the art of tight-rope walking; her tiny feet seemed to glide along the wire for play, as though the little sylph had had wings to bear her up.

It were idle to say Napoleona was the spoilt child of the family. She was worshipped by all, and she was fit to be. Her mother fondly cherished the thought that she would make a grand match some day. Is not that one of the contingencies of these people's nomadic life? Why might not Napoleona, grown up into a handsome young girl, come across a prince who would fall in love with her, and marry her?

"Just as in fairytales?" Mr. Cascabel would suggest, his turn of mind being more practical than his wife's.

"No, Cæser, just as in real life."

"Alas, Cornelia, the time is gone when kings married shepherdesses, and, my word! in these days of ours, I have yet to know that shepherdesses would consent to marry kings!"

Such was the Cascabel family, father, mother and three children. It might have been better perhaps, if a fourth olive branch had increased the number, seeing there are certain human-pyramid exercises in which the artists climb on top of each other in even numbers. But this fourth member did not appear.

Luckily, Clovy was there, the very man to lend a hand on extraordinary occasions.

In truth, Clovy was the complement of the Cascabels. He was not one of the show, he was one of the family; and he had every claim to the membership, an American though he was by birth. He was one of those poor wretches, one of those "nobody's children," born Heaven knows where,—they hardly know it themselves,—brought up by charity, fed as luck will have it, and taking the right road in life, if they happen to be rightly inclined, if their innate sense of what is good enables them to resist the evil examples and the evil promptings of their miserable surroundings. And should we not feel some pity for these unfortunates if, in the majority of cases, they are led to evil deeds, and come to an evil end?

Such was not the case with Ned Harley, on whom Mr. Cascabel had thought it funny to bestow the name of Clovy. And why? First, because he had as much spare fat about him as a dried clove; second, because he was engaged to receive, during the "parades," a greater number of five-fingered stingers than any cruciferous shrub could produce of cloves in a year!

Two years before, when Mr. Cascabel lighted upon him, in his round through the States, the unfortunate man was at death's door through starvation. The troupe of acrobats, to which he belonged, had just broken up, the manager having run away. With them, he was in the "minstrels," a sad business, even when it manages to pay, or nearly so, for the food of the wretch who plies it! Daubing your face with boot-blacking, "niggering" yourself, as they say; putting on a black coat and pants, a white vest and necktie; then singing stupid songs whilst scraping on a ludicrous fiddle in company with four or five outcasts of your kin, what a position that is in

16

society! Well, Ned Harley had just lost that social position; and he was but too happy to meet Providence on his path, in the person of Mr. Cascabel.

It happened just then that the latter had lately dismissed the artist who generally played the clown in the parade scenes. Will it ever be believed? This clown had passed himself off as an American, and was in reality of English origin! A John Bull in the troupe! A countryman of those heartless tormentors who—The rest of the story is known. One day, by mere chance, Mr. Cascabel heard of the intruder's nationality.

"Mr. Waldurton," said he to him, "since you are an Englishman, you'll take yourself off this very moment, or else it's not my hand on your face you shall get, a clown though you be!"

And a clown though he was, it is the tip of a boot he would have felt if he had not disappeared instantly.

It was then that Clovy stepped into the vacant berth. The late "minstrel" now engaged himself as a "man of all work"; he would perform on the boards, groom the horses, or, just as readily, do the kitchen work, whenever the mistress needed a helping hand. Naturally, he spoke French, but with a very strong accent.

He still was, on the whole, a simple-minded fellow, though now five-and-thirty years of age, as full of mirth when he gratified the public with his drolleries as he was melancholy in private life. He was rather inclined to view things on their dark side; and, to be candid, that was not to be wondered at, for it would have been hard for him to look upon himself as one of the favored ones here below. With his tapering head, his long-drawn face, his yellowish hair, his round, sheepish eyes, his phenomenal nose on which he was able to place half a dozen pairs of spectacles, a great source of laughter,—his flabby ears, his long neck like a stork's, his thin body stuck up on skeleton legs, he looked indeed a strange being. Still, he was not a man to complain, unless—this was his favorite way of qualifying a statement,—unless ill-luck gave him cause to complain. In addition, ever since his joining the Cascabels, he had become greatly attached to the good people, and they, on their part, could not have done without their Clovy.

Such was, if it may be put thus, the human element in this itinerant troupe.

As to the animal element, it was represented by two fine dogs, a spaniel—a first-rate hunter and a reliable watch-dog for the house on wheels—and a clever, intelligent poodle, sure to become a member of the "Institute," whenever the intellectual powers of the canine race are rewarded in France on a par with those of men.

Next to the two dogs, it is right we should introduce to the public a little ape that proved a worthy rival of Clovy himself when they vied with one another

17

in distorting their faces, and puzzled the spectators as to who should carry off the palm. Then, there was a parrot, Jako, a native of Java, who talked and prattled and sang and jabbered ten hours out of twelve, thanks to the teaching of his friend Sander. Lastly two horses, two good old horses, drew the wagon, and God knows if their legs, somewhat stiffened with years, had been stretched out over the miles and miles they had measured across country.

And, should you care to know the names of these two good steeds? One was called Vermont like Mr. Delamarre's winning horse, the other Gladiator like Count de Lagrange's.

Yes, they bore those names so famous on the French turf; yet they never had a thought of getting themselves entered for the Paris Grand Prix.

As to the dogs, they were called: the spaniel, Wagram, the poodle, Marengo; and, no need to tell who the godfather was to whom they were indebted for those renowned historical names.

The ape—why, he had been christened John Bull, for the simple reason that he was ugly.

What can be done? We must overlook this mania of Mr. Cascabel's, proceeding as it did, after all, from a patriotic sentiment which is very pardonable—even though at an epoch when such strong feelings are but little justified.

"Were it possible," he would say sometimes, "not to worship the man who exclaimed under a shower of bullets: 'Follow the white feather on my hat; you will ever find it, etc?'"

And, when he would be reminded that it was Henry IV who had uttered those beautiful words:

"That may be," he would reply; "but Napoleon could have said as much!"

18

CHAPTER III - THE SIERRA NEVADA

HOW many people have had dreams, at one time or other, of a journey performed in a movable house, after gypsy fashion! of a journey exempt of all worry concerning hotels, and inns, and unreliable beds, and still more unreliable cooks, when the country to be traversed is no more than besprinkled with hamlets or villages! That which wealthy amateurs do daily on board their pleasure yachts, surrounded by all the comfort of their transplanted home, few are the people who have done it by means of a vehicle ad hoc. And still, is not a carriage a movable house? Why do gypsies enjoy a monopoly of the pleasures of "yachting on terra firma?"

In reality, the showman's wagon constitutes a complete flat, with its various rooms and furniture; it is "home" on wheels; and Cæser Cascabel's was beautifully adapted to the requirements of his gypsy life.

The *Fair Rambler* was the name they had given it, as though it were a Norman schooner; and that name was justified after so many peregrinations through the length and breadth of the United States. They had bought it three years ago, with the first money they had saved, as a substitute for the old primitive van, just covered over with an awning and unsupported by a single spring, that had nestled them so long. Now, as it was over twenty years since Mr. Cascabel had begun visiting the fairs and markets of the United States, it is needless to say his wagon was of American manufacture.

The *Fair Rambler* rested on four wheels. Supplied with good steel springs, it combined lightness with strength. Well looked after, scrubbed and washed with soap, it shone in all the glow of its brightly-painted panels on which gold yellow blended harmoniously with cochineal red, and displayed to the public gaze the already famous trade name and mark:

THE CÉSAR CASCABEL FAMILY.

As to length, it would have been a match for those wagons that still ply the prairies of the Far West, in parts where the Great Trunk Railroad has not hitherto pushed its way. It is evident that two horses could only walk with so heavy a vehicle. In truth the load was no light one. Not to speak of its inhabitants, did not the *Fair Rambler* convey, on its roof, the canvas for the tent, and the poles, and the ropes, and, underneath between the fore and the hind wheels, a swinging board laden with various articles, a large drum and a smaller one, a horn, a trombone and other utensils and accessories, the real tools of the showman? Let us put on record likewise the costumes of a noted pantomine, "The Brigands of the Black Forest," on the repertory of the Cascabel family.

The internal arrangements were well devised, and we need not add that scrupulous cleanliness, Flemish cleanliness, reigned supreme, thanks to Cornelia, who could stand no trifling in this respect.

In the fore part, closing by means of a sliding glass-door, was the first compartment heated by the cooking-stove. Next came a drawing or dining-room, where the fortune-teller gave her consultations; then a bed-room with bunks, superposed on each other as on board ship, which, with a curtain for a division, afforded sleeping accommodation, on the right to the two brothers, and on the left to their little sister; lastly at the further end, Mr. and Mrs. Cascabel's room. Here, a bed with thick mattresses and a patchwork quilt, near which the famous safe had been deposited. All the recesses were taken up with little boards on hinges, which might be used as tables or toilet-stands, or with narrow cupboards where the costumes, the wigs and the false beards for the pantomine, were put by. The whole was lighted by two paraffine lamps, veritable ship lamps that swung to and fro with the motion of the vehicle when the roads were unlevel; moreover, so as to allow the light of day to penetrate the various compartments, half a dozen little windows, with lead-cased panes, light muslin curtains and colored bands, gave to the *Fair Rambler* the appearance of the saloon on a Dutch galliot.

Clovy, naturally easy to please, slept in the first compartment, on a hammock that he hung up at night and took down at day-break next morning.

We have yet to mention that the two dogs, Wagram and Marengo, in consequence of their being on night-duty, slept among the baggage under the wagon, where they tolerated the company of John Bull, the ape, in spite of his restlessness and his propensity for playing tricks, and that Jako, the parrot, was housed in a cage hooked on to the ceiling in the second compartment.

As to the horses, Gladiator and Vermont, they were quite free to graze round about the *Fair Rambler* nor was there any necessity to fetter them. And when they had done cropping the grass of those vast prairies where their table was ever laid, and their bed, or rather their litter ever ready, they had only to pick out a spot whereon to lay themselves to sleep, on the very ground that had supplied them with food.

One thing certain is, that, when night had closed around, what with the guns and the revolvers of its occupants, what with the two dogs that kept watch over it, the *Fair Rambler* was in perfect safety.

Such was this family coach. How many a mile it had rambled along for the past three years through the States, from New York to Albany, from Niagara to Buffalo, to St. Louis, to Philadelphia, to Boston, to Washington, down the Mississippi to New Orleans, all along the Great Trunk, up to the Rocky Mountains, to the Mormon district, to the furthermost ends of California! A healthy mode of traveling, if ever there was one, seeing that not one member of the little troupe had ever been ill, save and except John Bull, whose fits of indigestion were anything but few, his instinctive knavery making it easy for him to satisfy his inconceivable gluttony.

And how glad they would be to bring back the *Fair Rambler* to Europe, to drive it along on the highways of the old continent! What sympathetic curiosity it would awaken as it went through France, through the village homesteads of Normandy! Ah! seeing France again, "seeing his Normandie once more" as in Berat's well-known song, such was the aim of all César Cascabel's thoughts, the goal of all his aspirations.

Once in New York, the wagon was to be taken to pieces, packed up and put on board ship for Havre, where it would only need to be set up on its wheels again, to ramble away toward the French capital.

How Mr. Cascabel, his wife and children, longed to be off! and so, doubtless, did their companions, their four-footed friends we might say. That is why, at day-break, on the 15th of February, they left Circus Place in Sacramento, some on foot, others riding, each one to his fancy.

The temperature was very cool still, but it was fine weather. It may be surmised the anchor was not weighed without a due supply of biscuits on board, or if you like, without various preserves of meat and vegetables. As to that, it was an easy matter to renew the stocks in the towns and villages. And then, was not the country swarming with game, buffaloes, deer, hares and partridges? And would John be sparing of his gun or his shot when shooting was subject to no restriction, when no European gun license was demanded in those boundless wilds of the Far West? And a dead shot was John, I tell you; and Wagram, the spaniel, showed hunting qualities of no mean standard, if Marengo the poodle was deficient in that respect.

On leaving Sacramento, the *Fair Rambler* took a north-east course. The object was to reach the frontier by the shortest road, and to cross the Sierra Nevada, say, to travel a distance of about six hundred miles to the Sonora Pass, which opens on to the endless plains of the East.

This was not the Far West, properly so-called, yet, where villages are only to be found at long intervals; it was not the prairie with its far-distant horizon, its immense waste, its wandering Indians gradually driven back toward the less frequented parts of North America. Almost as soon as you were out of Sacramento, the land already began to rise. You already perceived the ramifications of the Sierra which so nobly enclasps old California within the dark frame of its pine-covered mountains, overtopped here and there with peaks 15,000 feet high. It is a barrier of verdure thrown up by nature around that country on which she had lavished such wealth of gold, now carried away by the rapacity of man.

21

Along the road followed by the *Fair Rambler* there was no lack of important towns: Jackson, Mokelumne, Placerville, the world-known outposts of the Eldorado, and the Calaveras. But Mr. Cascabel halted in these places barely long enough to make a few purchases, or to have a specially good night's rest, when needed. He longed to get to the other side of the Nevada, the Great Salt Lake district, and the huge rampart of the Rocky Mountains, where his horses would have many a hard tug to give. Then as far as the Erie or Ontario region, all they need do would be to follow, through the prairies, the trails already beaten by the feet of the horses and furrowed by the wagons of preceding caravans.

Still, progress was slow through these hilly districts. Unavoidable detours increased the length of the journey. And again, although the country lay in the thirty-eighth parallel, which, in Europe, is the latitude of Sicily and Spain, the last lingering chill of winter had lost none of its sting. In consequence, as the reader knows, of the deviation of the Gulf Stream—that warm current which, when leaving the Gulf of Mexico, winds obliquely toward Europe,—the climate of North America is much colder, on the same latitudes, than that of the old Continent. But, a few weeks more, and once again California would be the land exuberant among all others, that fruitful land, where cereals multiply a hundredfold, where the most varied productions, both of the tropics and of the temperate zone, luxuriate side by side, sugar cane, rice, tobacco, oranges, lemons, olives, pineapples, bananas. The wealth of the Californian soil is not the gold it contains, it is the marvelous vegetation it brings forth.

"We shall be sorry to leave this country," said Cornelia, who did not look with an indifferent eye on the good things of the table.

"You glutton!" her husband would answer.

"Oh, it is not for myself I speak, it is for the children!"

Several days were spent journeying along the edge of the forests, through prairies gradually resuming their fresh tint of green. Despite their numbers, the ruminants fed by these prairies are unable to wear out the carpet of grass that nature keeps on renewing for ever under their feet. Too great emphasis could not be laid on the vegetative power of that Californian soil, to which no other can be compared. It is the granary of the Pacific, and the merchant navy, that takes its produce away, cannot exhaust it. The *Fair Rambler* went on its way, at its usual speed, a daily average of eighteen or twenty miles—not more. It is at this rate it had already conveyed its freight throughout all the States, where the name of the Cascabels was so favorably known, from the mouth of the Mississippi to New England. True, they then stopped in every town of the Confederacy to increase the amount of their takings; while in this journey, from west to east, there was no thought of dazzling the populations.

No artistic tour was this; this time, it was the journey home toward old Europe, with the Norman farms away in perspective.

A merry journey it was, too! How many sedentary dwellings would have envied the happiness of this house on wheels? There was laughing, and singing, and joking; and at times the horn, on which young Sander exhibited all his skill, would set the birds to flight, just as noisy a tribe as our frolicsome troupe.

All this was very fine, but days spent traveling need not, of necessity, be schoolboys' holidays.

"My children," Mr. Cascabel would often say, "we must not get rusty for all this!"

And so, during the halts, if the horses took a rest, the family did not do so. More than once did the Indians eagerly watch John going over his juggling, Napoleona rehearsing a few graceful steps, Sander dislocating himself as though his limbs were India-rubber, Mrs. Cascabel indulging in muscular exercises, and Mr. Cascabel in ventriloquial effects, not to forget Jako prattling in its cage, the two dogs performing together, and John Bull exhausting himself in contortions.

Let it be noticed, however, that John did not neglect his studying by the roadside. Over and over again did he read the few books that made up the little library of the *Fair Rambler*, a small geography, a small arithmetic, and various volumes of travels; he it was, moreover, who wrote up the log-book, in which were pleasantly recorded the incidents of the cruise.

"You will know too much!" his father sometimes said to him. "Still, if your taste runs that way,—"

And far was it from Mr. Cascabel to thwart the literary instincts of his first-born. As a fact, his wife and himself were very proud to have a "scholar" in the family.

One afternoon, about the 27th of February, the *Fair Rambler* reached the foot of the Sierra Nevada gorges. For four or five days to come, this rugged pass through the chain would cause them much toil and labor. It would be no light task, for man or beast, to climb half-way up the mountain. The men would have to put their shoulders to the wheels along the narrow paths which skirt the giant's sides. Although the weather continued to grow milder, thanks to the early influence of Californian spring, the climate would still be inclement at certain latitudes. Nothing is to be dreaded more than the floods of rain, the fearful snowdrifts, the bewildering squalls you encounter at the turns of those gorges in which the wind gets imprisoned as in a gulf. Besides, the upper portion of the passes rises above the zone of the permanent snow, and you must ascend to a height of at least six thousand feet before reaching the downward slope toward the Mormon district.

Mr. Cascabel proposed to do as he had already done on similar occasions: he would hire extra horses in the villages or the farms on the mountain, as well as men, Indians or Americans, to drive them. It would be an additional expense, of course, but a necessary one, if they cared not to break down their own horses.

On the evening of the 27th, the entrance into the Sonora Pass was reached. The valleys they had hitherto followed presented but a slight gradient; Vermont and Gladiator had walked them up with comparative ease. But farther up they could not have gone, even with the help of every member of the troupe.

A halt was made within a short distance of a hamlet that lay in a gorge of the Sierra. Just a few houses, and, at a couple of gunshots' distance, a farm to which Mr. Cascabel determined to repair that very evening. There he would engage, for the following morning, some extra horses that Vermont and Gladiator would gladly welcome.

First, the necessary measures had to be taken for spending the night in this spot.

As soon as the camp was organized in the usual manner, the inhabitants of the hamlet were communicated with and readily consented to supply fresh food for the masters, and forage for the horses.

On this evening, the rehearsing of exercises was out of the question. All were worn out with fatigue. It had been a heavy day: for, in order to lighten the load, they had had to go on foot a great part of the journey. Manager Cascabel therefore granted absolute rest on this and every other night while they crossed the Sierra.

After the "master's searching eye" had been cast over the encampment, Cascabel took Clovy, and, leaving the *Fair Rambler* to the charge of his wife and children, made his way toward the farm over which ringlets of smoke were seen curling up through the trees.

This farm was kept by a Californian and his family by whom the showman was well received. The farmer undertook to supply him with three horses and two drivers. The latter were to pilot the *Fair Rambler* as far as where the eastward declivity begins, and then return with the extra horses. But, that would cost a deal of money.

Mr. Cascabel bargained like a man who is anxious not to throw his money away, and, eventually, a sum was agreed on, which did not exceed the subsidy allowed on the budget for this portion of the trip.

24

The next morning, at six o'clock, the two men arrived; their three horses were put to, in front of Vermont and Gladiator, and the *Fair Rambler* began climbing up a narrow gorge thickly wooded on each side. About eight o'clock, at one of the turnings of the pass, that marvelous land of California, which our travelers were not leaving without a pang, had entirely disappeared behind the Sierra.

The farmer's three steeds were fine animals, which could be relied upon in every way. Could the same be said of the drivers? The thing seemed, to say the least, doubtful.

Both were strong fellows, half-breeds, half Indian, half English. Ah! had Mr. Cascabel known it, how soon he had parted company with them!

Cornelia was anything but prepossessed by their looks on the whole. John held the same views as his mother, and these views were shared by Clovy. It did not seem as though Mr. Cascabel had made a good hit. After all, these men were but two, and they would find their match, should they harbor any evil design.

As to dangerous encounters in the Sierra, they were not to be dreaded. The roads should be safe by this time. The days were gone when Californian miners, the "loafers" and the "rowdies" as they were styled, joined the ranks of the criminals who had thronged here from every quarter of the globe, to become the plague of respectable people. Lynch law had succeeded in bringing them to reason.

However, as a prudent man, Mr. Cascabel determined to keep on the alert.

The men hired at the farm were skillful drivers; that could not be denied. The first day passed by without any accident: that was something to be thankful for, first of all. A wheel giving way, an axle tree in halves, and the occupants of the *Fair Rambler*, away from all human dwellings, without any means of repairing the damage, would have been in a sorry plight.

The pass now wore the wildest aspect. Nothing but black-looking pine trees, no vegetation but the moss hugging the soil. Here and there, enormous heaps of piled-up rocks necessitated many a detour, especially along one of the affluents of the Walkner, which came out of the lake of that name and bellowed its mad career into the precipices below. Far away, lost in the clouds, Castle Peak pointed to the skies, and looked down on the other spurs picturesquely shot upwards by the Sierra.

About five o'clock, when the shades of evening were already creeping up from the depths of the narrow gorges, they came to a sudden turn of the road. The gradient in this spot was so steep that it was found necessary to unload a portion of the freight and leave behind, for a time, most of the articles laid on the top of the wagon, as well as those underneath it.

Every one worked with a will, and, it must be confessed, the two drivers gave proofs of zeal in this circumstance.

Mr. Cascabel and his people had their first impression of those men slightly modified. Besides, in another couple of days, the highest point of the pass would be attained; their downhill journey would commence; and all that belonged to the farm would return thereto.

When the halting station had been agreed upon, whilst the drivers looked after the horses, Mr. Cascabel, his two sons and Clovy, walked back a few hundred paces for the things that had been left behind.

A good supper terminated the day, and nobody thought of aught else but a sound rest.

The "boss" offered to the drivers to make room for them in one of the compartments of the *Fair Rambler*; but they declined, assuring him that the shelter of the trees was all that they needed. There, well wrapped in thick rugs, they could watch all the better after their master's horses.

A few moments more, and the encampment was buried in sleep.

The following morning, all were on foot at the first dawn of day.

Mr. Cascabel, John and Clovy, the earliest risers in the *Fair Rambler*, went to the spot where Vermont and Gladiator had been penned up, the night before.

Both were there, but the three horses of the farmer had disappeared.

As they could not be very far off, John was about telling the drivers to go look for them; neither was to be seen about the camping-ground.

"Where are they?" said he.

"Very likely," answered his father, "they are running after the horses."

"Hallo! Hallo!" shouted Clovy in a tone of voice that should be heard a considerable distance away.

No answer came.

New cries were uttered, as loud as the force of human lungs would permit, by Mr. Cascabel and by John, who went a little way down the track.

No sign of the missing drivers.

"Could it be that their appearance only told too plainly what they were?"

"Why would they have run away?" asked John.

"Because they'll have done something wrong."

"What?"

26

"What? Wait a bit!—We shall soon know!"

And, with John and Clovy on his heels, he ran toward the *Fair Rambler*.

Jumping up the wagon step, opening the door, two strides through the compartments and on to the end room where the precious safe had been laid, all that was the work of an instant, and Mr. Cascabel reappeared, shouting:

"Stolen!"

"What, the safe?" said Cornelia.

"Yes, stolen by those ruffians!"

CHAPTER IV - A GREAT RESOLUTION

RUFFIANS!

This was indeed the only name suitable to such wretches. The robbery, however, was none the less an accomplished fact.

Each evening Mr. Cascabel had been in the habit of seeing whether the safe lay still in its nook. Now, the day before, well he remembered it, worn out with the hardships of the day and overpowered with sleep, he had omitted his habitual inspection. No doubt, while John, Sander and Clovy had gone down with him for the articles that had been left at the turning of the pass, the two drivers had made their way unnoticed into the inner compartment, removed the safe, and hidden it among the brushwood around the camping-ground. That was the reason why they had declined to sleep inside the *Fair Rambler*. They had afterward waited until everybody was asleep, and had then run away with the farmer's horses.

Out of all the savings of the little troupe, there was nothing left now but a few dollars that Mr. Cascabel had in his pocket. And was it not lucky that the rascals had not taken Vermont and Gladiator away as well!

The dogs, already grown accustomed to the presence of the two men for the past twenty-four hours, had not even given the alarm, and the evil deed had been done without any difficulty.

Where were the thieves to be caught, now that they had made for the Sierra? Where was the money to be recovered? And without the money, how was the Atlantic to be crossed?

The poor people gave vent to their grief, some with tears, others with outbursts of indignation. At the very first, Mr. Cascabel was a prey to a real fit of rage, and his wife and children found it very difficult to calm him down. But, after having thus given way to his passion, he recovered possession of himself, as a man who has no time to waste in vain recriminations.

"Accursed safe!" burst from Cornelia's lips in the midst of her tears.

"Sure enough!" said John, "if we had had no safe, our money—"

"Yes!—A brilliant idea I hatched that day, to go buy that devil of a chest!" exclaimed Mr. Cascabel. "I guess the best thing to do when you have a safe is to put nothing in it! A great boon, to be sure, that it was proof against fire, as the shopman told me, when it was not proof against thieves!"

It must be admitted, the blow was a hard one for the poor people, and it is no wonder they felt utterly crushed by it. Robbed of two thousand dollars that had been earned at the cost of so much toil!

"What shall we do now?" inquired John.

28

"Do?" replied Mr. Cascabel, whose gnashing teeth seemed to grind his words as he spoke. "It is very simple!—Nay, it is most uncommonly simple! Without extra horses we can't possibly go on climbing up the pass. Well, I vote we go back to the farm! It may be, those ruffians are there!"

"Unless they did not go back!" suggested Clovy.

And, truly, this was more than likely. However, as Mr. Cascabel said once more, the only course open to them was returning on their steps, since going ahead was out of the question.

Thereupon Vermont and Gladiator were put to, and the wagon began its journey down through the pass of the Sierra.

This was but too easy a task alas! You can put on speed when you go downhill; but it was with heads hanging down and without a word our folks jogged down, save and except when a volley of curses broke forth from Cascabel.

At twelve o'clock in the day the *Fair Rambler* stopped in front of the farm. The two thieves had not returned. On hearing what had taken place the farmer flew into a passion in which sympathy for the show-people played not the slightest part. If they had lost their money, he had been robbed of his three horses, he had! Once away in the mountain, the thieves must have cut across to the other side of the pass. A nice race he might have after them now! And the farmer, beside himself with excitement, had wellnigh held Mr. Cascabel responsible for the loss of his horses!

"That's a rich idea!" said the latter. "Why do you keep such scoundrels in your service, and why do you hire them to respectable people?"

"How did I know?" the farmer replied. "Not a word of complaint had I ever against them!"

In any case the robbery had been perpetrated, and the situation was heart-breaking.

But, if Mrs. Cascabel found it hard to master her own feelings, her husband with that solid foundation of gypsy philosophy so peculiarly his own, succeeded in recovering his coolness.

And when they were assembled together in the *Fair Rambler*, a conversation was engaged among all the members of the family,—a most important conversation, "out of which was to come forth a great resolution," so said Mr. Cascabel, strongly rolling his r's as he spoke:

"Children, there are circumstances in life, when a strong-willed man must be able to make up his mind on the spur of the moment. Indeed I have observed that those circumstances are generally unpleasant ones. Witness

29

those in which we now are, thanks to those rascals. Well, this is no time to hesitate to the right or to the left, the more so as we have not half a dozen roads before us. We have but one, and that's the road we shall take immediately."

"Which?" asked Sander.

"I am going to tell you what I have in my head," answered Mr. Cascabel. "But, to know if my idea is practicable, John must fetch his book with the maps in it."

"My atlas?" said John.

"Yes, your atlas. You must be a good fellow at geography! Run for your atlas."

"Straight off, father."

And when the atlas had been laid on the table, the father continued as follows:

"It is an understood thing, my children, that, although those ruffians have stolen our safe—why did I ever think of buying a safe!—it is an understood thing, I say, that we don't give up our idea of going back to Europe."

"Give it up?—never!" exclaimed Mrs. Cascabel.

"A good answer, Cornelia! We want to go back to Europe, and go back we shall! We want to see France again, and see her again we shall! It is not because we have been robbed by scoundrels that—I, for one, must breathe my native air once more, or I am a dead man."

"And you shan't die, César! We have made our start for Europe, we shall get there, no matter what—"

"And how shall we?" reiterated John. "How? I should like to know."

"How, that's the question," answered Mr. Cascabel, scratching his forehead. "Of course, by giving performances along the road, we shall be able to get day by day what will land the *Fair Rambler* in New York. But, when there, no money left to pay for our passage, no boat to take us across! And without a boat, no possibility of crossing the sea except we swim! Now, I fancy that will be rather hard."

"Very hard, boss," replied Clovy, "unless we had fins."

"Have you any?"

"Not that I know of."

"If so, hold your peace, and listen."

Then addressing his eldest son:

"John, open your atlas, and show us the exact spot where we are!"

John found out the map of North America, and laid it under his father's eyes. All eagerly looked whilst he pointed with his finger to a spot in the Sierra Nevada a little to the east of Sacramento.

"This is it!" he said.

"Very well," answered Mr. Cascabel. "And so, if we were on the other side of the range, we should have the whole territory of the United States to cross, right through to New York?"

"We should, father."

"And how many miles might that be?"

"Somewhere about four thousand miles."

"Very good; then we should have the ocean to cross?"

"Of course."

"And how many miles to the other side of that ocean?"

"Three thousand or thereabouts."

"And once on French soil, we may say we are in Normandy?"

"We may."

"And all that, put together, gives a total of—"

"Seven thousand miles!" cried out little Napoleona, who had been reckoning it to herself.

"See, the little one!" said Mr. Cascabel. "Isn't she quick at figures! So, we say seven thousand miles?"

"About that, father," answered John, "and I think I'm allowing good measure."

"Well, children, that little strip of ribbon would be nothing for the *Fair Rambler*, if there was not a sea between America and Europe, an unfortunate sea blocking up the road for the wagon! And that sea can't be got over without money, that is, without a boat—"

"Or without fins!" repeated Clovy.

"Clovy has got fins on the brain!" said Mr. Cascabel with a shrug of his shoulders.

"Well then, it is beyond all evidence," remarked John, "that we can't go home by the east!"

31

"Can't is the word, my son, as you say; the thing can't possibly be done. But, who knows if by the west?"

"By the west?" exclaimed John, looking up at his father.

"Yes! Look it up, will you? And show me what track we should follow by the west?"

"First, we should go up through California, Oregon and Washington Territory up to the Northern frontier of the United States."

"And from there?"

"From that time, we should be in British Columbia."

"Pugh!" said Mr. Cascabel. "And could we not avoid that Columbia by any means?"

"No, father."

"Well, go on! And after that?"

"After we had reached the frontier to the north of Columbia, we should find the province of Alaska."

"Which is English?"

"No, Russian—at least up to the present, for there is talk of its being annexed—"

"To England?"

"No! To the United States."

"That's right! And after Alaska, where are we?"

"In the Behring Strait, which separates the two continents, America and Asia."

"And how many miles to this strait?"

"Three thousand three hundred, father."

"Keep that in your head, Napoleona; you'll add it all up by and by."

"And so shall I?" asked Sander.

"And you too."

"Now, your strait, John, how wide might it be?"

"Maybe sixty miles, father."

"What! sixty miles!" remarked Mrs. Cascabel.

"A mere stream, Cornelia; we may as well call it a stream."

"How's that?--A stream?"

"Of course! Is not your Behring Strait frozen over in winter, John?"

"It is, father! For four or five months, it is one solid mass."

"Bravo! and at that time people might walk across it on the ice?"

"People can and do so."

"That's what I call an excellent strait!"

"But, after that," inquired Cornelia, "will there be no more seas to cross?"

"No! After that, we have the continent of Asia, which stretches along as far as Russia in Europe."

"Show us that, John."

And John took, in the atlas, the general map of Asia, which Mr. Cascabel examined attentively.

"Well! There is everything shaping itself as if to order," said he; "so long as there are not too many wild countries in your Asia?"

"Not too many, father."

"And Europe, where is it?"

"There," replied John, laying the tip of his finger on the Oural.

"And what is the distance from this strait—this little stream called Behring—to Russia in Europe?"

"They reckon nearly five thousand miles."

"And from that to France?"

"About eighteen hundred."

"And all that makes up, from Sacramento?"

"Ten thousand one hundred and sixty," cried at the same time Sander and Napoleona.

"You'll both get the prize!" said Mr. Cascabel. "So then, by the east we have about seven thousand miles?"

"Yes, father."

"And by the west, roughly speaking, ten thousand?"

"Yes, say a difference of three thousand miles."

"Three thousand miles more on the western route, but no sea on the road! Well, then, children, since we can't go one way, we must needs go the other, and that's what I vote we do, as any donkey would."

"A funny thing! Walking home backwards!" cried Sander.

"No, not backwards! It is going home by an opposite direction!"

"Quite so, father," replied John. "Still, I would have you bear in mind that, seeing the enormous distance, we shall never reach France this year, if we go by the west!"

"Why so?"

"Because, three thousand miles in the difference is something for the *Fair Rambler*,—and for its team!"

"Well, children, if we are not in Europe this year, we shall be next year! And, now I think of it, as we shall have to go through Russia, where are held the fairs of Perm, Kazan and Nijni, that I so often hear of, we shall stop in those places, and I promise you the famous Cascabel family will gather fresh laurels there, and a fresh supply of cash, too!"

What objections can you make to a man when he has his answer for everything?

In truth, it is with the human soul as with iron. Under repeated blows, its molecules get more firmly kneaded together, it becomes thoroughly wrought, it acquires a greater power of resistance. And that was exactly the effect now being produced on these honest show-people. In the course of their laborious, adventurous, nomadic life in which they had had so many trials to bear, they surely never had been in such a sorry plight, with all their savings lost, and their return home by the usual means a matter of impossibility. Yet this last blow of the sledge hammer of ill-luck had so mercilessly battered them that they now felt a match for anything the future might have in store for them.

Mrs. Cascabel, her two sons and her daughter all joined in unanimous applause of the father's proposal. And still, could anything seem more unreasonable? Mr. Cascabel must indeed have "lost his head" in his desire to return to Europe, to think of carrying such a plan into execution. Pshaw! What was it, to have to rough it across the West of America and the whole of Siberia, so long as it was in the direction of France!

"Bravo! Bravo!" exclaimed Napoleona.

"Encore! Encore!" added Sander, who could find no more suitable words to express his enthusiasm.

"Say, father," asked Napoleona, "shall we see the Emperor of Russia?"

"Of course we shall, if his Majesty the Czar is in the habit of coming to the Nijni fair to enjoy himself."

"And we shall perform before him?"

"No doubt!—if he will express the least desire to see us!"

"Oh, how I should love to kiss him on both cheeks!"

"You may have to be satisfied with one cheek, my little girlie!" answered Mr. Cascabel. "But, if you do kiss him, take good care you don't spoil his crown!"

As to Clovy, the feeling he experienced toward his master was nothing short of admiration.

And so, the itinerary being now regularly planned out, the *Fair Rambler* was to trail it up through California, Oregon and Washington Territory to the Anglo-American frontier. They had some fifty dollars left,—the pocket-money which, luckily, had not been put up in the safe. However, as so trifling a sum could not suffice to the daily wants of such a journey, it was agreed that the little troupe would give performances in the towns and villages. There was no regret to be felt, either, at the delay occasioned by these halts. Had they not to wait until the strait should be entirely frozen over and afford safe passage to the wagon? Now, this could not come to pass before seven or eight months.

"And, to wind up, it will be ill-luck with a vengeance," said Mr. Cascabel, "if we don't get a few good takings before we reach the end of America!"

In truth, throughout the whole of Alaska, "making money" among wandering tribes of Indians, was very problematical. But, as far as the western frontier of the United States, in that portion of the new continent hitherto unvisited by the Cascabel family, there was no doubt but the public, on the mere faith of its reputation, should gladly give its members the welcome they deserved.

Beyond that point, our travelers would be in British Columbia, and although, there, the towns were numerous, never, no, never would Mr, Cascabel stoop so low as to open his hands for English shillings or pence. It was bad enough already, it was too bad, that the *Fair Rambler* and its occupants should be compelled to journey a distance of over six hundred miles on the soil of a British colony!

As to Siberia, with its long desert steppes, all they would meet there would be perhaps some of those Samoyedes or Tchuktchis who seldom leave the coast. There, no takings in perspective; that was a foregone conclusion; proof evident thereof would be forthcoming in due time.

All being agreed upon, Mr. Cascabel decided that the *Fair Rambler* would start off next morning at daybreak. Meanwhile, there was supper wanted. Away Cornelia set to work with her usual heartiness, and while she was at her cooking-stove, with her kitchen-help Clovy:

"All the same," said she, "that's a grand idea of Mr. Cascabel's."

"I believe you, mistress, a grand idea like all those that simmer in his pot,— I mean, that gallop through his brain."

"And then, Clovy, no sea to cross on this road, and no sea-sickness."

"Unless—the ice should heave up and down in the strait!"

"That's enough, Clovy, and no ill omens!"

Meanwhile, Sander was doing a few somersaults, with which his father was delighted. Napoleona, on her side, was executing some graceful steps, while the dogs frisked about her. Nor was it needless now to keep in good form, since the performances were going to be resumed.

Suddenly, Sander called out:

"Why, the animals of the troupe! Nobody thought of asking their opinion about our great journey!"

And running to Vermont:

"Well, my old fellow, what do you think of it, eh? A little nine thousand miles of a jog?"

Then, turning toward Gladiator:

"What will your old legs say about it?"

Both horses neighed at the same time as if in token of cheerful assent.

It was now the turn of the dogs.

"Here, Wagram! here, Marengo, what jolly old capers you are going to cut, eh?"

A merry bark and a gambol seemed to supply the desired reply. It was plain that Wagram and Marengo were ready to go the wide world over at the beck of their master.

The ape was next called upon to speak his mind.

"Come, John Bull!" exclaimed Sander, "don't put on such a long face! You'll see lots of countries, my old boy! And, if you are cold, we'll put your warm jacket on you! And those funny faces of yours? I do hope you have not forgotten how to make them, have you?"

36

No! John Bull had not forgotten any such thing, and the antics he made there and then excited the laughter of all around him.

Remained the parrot.

Sander took it out of its cage. The bird strutted about, nodding its head and "squaring itself" on its legs.

"Well, Jako," asked Sander, "you say nothing? Have you lost your tongue? —We are going on such a glorious journey! Are you pleased, Jako?"

Jako drew from the depths of its throat a series of articulate sounds in which the r's rolled as if they had come out of Mr. Cascabel's powerful larynx. "Bravo!" cried Sander. "He is quite satisfied—Jako approves the motion! Jako votes with the ayes!"

And the young lad, his hands on the ground, and his feet up in the air, began a series of somersaults and contortions which gained him the applause of his father

Just then, Cornelia appeared.

"Supper is laid," she cried.

One moment later, all the guests were sitting down in the dining-room, and the meal was consumed to the last crumb of bread.

It would have seemed as though everything was forgotten already, when Clovy brought the conversation back to the famous safe:

"Why, the thought now strikes me, boss. What a sell for those two scoundrels!"

"How's that?" inquired John.

"As they haven't the word for the lock, they'll never be able to open the safe."

"And that's why I feel sure they'll bring it back!" answered Mr. Cascabel with an outburst of laughter.

And this extraordinary man, wholly absorbed by his new project, had already forgotten both the theft and the thieves!

CHAPTER V - ON THE ROAD

YES! on the road to Europe, but this time, according to an itinerary which is adopted by few only and which can hardly be recommended to travelers who are hardpressed.

"And, still, we are so," thought Mr. Cascabel to himself, "especially hard pressed for money!"

The start took place in the morning of the 2d of March. At early morn, Vermont and Gladiator were put to the *Fair Rambler*. Mrs. Cascabel took her place in the wagon with Napoleona, leaving her husband and her two sons to go on foot, whilst Clovy held the reins. As to John Bull, he had perched himself on the railing, and the two dogs were already running ahead.

It was beautiful weather. The new sap of spring swelled the early buds on the shrubs. Nature was beginning to unbosom those charms that she eventually unfolds in such profusion under Californian skies. The birds warbled in the foliage of the evergreen trees, the green oaks, and the white oaks, and the pine-trees whose slender trunks swung to and fro over huge sheaves of heather. Here and there clumps of dwarf chestnut-trees, and here and there one of those apple-trees, the fruit of which, under the name of manzanilla, is used for the making of Indian cider.

Whilst checking the adopted route on his map as he went along, John did not forget that it was his especial duty likewise to supply the kitchen with fresh game. Indeed, in case of need, Marengo would have given him a reminder. A good huntsman and a good dog are made for each other. And they are never in closer sympathy than where there is abundance of game, which was the case in the present instance. Rarely it was that Mrs. Cascabel had not to display her skill on a hare, a crested partridge, a heath-cock, or a few of those mountain quails with pretty little egrets, the sweet-scented flesh of which is such delicate eating. If game proved so plentiful all the way to Behring's Strait, right through the plains of Alaska, our traveling family would have but little expense to incur for their daily food. Beyond that, perhaps, on the continent of Asia, they might not be so well supplied. But they would see about it, when the *Fair Rambler* had entered the endless steppes of the Tchuktchis.

Everything was therefore going on for the best. Mr. Cascabel was not a man to neglect the favorable circumstances that the weather and the temperature afforded him just then. The utmost speed was made, compatible with the horses' powers of endurance, and every advantage taken of the roads that the summer rains would render impracticable a few months later. This resulted in an average of twenty to twenty-five miles per twenty-four hours, with a halt in the middle of the day for a meal and a rest, and a halt at six in the evening for the night encampment. The country was not as solitary as might be imagined. The field labors of spring-time called out the farmers, to whom this rich and generous soil procures a life of comfort which they would be envied in any other part of the globe. Frequently, besides, they came across farms, hamlets, villages and even towns, especially when the *Fair Rambler* followed the left bank of the Sacramento, through that region which once was pre-eminently the gold country and still continues to bear the significant name of Eldorado.

In conformity with the programme made out by the leader, the troupe gave performances wherever an opportunity presented itself for the display of its talents. It had not been heard of yet in this part of California; and do you not find everywhere people who ask nothing better than to enjoy themselves? At Placerville, at Auburn, at Marysville, at Tehama, and other more or less important cities, somewhat weary of the ever-recurring American circus which visits them at periodical intervals, the Cascabels received an equal proportion of applause and of cents, the latter mounting up to a few dozen dollars. Napoleona's gracefulness and courage, Sander's extraordinary suppleness, John's marvelous skill as a juggler, not to forget Clovy's drolleries and tricks, were appreciated by good judges as they deserved to be. The very dogs did wonders in company with John Bull. As to Mr. and Mrs. Cascabel, they proved themselves worthy of their fair fame, the former in muscular exercises, the latter in open-hand wrestling encounters in which she brought to the ground such amateurs as ventured to meet her.

By the 12th of March, the *Fair Rambler* had reached the little town of Shasta, on which the mountain of the same name looks down from a height of fourteen thousand feet. Toward the west could be noticed the ill-defined outline of the Coast Ranges, which, luckily, had not to be crossed to reach the frontier of Oregon. But the country was very hilly; the route lay between the whimsical easterly offshootings of the mountain, and along those scarce-trodden roads the wagon proceeded but slowly. Moreover, the villages were becoming few and far between. Naturally it would have been better to journey along through the territories close to the coast where natural obstacles were less numerous, but these lie on the other side of the Coast Ranges, and the passes of the latter are so to say impracticable. It therefore appeared a wiser plan to travel northward, and only to touch the very edges of the Ranges, at the frontier of Oregon.

Such was the advice given by John, the geographer of the troupe, and it was deemed prudent to adopt it.

On the 19th of March, when Fort Jones had been left behind, the *Fair Rambler* halted in view of the little town of Yreka. Here, a warm welcome, and not a few dollars. It was the first appearance of a French troupe in this part. Every one to his taste! In those far away districts of America, the children of France excite none but friendly feelings. They are always received with open arms, and a great deal better, most assuredly, than they would be by certain of their European neighbors.

In this locality they were able to hire, at a moderate price, a few horses that proved a help to Vermont and Gladiator. Thus the *Fair Rambler* was enabled to cross the chain at the foot of its northern extremity, and this time without being pillaged by its drivers.

Although not exempt from obstacles and delays, this part of the journey was accomplished without any accidents, thanks to the measures of precaution that were adopted.

At last, on the 27th of March, at a distance of some three hundred miles from the Sierra Nevada, the *Fair Rambler* crossed the frontier of the Oregon Territory. The valley was bounded to the east by Mount Pitt, standing up like a style on the surface of a sun-dial.

Horses and men had worked hard. A little rest was needed at Jacksonville. Then the Rogue river having been crossed, the caravan followed a track that meandered as far as the eye could reach along the sea-coast toward the north.

The country was rich, hilly still, and very favorable to agriculture. On all sides, meadows and woods; practically a continuation of the Californian region. Here and there were bands of Shastas and Umpqua Indians, roving about the country. There was nothing to be feared at their hands.

It was at this time that John, who kept on reading the books of travels of his little library,—for he was determined to turn his studies to profit—thought fit to give his people a warning which it was deemed opportune to heed.

They were a few miles to the north of Jacksonville, in the middle of a district covered with immense forests and protected by Fort Lane which stands on a hill at a height of two thousand feet.

"We shall have to be very careful," said John, "for this country swarms with serpents."

"Serpents!" screamed Napoleona with affright, "serpents! Let us go away, father!"

"Don't be uneasy, child!" answered Mr. Cascabel. "We shall get on all right, if we only take some precautions."

"Are those nasty things dangerous?" inquired Cornelia.

"Very dangerous, mother," replied John. "They are rattlesnakes, the most dangerous of serpents. If you avoid them, they do not attack you; but if you touch them, if you knock against them unintentionally, they stand up, swoop down on you and bite you; and their bites are almost always fatal."

"Where do they lie?" asked Sander.

"Under dry leaves where they are not easily noticed," replied John. "Still, as they make a rattling sound by shaking the rings on their tail, you have time to avoid them."

"If so, then," said Mr. Cascabel, "let us mind our p's and q's (the serpent's q's, of course) and keep our ears open!"

John had been quite right to draw attention to this fact; serpents were very numerous in Western America. Not alone did the Crotalidæ abound, but the Tarentulæ likewise, the latter almost as dangerous as the former.

Needless to add that the utmost caution was used, and each one looked on the ground as he walked. There was an eye to be kept, moreover, to the horses and the other animals of the troupe, no less exposed than their masters to the attacks of the insects and the reptiles.

Besides, John had thought it his duty to add that these dreaded snakes had a deplorable habit of creeping their way into houses, and, doubtless, were equally disrespectful of carriages. A possibility of their paying an unpleasant visit to the *Fair Rambler* was therefore to be feared.

And so, when the evening had come, how carefully they looked under the beds, under the furniture, in every nook and corner! And what screams Napoleona would utter when she fancied she saw one of those ugly reptiles and mistook some coil of rope or other for a crotalus, deprived though it was of a triangular head! And the fits of terror she had when, in semi-wakefulness, she imagined she heard the noise of a rattle at the other end of the compartment! It must be said that Cornelia was hardly braver than her daughter.

"Look here," exclaimed her husband, losing patience one day, "the devil take both the snakes that frighten the women, and the women that are afraid of snakes! Mother Eve was not such a coward, and many a chat she had with them!"

"Oh!—that was in the earthly paradise!" said the little girl.

"And that was not the best thing she ever did, either!" added Mrs. Cascabel.

This state of things kept Clovy busy every night. At first, he had hit upon the plan of lighting large fires, for which the forest supplied the necessary fuel; but John suggested to him that if the light of the fire was able to keep the serpents away, it was likely to attract the tarentulæ.

On the whole, our travelers felt really easy in their minds only in the villages where now and then the *Fair Rambler* halted to spend a night; there, danger was infinitely less.

Nor were these villages very far apart from each other; witness Cannonville on the Cow Creek, Roseburg, Rochester, Yoculla where Mr. Cascabel pocketed more dollars. All things considered, as he earned more than he spent, the prairies supplying him with grass for his horses, the forest with game for his kitchen, the streams with fish for his table, the journey really cost nothing. And the produce of the performances kept on heaping up. But, alas! how far they were from the two thousand dollars, stolen in the Sierra Nevada Pass!

However, if the little troupe eventually escaped the bites of the snakes and of the tarentulæ, they were to be visited in a different way. And it happened just a few days later; so numerous and manifold are the means devised by nature to test the patience of poor mortals here below!

The wagon, ever rumbling up through the Oregon district, had just passed Eugene City. This name had proved a source of genuine pleasure, pointing out, as it did, the French origin of the settlement. Mr. Cascabel would have been glad to know that countryman of his, that Eugene who was doubtless one of the founders of the said town. He must have been a worthy man, and, if his name does not appear among the modern names of French kings, the Charles, the Louis, the Francis, the Henrys, the Philippes,—and the Napoleons, it is French none the less, thoroughly French!

After a halt in the towns of Harrisburg, Albany and Jefferson, the *Fair Rambler* "dropped anchor" before Salem, a rather important city, the capital of Oregon, built on one of the banks of the Villamette.

It was the 3rd of April.

There, Mr. Cascabel allowed twenty-four hours' rest to his staff,—at least in so far as they were travelers; for the public square of the town was turned to advantage by the artists, and a round sum rewarded their exertions.

During their leisure moments John and Sander, hearing that the river was looked upon as abounding in fish, had gone and enjoyed the pleasure of angling.

But, the following night, behold father, mother, children all suffering such tortures, from a feeling of itching right over the body, as to suggest the possibility of their being the victims of one of those old practical jokes still played at country weddings.

And great was their wonderment, on the next morning, when they looked at each other!

"Why, I am as red as a Far West Indian!" exclaimed Cornelia.

"And I am swelled out like a gold beater's skin," cried Napoleona.

42

"And I am one mass of blisters from head to foot!" said Clovy.

"What does it all mean?" asked Mr. Cascabel. "Have they got the plague in these parts?"

"I think I know what it is," answered John, as he examined his arms, speckled with reddish spots.

"What?"

"We have caught the yedra, as it is called here."

"The devil take your yedra! Come, John, will you tell us the meaning of it?"

"The yedra, father, is a plant which you have only to smell, to touch, or even, so they say, to look at, to suffer from its evil power. It poisons you at a distance."

"How is that? We are poisoned," asked Mrs. Cascabel, "poisoned!"

"Don't be afraid, mother," John hastened to reply. "We shall get over it with a little itching and perhaps a little fever: that will be all."

The explanation was the correct one. This yedra is a dangerous, an extremely venomous plant. When the wind is loaded with the almost impalpable pollen of this shrub, if the skin be but touched by it, it reddens, gets covered with pimples, and becomes marbled with blotches. Probably, while crossing the woods in the neighborhood of Salem, Mr. Cascabel and his people had happened to be in a current of yedra. On the whole, the pustular eruption they suffered from hardly lasted twenty-four hours, during which time, it is true, there was such general scratching and rubbing as to excite the jealousy of John Bull, on whose favorite and continual occupation, this seemed an encroachment on the part of mankind.

On the 5th of April, the *Fair Rambler* left Salem, bringing away a very lively remembrance of the few hours spent in the forests of the Villamette,—a pretty name for a river, for all that, and one with a pleasant sound for French ears.

By the 7th of April, after calling at Fairfield, at Clackamas, Oregon City, Portland, towns already grown into importance, the troupe reached without any other accident, the banks of the Columbia River, on the frontier of that state of Oregon, three hundred and fifty miles of which they had just traveled over.

To the north stretched out Washington Territory.

It is mountainous in that portion lying east of the route followed by the *Fair Rambler* in its endeavors to reach Behring Strait. Here are developed the ramifications of the Cascade Ranges, with peaks such as St. Helens, nine thousand seven hundred feet in height, those of Mt. Baker and Mt. Rainier eleven thousand feet high. It seems as though nature, having spent herself in endless plains ever since she left the coast of the Atlantic, had preserved all her upheaving power to throw up the mountains with which the west of the new continent bristles. If we were to look upon these countries as a sea, we might say that this sea, still, unruffled, almost asleep on the one side, is stormy and angry on the other, and that the crests of its waves are mountain peaks.

This was John's remark, and the father was greatly pleased with the comparison.

"That's right, that's quite right!" he answered. "After the sun comes the storm! Pshaw, our *Fair Rambler* is not weak about the knees! She'll weather the storm, she will! All sails up, lads, all sails up!"

And the sails were set, and the Rambler continued her cruise through these billowy regions. In truth,—to keep up the simile,—the sea was beginning to calm down, and, thanks to the exertions of the crew, the fair ship of the Cascabels pulled through the worst passes unhurt. If, at times, speed had to be slackened, they succeeded, at least, in avoiding the reefs.

Then, a warm and sympathetic welcome always awaited them in the little townships, at Kalama, at Monticello, as well as at the forts, which are, strictly speaking, nothing else but military stations. In vain would you look for ramparts there, a paling at most; still the little garrisons occupying these posts are sufficient to keep in due awe the wandering Indians who roam about through the country.

That is why the *Fair Rambler* was threatened neither by the Chinooks nor by the Nesquallys when it ventured into the Walla-Walla country. When the shades of evening fell and these Indians collected around the encampment, they never showed any evil disposition. By far the greatest source of surprise for them was John Bull, whose ludicrous faces excited their laughter. They had never seen an ape, and doubtless they took this one for one of the members of the family.

"Why, of course! He is a little brother of mine!" Sander would say to them, in spite of Mrs. Cascabel's most indignant protestations.

At last they arrived in Olympia, the capital town of Washington Territory, and there "by general desire" was given the last performance of the French troupe in the United States. Now, the road would lie along the coast of the Pacific, or rather those numerous sounds, those capricious and manifold straits sheltered by the large islands of Vancouver and Queen Charlotte.

After a call at Steilacoom, they had to wind round Puget Sound, in order to reach Fort Bellingham, situated near the strait which separates the islands from the mainland.

Then came Whatcom station, with Mt. Baker pointing upward through the clouds at the horizon, and Simiamoo station, at the mouth of Georgia Strait.

At length, on the 27th of April, after a trip of over a thousand miles from Sacramento, the *Fair Rambler* reached the frontier line which was adopted by the 1847 treaty and still marks the limit of British Columbia.

CHAPTER VI - THE JOURNEY CONTINUED

FOR the first time, Mr. Cascabel, the natural, the implacable enemy of England, was about setting his foot on an English possession. For the first time the sole of his shoe would tread on British soil and be defiled with Anglo-Saxon dust. Let the reader forgive us such very strong language; most undoubtedly such was the somewhat ludicrous form of expression under which the thought presented itself to our showman's mind, so tenacious in its now unjustifiable patriotic hatred.

And still, Columbia was not in Europe. It was no portion of that group formed by England, Scotland and Wales and bearing the special name of Great Britain. But it was none the less British, just as India, Australia, New Zealand; and, as such, it was repulsive to César Cascabel.

British Columbia is a part of New Britain, one of the most important colonies of the United Kingdom, comprising as it does Nova Scotia, Upper and Lower Canada, as well as the immense territories ceded to the Hudson Bay Company. In width, it stretches from one ocean to the other, from the coasts of the Pacific to those of the Atlantic. To the south it is bounded by the frontier of the United States, a line running from Washington Territory to the coast in the State of Maine.

Columbia was therefore, on all counts, English soil, and the necessities of the journey left our travelers no chance of avoiding it. When all was added up, it was only a matter of six hundred miles to the southern extremity of Alaska, that is to say to the Russian possessions in Western America. Still, a trip of six hundred miles on "that hated soil," although a mere nothing for the *Fair Rambler* with its record of untold mileage, was six hundred times too much, and Mr. Cascabel was determined to clear that distance in the shortest possible time.

Henceforth, no halting save for meals. No exercising for the equilibrist or the gymnast, no more dancing, no more wrestling. The Anglo-Saxons would have to go without it. The Cascabels felt nothing but contempt for any coin bearing the effigy of the queen. Better a paper dollar than a silver crown or a gold sovereign!

Under these conditions, it will be understood that the *Fair Rambler* carefully kept away from the villages and gave a wide berth to the towns. If the game by the roadside could supply the wants of the troupe, it would save them from aiding the home trade of this abominable country.

Let it not be imagined that this attitude was but a kind of theatrical pose on the part of Mr. Cascabel. No! It was natural with him. This same philosopher, who had so stoically borne the blow of his late misfortune, who had so quickly recovered his usual merry temper after the robbery in the Sierra

Nevada, became gloomy and speechless as soon as he stepped into New Britain. He trudged along with downcast eyes and a scowling look, his cap drawn down to his ears; and wicked were the glances he cast on the inoffensive travelers who happened to cross his path. That he was in no mood for jokes was plainly shown one day when Sander drew on himself a severe rebuke for his ill-timed mirth.

That day, sure enough, behold the youngster taking it into his head to walk a good quarter of a mile, backwards, in front of the horses, with a thousand and one contortions and grimaces.

On his father's inquiring the reason of this mode of locomotion, which should be, to say the least, very fatiguing:

"Why, father! Aren't we going home backwards?" he replied with a wink of his eye.

And all burst out with laughter—even Clovy, who thought the answer was very funny,—unless it should turn out to be very silly.

"Sander," said Mr. Cascabel angrily, and with his stagey air, "if ever again you indulge in such frolic at a time when we are so little inclined to merriment, I'll pull your ears for you, and stretch them to your very heels!"

"Well now, father—"

"Silence under arms! I forbid you to laugh in this Englishmen's land!"

And no one now thought of smiling or showing his teeth in the presence of the terrible boss, although his anti-Saxon ideas were far from being shared to that extent.

That portion of British Columbia which lies next to the coast of the Pacific is very uneven. It is enclosed, to the east, by the Rocky Mountains, which almost stretch to the polar region; and the deep indentations of the Bute coast, to the west, give it the appearance of a Norwegian coast with its numerous fiords over which a range of mountains raises its picturesque summits. There stand peaks unparalleled in Europe, even in the middle of the Alpine region, glaciers the depth and extent of which surpass all the glories of Switzerland. Such are Mt. Hooker, with an altitude of seventeen thousand four hundred feet,—say three thousand feet higher than the loftiest plateau on Mt. Blanc— and Mt. Brown, higher likewise than the giant of the Alps.

Along the itinerary of the *Fair Rambler* between the eastern and the western ranges, lay a wide and fertile valley with a succession of open plains and magnificent forests. The water-course of this valley gave passage to the Fraser, an important stream, which, after a run of some three hundred miles from south to north, flows into a narrow arm of the sea, bounded by the coast of Bute, Vancouver's Island, and the archipelago it commands.

This Vancouver's Island is two hundred and fifty miles long and seventy-three wide. Originally purchased by the Portuguese, it was seized upon by tho Spaniards, and passed into their hands in 1789. Three times recognized by Vancouver at a time when it was still called Noutka, it bore both the name of the English navigator and that of Captain Quadra, and eventually became the property of Great Britain toward the end of the eighteenth century.

Its present capital is Victoria, its chief town Nanaimo. Its rich coal mines, at first worked by agents of the Hudson Bay Company, constituted one of the most active branches of the trade of San Francisco with the various ports along the western coast.

A little to the north of Vancouver, the mainland is sheltered by Queen Charlotte Island, the most important of the archipelago of that name, and the last of the British possessions in this part of the Pacific.

It will be readily guessed that Mr. Cascabel had no more a thought of visiting this capital than he dreamt of calling at Adelaide or Melbourne in Australia, at Madras or Calcutta in India. His only care was going up the valley of the Fraser as swiftly as his horses could go, holding intercourse, meanwhile, with none but Indian natives.

Indeed on their journey northward through the valley, our travelers easily found the game necessary to their sustenance. There was an abundance of deer, hares and partridges, and "on this occasion at least," Mr. Cascabel would say, "it was respectable people were fed by the game so surely and safely brought down by the gun of his eldest son. That game had no Anglo-Saxon blood in its veins; a Frenchman might partake of it without remorse!"

After passing Fort Langley, the wagon had already sunk deeply in the valley of the Fraser. It had been vain to look for a carriage road on this soil which man seemed to leave almost entirely to itself. Along the right bank of the river, stretched out wide pasture lands extending to the forests in the west, and enclosed far away with a horizon of mountains the summits of which stood out in bold relief on an ever gray sky.

It should be mentioned that, near Westminster, one of the chief towns along the coast of Bute, almost at the mouth of the Fraser, John had taken care to bring the *Fair Rambler* across the river, on the ferry that plies there between the two banks. And an excellent precaution it was; now, after going up the river to its spring, the party would only have to bear somewhat to the west. It was the shortest, the most practical way to reach that portion of Alaska which is adjacent to the Columbian frontier.

Over and above this, Mr. Cascabel had had the good luck to meet with an Indian who had offered to guide him to the Russian possessions, and the trust he had placed in this native was not to prove unmerited. Of course this was additional expense; but it was best not to look at a few dollars more or less, when the security of the travelers and the rapidity of the journey were in question.

This guide was called Ro-No. He belonged to one of those tribes whose tyhis, or chiefs, have frequent intercourse with Europeans. These Indians are in every way different from the Chilicots, a deceitful, cunning, savage tribe, against whom travelers should be on their guard in the northwest of America. A few years before, in 1864, these savages had had their share in the slaughter of a whole company of men who had been sent to the coast of Bute for the laying down of a road. Was it not under their blows that Engineer Waddington had fallen, whose death was so universally regretted throughout the colony? Was it not said that, at that very time, these Chilicots had torn out the heart of one of their victims, and had devoured it, like so many Australian cannibals?

John, who had read the tale of this frightful tragedy in Frederick Whymper's travels through North America, had thought it his duty to warn his father of the danger of an encounter with the Chilicots; but naturally no mention of it had been made to the other members of the family, whom it was needless to frighten. Indeed, since this shocking event, these redskins had kept prudently out of the way, awed as they had been by the hanging of a few of their number, who had been more directly implicated in the affair. This belief was corroborated by guide Ro-No, who impressed it on the travelers that they had no cause for anxiety while going through British Columbia.

The weather continued to keep fair. Already indeed the heat began to be severely felt for a couple of hours in the middle of the day. The buds commenced to expand along the branches swollen with sap; leaves and flowers soon blended their vernal tints.

The country presented that aspect so characteristic of northern zones. The valley of the Fraser was encased in the midst of forests abounding with the scented trees of the north, cedars and firs, and likewise those Douglas pines whose trunks measure forty-five feet in circumference and whose tops rise to a height of over a hundred feet above the ground. Both the woods and the valley were plentifully stocked with game, and, without going much out of his way, John easily supplied the daily requirements of the kitchen.

Nor did the district in any way bear the look of a desert. Here and there were villages in which the Indians seemed to live in comparative amity with the Anglo-Saxon administration. Up and down the river glided little flotillas of canoes made of cedar wood, borne down by the current itself, or propelled against it with paddle and sail.

Frequently, too, they fell in with bands of redskins, on the tramp southward. Wrapped in their white woolen cloaks, they would exchange a few words with

Mr. Cascabel, who managed, somehow, to make out something of what they said; for they used a singular dialect, the Chinook, a mixture of French, English, and the native language.

"There!" he would exclaim, "who would have thought I knew Chinook! Another language I can talk without ever having learnt it!"

Chinook is, indeed,—so Ro-No said,—the name given to that language throughout Western America, and it is used by the various tribes in those parts, right into the Alaskan provinces.

By this time, the warm season having thus far advanced, it is needless to say that the snows of winter had completely disappeared, although they sometimes keep on to the last days of April. And so the journey was progressing under favorable circumstances.

Short of overtiring them, Mr. Cascabel urged on his horses as much as he prudently could, so desirous was he of leaving Columbian territory. The temperature was rising gradually, a fact that would have been evident, were it but by the number of mosquitoes, which soon became unbearable. It was very hard to keep them out of the *Fair Rambler*, even with the precautionary measure of having no lights after darkness had fallen.

"You villainous creatures!" cried Mr. Cascabel one day, after an unsuccessful chase with these exasperating insects.

"I should like to know what use are those horrible flies?" asked Sander.

"They are of use,—to eat us up," replied Clovy.

"And especially to eat the English residents of Columbia," added Mr. Cascabel. "So, children, I positively forbid you to kill a single one of them! There will never be too many for my English lords, and that's a consolation for me!"

During this portion of the journey our marksman's gun was more productive than ever. The game often "rose" of themselves, and more especially the deer, which came from the forests to the plain to quench their thirst in the cool waters of the Fraser. With Wagram forever at his heels, John was able to bring down a few without having to go farther out of his road than might have been prudent,—which would have been a source of anxiety to his mother. Sander would sometimes go with him, happy to try his first shots under his big brother; and it would not have been easy to tell which was the fleeter or the longer-winded runner, the young hunter or his spaniel.

However, John had had but a few deer on his record, when he was lucky enough, one day, to kill a bison. On that occasion, it is true, he ran real danger; for the animal, merely wounded by his first shot, made a dart toward him, and he barely had time to spot him with a second bullet in the head, ere he himself would have been knocked to the ground and torn to pieces by the brute. As may be imagined, he refrained from giving any details of this adventure. But the exploit having been accomplished within a few hundred paces of the Fraser, the horses had to be taken down to the spot, to drag home the enormous buffalo, whose bushy mane gave it the appearance of a lion.

The reader knows how useful this ruminant is to the prairie Indian, who never hesitates to attack it with his spear or his arrows. His hide is the bed of the wigwam, the clothing of the family; some of those "garments" there are which will fetch twenty piastres. As to the flesh, the natives dry it in the sun and then cut it in long slices: a precious reserve for times of famine.

If, generally speaking, Europeans eat only the tongue of the bison,—and, in truth, it is an exquisite tid-bit,—the staff of the little troupe exhibited much less epicurean taste. Nothing was thought fit to be despised for those young digestive organs. Besides, served up in Cornelia's happy style, the bison's flesh, whether toasted, roasted, or boiled, was pronounced excellent, and was sufficient for a number of meals. Of the animal's tongue, each one could have but a small morsel, and it was unanimously agreed nothing choicer had ever been tasted.

During the first fortnight of the journey through Columbia no other incident worthy of notice occurred. However, there were signs of a coming change in the weather, and the time was not far distant when downpours of torrents of rain would, if not check, at least delay, any advance northward.

There was also to be dreaded a possibility of the swollen Fraser overflowing its banks. Now, such an overflow would have placed the *Fair Rambler* in the greatest dilemma, not to say the greatest danger.

Fortunately, although, when the rain fell, the Fraser did swell with great rapidity, it only rose to the level of its banks. Thus the plains escaped being flooded right to the edge of the forests that begin rising, in terrace fashion, from the first upheaving of the valley. Of course, the wagon proceeded now but very slowly, its wheels sinking into the softened ground, but under its strong and taut roof, the Cascabels continued to find that safe shelter it had already afforded them so often against the gale and the storm.

CHAPTER VII - THROUGH CARIBOO

GOOD honest Cascabel, why had you not come a few years sooner, and visited then the country you are about to travel through in this part of British Columbia? Why had not the ups and downs of your nomadic life brought you here when gold lay on the ground, and all that was needed was to stoop and pick it up! Why should the tale, told by John to his father, concerning that extraordinary period, be the story of the past, not the history of the present!

"This, now, is the Cariboo, father," said John, that day; "but you may not know, perhaps, what the Cariboo is?"

"Not the slightest idea," answered Mr. Cascabel. "Is it a biped, or a four-footed animal?"

"An animal?" exclaimed Napoleona. "Is it a large one? And is it very cruel? And does it bite?"

"Cariboo is indeed the name of an animal," replied John; "but in this instance it is simply a district bearing that name; it is the gold country, the Eldorado of Columbia. What wealth it contained once! And how many people it has enriched!"

"And how many it has beggared at the same time, I guess!" added Mr. Cascabel.

"No doubt, father, and, we may be sure, that was the majority. Still, there were miners' associations whose takings went up to two thousand marks a day. In a certain valley of this Cariboo, William Creek valley, gold was picked up in handfuls."

And yet, considerable as was the yielding of this auriferous valley, too many people had come to work it. And so, owing to the accumulation of gold-seekers and the mob they attract along with them, life soon became a matter of difficulty there, not to speak of the prodigious rise in the price of everything. Food was priceless; bread was a dollar a pound. Contagious diseases broke out in the midst of these unhealthy surroundings. Finally came misery, and, in its train, death, for the greater number of those who had flocked to this spot. Was this not a repetition of what had taken place, a few years before, in Australia and in California?

"Father," said Napoleona, "all the same it would be nice to find a big lump of gold on our road!"

"And what would you do with it, pet?"

"What would she do with it?" Cornelia replied. "She would bring it to dear little mother and she, I guess, would very soon have it exchanged for its value in current money!"

"Well, let us have an eye open," said Clovy, "and for sure, we can't but find something, unless—"

"Unless we find nothing, you were going to say," said John. "And that is just what will happen, my poor Clovy; the gold box has been emptied,—regularly emptied clean out."

"Well!—Well!" replied Sander, "we shall see!"

"That's enough, children!" exclaimed Mr. Cascabel, in his most imperative tone of voice. "I forbid any of you to enrich himself in that manner. Gold picked up on English soil! Fie! Let us pass on,—let us pass on, I say, without stopping, without stooping to pick up a nugget, even if it were the size of Clovy's head! And when we get to the frontier, should there be no card stuck up, with the words 'Please wipe your feet,' we shall give ours a good wiping, my children, so as to take away no part or parcel of this Columbian soil with us!"

Always the same Cæser Cascabel! But let him be easy in his mind! It is probable that not one member of his family will have the least chance of picking up the smallest particle of gold.

For all that, and notwithstanding Mr. Cascabel's prohibition, many a side glance was cast on the ground, along the road. A pebble of any sort seemed to Napoleona, and especially to Sander, as though it should be worth its weight in gold. And why not? In the list of auriferous countries, does not North America hold the foremost rank? Australia, Russia, Venezuela, China, are only next to her.

Meanwhile, the rainy season had set in. Every day heavy showers came down, and progress became the more arduous.

The Indian guide spurred the horses onward. He feared lest the rios or creeks, affluents of the Fraser, hitherto almost dry, should suddenly fill up; and, how would they be crossed over if no fords could be found? The *Fair Rambler* would run the risk of standing still, in distress, for the several weeks that the rainy season lasts. All speed then should be made to get out of the valley of the Fraser.

We said the natives in these parts were no longer to be dreaded since the Chilicots were driven to the east. This was quite true; but there were certain formidable animals—bears amongst others—an encounter with which would have proved really dangerous.

This fact Sander learned by experience, on an occasion when he well-nigh paid dearly the fault he had committed of disobeying his father.

It was on the afternoon of the 17th of May. A halt had been made some fifty paces beyond a creek that the party had just crossed dry-footed. This creek, deeply buried as it was, would have proved an insurmountable obstacle, if perchance a sudden rise of the waters had transformed it into a torrent.

The halt was to be of a couple of hours' duration. John went ahead in search of game; and Sander, although ordered not to leave the encampment, crossed back the creek unnoticed and went back along the road, carrying nothing with him but a rope, about a dozen feet long, coiled around his waist.

The lad had an idea in his head: he had noticed, by the roadside, a beautiful bird with many-colored plumage; he meant to chase it home so as to find out its nest; then with the help of the rope, he would have little trouble in climbing up any tree to possess himself of it.

In thus betaking himself away Sander committed an error all the greater as the weather was threatening. A dark cloud was gathering overhead. But what will stop a lad running after a bird?

In a few moments Sander was rushing down a thick forest, the first trees of which bordered the left bank of the creek. The bird fluttering, from branch to branch, seemed to take a delight in enticing him along.

Sander, his mind full of his chase, was forgetting that the *Fair Rambler* should start off again in two hours' time; and, within twenty minutes of his leaving the camp, he had dived a couple of miles into the depths of the forest. Here no roads, nothing more than narrow paths, netted over with brushwood, at the foot of the cedars and the pine trees.

The bird, with many a merry twitter, winged it lightly from tree to tree, and Sander ran and leaped like a young wild-cat. Such efforts, however, were doomed to be fruitless: the bird eventually disappeared in the undergrowth.

"Well, go to Jericho!" exclaimed Sander, as he stopped short, annoyed at his failure.

Then, only, through the foliage, he noticed the cloudy sky above. Sheets of light fitfully brightened the darkened verdure around.

They were the first flashes of lightning, quickly followed by long peals of thunder.

"It is high time to go home," the young lad thought to himself, "and what will father say?"

Just then his attention was attracted by a singular-looking object, a peculiarly shaped stone, of the size of a pine-cone, and bristling with metallic points.

Of course, in our youth's mind, this was a nugget, forgotten by somebody in this part of Cariboo. And with a cry of joy, he stoops for it, weighs it in his hand, and consigns it to his pocket, promising himself not to breathe a word about it to anybody.

"We shall see what they will say about it some day, when I have changed it for fine gold coins!"

Sander had scarcely pocketed his precious stone, when the storm burst with a terrific thunderclap. And its last echoes still lingered in the air, when a wild roar was heard.

At a distance of twenty paces, in the middle of the thicket, stood up a huge grizzly bear.

Full of courage as he was, Sander took to flight with all his might, in the direction of the creek. Instantly, the bear was after him.

If Sander could only reach the bed of the stream, get to the other side and away to the camp, he was saved. His people would be well able to keep the grizzly at a respectful distance on the left bank of the creek, or perhaps to level him to the ground and make a bed-room rug of him.

But the rain now fell in torrents, the flashes of lightning were more frequent, and the heavens shook with the roars of thunder. Sander, drenched to his skin, hindered in his flight by his wet garments, was in danger of stumbling at every step, and a fall would have left him at the mercy of the brute. Still he managed to keep his distance, and in less than a quarter of an hour he was on the bank of the creek.

Here he now faced an insurmountable obstacle. The creek, transformed into a veritable torrent, whirled along stones, trunks and stumps of trees torn away by the violence of the flood. The waters had risen to the level of the banks. Plunging into this whirlpool was rushing to death without a chance of escape.

To return on his steps, Sander dared not venture. He felt the bear on his heels, ready to take him in his grasp. And the *Fair Rambler* was hardly visible, yonder under the trees; letting its occupants know of his presence here was out of the question.

Almost without a thought on his part, instinct suggested to him the only thing that might save him perhaps.

A tree stood there, within five paces of him, a cedar, the lowest branches of which overhung the creek.

Making a dart for it, clasping its trunk in his arms, hoisting himself up to the fork with the help of the bumps on the bark, and gliding along through the inferior horizontal branches, all this was for the lad the work of an instant. An ape would not have been more clever or more supple. Nor was this surprising on the part of a little clown; and now, he could think himself safe.

Alas, it was not for long. The bear, who had taken up a position at the foot of the tree, was preparing to climb up, so that it would be very hard to escape him, even by taking refuge among the highest branches.

Sander lost none of his presence of mind. Was he not the worthy son of the famous Cascabel, with whom getting safe and sound through the hardest passes had grown into a habit?

Leave the tree, he should, of necessity; but how? And afterward, get across the torrent; but in what way? Thanks to the rise occasioned by the deluge of rain, the creek was now overflowing, and its waters spread over the right bank in the direction of the camp.

Calling for help?—His cries could not possibly be heard in the deafening crash of the furious storm. Besides, supposing that Mr. Cascabel, John or Clovy had set out in search of the missing youth, they must have gone on ahead along the road. How could they have guessed that Sander had gone back across the creek?

Meanwhile the bear was climbing up—slowly; still he was gradually coming up, and he soon would reach the fork of the cedar whilst the boy endeavored to make his way to the top.

It is at this moment an idea struck the lad. Seeing that some of the branches stretched for a distance of some ten feet over the creek, he quickly got out the rope he had brought around his waist, and, with a loop at the end of it, skillfully lassoed the extremity of one of these horizontal branches; the latter he bent upward by hauling the rope toward himself and maintained it in this vertical position.

All this had been done cleverly, quickly and with the utmost coolness.

There was no time, indeed, to be lost. The bear was hugging the fork and thence smelling his way among the boughs.

But just then, firmly grasping the top of the strained branch, Sander let it go back like a spring, and he himself was hurled over the creek like a stone shot by a catapult. Then, turning a splendid somersault, he landed himself on the edge of the right bank of the creek, while the bear, in silly amazement, looked at his prey escaping him in mid-air.

"You rascally boy!" It was thus Mr. Cascabel greeted the thoughtless youth on his "landing," just as he himself arrived at the creek with John and Clovy, after looking in vain for the lad round about the camp.

"You rascal!" he repeated. "How anxious you made us!"

"Well, father, do pull my ears!" answered Sander. "I have deserved it richly!"

But instead of settling accounts with his ears, Mr. Cascabel could not resist kissing both his cheeks, saying:

"Well, don't do it again, or, if you do—"

"You'll kiss me again!" said Sander, giving a hearty kiss to his father.

Then he added:

"I say!—What a sell for the bear! Doesn't he look sheepish, eh?—for all the world as if he came out of the damaged goods department of a grizzly store!"

John would have dearly liked to have a shot at the bear, who had climbed down and was now skulking away; but going after him was not to be thought of. The flood was still rising; there was nothing more urgent than to avoid it; and all four returned to the *Fair Rambler*.

CHAPTER VIII - KNAVES' VILLAGE

A WEEK after, on the 26th of May, our party had reached the springs of the Fraser. Night and day the rain had kept coming down, but this bad weather should soon come to a stop, so said the Indian guide.

A détour round the springs of the river, through a somewhat hilly country, and the *Fair Rambler* now turned due west.

A few days more and Mr. Cascabel would be at the Alaska frontier.

For a week past, not a village, not a hamlet had been seen along the track selected by Ro-No. Indeed they had every reason to prize the services of this native; he knew the country thoroughly.

On that day, the guide informed Mr. Cascabel that he might, if he chose, halt at a village, a short distance off, where twenty-four hours' rest would not be thrown away on his horses, overworked as they had been.

"What is this village?" inquired Mr. Cascabel, always distrustful when the Columbian population was in question.

"Kokwin village," replied the guide.

"Kokwin?" exclaimed Mr. Cascabel. "That, in French, would be Knaves' Village."

"Yes," said John, "such is the name given in the map; it must be the name of some Indian tribe."

"Very well! very well! Not so many explanations," answered Mr. Cascabel. "A most suitable name it is for that village, if it is inhabited by English people, were it but by a half dozen of them!"

In the course of the evening, the *Fair Rambler* did halt at the entrance into the village. Three days at most now separated it from the geographical frontier between Alaska and Columbia.

Thenceforth Mr. Cascabel would speedily recover that happy temper of his, so severely tried on the territory of her Britannic Majesty.

Knaves' Village was occupied by Indians; but there were not a few Englishmen, professional huntsmen or mere amateurs, who stayed here only during the hunting season.

Among the officers of the Victoria garrison, who happened to be there, was a baronet, Sir Edward Turner by name, a haughty personage and a bully, infatuated with the magical power of his nationality,—one of those "gentlemen" who imagine anything is lawful for them, because of their being Englishmen. Needless to say he hated the French quite as much as Mr. Cascabel hated his countrymen. These two were a match, it is evident.

Now the very evening on which the halt took place, while John, Sander, and Clovy were gone in search of provisions, it happened that the baronet's dogs fell in with Wagram and Marengo in the vicinity of the *Fair Rambler* and it was apparent that the two French bow-wows shared the national antipathies of their master.

Hence a disagreement between the spaniel and the poodle on one hand, and the pointers on the other; hence a good deal of barking and snarling, then a regular fight, and finally the intervention of the respective owners.

On hearing the noise, Sir Edward had rushed out of the house which he tenanted on the outskirt of the village, and threatened Mr. Cascabel's dogs with his whip.

The latter immediately found a protector in their master, who made straightway for the baronet.

Sir Edward Turner—he spoke very good French—soon found out the kind of a man he had to deal with, and breaking open the flood-gates of his arrogance, began to treat, à la British, our showman in particular and his countrymen in general.

Mr. Cascabel's feelings, on hearing such language, may easily be imagined. However, as he had no wish—especially in an English country—to get into difficulties which might delay his journey, he bit his lips and said in a tone of voice in no way objectionable:

"It was your dogs, sir, that began to attack mine!"

"Your dogs!" sneered the baronet. "A showman's curs!—What are they good for but to be snarled at by my pointers or cut by my whip!"

"I'll pray you to observe," said Mr. Cascabel, warming up despite his intention to keep cool, "that what you say there is unworthy of a gentleman!"

"Still, what I say is the only answer that one of your sort deserves."

"I speak politely, sir,—you prove yourself but a cad."

"I advise you to take care, you who bandy words with Sir Edward Turner."

Mr. Cascabel filled with passion; with blanched cheeks, eyes aglow, and clenched fists, he was stepping up to the baronet, when Napoleona stood by him:

"Father, do come!" said she. "Mamma wants you!"

Cornelia had sent her daughter to fetch Mr. Cascabel home to the *Fair Rambler*.

"Presently!" replied the father. "Tell mamma to wait till I have done with this gentleman, Napoleona!"

At the mention of this name, the baronet indulged in a sarcastic peal of laughter,

"Napoleona!" he repeated, "Napoleona!—That little lass is called after the monster who—"

This was more than Mr. Cascabel could bear. He stepped forward until his folded arms grazed the baronet's chest.

"You insult me!" cried he.

"I insult you,—you?"

"Yes, me, as well as the great man who would have made but one mouthful of your island if he had only landed there!"

"Indeed?"

"Yes, would have gobbled it up like an oyster!"

"Contemptible clown!" exclaimed the baronet.

And he had moved one step back in the attitude of the boxer who stands on the defensive.

"Yes, you do insult me, Mr. Baronet, and you shall give me an account of it."

"Settle accounts with a showman!"

"When you insulted the showman, you made him your equal, sir. And fight we shall, with the sword or the pistol, anything you like,—even with our fists!"

"Why not with bladders like the clowns on your trestles?"

"Ready, sir—"

"Can I have a fight with a tramp?"

"Yes!" shouted Cascabel, beside himself with rage, "yes! a fight—or a sound drubbing!"

And without minding that he was likely to have heavy odds against him in a boxing encounter with his "gentlemanly" opponent, he was about to dash at him, when Cornelia herself intervened.

At the same time appeared some officers of Sir Edward Turner's regiment, his hunting companions; they naturally sided with the baronet, determined as they were not to permit him to measure himself with a fellow of that "tribe," and heaped their insults on the Cascabel family. Indeed these insults were powerless to move the self-composed Cornelia—at least outwardly. She contented herself with throwing on Sir Edward Turner a glance that was anything but reassuring for the man who had insulted her husband.

John, Clovy, and Sander had also appeared on the scene, and the dispute would have degenerated into a general battle, when Mrs. Cascabel cried out:

"Come, Cæser; come along, children!—Now then, all of us to the *Fair Rambler*, and quicker than that!"

There was such an imperative ring in the tone of her voice, that no one thought of disobeying the order.

What an evening Mr. Cascabel spent! His anger could not cool down! He, touched in his honor, touched in the person of his hero! Insulted by an Englishman! He would go to him, he would fight him, he would fight all his companions, and all the knaves of Knaves' Village! And his children were but too ready to go and back him. Clovy himself talked of nothing short of eating an Englishman's nose,—unless it were his ear!

In truth, Cornelia found it no easy task to calm down all her enraged folks. In her heart, she knew that all the wrong was on Sir Edward Turner's side; she could not deny that her husband first, and every member of the family after him, had received such treatment as showmen of the lowest type would not give each other at a fair!

Still, as she would not let matters grow worse, she would not give in; she showed a bold front to the storm, and when he expressed what she thought would be his final determination to go and give the baronet such a drubbing as would,—she said to him:

"Cæser, I forbid you!"

And Mr. Cascabel, gnawing his heart, had to yield to his wife's command.

How Cornelia longed to see the dawn of the next day, when they would leave the unlucky village! She would not feel easy until her family would be a few miles farther to the north. And, so as to be sure that nobody would leave the wagon during the night, not only did she carefully lock the door of the *Fair Rambler* but she mounted guard outside, herself.

The next day, the 27th of May, at three in the morning, Cornelia awoke the whole troupe. By way of greater safety, she was anxious to be off before dawn, when all the villagers, Indians or Englishmen, would still be sleeping. This was the best way to prevent a fresh resuming of hostilities. Even at that early hour—a detail worth noticing—the good woman seemed in a singular hurry to raise the camp. All agitation, with anxious features and beaming eyes, prying to the right and to the left, she urged, harassed, and scolded her husband, her children, and Clovy, who were not half quick enough to please her.

"In how many days shall we have crossed the frontier?" she asked of the guide.

"In three days," replied Ro-No, "if we have no hindrance on the road."

"Now then, forward, march!" she cried. "And above all, let no one see us going away!"

It should not be imagined that Mr. Cascabel had swallowed the insults thrust down his throat the previous night. Leaving this village without squaring up that little account with the baronet was indeed hard for a Norman, and a patriotic Frenchman, to boot.

"That's what it is," he kept on repeating, "to set your foot in one of John Bull's possessions."

Still, longing as he was to run down to the village in the hope of coming across Sir Edward Turner, many though the glances were that he cast toward the closed shutters of the house inhabited by that gentleman, he dared not go away from the terrible Cornelia. Not an instant did she leave his side.

"Where are you going, Cæser?—Cæser, stay where you are!—I forbid you stirring, Cæser!"

Mr. Cascabel heard nothing else. Never had he been so completely under the control of his excellent and self-willed wife.

Fortunately, thanks to oft-repeated injunctions, all preparations were soon completed, and the horses stood ready in the shafts. By four o'clock, the dogs, the monkey and the parrot, the husband, the sons and the daughter, were all secured inside the *Fair Rambler*, and Cornelia took a seat by the front railing. Then, as soon as Clovy and the guide were ready at the horses' heads, the signal was given for the start.

A quarter of an hour later Knaves' Village had disappeared behind the curtain of tall trees with which it was encircled. It was scarcely daylight. All was silence. Not a living soul was to be seen along the vast plain that stretched forth toward the North.

At last, when it was evident that the departure had been accomplished without attracting the attention of any one in the village, when Cornelia felt perfectly satisfied that neither the Indians nor the English thought of preventing their escape, she heaved a deep sigh of relief, at which her husband felt somewhat hurt.

"How greatly frightened you seemed of those people, Cornelia!" he remarked.

"Yes, greatly," was her simple reply.

The next three days passed by without any incident, and, as the guide had said, the extreme end of Columbia was reached.

And having safely crossed the Alaska frontier, the *Fair Rambler* was now at liberty to rest.

Once there, the travelers had only to pay off the Indian, who had proved as zealous as faithful, and to thank him for his services. Then Ro-No took leave of the family, after explaining the course they should follow to reach Sitka, the capital of the Russian possessions, as speedily as possible.

Now that he was on English soil no longer, Mr. Cascabel should have breathed more freely! Well, it was not so! At the end of three days, he was still under the influence of the exciting scene at Knaves' Village. It still weighed heavily on his chest:

"Look here," he could not refrain from saying to Cornelia, "you should indeed have let me go back and settle accounts with my English lord—"

"They had been settled before we left, César!" simply answered Mrs. Cascabel.

And settled they had been, in truth,—settled and squared right even!

During the ensuing night, whilst all her people were asleep at the camp, Cornelia had gone for a stroll round the baronet's house, and perceiving him on his way to the woods to lie in wait for game, she had followed him a few hundred paces. Then, once under cover of the forest, "the champion of the Chicago female encounters" had administered him one of those "floorers" that leave a man sprawling on the ground. Sir Edward Turner, well thrashed and sore, had got on his legs the next morning only, and must have felt for a long time after, unpleasant reminders of his meeting with this amiable woman.

"Oh, Cornelia! Cornelia!" exclaimed her husband, as he pressed her in his arms, "you have avenged my honor. You were worthy, indeed, to be a Cascabel!"

CHAPTER IX - CAN'T PASS THROUGH!

ALASKA is that portion of the continent comprised, to the northwest of North America, between the fifty-second and the seventy-second degree of latitude. It is transversely cut by the line of the Arctic polar circle which curves through Behring Strait.

Look at the map with a little attention, and you will recognize without much trouble the outline of a head, of the Israelite type. The forehead is developed between Cape Lisbon and Barrow Point; the orbit of the eye is Kotzebue Sound; the nose is Cape Prince of Wales; the mouth is Norton Bay; and the traditional beard is the Alaska peninsula, continued on by that sprinkling of Aleutian Islands which dots the Pacific Ocean. As to the head, it ends with the termination of the ranges, the last slopes of which die off into the Ice Sea.

Such is the country about to be crossed obliquely by the *Fair Rambler* over a distance of eighteen hundred miles.

Of course, John had carefully studied the map, its mountains, its watercourses, the shape of the coast line, in fine the whole itinerary to be followed. He even had delivered a little lecture on the subject, a lecture listened to with the utmost interest by the whole family.

Thanks to him, everybody—not forgetting Clovy—knew that this country, the northwestern extremity of the American continent, had first been visited by the Russians, then by the Frenchman Lapérouse and by the Englishman Vancouver, and lastly by the American McClure, at the time of his expedition in search of Sir John Franklin.

In reality, the district had already been known—though partly only—thanks to the explorations of Sir Frederick Whymper and of Colonel Bulkley, in 1865, when there had been a question of laying a submarine cable between the old and the new worlds through Behring Strait. Up to this time, the interior of Alaska had hardly been journeyed through except by the travelers of houses in the fur and hide trade.

It was then that Monroe's famous doctrine made its reappearance in international politics, a doctrine in accordance with which America should be the exclusive property of Americans. If the colonies of Great Britain, Columbia, and the Dominion, were fated to remain non-American for a more or less lengthened period, Russia, perhaps, might be induced to cede Alaska to the Union, say a hundred and thirty-five thousand square feet[1] of territory. And with this object in view, correspondence was entered into with the Muscovite government.

No little sneering was raised at first, in the United States, when Secretary of State Seward proposed the purchase of this "Walrus Sea," which seemed likely to prove a white elephant for the Republic. Still, Seward plodded on, with Yankee obstinacy, and in 1867 things had made considerable progress. Indeed it may be said that, if the convention between America and Russia was not signed, it was expected to be from one day to another.

It was on the evening of the 31st of May that the Cascabels had halted at the frontier, under a grove of tall trees. In this spot, the *Fair Rambler* stood on Alaskan territory, fully under Russian dominion, and no longer on the soil of British Columbia. Mr. Cascabel might be free from all uneasiness on this score.

And his good-humor had returned, and in so contagious a manner that it was shared by all his people. Now, all along as far as the boundary of Russia in Europe, the road should lie unceasingly on Muscovite territory. Be they called Alaska, or Siberia, did not these immense countries belong to the Czar?

Supper was unusually gay. John had killed a fine hare, fat and plump, that Wagram had raised in the thicket; a real Russian hare, if you please!

"And we shall drink a good bottle!" said Mr. Cascabel. "On my honor, I fancy my lungs breathe better this side of that frontier! It looks to me like a mixture of Russian and American air! Breathe the full of your chests, my children! Don't stint yourselves! There is enough for everybody—even Clovy, in spite of that thirty-six-inch nose of his! Why, I have been stifling these five weeks past, coming through that cursed Columbia!"

Supper over, and the last drop of the good bottle gone, each one repaired to his bunk and his little bed. The night was spent in the greatest calm. It was disturbed neither by the approach of dangerous animals nor by the apparition of wandering Indians. Next morning, horses and dogs had completely recovered from their fatigue.

The camp was raised at early morn, and the guests of hospitable Russia, "that sister of France," as Mr. Cascabel said, prepared for their journey. Nor was much time needed. A little before six in the morning, the *Fair Rambler* was making headway, northwest, toward Simpson River, which it would be easy to ferry across.

This spur, which Alaska shoots forth toward the south, is a narrow strip, known under the general name of Thlinkilthen, and flanked, to the west, by a certain number of islands and archipelagos, such as the isles of the Prince of Wales, of Crooze, of Kuju, of Baranoff, of Sitka, etc. It is in the latter island that the capital of American Russia is situated, called likewise New Archangel. As soon as the *Fair Rambler* had arrived at Sitka, Mr. Cascabel intended halting for a few days, first of all to take some rest, and secondly to prepare for the completion of that first portion of his journey which was to bring him to Behring Strait.

This itinerary obliged them to follow a strip of land which skirted in capricious zigzags the mountains of the coast line.

Mr. Cascabel started then; but he had not advanced a step on Alaskan soil, when he was stopped short by an obstacle which had every appearance of proving insurmountable.

Friendly Russia, the sister of France, did not seem disposed to extend her hospitality to those French brethren who constituted the Cascabel family.

For, Russia suddenly stood before them under the shape and form of three frontier guards, muscular fellows, with thick beard, large heads, "tip-tilted" noses, a decidedly Kalmuk look about them, wearing the dark uniform of the Muscovite official, and that flat cap which strikes wholesome fear into the hearts of so many millions of human beings.

At a signal from the chief of these guards the *Fair Rambler* stood still, and Clovy, who drove the horses, called to his master.

Mr. Cascabel appeared at the door of the first compartment and was joined by his sons and his wife. And, somewhat uneasy at the sight of these uniforms, all alighted.

"Your passports!" demanded the officer in Russian—a language Mr. Cascabel understood but too well on this occasion.

"Passports?" he repeated.

"Yes, there is no entering the possessions of the Czar without passports."

"Why, we have none, dear sir," politely answered Mr. Cascabel.

"Then, you'll stay where you are!"

This was clear and to the point, just like a door slammed in an intruder's face.

Mr. Cascabel winced. He knew how severe are the regulations of the Muscovite administration; and a friendly compromise was a very doubtful eventuality. In truth, it was incredible ill-luck to have come across these guards at the very moment when the *Fair Rambler* had crossed the frontier.

Cornelia and John, in great anxiety, were awaiting the result of the conversation, on which depended the accomplishment of their journey.

"Brave Muscovites," Mr. Cascabel began, bringing out the full power of his voice and the eloquence of his gestures to give more emphasis to his usual oratory, "we are French people, traveling for our pleasure, and, I presume to say, for the pleasure of others, more especially that of the noble Bojars, when they condescend to honor us with their presence! We had imagined that papers could be dispensed with in the case of the dominions of His Majesty the Czar, Emperor of all the Russias."

"Entering the Czar's territory without a special permit," was the answer, "such a thing was never seen,—never!"

"Might it not be seen once,—just on one little occasion?" suggested Mr. Cascabel in his most insinuating manner.

"No," replied the agent, stiff and dry. "And so, back you go, and no comments!"

"Still, may I ask where passports may be had?" inquired Mr. Cascabel.

"That's your business!"

"Let us pass on, as far as Sitka, and there, through the intervention of the consul of France—"

"There is no French consul at Sitka! And besides, where do you come from?"

"From Sacramento."

"Well, you should have supplied yourselves with passports at Sacramento! Now, it is no use saying any more."

"It is very great use, on the contrary," replied Cascabel, "as we are on our way home to Europe."

"To Europe!—and by what road?"

Mr. Cascabel felt that his remark was likely to arouse suspicions about him, for, returning to Europe by this route was rather extraordinary.

"Quite so," he added. "Certain circumstances have compelled us to come this round."

"After all, that is beside the question," remarked the officer. "Russian territories are closed to travelers without passports!"

"If the only thing needful is the payment of certain dues," continued Mr. Cascabel, "we might come to an understanding perhaps."

And a knowing wink accompanied this gentle hint.

But an understanding was not to be arrived at, even on these conditions.

"Brave Muscovites," reiterated Cascabel, as a drowning man who clutches at a straw, "have you never heard of the Cascabel family?"

And he spoke the words as though the Cascabel family were on a foot of equality with the Romanoff House!

The hit proved as utter a failure as the rest. They had to turn the horses round and retrace their steps. The guards even carried their strict orders out to the extent of accompanying the *Fair Rambler* to the other side of the frontier, with a distinct injunction to the travelers never to cross it again. And the consequence was that Mr. Cascabel found himself once more, with a very long face, on the territory of British Columbia.

It will be confessed this was an unpleasant position, nay, a most alarming one. All the plans were now upset. The itinerary, adopted with such enthusiasm, should now be laid aside. The journey home through the west, the return to Europe by Siberia, became an impossibility for want of passports. Going back to New York through the Far West could be done in the usual way. But how was the Atlantic Ocean to be crossed without a boat, and where was the boat to be had without money to pay the passage fare?

As to earning, along the road, a sum sufficient to cover that amount, it would have been unwise to expect it. Besides, how long would it have taken them to save it up? The Cascabel family—why not hit the nail on the head?—must be well-nigh overdone by this time in the United States. For the past twenty years there was hardly a town or a village that; the Cascabels had not "worked" all along the Great Trunk. They would not now take in as many cents as they formerly took dollars. No, the eastern route was beset with endless delays; years perhaps would roll by before they could take ship for Europe. At any cost, combinations should be found which would enable the *Fair Rambler* to reach Sitka. Such were the thoughts, such was the language, of the members of this interesting family when they were left to their painful meditations.

"Well, here we are in a pretty pass!" said Cornelia, with a shake of her head.

"It is not a pass at all," retorted her husband, "you can't pass through, it's a blind alley!"

Now then, old wrestler, you the Hercules of the popular arena, will you lack the means to get the better of your evil fortune? Will you let yourself be nonplussed by ill-luck? You have all the showman's tricks and dodges at your fingers' ends, will you not succeed in juggling yourself out of this difficulty? Is your bag of tricks really emptied out? Can it be that your imagination, so fruitful in expedients, will not carry off the victory in this struggle?

"César," said Cornelia, "since those wretched guards happened to be on our path just in time to prevent us stepping into the country, let us apply to their superior officer!"

"Their superior officer!" exclaimed Mr. Cascabel. "No doubt, that is the Governor of Alaska, some Russian colonel, as unmanageable as his men, and who will send us to the devil!"

"Besides, his residence must be at Sitka, and Sitka is the very place they wont let us go to."

"Who knows," suggested Clovy with no little judgment, "perhaps these frontier-men might not object to bring one of us to the Governor."

"Why, Clovy is right," answered Mr. Cascabel. "That's a good idea!"

"Unless it's not worth a clove," added the clown with his habitual qualifying clause.

"It is worth trying before we retrace our steps," replied John, "and, if you like, father, I shall go—"

"No, I had better go," said Mr. Cascabel. "Is it a far cry to Sitka?"

"Some three hundred miles."

"Well, in the course of nine or ten days I can be back here again. Let us have a sleep over it, and to-morrow we shall make the venture!"

Next morning, at break of day, Mr. Cascabel went out in search of the guards. His search proved neither hard nor of long duration, for they had remained on the look-out in the vicinity of the *Fair Rambler*.

"Why, there you are again?" they cried to him in a threatening tone of voice.

"Here I am again," he replied, trying the effect of his most bewitching smile.

And with a running accompaniment of compliments to the Russian authorities, he expressed his wish to be brought to the presence of His Excellency the Governor of Alaska. He offered to pay all the traveling expenses of the "honorable officer" who would be kind enough to accompany him, and even hinted at a handsome remuneration in hard cash for the generous and noble-hearted man who would,—etc.

The proposal fell through. Even the perspective of the handsome remuneration proved of no avail. It is probable that the guards, as obstinate as custom-officers, and stubborn as tax-gatherers, were beginning to look upon this persistent desire to cross the Alaskan frontier as extremely suspicious. In truth, one of them cut matters short by ordering Cascabel to return to where he came from, forthwith, and added:

"If we ever find you again on Russian territory, it is not to Sitka we shall bring you, but to the nearest fort. And once you get in there, you never know how or when you will get out."

Mr. Cascabel, not without being somewhat roughly handled, was immediately conducted back to the *Fair Rambler*, where his disappointed look told the tale of his failure.

Had the day really come when the home on wheels of the Cascabels was about to be transformed into a sedentary dwelling? Was the skiff, that carried the showman and his fortune, to remain stranded on the Columbo-Alaskan frontier like a boat that the outgoing tide leaves high and dry on the rocks? To all appearance, there was but too much fear of it.

How sad and gloomy the first day that was spent in these conditions, how sad the days that wore their weary length away, ere the wanderers could resolve on a new course!

Luckily, there was no lack of food; of the provisions that they expected to renew at Sitka a sufficient stock still remained. Besides, it was surprising to see the abundance of game in the neighborhood. Only, John and Wagram took good care not to venture out of the Columbian territory. It would have meant much more for the youth than the confiscation of his gun and a fine to the benefit of the Muscovite treasury.

Meanwhile, grief "clawed in its chilly clutch" the hearts of our friends. The very animals themselves seemed to feel their share of sorrow. Jako jabbered less than usual. The dogs indulged in dismal fits of howling. John Bull was forgetting his antics and grimaces. Vermont and Gladiator alone seemed to accept their situation without a murmur, having nothing to do but graze the rich, fresh grass supplied to them by the surrounding plain.

"For all that, and all that, we must make up our minds one way or the other!" Mr. Cascabel would often say, folding his arms across his chest.

That was evident, but which way?—which way? This should not have puzzled Mr. Cascabel; for, in truth, he had no choice in the matter. Seeing that he was forbidden going on ahead, the only alternative was moving back and giving up that trip westward that he had so courageously undertaken. Return he should on that hated soil of British Columbia, thence away through the prairies of the Far West, and on to the coast of the Atlantic! Once in New York, what would they do? Perhaps a subscription might be set on foot by some charitable souls, to enable them to pay their voyage home? How humiliating for these brave-hearted folks, who had always lived by their labor and never held out a begging hand, to come down so low as to be the recipients of charity! What wretches they were who had robbed them of their little all, in the passes of the Sierra!

"If they don't get hanged in America, garroted in Spain, guillotined in France, or impaled in Turkey," Mr. Cascabel used to say, "justice has fled this nether world."

And at length his mind was made up.

"We shall be off to-morrow!" he said during the evening of the 4th of June. "We shall go back to Sacramento, and then—"

He said no more. In Sacramento, they would see. As to setting off, everything was ready. There was nothing to do but putting the horses to the wagon and turning their heads to the south.

This last evening on the frontier of Alaska was still sadder than the rest. Each one sat in his corner, without a word. Outside, darkness was intense. Heavy clouds hovered to and fro through the sky like icebergs sent adrift by the gale toward the east.

In vain would the eye seek a single star, and the crescent of the new moon had just disappeared behind the lofty mountains at the horizon.

It may have been nine o'clock when Mr. Cascabel gave the order to go to bed. Next morning they should start before daybreak. The *Fair Rambler* would resume the track it had followed from Sacramento, and even without a guide, it would not be a difficult matter to get along. Once at the springs of the Fraser, the valley would bring them straight on to the frontier of Washington Territory.

And accordingly Clovy was preparing to lock the door of the outer compartment, after saying good-night to the two dogs, when a sudden report was heard within a short distance.

"That sounded uncommonly like a shot!" exclaimed Mr. Cascabel.

"Yes, it was a shot," answered John.

"Some sportsman, no doubt!" said Cornelia.

"A sportsman—this dark night?" observed John. "That's hardly likely!"

Just then, a second report broke the stillness of the night, and cries were heard.

CHAPTER X - KAYETTE

ON hearing the cries, Mr. Cascabel, John, Sander, and Clovy rushed out of the wagon.

"It is this way," said John, pointing to the edge of the forest which bordered the frontier line.

"Let us listen again!" said Mr. Cascabel.

This was useless. No other cry was uttered, no other detonation followed the first two that had been heard.

"Might it be an accident?" suggested Sander.

"In any case," answered John, "one thing certain is, that the cries we heard were cries of distress, and that, somewhere about here, there is somebody in danger."

"You must go and bring help!" said Cornelia.

"Yes, lads, come along," answered Mr. Cascabel, "and let us be well armed!"

After all, it might not be an accident. A traveler might have been the victim of a murderous assault on the Alaskan frontier. Hence it was prudent that they should be prepared to defend themselves as well as to defend others.

Almost without losing an instant, Mr. Cascabel and John, each supplied with a gun, and Sander and Clovy, with a revolver, left the *Fair Rambler* to the keeping of Cornelia and the two dogs.

For five or six minutes they followed the edge of the wood. Now and then they stopped to listen: no noise disturbed the silence of the forest. They felt sure, none the less, that the cries had come from this direction, and from no great distance.

"Unless we were the dupes of an illusion?" hinted Mr. Cascabel.

"No, father," replied John, "that could not be! Hark!—do you hear?"

This time, there was indeed a call for help; it was not the voice of a man, as in the first instance, but that of a woman or a child.

The night was still very dark, and, under the canopy of the trees, nothing could be discerned beyond a few yards.

Clovy had at first suggested taking one of the wagon lamps with him; but Mr. Cascabel had objected to it on the score of prudence, and, on the whole, it was better for them not to be seen going along.

Besides, the cries were now getting very frequent, and sufficiently distinct to guide our relief party.

Indeed it seemed likely that there would be no necessity for going very deep into the woods.

Sure enough, five minutes later, Mr. Cascabel and his three companions had come to a little clearing in the forest. There, two men lay on the ground. A woman, kneeling near one of them, held up his head between her arms.

This was the woman whose cries had last been heard, and, in the Chinook dialect, of which Cascabel had a smattering, she called out:

"Come!—Come!—They have killed them!"

John drew near to the scared woman all besprinkled with the blood flowing from the breast of the unfortunate man that she endeavored to bring back to life.

"This one breathes still!" said John.

"And the other?" inquired Mr. Cascabel.

"The other—I don't know about him!" replied Sander.

Mr. Cascabel stooped to see if the throbbing of the heart or the breathing through the lips betrayed the least remnant of life in the man.

"He is quite dead!" he said.

And it was but too true; a bullet had struck him in the temple; his death must have been instantaneous.

And now, what was this woman, whose language proclaimed her Indian origin? Was she young or old? This could not be seen in the dark, under the hood drawn over her head. But, it would be ascertained later on; she would tell whence she came, as well as the circumstances under which this two-fold murder had been committed. The first thing to be done was to convey to the camp the man who was still breathing and to give him such immediate tending as might perchance save his life. As to his dead companion, they would come and pay the last duties to him on the following day.

With the aid of John, Mr. Cascabel raised the wounded man by his shoulders, whilst Sander and Clovy took him up by his feet. Then turning to the woman:

"Follow us," said he to her.

And the latter, without any hesitation, walked by the side of the body, stanching with a kerchief the blood still flowing from the wound.

Progress was slow. The man was heavy; and above all, care should be taken to avoid jolting him, It was a living man Mr. Cascabel meant to bring to the *Fair Rambler*, not a corpse.

At last, at the end of twenty minutes, the whole party reached the wagon without any mishap.

Cornelia and little Napoleona, thinking they might have been attacked, were awaiting their return in deep anxiety.

"Quick, Cornelia!" cried Mr. Cascabel, "some water, some linen, everything that is wanted to stop a hemorrhage or else this unfortunate man will lose all consciousness."

"All right, all right," replied Cornelia. "You know I am good at that, Cæser. Not so much talking, and leave him to me!"

She was good at it, was Cornelia; and many were the wounds she had dressed, in the course of her professional career.

Clovy spread out, in the first compartment, a mattress on which the body was laid, the head slightly raised with a bolster. By the light of the lamp in the ceiling, they were then able to see the man's face, already blanched by approaching death, and likewise the features of the Indian woman who was kneeling by his side.

She was a young girl; she did not seem over fifteen or sixteen years of age.

"Who is this child?" asked Cornelia.

"It is she we heard calling for help," replied John; "she was near the wounded man."

The latter might be forty-five years old; his beard and hair were turning gray; he was above the middle height, of a sympathetic cast of features, and the firmness of his character could be read even through his closed eyelids, despite the deathly pallor of his face. From time to time, a sigh broke through his lips, but not a word escaped him that would denote his nationality.

When his chest was laid bare, Cornelia was able to see that it had been transpierced by a poniard between the third and fourth ribs. Was the wound a fatal one? A surgeon alone could have said so. What was beyond a doubt was its severity.

However, as the attendance of a surgeon was out of the question under existing circumstances, they should remain satisfied with such attentions as lay in Cornelia's power and such drugs as were contained in their little traveling pharmacy.

This was done, and the hemorrhage, from which death would have quickly followed, was effectually stopped. Later on they would see if, absolutely prostrated as he was, this man might be conveyed to the nearest village or not. And this time, Mr. Cascabel would not trouble to inquire whether it was Anglo-Saxon or not.

After carefully washing the lips of the wound with cold water, Cornelia laid on it some strips of linen steeped in arnica; and this dressing proved sufficient to stop the blood, which the wounded man had lost in such quantity from the time of the attempted murder to his arrival at the camp.

"And now, Cornelia," inquired Mr. Cascabel, "what can we do?"

"Well, we shall lay this poor man on our bed," replied Cornelia, "and I shall keep watch over him, to renew the dressing when needs be."

"We shall all watch him," said John. "Could we go asleep, do you think? Besides, we must keep on the lookout! There are murderers about!"

Mr. Cascabel, John, and Clovy took the man and laid him on the bed in the inner room.

And while Cornelia stood by the bedside, spying a word that was not spoken, the young Indian, whose dialect Mr. Cascabel did his best to interpret, related her history.

She was, as had been surmised, a native, belonging to one of the independent tribes of Alaska. In this province, to the north and to the south of the big river Yukon which waters it from east to west, you come across numerous tribes, some wandering, others sedentary, and, among them, the Co-Yukons, the chief and the most cruel perhaps, then the Newicarguts, the Tanands, the Kotch-a-Koutchins, and also, more especially near the mouth of the river, the Pastoliks, the Kaveaks, the Primosks, the Malemutes, and the Ingeletes.

It was to this last tribe that the young Indian woman belonged, and her name was Kayette.

Kayette had lost her father and her mother, and had not one relative left. Nor do families alone thus utterly disappear among the natives; whole tribes do so, no trace of which is to be found afterwards in the territory of Alaska.

Such the Midland tribe, which formerly occupied the north of the Yukon.

Kayette, thus left an orphan, had started off toward the south, through those countries of which she had a certain knowledge thanks to her previously visiting them with the wandering Indians. Her intention was to go to Sitka, where she hoped to be engaged as a servant by some Russian official. And surely she ought to have been engaged on the mere recommendation of her gentle, pleasing, honest countenance. She was very handsome, with the least tinge of red in her complexion, dark eyes with long lashes, and a luxuriance of dark hair held up in the hood of fur that she wore over her head.

Of middle height, she seemed graceful and light in spite of her heavy cloak.

Among these Indian races of North America, as is known, the bright and merry-tempered children grow up quickly. At ten years of age, the boys can use the gun and the hatchet skillfully. At fifteen, young girls marry, and, even at that age, prove devoted mothers. And so Kayette was more sober, stronger-willed likewise, than her age would imply; and the long journey she had just undertaken was very evident proof of her strength of character. For a month already she had been on the tramp toward the southwest of Alaska; and she had reached the narrow strip of land, close to the island in which the capital is situated, when, journeying along the edge of the forest, she had heard two reports of fire-arms, followed by cries of despair, at a distance of a few hundred paces.

These were the cries that had reached the ears of the occupants of the *Fair Rambler*.

Instantly Kayette had courageously plunged into the wood.

And no doubt her approach must have given the alarm, for she barely had time to get a glimpse of two men running away through the thicket. But evidently the wretches would have noticed very soon that they had been scared by a child; and, as a matter of fact, they were already returning to the clearing to rob their victims, when the coming of Mr. Cascabel and his party had frightened them—and, this time, frightened them right away.

In the presence of these two men lying on the ground, one a corpse, the other still breathing, young Kayette had called for help, and the reader knows what had taken place subsequently. The first cries heard by Mr. Cascabel were those of the assaulted travelers, the second had been uttered by the young Indian woman.

The night passed by. Our friends had no occasion to repel an attack on the part of the murderers; they, doubtless, had hastened to leave the scene of their crime.

Next morning, Cornelia could report no change in the state of the wounded man, no cause for less anxiety.

It was now that Kayette proved of great utility by going and gathering certain herbs of which she knew the antiseptic properties. She made an infusion of these, and, steeped in this liquid, the dressing did not allow one drop of blood to ooze through.

In the course of the morning, it was noticed that the wounded man was commencing to breathe more freely; but, as yet, they were only sighs—not even broken words—that escaped his lips. And so, it was impossible to learn who he was, whence he came, where he was going, what his business was on the Alaskan frontier, under what circumstances his companion and he were attacked, and who their aggressors were.

In any case, if money had been the motive of their crime, the scoundrels, in their hurried flight on the approach of the young Indian, had missed a fortune the like of which they would hardly ever find again in these solitary parts.

For, Mr. Cascabel having undressed the wounded man, had found, in a leather belt closely fitted around his waist, a quantity of gold coins of American and of Russian currency. The whole amounted to about fifteen thousand francs. This sum was carefully put aside, to be restored to its owner as soon as possible.

As to papers, there were none, save a pocket-book with a few notes, some scribbled in Russian, some in French. Nothing there was, that would help to ascertain the identity of the stranger.

That morning, about nine o'clock, John said:

"Father, we have a last duty to perform toward that unburied corpse."

"You are right, John, come on. Maybe we shall find on him some writing that may help us. You, Clovy, you had better come, too. Bring a pick and a shovel with you."

Supplied with these tools, and careful to take their firearms with them, the three men left the wagon, and made their way along that same edge of the wood that they had followed the previous night.

In a few minutes' time, they had reached the spot where the murder had been committed.

What seemed to permit of little doubt was that the two wayfarers had encamped there for the night. There were still the signs of a halt, the remnants of a fire, the ashes of which were still alive. At the foot of a huge fir-tree a quantity of grass had been heaped up, so that the two travelers might have a soft bed to lie on, and indeed they may have been asleep when they were attacked.

As to the dead man, the rigor mortis had already set in.

To judge by his dress, his features, his hard hands, it was easy to see that this man—he might have been thirty at most—was the other's servant.

John searched his pockets. He found no paper. No money was there either. From his belt hung a revolver, of American make, that the poor fellow had not had time to use.

Evidently the attack had been sudden and unforeseen, and the two victims had fallen at the same time.

At this hour, round about the neighborhood of the clearing, the forest was undisturbed by a living soul. After a short exploration, John returned without seeing anybody. It was plain the murderers had not come back, for they surely would have taken the garments of their victim, or at the very least the revolver still hanging on his belt.

Meanwhile, Clovy had dug a grave deep enough to prevent the wild animals clawing out the corpse. The dead man was lowered into it, and John said a few words of a prayer when the clay had been shoveled back over him.

Whereupon Mr. Cascabel, his son, and Clovy returned to the camp. There, while Kayette remained by the wounded man, John, his father, and his mother held a consultation among themselves.

"It is certain," began Mr. Cascabel, "that if we turn our steps toward California, our man will never get there alive. We have hundreds upon hundreds of miles to get over. The best thing would be to make a shot for Sitka, if those hangable police-folk did not forbid us to set our foot on their territory!"

"And do what they like, to Sitka it is that we must go," answered Cornelia resolutely, "and to Sitka we will go!"

"And how can we? We wont have gone a mile of ground before we are arrested."

"No matter, César! Go we must, and with a bold face! If we meet the guards, we shall tell them what has happened, and surely they could not refuse to this unfortunate man what they did refuse us!"

Mr. Cascabel shook his head with an air of doubt.

"Mother is right," said John. "Let us endeavor to push on to Sitka, even without seeking at the hands of the officials a permit that they will not give us. It would be a loss of time. Besides, it is just possible that they think we are on the way to Sacramento and that they have gone about their business. For the last twenty-four hours we have not seen one of them."

"That is right," answered Mr. Cascabel, "I should not be surprised if they were gone."

"Unless—" remarked Clovy, who had just joined the discussion.

"Yes—unless—We know the rest!" replied Mr. Cascabel.

John's remark was quite correct, and there was perhaps nothing better to do than take the road to Sitka.

A quarter of an hour after, Vermont and Gladiator were in harness.

After their good rest during this prolonged halt at the frontier, they could measure a fair extent of ground for their first day's work. The *Fair Rambler* started, and it was with undisguised pleasure that Mr. Cascabel left Columbian territory.

"Children," said he, "let us keep our eye open, and let it be our weather eye. As to you, John, silence your gun! It is quite needless to proclaim our passage."

"As to that, the kitchen has no chance of running short!" added Mrs. Cascabel.

The country north of Columbia, though rather uneven, is easy for a vehicle, even when you follow the numerous channels which separate the archipelagos on the edge of the continent. No mountains in view, to the furthest limits of the horizon. Now and then, but very seldom, a solitary farm, to which our party carefully refrained from paying a visit. Having studied the map of the country thoroughly, John found out his way easily, and he was in hopes of reaching Sitka without needing the services of a guide.

What was of the utmost importance was to avoid a meeting with any officials whether frontier guards or inland police. Now, along the first stages of the journey, the *Fair Rambler* seemed to be left entirely free to ramble away as it chose. This was a remarkable thing. And Mr. Cascabel's surprise was only equaled by his satisfaction.

Cornelia put down the gratifying fact to the credit of Providence, and her husband was inclined to do the same. As to John, he was under the impression that some circumstance or other must have altered the proceedings of the Muscovite administration.

Things went on in this way throughout the length of the 6th and of the 7th of June. They were drawing near to Sitka. The *Fair Rambler* might have made greater speed perhaps, but Cornelia dreaded the jolting for her invalid, whom Kayette and herself continued to tend, one as a mother, the other as a daughter. If, on the one hand, he had not grown worse, it could not be said either that he was much better. The scanty resources of the little pharmacy, the trifle that the two women were able to do for so serious a case and when the aid of a medical man would have been a necessity, all that could hardly be sufficient. Tender care could not prove a substitute for science,—and alas that it should be so! for never did sisters of charity display greater self-denial.

Indeed, the young Indian's zeal and intelligence had been appreciated by all. She looked as though she were already a member of the family. She was, in a sort of way, a second daughter that heaven had sent to Mrs. Cascabel.

On the 7th, in the afternoon, the *Fair Rambler* forded across Stekine River, a little stream which flows into one of the narrow passes between the mainland and the Isle of Baranoff, a few leagues only from Sitka.

In the evening, the wounded man was able to utter a few words:

"My father—yonder—see him again!" he murmured.

These words were said in Russian; Mr. Cascabel had understood them clearly.

There was likewise a name that was repeated several times: "Ivan—Ivan—"

No doubt this was the name of the luckless servant who had been murdered by the side of his master. It was very probable that both of them were of Russian origin.

However that might be, as the wounded man was now recovering both his power of speech and his memory, it would not be long ere the Cascabels knew his history.

On that day, the *Fair Rambler* had gone as far as the banks of the narrow channel that must be crossed to reach the Isle of Baranoff. And accordingly it became a necessity to have recourse to the boatmen who ply ferries across these numerous straits. Now, Mr. Cascabel could never hope of opening negotiations with the natives of the country without betraying his nationality. It was to be feared that the awkward question of passports should crop up once more.

"Well," said he, "in any case our Russian will have come to Sitka. If the police send us back to the frontier, they surely will keep their own countryman, and since we began his recovery, it will be the devil if they can't manage to set him right on his feet."

All this sounded very reasonable; still our travelers were anything but free from anxiety concerning the welcome that was awaiting them. It would be such a cruel blow, now they were in Sitka, to have to turn round and face the road to New York.

Meanwhile, whilst the wagon stood waiting on the bank of the canal, John had gone to make the necessary inquiries about the ferry and the boatmen.

Just then, Kayette came and told Mr. Cascabel that his wife wanted him, and he hastened toward her.

"Our invalid has quite recovered consciousness," said Cornelia. "He talks, César, and you must try and understand what he says!"

As a matter of fact, the Russian had opened his eyes and surveyed with an inquiring look the people he saw for the first time about him. Now and then, incoherent words fell from his lips.

And then, in a tone of voice so weak as to be scarcely audible, he called his servant Ivan.

"Sir," said Cascabel, "your servant-man is not here, but we are—"

At these words, spoken in French, the wounded man replied in the same language:

"Where am I?"

"With people who have taken care of you, sir."

"But in what country?"

"In a country where you have nothing to fear, if you are a Russian."

"A Russian—yes—a Russian!"

"Well, you are in the province of Alaska, within a short distance of the capital."

"Alaska!" murmured the stranger.

And you would have fancied that a feeling of terror had overclouded his features.

"The Russian possessions!" he repeated.

"No! An American possession now!" cried John as he entered the room.

And, through the little open window of the *Fair Rambler*, he showed the American stars and stripes waving from the flag-post on the coast.

Sure enough, the province of Alaska had ceased to be Russian three days before.

Three days previous, the treaty by which it was ceded to the United States had been signed. Henceforth the Cascabels had nothing more to apprehend at the hands of Russian officials. They were on American ground!

CHAPTER XI - SITKA

SITKA, or New Archangel, situated on Baranoff Island, in the middle of the archipelagos of the western coast, is not only the capital of the island, it is likewise the capital of the whole province which had just been ceded to the Federal government. There was no city of greater importance in this region, where the traveler finds but few towns, mere villages indeed, scantily sprinkled at long intervals. It would be even more accurate to designate these villages as settlements or trading stations. For the most part they belong to American companies; a few are the property of the English Hudson Bay Company. It is then easily understood that the means of communication between these stations are very difficult, especially during the bad season, in the midst of all the hardships of the Alaskan winter.

A few years ago, Sitka was still but an unfrequented commercial center, where the Russo-American Company kept its stores of furs and hides.

But thanks to the discoveries made in that province, which is contiguous to the polar regions, Sitka very soon underwent a considerable development; and, under its new administration, it will become an opulent city, worthy of this new State of the Confederacy.

At this time already, Sitka possessed all those edifices which constitute what is called a "town," a Lutheran church, a very simple edifice whose architectural style does not lack grandeur; a Greek church with one of those cupolas that are so little in harmony with a fog-laden sky, so different from the Eastern skies; a club, the Club Gardens, a sort of Parisian Tivoli where the habitual visitor and the traveler find restaurants, cafes, bars, and amusements of all kinds; a club-house, the doors of which are open to single men only; a school, a hospital, with fine houses, villas, and cottages picturesquely grouped on the surrounding hillocks. This landscape is horizoned by a vast forest of resinous trees which encase it in their eternal verdure, and beyond, a ridge of lofty mountains, the summits of which are lost in the clouds, and, lording it over all of them, Mt. Edgecumb, the giant of Crooze Island, to the north of Baranoff Island, the peak of which rises to a height of eight thousand feet above the level of the sea.

On the whole, if the climate of Sitka is not very severe, if the thermometer hardly ever goes below seven or eight degrees centigrade—although the town be crossed by the fifty-sixth parallel—it would deserve to be called the "watering town" par excellence. In truth, on Baranoff Island, it always rains, you may say, unless it snows. Let it surprise no one, therefore, if after crossing the canal in a ferry with all its household and belongings, the *Fair Rambler* entered Sitka under a torrent of rain. And still Mr. Cascabel had no thought of complaining, since he had reached the town at the very time of a transaction which enabled him to enter it without a passport. "Many a bit of good luck I have had in my day, but never such luck as this!" he went on repeating. "We were just at the gate, unable to get in, and slambang goes the door, of itself, just in time, before us!"

The treaty of the cession of Alaska had been signed opportunely, indeed, to enable the *Fair Rambler* to cross the frontier. And on this soil, now American, none of those unmanageable officials, none of those formalities in regard to which the Russian administration shows such severity.

And now it would have been the simplest thing on earth to bring our Russian either to the Sitka hospital where all due care would have been bestowed upon him, or to a hotel where he might have the attendance of a doctor. Still, when Mr. Cascabel proposed the matter to him:

"I feel better, my friend," he replied, "and if I am not in your way—"

"In our way, sir!" exclaimed Cornelia. "And what do you mean by being in our way?"

"You are at home here," added Mr. Cascabel, "and if you think—"

"Well, I think it is best for me not to leave those who have picked me up— who have devoted themselves—"

"All right, sir, all right!" answered Cascabel. "Still you must lose no time in seeing a medical man."

"Might I not see him here?"

"By all means, and I am off, myself, to fetch you the best in the town."

The *Fair Rambler* had stopped at the entrance into the town, at one end of an avenue planted with trees which stretches on to the forest. There Doctor Harry, who had been named to Mr. Cascabel, came and visited the Russian.

After a careful examination of the wound the doctor declared it was in no way dangerous, the poniard having glanced off on a rib. No important organ had been touched, and thanks to the cold-water dressing, thanks to the juice of the herbs gathered by the young Indian, the healing process, already commenced, would soon be sufficiently advanced to allow the patient to get up in a few days. He was therefore progressing as favorably as possible, and he might, from now, begin to take some food. But most assuredly, had not Kayette tended him, had not the hemorrhage been stopped by Mrs. Cascabel, he would have been a dead man a few hours after the attack of which he had been the victim.

Dr. Harry then added that, in his opinion, the murder must have been the deed of some members of Karnof's gang, if not that of Karnof himself, whose presence had been reported in the eastern part of the province. This Karnof was a criminal, of Russian or rather Siberian origin, who had under his orders a gang of those deserters from the Czar's army, so numerous in the Russian possessions of Asia and America. In vain had the police sent its best "ferrets" after him. In vain had rewards been offered for the capture of the band. These ruffians, as dreaded as they deserved to be, had hitherto escaped punishment. And still, frequent crimes, thefts, and murders had spread terror around, especially in the southern portion of the territory. The safety of the travelers, the traders, the agents of fur companies, was in continual jeopardy; and undoubtedly this new crime should be attributed to Karnof's gang.

On withdrawing. Dr. Harry left the family quite free from anxiety concerning their guest.

Whilst on his way to Sitka, Mr. Cascabel had always intended taking a few days' rest there, a rest his troupe was well entitled to, after a journey of almost two thousand one hundred miles since the time of leaving the Sierra Nevada. Besides he expected to increase his exchequer by two or three good performances in this town.

"Lads, we are no longer in England here," he would say, "we are in America, and before Americans we are quite at liberty to work!"

Mr. Cascabel felt sure, moreover, that the name of his family was a household word among the Alaskan population, and that the cry was going round Sitka:

"The Cascabels are within our walls!"

However, after a conversation which took place a couple of days after between the Russian and his host, these plans were slightly modified, except in so far as they concerned the few days' rest, an absolute necessity after the hardships of the journey. This Russian—in Cornelia's mind he could be no other than a prince—now knew what the good people were who had saved him, poor itinerant artists traveling through America. All the members of the family had been presented to him, including the young Indian to whom he was indebted for his being now alive.

One evening, as they were all sitting round together, he told them his history, or at least such portion of it as interested them. He spoke French very fluently, as if that language had been his own, with the only peculiarity that he rolled his r's a little, which gives to the Muscovite tongue an inflexion at the same time soft and manly in which the ear finds a great charm.

Besides, what he related was extremely simple. Nothing very adventurous, nothing romantic either.

His name was Sergius Wassiliowitch—and from that day, with his permission, he went by no other name than "Mr. Sergius" among the Cascabels. Of all his relatives, his father alone was still alive, and resided on a domain situated in the Government of Perm, within a short distance of the town of that name. Mr. Sergius, actuated by his traveling instincts, and his taste for geographical discoveries and researches, had left Russia three years before. He had visited the Hudson Bay territories and was preparing an exploring tour through Alaska, from the course of the Yukon to the Arctic Sea, when he was attacked under the following circumstances:

His servant Ivan and he had just settled their little encampment on the frontier, on the evening of the 4th of June, when they were suddenly fallen upon, during their first sleep. Two men were upon them. They awoke, stood up, and meant to defend themselves. It was useless: almost instantly poor Ivan fell dead, struck by a bullet through his head.

"He was a brave fellow, a faithful servant!" said Mr. Sergius. "We had lived together for ten years! He would have done anything for me; I mourn him not as a servant, but a friend!"

And so saying, Mr. Sergius made no effort to conceal his emotion, and every time he spoke of Ivan, his tearful eye showed how sincere was his grief for his loss.

Then he added that, being stabbed in the chest himself, he had lost consciousness, and no longer remembered anything, until, coming back to life but unable to express his gratitude, he had understood that he was with kind-hearted people who were nursing him.

When Mr. Cascabel told him that the deed was attributed to Karnof or to some of his accomplices, Mr. Sergius did not feel surprised, for he had been informed that the gang was haunting the frontier.

"You see," said he, in the end, "my history is not very entertaining, yours must be more so. My campaign was to end with the exploration of Alaska. Thence, I was to return to Russia, go home to my father, and leave him no more. Now let us talk about you, and first, let me ask how and why French people, like you, find themselves so far away from home in this part of America?"

"Do not showmen ramble the wide world over, Mr. Sergius?" Cascabel replied.

"Quite so, but none the less I may feel somewhat surprised to see you at such a distance from France."

"John," said Mr. Cascabel, turning to his eldest son, "tell Mr. Sergius how it is that we are here, and by what route we are returning to Europe."

John related everything that had happened the occupants of the *Fair Rambler* since they had left Sacramento, and, so as to be understood by Kayette, he told his tale in English, Mr. Sergius giving supplementary explanations in the Chinook dialect. The young Indian woman listened with the greatest attention. In this way she learnt what was this Cascabel family to which she had become so fondly attached. She heard how the show people had been robbed of all they possessed as they were crossing the pass of the Sierra Nevada on their way to the coast of the Atlantic, and how, for want of money, compelled to alter their plans, they had attempted by a westward road what they were unable to do by the east. After having faced their house on wheels toward the setting sun, they had traversed the State of California, Oregon, Washington Territory, Columbia, and had stopped on the frontier of Alaska. There they had found it impossible to move farther, thanks to the strict orders of the Muscovite administration—a fortunate draw-back, after all, since it had given them an opportunity to come to Mr. Sergius's help. And that was how a troupe of artists, French by birth, and Norman by their leader, were now in Sitka, the annexation of Alaska to the United States having opened wide, for them, the gates of the new American possession.

Mr. Sergius had listened to the young man's story with the keenest interest, and when he heard that Mr. Cascabel intended reaching Europe through Siberia, a little movement of surprise escaped him which, indeed, no one could have understood at the time.

"And so, my friends," said he, when John had finished, "your intention, on leaving Sitka, is to make for Behring Strait?"

"It is, Mr. Sergius," replied John, "and to ride over the strait when it will be frozen."

"The journey you undertake there is a long and laborious one, Mr. Cascabel."

"A long one, it is, Mr. Sergius! A laborious one, it shall be, no doubt. But what can be done? We have no choice in the matter. Besides, itinerant artists trouble themselves but little about the labor, and we have got accustomed to roving."

"I suppose that, under these conditions, you have no expectation of reaching Russia this year?"

"No," said John, "for the strait will not be frozen over before the beginning of October."

"In any case," repeated Mr. Sergius, "it is a bold and venturous scheme."

"That may be," replied Mr. Cascabel, "but there is no other way out of the difficulty. Mr. Sergius, we are homesick! We long to go back to France, and go home we must! And since we shall be going through Perm and Nijni at the time of the fairs,—well, the Cascabel family will do its best not to disgrace itself."

"Very well, but what are your resources?"

"A little money we made, coming along, and the takings of two or three performances that I propose to give in Sitka. As it happens, there are public rejoicings over the annexation, and I imagine the Sitkans will take an interest in the exercises of the Cascabel family."

"My friends," said Mr. Sergius, "how pleased I should have been to share my purse with you, if I had not been robbed."

"Why, you have not been robbed, Mr. Sergius," exclaimed Cornelia.

"Not to the extent of half a rouble!" added Cascabel.

And he brought the belt in which Mr. Sergius's money had remained untouched.

"Then, my friends, you will be good enough to accept—"

"No such thing, Mr. Sergius!" answered Mr. Cascabel. "I'll not have you run the risk of getting into difficulties by trying to get us out of our own."

"You decline to share with me?"

"Most positively!"

"Well, well, those French people!" said Mr. Sergius, stretching his hand to him.

"Long live Russia!" cried out young Sander.

"And long live France!" responded Mr. Sergius.

It was the first time, no doubt, that those cries were interchanged in those distant lands of America!

"And now, that's enough talking for once, Mr. Sergius," said Cornelia. "The doctor has recommended that you should keep very quiet, and patients must always obey their medical advisers."

"Your obedient servant then, Madame Cascabel," replied Mr. Sergius. "Still, I have one more question to ask you, or rather a request to make."

"At your service, sir."

"Indeed it is a favor I am expecting at your hands."

"A favor?"

"Since you are bent on going to Behring Strait, will you permit me to accompany you thus far?"

"Accompany us?"

"Yes! this will complete my exploration of Alaska in the West."

"And our answer to that request is: With the greatest pleasure, Mr. Sergius!" exclaimed Cascabel.

"On one condition," added Cornelia.

"What condition?"

"That you will do everything that will be necessary to your recovery,— without a single word."

"And on condition, too, that as I am your fellow-traveler I shall contribute toward the expenses of the journey?"

"That's as you like, Mr. Sergius!" answered Cascabel.

Everything was now settled to the satisfaction of all parties. However, the "manager" of the troupe did not think he should give up his idea of having two or three performances on the principal square in Sitka—performances from which he was to derive both glory and profit. Fetes were held throughout the province anent the annexation, and the *Fair Rambler* could not have appeared on the scene at a more opportune moment.

Of course Mr. Cascabel had communicated to the authorities the murderous attack of which his guest had been the victim, and orders had been issued for a more active chase after Karnof's band along the Alaskan frontier.

On the 17th of June, Mr. Sergius was able to go into the open air for the first time. He felt much better, and his wound was quite healed, thanks to Dr. Harry's attentions.

It was then he made acquaintance with the animal portion of the troupe: the two dogs came and rubbed against his legs, Jako greeted him with a "You're better, Mr. Sergius?" that Sander had taught him, and John Bull presented him with his choicest grimaces. The two good old horses themselves, Vermont and Gladiator, joyfully neighed their thanks to him for the lumps of sugar he gave them. Mr. Sergius was now a member of the family, just as Kayette was. He had already noticed that serious turn of mind, that love of study, that yearning upwards which characterized the eldest son. Sander and Napoleona charmed him with their graceful playfulness. Clovy amused him with his harmless nonsense. As to Mr. and Mrs. Cascabel, he had, long since, appreciated their domestic virtues.

Truly noble-hearted people were those among whom he had fallen.

However, they were actively pushing on the preparations for their forthcoming departure. Nothing was to be omitted that could insure the success of those fifteen hundred miles of a journey from Sitka to Behring Strait. This almost unknown country did not threaten them with any great dangers, it is true, either on the part of wild beasts, or at the hands of the Indians, whether wandering or sedentary; and nothing would be easier than to halt at the trading stations occupied by the agents of fur companies. What was of importance, was to minister to the daily necessities of life in a country whose resources, with the exception of the game, were likely to be null.

It followed, therefore, that all these questions had to be discussed with Mr. Sergius.

"First of all," said Cascabel, "we must take this into consideration, that we shall not have to travel during the bad season."

"That is fortunate," answered Mr. Sergius, "for they are indeed cruel, those Alaskan winters on the verge of the polar circle."

"And then, we shall not grope along like blind people," added John. "Mr. Sergius must be a learned geographer."

"Oh," replied Mr. Sergius, "in a country that he is not acquainted with, a geographer is often puzzled to find out his road. But, with his maps, my friend John has been able to make his way hitherto, and if we put our two heads together I am in hopes we shall get on all right. Besides, I have an idea, which I shall tell you about one day."

If Mr. Sergius had an idea, it could not fail being an excellent one, and so they allowed him all the time necessary to ripen it before carrying it into execution.

There being no lack of money, Mr. Cascabel renewed his stock of flour, grease, rice, tobacco, and especially tea, a very large consumption of which is made throughout Alaska; he likewise took in hams, corned beef, biscuits, and a certain quantity of preserved ptarmigan from the Russo-American Company's store. They would not run short of water along the affluents of the Yukon, but the water could not but be improved by the addition of a little sugar and cognac, or rather "vodka," a sort of brandy highly appreciated by the Russians; and accordingly a purchase was made of sufficient quantities of sugar and vodka. As to the fuel, although the forests might be depended upon, the *Fair Rambler* stowed in a ton of good Vancouver coal, a ton and no more, for the wagon should not be loaded to excess.

In the meantime, an additional bunk had been fitted into the second compartment, which Mr. Sergius declared quite sufficient for him, and which was comfortably supplied with bedding. Blankets were not forgotten, nor yet those hareskins so generally used by the Indians during winter. Finally, in the event of their having to make any purchases along the road, Mr. Sergius supplied himself with those glass trinkets, strips of cotton stuff, cheap knives and scissors, that constitute the usual currency between traders and natives.

As game might be relied upon, both large and small, since the deer and the hares, heathcocks, geese, and partridges abound in those parts, a proportionate stock of powder and shot was bought. Mr. Sergius even succeeded in finding two guns and a carbine, which completed the arsenal of the *Fair Rambler*. He was a good shot, and would delight in going out in search of game with his friend John.

It was not to be forgotten, either, that Karnof's gang might be roaming about Sitka perhaps, that they should be on the watch for a possible attack on their part, and, should the opportunity present itself, receive them as they deserved.

"Now," remarked Mr. Cascabel, "to the requests of such intruders I know of no better answer than a bullet, fair in the chest."

"Unless it be one fair in the head!" added Clovy, not unreasonably.

In a word, thanks to the trade carried on by the capital of Alaska with the various towns in Columbia and the ports of the Pacific, Mr. Sergius and his companions were able to purchase, without paying exorbitant prices, all that they thought necessary for their long journey through a desert country.

These arrangements were not completed before the last week but one in June, and it was decided they should start on the 26th. As they could not dream of crossing Behring Strait before it was completely frozen, they had ample time before them. Still, possible delays, unforeseen obstacles, were to be taken into account, and it would be better to arrive too soon than too late. At Port Clarence, on the very coast of the strait, they should rest and await the right moment for crossing over to the Asiatic shore.

Meanwhile, what was the young Indian girl doing? Nothing but what was very simple. She aided Mrs. Cascabel, with a deal of intelligence, in all the preparations for the journey. The good woman loved her with a mother's love: she loved her as she did Napoleona, and every day she grew more and more attached to her second daughter. Every one, indeed, was really fond of Kayette, and, no doubt, the poor girl enjoyed a happiness she had never tasted among the nomadic tribes, under the tents of the Indians. Sad did each one feel at the thought that the time was drawing near when Kayette would part with the family. But, alone as she now was in the world, should she not remain in Sitka, since she had left her people for the very purpose of coming here and entering service, even though under wretched conditions perhaps?

"Still and all," Mr. Cascabel would sometimes Say, "if that pretty Kayette —my little Kayette, I was going to say—had a taste for dancing, who knows but we might make her an offer? What a handsome dancer she would make, eh? And what a graceful rider, if she cared to make her début in a circus! I bet you, she would ride like a centaur!"

It was one of Mr. Cascabel's articles of faith that the centaurs were excellent riders, and it would have been dangerous to cross words with him on this subject.

Seeing how John shook his head, when his father spoke thus, Mr. Sergius understood plainly that the steady, reserved lad was far from sharing the paternal view of acrobatic performances or of the other practices of an itinerant artist's life.

In short, a great deal of thinking was bestowed on Kayette, on what would become of her, on the life that was awaiting her at Sitka,—and that thinking was not of the pleasantest kind,—when, the day before the departure, Mr. Sergius took her by the hand and presented her to the whole assembled family, saying:

"My friends, I had no daughter; now I have one, an adopted daughter! Kayette agrees to look upon me as her father, and I ask you for a little room for her in the *Fair Rambler!*"

Cries of joy greeted Mr. Sergius, and the fondest of caresses were lavished on "little Kayette." The happiness with which she, on her side, had accepted the proposal, is not to be told.

"You are a good heart, Mr. Sergius!" cried out Cascabel, not without emotion.

"Why so, my friend? Have you forgotten what Kayette has done for me? Is it not natural she should become my child, when I owe my life to her?"

"Well then, let us have a share!" said Cascabel. "Since you are her father, Mr. Sergius, I want to be her uncle!"

CHAPTER XII - FROM SITKA TO FORT YUKON

ON the 26th of June, at daybreak, the "Cascabel chariot raised anchor," to use one of the favorite metaphors of the captain. It remained to be seen,—in order to complete the metaphor with the immortal Prudhomme's figure of speech,—if the skiff was not going to cruise on a volcano. There was nothing impossible in that—figuratively, first, for the difficulties of the journey would not be trifling,—physically, moreover, for there is no lack of volcanoes, extinct or otherwise, on the northern coast of Behring Sea.

The *Fair Rambler*, then, left the Alaskan capital, in the midst of the many and noisy good wishes for a safe journey that accompanied its departure. They came from the numerous friends whose applause and roubles the Cascabels had received during the few days they had spent at the gates of Sitka.

The word "gates" is more accurate than might be thought. For the town is surrounded with a palisade of stout build and with very few openings, which it would be hard to get over by force.

The reason of it is that the Russian authorities had had occasion to protect themselves against the influx of Kalosch Indians, who usually come and squat between the Stekine and the Chilcat rivers in the vicinity of New Archangel. There stand scattered their very primitive-looking huts; a low door opens into a circular room, sometimes divided into two compartments; and one hole, made overhead, allows the light to come in and the smoke of the fire to go out. The aggregation of these huts constitutes a suburb, a suburb extra muros, to the town of Sitka. After sunset, no Indian may remain in the town; a restriction not without a just motive, one necessitated, indeed, by the frequently unpleasant relations existing between the redskins and the palefaces.

Beyond Sitka, the *Fair Rambler* had at first to cross a number of narrow passes, by means of ferries ad hoc, so as to reach the furthest extremity of a sinuous gulf, terminated in a point, called Lynn canal.

Thenceforth, the road lay on terra firma.

The plan of the journey, or rather the itinerary, had been carefully studied by Mr. Sergius and John on large scale maps which they had easily procured at the Gardens Club. Kayette's knowledge of the country had been called into requisition in this circumstance; and her bright intelligence had enabled her to understand the indications of the map that was laid under her eyes. She expressed herself half in Indian, half in Russian, and her remarks were very useful in the discussion. The question was to find, if not the shortest, at least the easiest road to Port Clarence, situated on the east shore of the strait. It was therefore agreed that the *Fair Rambler* should make straight for the great Yukon River, at the height of the fort that has taken its name from this important stream. This was a point about midway along the itinerary, say seven hundred and fifty miles from Sitka. They would thereby avoid the difficulties that would be encountered along the coast line where not a few mountains are to be met. On the contrary, the Yukon valley stretches, wide and clear, between the intricate chains of the West and the Rocky mountains, which separate Alaska from the valley of the Mackenzie and the territory of New Britain.

It follows, therefore, that a few days after setting out, the Cascabels had seen, away to the southwest, the last outline of the uneven coast over which stand, at an immense height. Mount Fairweather and Mount Elias.

The carefully preconcerted division of time, for labor and for rest, was strictly adhered to. There was no occasion for increased speed toward Behring Strait, and it was better to go piano in order to be sure to go sano. The important point was to spare the horses, who could not be replaced, except by reindeer, if ever they broke down, an eventuality that should be warded off at any cost. Accordingly, each morning the start was made about six o'clock, then a two hours' halt at noon, another spur onward till six, and then rest for the whole night; which gave an average of fifteen or eighteen miles per day.

Had it been necessary to travel at night, nothing could have been easier, for, according to Mr. Cascabel's way of putting it, the Alaskan sun was not overfond of his bed.

"He has hardly gone to bed when he gets up again!" he used to say. "Twenty-three hours' continuous light, and no extra charge!"

Sure enough, at this time of the year, that is, about the summer solstice, and in this high latitude, the sun disappeared at seventeen minutes past eleven at night and reappeared at forty-nine minutes past eleven—let us say after thirty-two minutes' eclipse beneath the horizon. And the twilight that was left after its disappearance blended its light tints, without a break, with those of the succeeding dawn.

As to the temperature, it was hot, at times stifling. Under such conditions, it would have been more than imprudent not to suspend work during the heat of noontide. Both man and beast suffered intensely from this excessively high temperature. Who could believe that, on the edge of the polar circle, the thermometer registers thirty degrees centigrade above zero? Still, such is the simple truth!

Nevertheless, if the journey was progressing safely and without any great difficulties, Cornelia, severely tried by the unbearable temperature, complained not without cause.

"You will soon regret what you now think so hard to bear!" said Mr. Sergius to her one day.

"Regret such heat? Never!" she replied.

"Quite so, mother," added John; "you will suffer very differently from the cold, the other side of Behring Strait, when we shall be going through the steppes of Siberia."

"I believe you, Mr. Sergius," Cascabel would answer. "But if there is no help against the heat, you can fight against the cold with the aid of fire."

"No doubt, my friend, that is what you will have to do in a few months, for the cold will be terrific, bear it in mind!"

Meanwhile, by the 3d of July, after meandering through the narrow gorges, the canons, whimsically carved among hillocks of medium height, the *Fair Rambler* saw nothing on its road but a perspective of ever-lengthening plains between the scanty woods of this territory.

On that day, they had to follow the bank of a little lake, from which sprang the Rio Lewis, one of the chief tributaries of the lower Yukon.

Kayette recognized it and said:

"Yes, that is the Cargut, that flows into our big river!"

She had told John that in the Alaskan dialect this word "cargut" was the very word for "little river."

And, during this journey, free from obstacles and exempt of fatigue, did the artists of the Cascabel troupe neglect rehearsing their exercises, keeping up the strength of their muscles, the suppleness of their limbs, the agility of their fingers? No, assuredly; and unless the heat would forbid it, each evening the camping ground was transformed into an arena whose only spectators were Mr. Sergius and Kayette. Both admired the achievements of the hard-working people—the Indian girl, not without some astonishment; Mr. Sergius with kindly interest.

One after the other, Mr. and Mrs. Cascabel lifted heavy weights with outstretched arms and juggled with dumb-bells; Sander practised the dislocations and contortions that were his specialty; Napoleona ventured on a rope stretched between two trestles and showed her dancing skill and grace, while Clovy went through his parade buffoonery before a purely imaginary public.

Surely, John would have preferred remaining with his books, improving himself by conversing with Mr. Sergius, and giving lessons to Kayette, who, thanks to him, was rapidly getting acquainted with the French language; but his father insisted on his losing nothing of his remarkable skill as an equilibrist, and, for obedience sake, he twirled through the air his glasses, his rings, his balls, his knives, and his sticks—with his mind engaged on very different thoughts, poor lad!

One thing that had given him great satisfaction, was that his father had had to abandon his idea of making an "artist" of Kayette. From the day when she had been adopted by Mr. Sergius, a wealthy, educated man, who belonged to the best society, her future prospects had been assured, and that, under the most favorable conditions. Yes, he felt happy to think of it, good honest John did, although he experienced a pang of real sorrow at the thought that Kayette would leave them when they reached Behring Strait. And leave them she would not have had to, if she had joined the troupe as a dancer!

For all that, John felt too genuine a friendship for her, not to rejoice at the fact that she was the adopted child of Mr. Sergius. Did he not long most ardently, himself, to change his position? Under the impulse of his loftier instincts, he felt himself unfit for the showman's life he led, and how many a time, on the public square, he had felt ashamed of the applause lavished on him for his uncommonly clever performances!

One evening, walking alone with Mr. Sergius, he opened his heart to him, laid bare before him his intimate yearnings and regrets, told him what he fain would have been, what he thought he might fairly aspire to. Perhaps by dint of roaming the world over, exhibiting themselves before popular gatherings, keeping up their calling as gymnasts and acrobats, securing the aid of jugglers and clowns, his parents might, in the end, reach a certain ease and comfort, he himself might eventually acquire a little fortune. But, it would be too late, then, to engage in a more honorable career.

"I do not feel ashamed of my father and mother, sir," he added. "By no means! I should be an ungrateful son, if I did! Within the limits of their ability, they have done everything! They have been good indeed to their children! Still, I feel I have in me the making of a man, and I am fated to be but a poor showman!"

"My friend," Mr. Sergius said to him, "I understand you. But let me tell you that, whatever a man's trade may be, it is no trifle to have carried it on honestly! Are you acquainted with more respectable people than your father and mother?"

"I am not, Mr. Sergius!"

"Well, continue to esteem them as I esteem them myself. Your desire to rise out of your present sphere is evidence of noble instincts. Who knows what the future may have in store for you? Be brave-hearted, my child, and rely on me to help you. I shall never forget what your people have done for me, no, I never shall! And some day, if I can—"

And as he spoke, John observed that his brow darkened, that his voice faltered. He seemed to look anxiously to the future. A momentary silence followed, which the lad interrupted, saying:

"When we are at Port Clarence, Mr. Sergius, why would you not continue the journey with us? Since your intention is to return to Russia, to your father —"

"That is out of the question, John," replied Mr. Sergius. "I have not completed the work of exploration I began in the territories of West America."

"And Kayette will remain with you?" inquired John, almost in a whisper.

There was so much sadness in the whispered inquiry, that Mr. Sergius could not hear it without being deeply moved.

"Must she not come with me," he replied, "now that I have taken her into my charge?"

"She would not leave you, then, sir; and when in your country—"

"My child," was the answer, "my plans are not definitely settled yet. That is all I can say to you for the present. When we are at Port Clarence, we shall see. Perhaps I may then make a certain proposal to your father, and on his answer will depend, no doubt,—"

John noticed once more the hesitation he had already observed in his companion's way of speaking. This time he refrained from further comment, feeling that an extreme reserve was a duty for him. But, ever since this conversation, there was a more intimate sympathy between them. Mr. Sergius had ascertained all that there was of good, of trustworthy, of noble in that young man so upright, so openhearted. He therefore applied himself to instruct him, to guide him in those studies for which he was inclined. As to Mr. and Mrs. Cascabel, it was with a grateful heart they watched what their guest was doing for their son.

Nor did John neglect his duties as purveyor. Very fond of hunting, Mr. Sergius accompanied him most of the time, and, between two shots, how many things can be said! Indeed there was an abundance of game in these plains. Of hares there were enough to feed a whole caravan. And it was not as eatables only that they proved useful.

"Those things you see skipping about here are not only dainty bits and ragouts, they are cloaks too, and muffs, and boas, and blankets!" said Mr. Cascabel one day.

"You are right, friend," Mr. Sergius made answer, "and after they have appeared in one character, in your meat safe, they will play quite as useful a part in your wardrobe. We could not be too plentifully supplied against the hardships of the Siberian climate!"

And accordingly they gathered quite a stock of the skins, and spared the preserved meat for such time as winter would drive the game away from the polar regions.

As for that, if perchance the sportsmen brought home neither partridge nor hare, Cornelia did not disdain putting a raven or a crow into the pot, after Indian fashion, and the soup was none the less excellent.

At other times, it might happen that Mr. Sergius and John drew forth from their bag a magnificent heathcock, and the reader will readily imagine how well the roasted bird looked on the table.

There was no fear of starvation, in fine, on board the *Fair Rambler*; true it is, she still was in the smoothest part of her adventurous voyage.

One annoyance, it must be said,—indeed, a source of pain and suffering,— was the continual worrying of the mosquitoes. Now that Mr. Cascabel was no longer on British soil, he found them unpleasant. Doubtless, they would have increased and multiplied beyond measure, had not the swallows made an extraordinary consumption of them. But, yet a little while, and the swallows would migrate toward the south; for, short indeed is their lingering about the limit of the polar circle!

On the 9th of July, the *Fair Rambler* reached the confluence of two streams, the one a tributary to the other. It was the Lewis River, flowing into the Yukon through a large widening of its left bank. As Kayette remarked, this river, in the upper portion of its course, also bears the name of Pelly River. From the mouth of the Lewis it takes a direction due northwest, and then curves to the west to go and pour its waters into a vast estuary of the sea of Behring.

At the confluence of the Lewis stands a military post, Fort Selkirk, less important than Fort Yukon, which is situated some three hundred miles up the river on its right bank.

Since they had left Sitka, the young Indian woman had rendered the little troupe valuable services by guiding them with marvelous accuracy. Once already during her nomadic life, she had traveled these plains watered by the great Alaskan river. Questioned by Mr. Sergius on the way her childhood had been spent, she had related the hardships of her life, when the Ingelete tribes migrated from one point to another in the valley of the Yukon, and how her tribe had been scattered, and how her parents and relatives disappeared. And, again, she told how, left alone in the world, she had seen herself reduced to seek an engagement as a servant to some official or agent in Sitka. More than once had John made her go over her sad history, and each time he had heard it with the same thrill of emotion.

It was in the neighborhood of Fort Selkirk that they fell in with some of those Indians who roam along the banks of the Yukon, and particularly the Birchmen, a tribe whose name was more fully developed in Kayette's language: "the rovers by the birch trees." As a matter of fact, the birch tree is very common among the firs, the Douglas pines, and the maple trees with which the center of the province of Alaska is besprinkled.

Fort Selkirk, occupied by some agents of the Russo-American Company, is, in reality, but a fur and peltry store where the traders along the coast come and make their purchases at certain seasons of the year.

These agents, delighted with a visit which varied the monotony of their lives, gave a hearty welcome to the occupants of the *Fair Rambler*. And in consequence Mr. Cascabel decided to take a rest here for twenty-four hours.

However, it was arranged that the wagon would cross the Yukon River at this spot, so as not to have to do so farther on, and perhaps under less favorable circumstances. Sure enough, its bed grew wider and its stream more swift in proportion as it flowed westward.

This advice was given by Mr. Sergius himself after he had studied on the map the course of the Yukon, which cut across their route some six hundred miles ahead of Port Clarence.

The *Fair Rambler* was therefore ferried to the right bank with the aid of the agents and that of the Indians who encamp round about Fort Selkirk, and seek an easy prey in the waters of the river.

Indeed, the advent of the troupe did not prove useless, and, in return for the services of the natives, they were enabled to render them one, the full importance of which was duly appreciated.

The chief of the tribe was then grievously ill—at least he might have been thought so. Now, he had no other physician or other remedies than the traditional magician and the magical incantations in use among native tribes. Accordingly, for some time past, the chief had lain in the open air, in the center of the village, with a huge fire burning night and day by his side. The Indians gathered around him sang in a chorus an invocation to the great Manitou, whilst the magician tried all his best charms to drive away the evil spirit that had taken up his abode in the body of the sick man. And, the better to succeed, he endeavored to introduce the said spirit into his own person; but the latter, a stubborn spirit, would not move an inch.

Fortunately, Mr. Sergius had a smattering of the medical art, and was able to give the Indian chief such a remedy as his condition required.

On examination, he had no difficulty in finding out the ailment of the august patient; and calling the little pharmacy into requisition, he administered to him a violent emetic, for which all the magician's incantations could not have proved a substitute.

The truth is that the chief suffered from a frightful fit of over-feeding, and the pints of tea he had been swallowing for the past two days were powerless in such a state of things.

And so, the chief did not die, to the great joy of his tribe—which deprived the Cascabels of an opportunity to witness the ceremonies attendant on the burial of a sovereign. Burial is not the right word, perhaps, when Indian funerals are in question. For the corpse is not interred, but suspended in mid-air, a few feet over the ground. There, at the bottom of his coffin, and intended for his use in the other world, are laid his pipe, his bow, his arrows, his snow-shoes, and the more or less valuable furs he wore in winter. And there, as a child in his cradle, he is rocked by the breeze during that sleep from which there is no awakening.

After twenty-four hours spent at Fort Selkirk, the Cascabels took leave of the Indians and the agents, and brought away pleasant recollections of this first halt on the bank of the river. They had to toil up the Pelly River along a somewhat rugged track, which was the cause of no little fatigue to the horses. At length, on the 27th of July, seventeen days after leaving Fort Selkirk, the *Fair Rambler* arrived at Fort Yukon.

CHAPTER XIII - CORNELIA CASCABEL HAS AN IDEA

IT was along the right bank of the river that the *Fair Rambler* had accomplished that portion of the journey which lay between Fort Selkirk and Fort Yukon. It had kept at a shorter or a longer distance from it so as to avoid the many detours the course of the river would have necessitated, cut into, as it is, by innumerable clefts, and rendered inaccessible at times by marshy lagoons. Things were so, at least, on this side; for, on the left, a few low hills encase the valley and stretch to the northwest. It might have been difficult to get over certain small affluents of the Yukon, among others the Stewart, which has not a single ferry, if, during the warm season, it had not been possible to ford it, with water half-way up to the knee only. And even then, Mr. Cascabel and family would have been sorely puzzled but for Kayette who, knowing the valley well, was able to guide them to the exact spots.

It was indeed a piece of good fortune for them to have the young Indian girl for a guide. She was so happy, too, to oblige her new friends, so pleased to find herself in a new home, so grateful for those caresses of a mother, that she had thought she would never more enjoy!

The country was pretty woody in its central part, with here and there a rise, swelling the surface of the ground; but it already bore a different aspect from that of the neighborhood of Sitka.

As a fact, the severity of a climate subjected to eight months of Arctic winter is an absolute check to vegetation. Hence, with the exception of a few poplars, the tops of which curve down in the shape of a bow, the only families of fragrant trees to be met with in these parts are the firs and the birches. Beyond these you see nothing but a few clumps of those melancholy, stunted, and colorless willows that the breeze from the Ice Sea very quickly strips of their leaves.

During the trip from Fort Selkirk to Fort Yukon, our sportsmen having been rather fortunate, it had not been necessary to draw on the reserve stock for the daily requirements. Hares there were, as many as could be wished for, and, if the truth must be told, the guests at our table were almost beginning to have too much of one good thing. True, the bill of fare had been varied with roast geese and wild ducks, not to mention the eggs of those birds whose nests Sander and Napoleona were so clever at finding, deeply buried in holes. And Cornelia had so many recipes for cooking eggs—she prided herself on it too —that it was a succession of ever new treats.

"Well, on my word, this is a country where living is good!" exclaimed Clovy one day, as he finished picking the backbone of a splendid goose. "It is a pity it is not situated in the center of Europe or of America!"

"If it were in the center of thickly populated countries," answered Mr. Sergius, "it is probable that game would not be so plentiful."

"Unless—" began Clovy.

But a look from his master closed his lips and spared him the nonsensical remark he was certainly going to make.

If the plain swarmed with game, it must be noted likewise that the creeks, the rios, the tributaries of the Yukon supplied excellent fish, which Sander and Clovy caught with their rods, and more especially magnificent pikes. The only trouble, or rather pleasure, they need give themselves was to freely indulge their taste for fishing, for not a sou or a cent had they ever to spend.

Spending, indeed! that would have weighed very little on Master Sander's mind! Were not the Cascabels sure to pass their old age in comfort and luxury, thanks to him? Had he not his famous nugget in his possession? Had he not concealed, in a corner of the wagon, unknown to all but himself, the precious stone he had found in the Cariboo forest? He had; and to this day, the youngster had had sufficient control over himself to say nothing about it to anybody, patiently waiting for the day when he could turn his nugget into current gold. And then, would he not be proud to show off his fortune! Not indeed, gracious heavens! that the selfish thought had entered his head to keep the money for himself! His father and mother it was, for whom he kept it; and with that, they would be largely compensated for the robbery committed on them in the Sierra Nevada!

When the *Fair Rambler* reached Fort Yukon, after several hot days, all the travelers were really tired. It was therefore agreed that they would stay here for a whole week.

"You can do so all the more unbegrudgingly," remarked Mr. Sergius, "as we are only six hundred miles from Port Clarence. Now to-day is the 27th of July, and we cannot possibly cross the strait on the ice before two months', perhaps three months' time."

"That is a settled matter," said Mr. Cascabel; "since we can afford the time, halt!"

This command was greeted with equal satisfaction by the whole troupe, the professional bipeds as well as the four-footed staff of the *Fair Rambler*.

The foundation of Fort Yukon goes back to the year 1847. This, the most westerly post in the possession of the Hudson Bay Company, is situated almost on the limit of the polar circle. But as it stands on Alaskan territory this Company is obliged to pay a yearly indemnity to its rival, the Russo-American Company.

In 1864 only were the present buildings and their belt of palisades commenced, and they had been but lately completed when the Cascabel family halted at the fort for a few days' stay.

The agents readily offered them hospitality within the precincts of the fort. There was no lack of room in the yards and under the sheds. Mr. Cascabel, however, poured forth his thanks in a few pompous sentences: he preferred not to leave the roof of his comfortable *Fair Rambler*.

In reality if the garrison of the fort consisted only of a score of agents, mostly Americans, with a few Indian servants, the natives round about the Yukon were reckoned by hundreds.

For as a matter of fact, it is in this central point of Alaska that the most largely frequented market is held for the traffic in furs and hides. Thither flocked the various tribes of the province, the Kotch-a-Kutchins, the An-Kutchins, the Tatanchoks, and, foremost among them all, the Co-Yukons, who dwell by the banks of the big river.

The truth is, that the situation of the fort is most advantageous for the exchange of goods, standing as it does at the angle formed by the Yukon at the confluent of the Porcupine. Here the river divides into five streams, which enables traders to penetrate more easily into the interior and to barter goods even with the Eskimos by the Mackenzie River.

This network of streams is, accordingly, furrowed with skiffs, gliding up or down, and especially with numbers of those "baidarras," light boat-frames covered with oiled skins, the seams of which are greased, so as to render them more water-tight. On board these frail boats the Indians do not hesitate to venture on long voyages, thinking nothing of carrying them on their shoulders when rapids or natural dams happen to impede their progress. However, these skiffs cannot be used more than three months at most. For the rest of the year the waters are imprisoned under a thick covering of ice. The baidarra then changes its name and becomes a sleigh. This vehicle, whose curved extremity, recalling the prow of a boat, is held in position by strips of leather from the hide of the moose, is drawn by dogs or reindeer, and travels quickly. As to foot-travelers, with their long snow-shoes, they move along more swiftly still. Always in luck, was our Cæser Cascabel! He could not have reached Fort Yukon at a better moment. The fur and hide fair was at its highest; several hundreds of Indians had already pitched their tents near the trading station.

"Hang me," he exclaimed, "if we don't make something by it! This is a regular fair, and we must not forget that we are fair artists! Is not this the time, if ever, to display our talents? You see no objection to it, Mr. Sergius?"

"None, my friend," replied the latter, "but I see no great chance of heavy takings!"

"Why, they'll surely cover our expenses, seeing we have none!"

"Quite true. But, let me ask you, in what way do you hope these good natives will pay you for their seats, since they have no American money, no Russian money."

"Well, they'll give me muskrats' skins, beavers' skins, anything they like! In any case, the immediate result of these performances will be to unbend our muscles, for I am always afraid our joints will get stiff. And, you know, we have a name to keep up at Perm, at Nijni, and I would not for the world expose my troupe to a fiasco when we make our first appearance on your native soil. It would be the death of me, Mr. Sergius,—yes, it would be my death!"

Fort Yukon, the most important in these regions, occupies a pretty large site on the right bank of the river. It is a sort of oblong quadrilateral construction, strengthened at each corner with square towerets not unlike those windmills resting on a pivot that are to be seen in the north of Europe. Inside are several buildings, for the lodging of the agents of the company and their families, and two vast inclosed sheds, where a considerable stock is kept of sable furs and beavers' skins, and black and silver-gray foxes' skins, not to speak of less valuable goods.

A monotonous life, a painful life too, is the life of these agents. The flesh of the reindeer sometimes, but more frequently that of the moose, toasted, boiled, or roasted, is their main article of food. As to other kinds of victuals, they must be fetched from the trading-station at York, in the region of Hudson Bay, that is to say from a distance of some two thousand miles; and, of necessity, the arrival of such supplies is an unfrequent occurrence.

In the course of the afternoon, after having arranged their encampment, Mr. Cascabel and family went and paid a visit to the natives who had squatted between the banks of the Yukon and the Porcupine.

What a variety in those temporary dwellings according to the tribe to which they belonged! Huts of hides and barks of trees, held up on poles and covered over with foliage, tents made of the cotton stuff manufactured by the natives, wooden cabins that can be taken down or set up according to requirements.

And what quaint mixture of colors in the dresses! Some wore fur clothing, others cotton garments; all had a garland of leaves around their heads to preserve themselves against the bite of the mosquito. The women wear square-cut petticoats, and adorn their faces with shells. The men wear shoulder clasps and use them, in winter, to hold up their long robe of moose's skin, the fur of which is on the inside. Both sexes, moreover, make a great show of fringes of false pearls, the size of which is the only standard by which they are valued. Among these various tribes, were distinguished the Tananas, easily known by the bright colors painted on their faces, the feathers on their headdress, the little pieces of red clay stuck on their egrettes, their leather vests, their pants of reindeer skin, their long flint guns, and their powder pouches carved with extreme delicacy.

By way of coin, these Indians use the shells of the dentalium, which are found even among the natives of the Vancouver Archipelago; they hang them on the cartilage of their noses, and take them down when they want to pay for anything.

"That is a handy way to carry your money," said Cornelia. "No fear of losing your purse."

"Unless your nose drops off!" justly remarked Clovy.

"And that might easily come to pass in such severe winters!" added Mr. Cascabel.

On the whole, this gathering of natives offered a curious spectacle.

Of course, Mr. Cascabel had entered into conversation with several of the Indians, by means of the Chinook tongue with which he was slightly acquainted, whilst Mr. Sergius questioned and answered them in Russian.

For several days, a brisk trade was carried on between the natives and the representatives of the Company, but hitherto the Cascabels had not availed themselves of their talents for a public performance.

Meanwhile, however, the Indians soon became aware that the troupe was of French origin, that its various members enjoyed a wide reputation as athletes, acrobats, and jugglers. Each evening they flocked, in wondering crowds, around the *Fair Rambler*. They had never seen such a vehicle, one with such gaudy coloring above all. They chiefly praised it because it moved about easily,—a peculiarly pleasing feature in the eyes of nomadic people. Who knows if, at some future time, Indian tents mounted on wheels will not be a common sight? After houses on wheels, we may have villages on wheels,— why not?

It was a natural consequence of such a state of things that an extraordinary performance should be given by the new-comers. And accordingly the giving of such a performance was resolved upon "at the general requests of the Indians of Fort Yukon."

The native with whom Mr. Cascabel had made acquaintance very soon after his arrival was a "tyhi," that is to say the chief of a tribe. A fine fellow, some fifty years old, he seemed full of intelligence; nay, there was a very "knowing" look about him. Several times he had visited the *Fair Rambler*, and had given to understand how glad the natives would be to witness the exercises of the troupe.

This tyhi was mostly accompanied by an Indian, some thirty years of age, named Fir-Fu, a graceful type of the more refined native, who was the magician of the tribe and a remarkable juggler, well known as such throughout the Yukon province.

"He is a colleague of ours then?" said Mr. Cascabel the first time that he was presented to him by the tyhi.

And all three, having drunk together some of the liqueurs of the country, had smoked the calumet of peace.

As the outcome of these conversations, in the course of which the tyhi had pressed Mr. Cascabel for a performance, the latter was appointed to take place on the 3d of August. It was agreed that the Indians would lend their aid, for they would not be thought inferior to Europeans in strength, skill, or agility.

This indeed is not surprising; in the Far West, as in the province of Alaska, the Indians are very fond of gymnastic and acrobatic displays, and with these they intermix comedies and masquerades, at which they are great adepts.

And accordingly, on the appointed date, when a large audience had been gathered together, you could have seen a group of half a dozen Indians whose faces were hid under large wooden masks of unspeakable hideousness. After the fashion of the "big heads" at pantomimes, the mouth and eyes of these masks were set in motion by means of strings,—which gave an appearance of life to these horrible faces, most of which ended in birds' beaks. It were difficult to imagine what a degree of perfection they had attained in the art of making grimaces, and John Bull (the ape of course) might have taken some good lessons from them.

Needless to say that Mr. and Mrs. Cascabel, John, Sander, Napoleona, and Clovy had all donned their gala dresses for this occasion.

The spot selected was an immense meadow surrounded by trees, of which the *Fair Rambler* occupied the background, as though a part of a stage scenery. The front rows had been reserved for the agents of Fort Yukon with their wives and children. On the sides several hundreds of Indians, men and women, formed a semi-circle, and smoked the time away, waiting for the performance.

The masked natives who were to join in it stood by themselves, somewhat out of the way.

Punctual to the time, Clovy appeared on the platform of the wagon, and proceeded to deliver his usual address:

"Indian gentlemen and Indian ladies, you are about to see what you shall see!"—etc., etc.

But as Chinook "was to him unknown," it is very probable that his witticisms were all thrown away on the audience.

What they did understand was the traditional shower of blows leveled at him by his boss, and the kicks he received from behind with all the resignation of a clown who is paid for that very purpose.

The prologue over:

"Now, for the quadrupeds!" said Mr. Cascabel, bowing to the audience.

Wagram and Marengo were trotted out to the open space that had been reserved in front of the *Fair Rambler* and astonished the natives, little accustomed as they were to any labor that brings out the intelligence of animals. Then, when John Bull came and went through his vaulting exercises over the spaniel and the poodle, he did so with such nimbleness, and such droll attitudes, as to unwrinkle the grave-faced Indians.

Meanwhile, Sander did not cease blowing into the horn with all the might of his lungs, and Cornelia and Clovy kept beating their respective drums. If, after that, the Alaskans did not appreciate all the effect that can be produced by a European orchestra, the fact can only be explained by their lacking all sense of what is artistic.

Until now, the masked group had been motionless, deeming, no doubt, that the time for action had not come yet: they were keeping themselves in reserve.

"Mademoiselle Napoleona, the high rope dancer!" shouted Clovy through a speaking-trumpet.

And the lassie, presented by her father, made her appearance before the public.

First she danced with such grace as brought her warm applause, not expressed, indeed, by shouts or the clapping of hands, but by simple nods of the head which were not less significant. And these signs of gratification were renewed when she was seen to dart up on a rope, stretched between two trestles, and there, walk, run, and skip about, with an ease which particularly admired by the Indian women.

"Now is my turn!" exclaimed young Sander.

And behold him coming forward, saluting the public with a tap on his nape, then twirling, twisting, dislocating himself, reversing his joints in all kinds of manner, transforming his legs into his arms, and his arms into his legs, now walking like a lizard, then hopping like a frog, and eventually terminating the whole with a double somersault.

He, too, received his meed of applause; but he had scarcely bowed his thanks by bringing his head on a level with his feet when an Indian, of his own age, stepping out of the group of native performers came forward in the ring, and took off his mask.

Every exercise executed by Sander, the young native then went through with such suppleness in his joints, such accuracy in his movements as to leave nothing to be desired from the acrobatic point of view. If he was less graceful than the younger of Cascabel's sons, he was not less astonishing than he. And his exploits accordingly excited among the natives the most enthusiastic nods.

Needless to say that the staff of the *Fair Rambler* had the good taste to add their applause to that of the public. But, unwilling to be beaten, Mr. Cascabel beckoned to John to proceed with his juggling, an art in which he considered him as having no equal.

John felt he had the honor of the family to keep up. Encouraged by a gesture from Mr. Sergius, and a smile from Kayette, he took up, in turn, his bottles, his plates, his balls, his knives, his disks, and his sticks, and it may be said he surpassed himself.

Mr. Cascabel could not help casting upon the Indians a look of proud complacency in which could be seen something like a challenge. He seemed to be saying to the members of the masked group:

"Well, you fellows, beat that if you can!"

His thought was, no doubt, understood; for, at a beck of the tyhi's, another Indian, pulling off his mask, walked out of the group.

This was the magician Fir-Fu; he, too, had his reputation to keep up, on behalf of the native race.

Then, seizing, one after the other, the various articles used by John, he repeated each and every one of his rival's exercises, crossing the knives and the bottles, the disks and the rings, the balls and the sticks, and all this, it must be confessed, with as graceful an attitude, as unerring a hand, as John Cascabel's.

Clovy, accustomed to admire no one but his master and his family, was literally bewildered.

This time Cascabel applauded merely as a matter of courtesy and with the tips of his fingers.

"My word!" he murmured. "They are no joke, those redskins aren't! People without schooling, too! Well! We shall teach them a thing or two!"

On the whole, he was not a little disappointed to have found rivals where he had expected admirers only. And what rivals? Simple natives of Alaska,—

savages, you might say. His pride as an artist was stung to the quick. After all! you are a showman, or you are not!

"Now then, children," he thundered, "now for the human pyramid!"

And all rushed toward him, as if to the assault. He had taken a firm stand, his legs wide open, his hips bulging out well, his bust fully developed. On his right shoulder John had lightly stepped, holding out a hand to Clovy, who stood on Cascabel's left shoulder. In his turn, Sander had taken up his stand on his father's head, and, above him, Napoleona crowned the edifice, circling her two arms to send kisses to the audience.

The French pyramid had scarcely been up when another, the native one, rose beside it. Without even removing their masks, the Indians had stood on each other, not five, but seven deep; their structure overtopped the other by one man. Pyramid vied against pyramid.

Shouts and hurrahs were now uttered by the Indian spectators in honor of their tribes. Old Europe was beaten by young America, and what America?— The America of the Co-Yukons, of the Tananas, and the Tatanchoks!

Mr. Cascabel, full of shame and confusion, made a wrong movement and well-nigh hurled his co-workers to the ground.

"Ah! That's the way, is it?" he grumbled, after ridding himself of his human load.

"Be calm, my friend," said Mr. Sergius to him. "It is really not worth while to—"

"Not worth while, indeed! It is easily seen you are not an artist, Mr. Sergius!"

Then, turning to his wife:

"Come, Cornelia, an open-hand wrestling match!" he cried. "We shall see which of these savages will dare to face the 'Chicago champion'!"

Mrs. Cascabel did not move.

"Well, Cornelia?"

"No, Cæser."

"How? No? You won't wrestle with those apes, and rescue the honor of the family?"

"I shall rescue it," simply replied Cornelia. "Leave it to me. I have an idea!"

And when this wonderful woman had an idea, it was best to let her carry it out as she pleased. She felt quite as much humiliated as her husband by the success of the Indians, and it was probable she was about paying them off in her own coin.

She had returned to the *Fair Rambler*, leaving her husband somewhat uneasy, despite all the reliance he placed in the resources of her intelligence and imagination.

Two minutes later, Mrs. Cascabel reappeared and stood before the group of the Indian performers who gathered around her.

Then addressing the principal agent of the fort, she prayed him to kindly repeat to the natives what she was going to say.

And this is what was translated by him, word for word, in the vernacular tongue of the province of Alaska:

"Indians, you have exhibited, in these displays of muscle and of skill, talents that are worthy of a reward. That reward, I bring it to you."

The audience listened with breathless attention.

"You see my hands?" continued Cornelia. "More than once they have been pressed by the most august personages of the old world. You see my cheeks? Many a time and oft they have received the kisses of the mightiest sovereigns of Europe! Well! these hands, these cheeks, they are yours! American Indians, come and kiss these cheeks, come and press these hands!"

And, in very truth, the natives did not wait to be asked twice. Never again would they have the like opportunity with so fine a woman!

One of them, a good-looking Tanana, came forth and seized the hand that she held out to him—

What a yell burst from his lips when he felt a shock that made him wriggle in a thousand contortions.

"Ah, Cornelia!" whispered Mr. Cascabel, "Cornelia, I understand you, and I admire you."

And Mr. Sergius, John, Sander, Napoleona, and Clovy were in convulsions of laughter at the trick played on the natives by this extraordinary woman.

"Another!" she called, her arms stretched toward the audience,—"another!"

The Indians hesitated; something supernatural must have happened there, they thought.

However, the tyhi seemed to be making up his mind; he walked slowly up toward Cornelia, stood still a couple of steps away from her imposing person, and surveyed her with a look that bespoke anything but a fearless heart within.

"Now then, old fellow!" cried Cascabel to him. "Now then, a little courage! —Kiss the lady! It's the easiest thing out, and it's so sweet!"

The tyhi, stretching out his hand, barely touched the European belle with his finger.

A second shock, a second series of screams, uttered this time by the chief, who well-nigh measured his length backwards on the ground, and awful stupefaction of the public. If people were so roughly handled for merely touching Mrs. Cascabel's hand, what would come to pass if they ventured to embrace this astonishing creature, whose cheeks "had received the kisses of the mightiest sovereigns of Europe?" Well! there was one bold man, venturesome enough to run the risk. That man was the magician Fir-Fu. He, at least, should believe himself proof against all malefices! And so, he planted himself in front of Cornelia. Then, having walked right round her, and encouraged by the incentives of his countrymen, he took her in his two arms and gave her a formidable kiss, full on her cheek.

What followed this time was not a shock, but a series of leaps and jumps. The juggler had suddenly become an acrobat! And after two somersaults, as wonderfully per formed as they were involuntary, he dropped into the midst of his amazed companions.

To produce this effect on the magician, as well as on the other natives, Cornelia had merely to press the knob of a little electric pile she had in her pocket. Yes!—a little pocket pile with which she acted "the electrical woman!"

"Ah! wifie!—wifie!" exclaimed her husband, as he pressed her in his arms with impunity before the stupefied Indians. "Is she clever, eh? Is she clever?"

"As clever as electrical!" added Mr. Sergius.

In truth, what could the natives think, if not that this supernatural woman disposed of the thunder at her will? How was it that, for merely touching her hand, you were knocked to the ground? Surely, she could be no one else but the wife of the Great Spirit, who had condescended to come down on earth and take Cascabel for her second husband!

CHAPTER XIV - FROM FORT YUKON TO PORT CLARENCE

THAT same evening, in the course of a conversation at which the whole family circle was present, it was decided they would resume their journey two days after this memorable performance.

Evidently,—this was Mr. Cascabel's own judicious remark,—had he been desirous to add recruits to his troupe, his only trouble would have been the abundance of the materials at his disposal. Though not without a sting for his personal pride, he was forced to acknowledge that these Indians had a wonderful aptitude for acrobatic exercises. As gymnasts, clowns, jugglers, or equilibrists, they would have met with immense success in any country. No doubt, practice was a great element in their talent, but they had to thank nature even more for making them muscular, supple, and nimble. Denying their having proved themselves equal to the Cascabels had been an injustice. Fortunately, the honor of the day had been saved for the troupe by the presence of mind of the "Queen of electrical women"!

It must be said that the agents at the fort—poor fellows without any education, most of them—had been no less astounded than the natives at what had taken place before them. It was agreed, however, that they should not be told the secret of the phenomenon, in order to leave with Cornelia the laurels she had won. The next morning, accordingly, when they came to pay their usual visit, they were afraid to draw too close to the "thunderbolt woman," although she greeted them with a world of smiles. They hesitated somewhat before they took her proffered hand, and so did the tyhi and the magician, who would fain have known the mystery,—useful as it would have proved to them, to increase their prestige with the native tribes.

The preparations for the departure being completed, Mr. Cascabel and his people took leave of their hosts in the forenoon of the 6th of August, and the horses now well rested, started down the river-side, following the direction of the stream toward the west.

Mr. Sergius and John had carefully studied the map, availing themselves of the accurate indications given to them by the young Indian. Kayette knew most of the villages they would have to cross, and, from what she said, there were no streams ahead that would be a serious hindrance to the progress of the *Fair Rambler*.

Besides, there was no question, as yet, of leaving the Yukon valley. After following the right bank of the river as far as the station at Nelu, they would call at Nuclukayette village, and thence to Nulato Fort would be about two hundred and forty miles. The wagon would then leave the Yukon, and journey due west.

The season still kept favorable; the days were pretty warm, whilst the nights gave unmistakable signs of a falling in the temperature. So, barring unforeseen obstacles, Mr. Cascabel felt sure of reaching Port Clarence before winter had heaped insurmountable obstacles on his path.

Surprise may be felt at the comparative ease with which such a journey could be accomplished. But is not this the case in flat countries, when the fine season, the length of the days, the mildness of the climate are in the traveler's favor? Things would be altogether different, on the other side of Behring Strait, when the Siberian steppes would stretch away to the horizon, when they would be buried under the winter snow as far as the eye could reach, and when gusts of the winter blast would plow their surface.

One evening, as they were chatting of dangers to come:

"Well, well," said the sanguine Cascabel, "we shall manage to pull through, never mind!"

"I hope so," answered Mr. Sergius. "But as soon as you set foot on the Siberian coast, I advise you to make for the southwest of the province immediately. In the more southerly parts, you will suffer less from the cold."

"That is what we mean to do, Mr. Sergius," answered John.

"And with all the more reason, my friends, as you have nothing to fear from the Siberians, unless—as Clovy would say—unless you ventured among the tribes on the northern coast. In truth your greatest enemy will be the cold."

"We are prepared against it," said Mr. Cascabel, "and we shall get on all right; our only regret being that you will not continue the journey with us, Mr. Sergius."

"Our only regret, but a very keen one," added John.

Mr. Sergius felt to what an extent these people had grown attached to him, and how fond he himself had become of them. Sure enough, as one day after another was spent in the intimacy we have described, the bonds of friendship grew closer and closer between them and him. The parting would be painful; and would they ever meet again, throughout the haphazard eventualities of two courses of life so different from each other? And then, Mr. Sergius would bring Kayette away with him, and he had already noticed that John's friendship for the young Indian girl was deserving of another name. Had Mr. Cascabel remarked what was going on in the heart of his son? Mr. Sergius did not feel sure of it. As to Cornelia, as the good woman had never opened her mind on the subject, he had thought it his duty to keep equally reserved. Of what use would an explanation have been? Quite a different future was in store for Mr. Sergius's adopted daughter; and poor John was now indulging in hopes that could not be realized.

In fine, the journey was proceeding without too many obstacles, without too much toiling. Port Clarence would be reached before Behring Strait had been frozen into a roadway, and there, very probably, they would have to make a stay of several weeks. No necessity, therefore, to overwork men or beasts.

Still, they were always at the mercy of a possible accident. One of the horses hurt or sick, a broken wheel, and the *Fair Rambler* would have been in an alarming position. The observance of the greatest caution was therefore obligatory.

For the first three days, the route continued to follow the course of the river, which flowed toward the west, as we have said; but the Yukon began to bend southward, and it was thought right to keep along the line of the seventy-fifth parallel.[1]

About this spot, the river was very sinuous, and the valley became visibly narrower, ensconced by hills of medium height, which the map designates under the name of "ramparts" on account of their bastion-faced appearance.

Some difficulty was experienced in getting out of this maze, and all sorts of precautions were taken to save the wagon from accident. They took a portion of the load down when the road was too steep, and frequently put their shoulders to the wheels, the more so, according to Mr. Cascabel's expression, "as wheelwrights seemed rather scarce in these parts!"

There were likewise not a few creeks to cross, among others the Nocotocargut, the Shetehaut, the Klakinicot. Fortunately, at this season, these streams were shallow, and it was easy to find available fords.

As to the Indians, there were few or none at all in this part of the province, once occupied by the tribes of the Midland Men, tribes now almost extinct. From time to time, a family, at most, passed by, on their way to the southwest coast for the autumn fishing season.

At other times, likewise, traders met our friends from the opposite direction, coming from the mouth of the Yukon, and pushing on toward the various stations of the Russo-American Company. They contemplated, not without some surprise, both the gayly painted wagon and the freight it carried. Then, with a "Safe home!" they continued their tramp eastward.

On the 13th of August, the *Fair Rambler* arrived at the village of Nuclakayette, three hundred and sixty miles from Fort Yukon. It is in reality but another fur-trade station, the furthest station frequented by Russian agents. Starting from different points in Russia in Asia, and in Alaska, they meet here to set up a competition with the buyers of the Hudson Bay Company.

Hence Nuclakayette was a center to which the natives converged with the furs they had been able to gather during the winter season.

113

Having deviated from the river in order to avoid its numerous bends, Mr. Cascabel had met it again in the latitude of this village, which was pleasantly nestled among low hills within a gay curtain of green trees. A few wooden huts clustered around the palisade with which the fort was protected. Brooklets murmured through the grassy plain. Two or three skiffs lay by the bank of the Yukon. The whole landscape was gratifying to the eye and suggestive of rest. As to the Indians who frequented the neighborhood, they were Tananas, belonging, as was remarked above, to the finest type of the native in northern Alaska.

Enticing as this spot looked, the *Fair Rambler* only stopped twenty-four hours here. The rest seemed sufficient for the horses, seeing the care that was taken of them. Mr. Cascabel proposed to make a longer stay at Nulato, a more important and better-stocked fort, where various purchases would be made in view of the journey through Siberia.

Needless to say that Mr. Sergius and John, accompanied sometimes by young Sander, made good use of their guns, along the road. By way of heavy game, there were the reindeer and the moose which ran across the plains and sought the shelter of the forests, or rather the clumps of trees with which the country is rather sparingly dotted. In the marshy parts, the geese, the woodcocks, the snipes, and the wild ducks afforded many a good shot; and our sportsmen had even an opportunity of bringing down a couple of herons, little appreciated though these be from the eatable point of view.

And still, from what Kayette stated, the heron is greatly prized by the Indians as an article of food—especially when they have nothing else. A trial of these birds was made at breakfast, on the 13th of August. Despite all Cornelia's talent,—and that talent was marvelous,—the flesh of the heron seemed tough and leathery, and by none was it accepted without a protest but by Wagram and Marengo, who left not a bone.

It is true that, in times of dearth, the natives are glad of owls, falcons, and even of martens; but the reason of it is, it must be confessed, that they cannot help it.

On the 14th of August, the *Fair Rambler* had to slip through the windings of a narrow gorge between very steep hillocks by the bank of the river. This time, so steep was the pass, so rugged the track, as though it had been the ravine-bed of a torrent, that, despite all precautions, an accident happened. Luckily, it was not one of the wheels that was broken, but one of the shafts. The repairs took but little time, and a few pieces of rope set matters right again.

After passing, on one bank of the river, the village of Suquonyilla, and, on the other, the village of Newi-cargut, on the creek of the same name, the journey went on without any hindrance. Not a hill was to be seen. One immense plain spread out farther than the eye could reach. Three or four rios intersected it; at this season, when rain is scarce, their beds were quite dried up. At the times of storms and snow, it would have been impossible to keep up the itinerary in these parts.

When crossing one of these creeks, the Milo-cargut, in which there was barely a foot of water, Mr. Cascabel remarked that there was a dam across it.

"Well!" said he, "when they went to the trouble of damming this creek, they might as well have made a bridge over it! It would have been more useful in times of flood!"

"No doubt, father," answered John. "But the engineers who built this dam would not have been capable of constructing a bridge!"

"Why so?"

"Because they are four-footed engineers, otherwise called beavers."

John was not mistaken, and they were able to admire the work of these industrious animals, who take care to build their dam in conformity with the current and to regulate its height according to the usual low-water level of the creek. The very slope given to the sides of the dam had been calculated in view of a greater power of resistance to the force of the waters.

"And still," cried Sander, "these beavers never went to school to learn lessons."

"They had no need of going," answered Mr. Sergius. "Of what use is science, which is sometimes at fault, when you have instinct, which is always right? This dam, my child, the beavers have constructed it, just as ants make their nests, just as spiders weave their webs, just as bees contrive the combs in their hives, in fine just as trees and shrubs bring forth fruits and flowers. No fumbling about, on their part; no improving either. Indeed there are no improvements to make here. The beaver of our day is as perfect in his work as the first beaver that appeared on this globe. The power of improving does not belong to animals, it is man's own; he alone can rise from one improvement to another in the domain of art, of industry, and of sciences. Let us give free scope to our admiration for this marvelous instinct of animals, which nables them to create such things. But let us consider such accomplishments only as the work of nature!"

"Quite so, Mr. Sergius," said John, "I fully understand your remark. Therein lies the difference between instinct and reason. On the whole, reason is superior to instinct, although it be likely to err."

"Most undoubtedly, my friend," replied Mr. Sergius, "and the errings of reason, successively recognized and repaired, constitute but so much headway on the path of progress."

"In any case," repeated Sander, "I keep to what I said! Animals can do without going to school."

"Right, but men are only animals when they have not gone to school!" retorted Mr. Sergius.

"Very well, very well!" exclaimed Cornelia, always very practical in household matters. "Are your beavers good to eat?"

"Of course," said Kayette.

"I even read," added John, "that the tail of the animal is excellent!"

They were unable to verify the statement, for there were no beavers in the creek, or if there were any, they were not to be caught.

After leaving the bed of the Milo-cargut, the *Fair Rambler* went through Sachertelontin village, in the very heart of the Co-Yukon district. On Kayette's recommendation, certain precautions had to be taken by our friends in their intercourse with the natives owing to the thieving propensities of the latter. As they surrounded the vehicle rather closely, care had to be taken that they should not enter it. Besides, a few glass baubles, liberally offered to the principal chiefs of the tribe, produced a salutary effect, and the episode passed off without any unpleasantness.

The itinerary, however, became once more complicated with a certain amount of difficulties, skirting as it did the narrow base of the "ramparts"; but it had been impossible to avoid them without venturing into a more mountainous country.

The speed of the journey was affected thereby, and still it was now advisable not to tarry. The temperature began to feel coldish, if not during the day, at least at night—quite a normal occurrence at this season, since the region lay within a few degrees only of the polar circle.

The Cascabels had now reached a point where the river describes a rather sudden angle toward the north. They had to follow it up to the confluent of the Co-Yukuk, which joins it by means of two tortuous streams. One whole day was spent in finding a fordable spot, nor did Kayette make it out without trouble, as the level of the stream had already risen.

Once on the other side of this affluent, the *Fair Rambler* resumed its southerly course, and went down through a somewhat uneven district, to Nulato fort.

This post, the commercial importance of which is considerable, belongs to the Russo-American Company. It is the most northerly trading station in Western America, being situated, according to Sir Frederick Whymper's observations, in latitude 60°42'[2] and longitude 155°36'.

And yet, in this part of the Alaskan province, it would have been difficult to believe one's self in such high latitude. The soil was unquestionably more fertile than in the neighborhood of Fort Yukon. Everywhere trees of fair growth could be seen, everywhere pasture lands carpeted with green grass, not to speak of vast plains that might be profitably tilled, for the clayey soil is covered over with a thick layer of humus. The land is, moreover, abundantly watered, thanks to the meanderings of the river Nulato, whose general direction is southwest, and to the network of creeks or "carguts" stretching out toward the northeast. However, the only signs of vegetable production are a few bushes laden with wild berries, and utterly abandoned to the whims of nature.

The laying out of Fort Nulato is as follows: around the buildings, a belt of palisades, protected by two towerets, which Indians are forbidden to enter at night, and even during the day, when there are many of them together; within the precincts, huts, sheds, and wooden stores, with windows where the skin of the seal's bladder is a substitute for glass. Nothing more rudimentary, the reader will perceive, than these stations in far-away America.

There, Mr. Cascabel and his friends received a warm welcome. In those out-of-the-way spots on the new continent, outside the tracks of regular intercommunications, is not the advent of a few visitors always a relief to monotony, a real source of enjoyment, and are they not always welcome for the news they bring from such distances?

Fort Nulato was inhabited by a score of employes, of Russian or American origin, who placed themselves at the disposal of the Cascabels, to supply them with anything they might need. Not only do they receive regular supplies from the Company, but they are in a position to add to their resources during the fine season, either hunting the reindeer and the moose, or fishing in the waters of the Yukon. There they find abundance of certain fish, particularly of "nalima," a fish more generally used for the feeding of the dogs, but one the liver of which is rather valued by those who are accustomed to eat it.

Naturally the inhabitants of Nulato were somewhat surprised when they descried the *Fair Rambler*, and not less so, when Mr. Cascabel told them of his intention to return to Europe by way of Siberia. Really, those French folks doubt of nothing! As to the first portion of the journey, as far as Port Clarence, they stated their belief that there would be no obstacles to it, and that it would be completed before the plains of Alaska were gripped by the first chill of winter.

On the advice of Mr. Sergius, they resolved to purchase some of the articles necessary to the trip across the steppes. And first of all, it was advisable to get a few pair of those spectacles that are indispensable over immense tracts whitened with winter rime and snow. The Indians bartered a dozen of them against a few glass trinkets. They were only wooden spectacles without any glass, or rather they were a sort of winkers covering up the eye in such a way as to allow it to see but through a narrow chink. This is sufficient to enable you to get along without too much trouble, and saves you from the ophthalmia which would be a necessary consequence of the reflection from the snow. The whole staff made a trial of the winkers, and declared they could easily get accustomed to them.

Next to this sight-saving apparatus, a covering for the feet had to be thought of, for you do not promenade in thin boots or shoes through steppes subjected to the hardships of Siberian winters.

The Nulato stores supplied them with several pair of boots made of seal-skins—of those best suited to long journeys over an ice-bound soil, and rendered waterproof by a coating of grease.

This led Mr. Cascabel to make, in his sententious style, this very just remark:

"It is always advantageous to clothe yourself in the same way as the animals of the country you go through! Since Siberia is the land of seals, let us dress like seals."

"Seals with spectacles on!" added Sander, whose sally received the father's approbation.

Two days were spent by our party at Fort Nulato, a sufficient rest for spirited steeds. Port Clarence was eagerly wished for. On the 21st of August, the *Fair Rambler* started onward, and from this moment, finally withdrew from the right bank of the big river.

As a matter of fact, the Yukon was now flowing straight for the southwest, to empty itself into Norton Bay. If they had kept on with it in this new direction, they would have needlessly lengthened their journey, since the mouth of the river lies below Behring Strait. From there, they would have been obliged to turn up toward Port Clarence along a coast indented with fiords, bays, and creeks, where Gladiator and Vermont would needlessly have worn themselves out.

The cold was becoming more biting. If the very oblique rays of the sun still gave a great light, they gave very little heat. Thick clouds, gathering in a grayish mass, threatened to fall in a shower of snow. Small game was growing scarce, and the migratory birds were commencing their flight southward in search of milder winter quarters.

To this day,—a blessing to be thankful for—Mr. Cascabel and his party had not been too severely tried by the fatigues of the journey. In truth, they must have had iron constitutions,—the result, evidently, of their nomadic life, the habit of acclimatizing themselves under any and every sky, and the muscular training of their bodily exercises. There was then every hope that they all should reach Port Clarence safe and sound.

And it came to pass thus, on the 5th of September, after a trip of fifteen hundred miles from Sitka, and almost three thousand three hundred from Sacramento, say after a journey of over five thousand miles in seven months through western America.

CHAPTER XV - PORT CLARENCE

PORT CLARENCE is the most northwesterly port of northern America on Behring Strait. Lying to the south of Cape Prince of Wales, it is deeply sunk into that portion of the coast which forms the nose in the face profiled by the configuration of Alaska. This port affords very safe anchorage, and is therefore duly appreciated by seamen, especially by the whalers whose boats seek their fortune in the Arctic seas.

The *Fair Rambler* had taken up its camping ground near the inner shore of the harbor, close to the mouth of a small river, under shelter of tall rocks crowned with a cluster of stunted birch trees. There, the longest halt of the whole journey was to be made. There, the little troupe would take a lengthy rest,—a rest enforced by the condition of the strait, the surface of which had not become solid yet, at this time of the year.

Needless to say that the *Fair Rambler* could not possibly have crossed it on board the Port Clarence ferry-boats, mere fishing canoes of very small tonnage. It was then obligatory to adhere to the plan of getting over to the Asiatic side when the sea would be transformed into an immense ice-field.

This long halt was not to be regretted, previous to undertaking the second portion of the journey that would witness the commencement of the real physical difficulties, the struggle against the cold, the battling with the snowstorms—at least for so long as the *Fair Rambler* would not have reached the more accessible territories of southern Siberia. Until then some weeks, some months perhaps, of hardships would have to be passed, and it should be a cause of rejoicing to have plenty of time to complete the preparations for so severe an ordeal. For, if the Indians at Fort Nulato had been able to supply certain articles, there were others wanting still, which Mr. Cascabel expected to purchase either from the traders, or from the natives at Port Clarence.

The consequence was that his staff experienced a feeling of genuine satisfaction when he gave out his well-known word of command:

"Stand at ease!"

And this order, always welcomed on the march or in military maneuvers, was immediately followed by another, loudly called by young Sander:

"Dismiss!"

And the troupe did dismiss, you may believe it.

As may be imagined, the arrival of the *Fair Rambler* at Port Clarence had not escaped notice. Never had such a perambulating machine ventured so far, since it had now reached the very utmost confines of northern America. For the first time did French showmen appear to the wondering eyes of the natives.

There were then at Port Clarence, over and above its usual population of Eskimos and traders, not a few Russian officials. They were men who, consequent upon the annexation of Alaska to the United States, were under orders to cross the strait and repair either to the Tchuktchi peninsula on the coast of Asia, or to Petropaulovski, the capital of Kamtchatka. These officials joined the whole population in the hearty welcome they gave to the Cascabel family, and it is worthy of notice that the Eskimos' greeting, in particular, was most cordial.

They were the same Eskimos who were to be met in these parts, twelve years later, by the famous navigator Nordenskiold, at the time of that bold expedition in which he discovered the northeast passage. Even now, some of these natives were armed with revolvers and repeating guns, the first gifts of American civilization.

The summer season being scarcely over, the natives at Port Clarence had not returned to their winter dwellings yet. They were encamped under small tents, pitched not without elegance, made of thick, brightly variegated cotton cloth and strengthened with straw matting. Inside might be seen a number of utensils manufactured with cocoanut shells.

And when Clovy saw these utensils for the first time, he exclaimed:

"I say!—And cocoanuts grow here, then? in the Eskimos' forests?"

"Unless," answered Mr. Sergius,—"unless these nuts be brought here from the islands of the Pacific, and given in payment by the whalers who call at Port Clarence."

And Mr. Sergius was right. Indeed, the relations between the Americans and the natives were already progressing rapidly at this time, and a fusion was taking place between them, entirely to the advantage of the development of the Eskimo race.

In this connection, we may draw attention to the fact, which will be noticed hereafter, that there exists no conformity of type or manners between the Eskimos of American origin and the natives of Siberia in Asia. The Alaskan tribes do not even understand the language which is spoken west of Behring Strait. But their dialect having a very considerable admixture of English and Russian words, it was no very hard task to carry on a conversation with them.

It therefore follows that, immediately on their being settled, the Cascabels endeavored to hold intercourse with the natives scattered around Port Clarence. As they were hospitably received in the tents of these good people, they felt no hesitation in opening for them the doors of the *Fair Rambler*,— and neither party had cause to repent this interchange of friendly relations.

These Eskimos, besides, are much more civilized than is generally believed. They are popularly looked upon as a sort of speech-endowed seals, human-faced amphibious creatures, judging of them by the clothing they are in the habit of wearing, especially in winter time. But this is in no way concurrent with facts. At Port Clarence, the representatives of the Eskimo race are neither repulsive to behold nor unpleasant to associate with. Some of them even carry their regard for fashion to the extent of dressing almost after European style. Most of them obey a certain code of coquetry, which regulates the making of a garment in reindeer or in sealskin, the "pask" in marmot's fur, the tattooing of the face, that is, a few lines slightly drawn on the skin. The scanty beard of the men is cut short; at each corner of their lips three holes, skillfully drilled, enable them to hang thereby small carved-bone rings, and the cartilage of their noses receives likewise certain ornaments of the same kind.

In a word, the Eskimos, who came and paid their duties to the Cascabel family, wore by no means an objectionable appearance,—the appearance, for instance, but too often presented by the Samoyedes or the other natives of the Asiatic coast. The young girls wore strings of pearls in their ears, and, on their arms, iron or brass bracelets of very fair workmanship.

It should also be noted that they were honest people, full of good faith in their transactions, though they be given to bargaining and haggling to excess. Forsooth, upbraiding the natives of the Arctic regions for such a fault would be severe indeed.

The most perfect equality reigns among them. Their clans have even no chieftains. As to their religion, it is paganism. By way of divinities, they worship wooden posts, with carved faces painted red, which represent various sorts of birds whose wings are stretched out to their full, like so many fans. Their morals are pure; their sense of home duties highly developed; they respect their parents, love their children, and revere the dead. The remains of the latter are exposed in the open air, dressed in holiday attire, with their weapons and cayak lying by their side.

The Cascabels took great pleasure in their daily walks round about Port Clarence. Not unfrequently, likewise, they paid a visit to an old oil-factory, of American foundation, which was still working at this season.

The country is not without trees, nor does the appearance of the vegetating soil differ much from that which is presented by the peninsula of the Tchuktchis on the other side of the strait. This is due to the fact that along the coast of the New Continent there flows a warm current from the burning seas of the Pacific, whereas the cold current that bathes the Siberian coast comes from the basin of the boreal seas.

As a matter of course the thought of giving a performance to the natives at Port Clarence did not enter Mr. Cascabel's mind. He now felt misgivings on that point, and he had cause to. What if among them were acrobats, and jugglers, and clowns as expert in their art as those of the Indian tribes at Fort Yukon!

Better not run the risk of compromising the honor of the family once more!

Meanwhile the days passed by, and, in reality, the little troupe had a longer rest than it needed. No doubt but one week's rest at Port Clarence would have enabled them to attack the fatigues of their journey through Siberian wastes.

But the *Fair Rambler* was still forbidden the strait. By the end of September, and at this latitude, even though the mean temperature was already below zero, the arm of the sea which separates Asia from America was not frozen yet. True, numerous icebergs passed by, accumulated in the open sea on the verge of the basin of Behring, and were drifted northward along the Alaskan coast by the current from the Pacific. But these icebergs had to cohere into one solid mass ere they offered the gigantic, firm, and steady ice-field we spoke of, a veritable "carriage-drive" between the two continents.

It was evident that on this sheet of ice with a power of resistance sufficient to bear a train of artillery, the *Fair Rambler* and its occupants would run no risk. The strait, indeed, measured but some sixty miles across its narrowest width, from Cape Prince of Wales, somewhat above Port Clarence, to the little port of Numana, on the Siberian coast. "Verily, verily," said Mr Cascabel, "it is a great pity the Americans did not run up a bridge here."

"Sixty miles of a bridge!" exclaimed Sander.

"Why not?" remarked John. "It might be supported, in the middle of the strait, by the Isle of Diomede."

"The feat would not be impossible," rejoined Mr. Sergius; "and one may indulge the belief that it will be done some day, like everything that the intelligence of man can achieve."

"Why! They are even now talking of bridging the British Channel[1] over," said John.

"You are right, my friend," said Mr. Sergius. "Still, let us own it, a bridge across Behring Strait would not prove so useful as one from Calais to Dover. Positively, the former would not cover its expenses!"

"Although it were but of little use for the generality of travelers," suggested Cornelia, "to us at least it would be a boon."

"Why! Now that I think of it," answered Mr. Cascabel, "the bridge here does exist for two-thirds of the year, an ice bridge, as strong as any bridge made of iron or stone! Dame Nature it is who builds it every year when the ice breaks up at the pole, and she charges no toll on it!"

With his habit of taking things by their best side, Mr. Cascabel was quite right. What was the use of spending millions on a bridge, when both foot travelers and carriages need only await the favorable moment to obtain a safe thoroughfare?

And sure enough the thing would shortly come to pass now. A little more patience was all that was needed.

About the 7th of October it became apparent that winter had set in, in downright earnest. Snow showers were frequent. All trace of vegetation had disappeared. The few trees along the shore, spoiled of their last leaves, were covered with rime. Not one of those sickly-looking plants of the Boreal regions could be seen, so closely allied to those of Scandinavia; not one of those linnearia which make up the greatest part of the Arctic flora.

However, if the blocks of ice still floated through the strait, thanks to the swiftness of the current, they increased in breadth and thickness. Even as a good blast of heat is sufficient to solder metals, even so a good blast of cold was all that was now needed to solder together the pieces of the icefield. This blast might be expected from one day to another.

At the same time, if the Cascabels longed to be able to avail themselves of the strait and to leave Port Clarence, if it was a joy for them to think of setting their feet once again on the Old Continent, that joy was not unmingled with bitterness. That hour would be the hour of parting. They would leave Alaska, no doubt, but Mr. Sergius would remain in the country, since there was no question of his going further westward. And, winter over, he would resume his excursions through that portion of America of which he desired to complete the exploration and visit the districts lying north of the Yukon and beyond the mountains.

A cruel parting it would be for all; for, all were now bound, not by the bonds of sympathy alone but by a very close friendship!

The most aggrieved, it will be guessed, was John. Could he forget that Mr. Sergius would take Kayette away with him? And, still, was it not to the young girl's interest that her future prospects should be in the hands of her new father? With whom could they be in better keeping than with Mr. Sergius? He had made her his adopted daughter, he would bring her to Europe, he would get her educated, and would assure her a position that she would never have found in the home of a poor showman. In the face of such advantages, were it possible to hesitate? No, assuredly! and John was the first to acknowledge it. Still he none the less experienced a feeling of sorrow which his ever increasing sadness betrayed but too plainly. How could he have mastered his feelings? Part with Kayette, see her no more, see her no more even when she would be so far from him physically and morally, when she would have taken her place in the family circle of Mr. Sergius; give up the pleasant habit they had grown into of chatting together, working together, being always near one another, all this was heart-breaking. John loved Kayette; he loved her with a real love, a love he had revealed in the attentions he paid her, in the trembling of his voice when he spoke to her. That love was requited, perhaps, even unknown to the young girl! All that would be broken when they should part, part perhaps forever.

On the other hand, if John felt very wretched, his father and his mother, his brother and his sister, deeply attached to Kayette, could not grow accustomed to the thought of parting with her, or with Mr. Sergius either. They would have given "a big sum," as Mr. Cascabel put it, for Mr. Sergius to accompany them to the end of their journey. They would have a few months more, at least, to spend with him, and then—why, then—they would see.

We have mentioned above that the inhabitants of Port Clarence had taken a great liking for the Cascabels, and no little apprehension was felt on their behalf as the time drew near when they would venture among the too real dangers of their journey. But, interested as they were in these French people who had come from such a distance and were going so far away, some of the Russians, recently arrived at the strait, were inclined to observe the individual members of the party, and more especially Mr. Sergius, with a very different kind of interest.

The reader will not have forgotten that there sojourned, then, at Port Clarence, a certain number of officials recalled on Siberian territory, owing to the annexation of Alaska.

Among them were two agents entrusted with a very special supervision on the American territories subjected to the Muscovite administration. It was their mission to watch the political refugees to whom New Britain offered an asylum, and who might be tempted to cross the Alaskan frontier. Now, this Russian, who had become the guest and companion of a showman's troupe, this Mr. Sergius whose journey happened to terminate just at the very limit of the Czar's empire, had somewhat aroused their suspicions, and they watched him accordingly, but with sufficient caution to escape notice.

Little did Mr. Sergius dream of his being the object of suspicious watching. He, too, had his mind full of the approaching parting. Was he wavering between his project to resume his excursions through Western America, and the thought of giving it up, so as to follow his new friends to Europe? It would have been hard to say. However, seeing him very pensive, Mr. Cascabel determined to bring him to an explanation on this subject.

One evening, the 11th of October, after supper, turning to Mr. Sergius, as though he spoke of quite a new thing:

"By the way, Mr. Sergius," said he, "you know we shall soon start for your country?"

"Of course, my friends. That's agreed on."

"Yes! We are going to Russia; and, as luck would have it, we shall pass through Perm, where your father lives, if I mistake not."

"Quite so, and your departure excites both my regret and my envy!"

"Mr. Sergius," inquired Cornelia, "do you propose to stay much longer in America?"

"Much longer? I hardly know."

"And when you come back to Europe, which way will you come?"

"I shall return by the Far West, as my explorations will naturally bring me back toward New York, and it is there I shall take ship, with Kayette."

"With Kayette!" murmured John, as he looked toward the girl, who hung down her head.

A few moments' silence followed. Then Mr. Cascabel began again, hesitatingly:

"Now, Mr. Sergius, I am going to beg leave to make a proposal to you. Of course I am aware that it will be very hard to pull thorough that devilish Siberia! But with a good heart and a will—"

"My friend," replied Mr. Sergius, "be persuaded that I am frightened neither by the dangers nor by the fatigues, and I would share them with you willingly, if—"

"Why not complete our journey together?" asked Cornelia.

"It would be so nice!" added Sander.

"And I would give you such a kiss if you said yes!" exclaimed Napoleona.

John and Kayette had breathed not a word, but their hearts beat violently.

"My dear Cascabel," said Mr. Sergius, after a few moments' reflection, "I should like to have a chat with yourself and your wife."

"At your service, sir, this very moment."

"No, to-morrow," answered Mr. Sergius.

Thereupon, each one retired to his little bed, both very uneasy and singularly puzzled.

What motive had Mr. Sergius for this private conversation? Had he made up his mind to alter his plans, or, on the contrary, did he simply mean to enable the Cascabels to accomplish their journey under better conditions by making them accept some money?

Be that as it might, neither John nor Kayette had one hour's sleep that night.

Next day, in the course of the morning, the conversation did take place. Not through any distrust of the children, but for fear of being overheard by the natives or other people who continually passed by, Mr. Sergius asked Mr. and Mrs. Cascabel to accompany him a certain distance away from the encampment. Doubtless, what he had to say was important, and it was advisable to keep it secret.

All three walked up the beach in the direction of the oil factory, and this is how the conversation began:

"My friends," said Mr. Sergius, "listen to me, and ponder well ere you give your answer to the proposal I am about making to you. Of your good heart I have no doubt, and you have shown me to what extent your devotion can go. But, before you take one final resolution, you must know who I am."

"Who you are? Why, you are an honest man, of course!" cried Cascabel.

"Well, be it so, an honest man," repeated Mr. Sergius; "but an honest man who is desirous not to add, by his presence, to the dangers of your journey through Siberia."

"Your presence a danger, Mr. Sergius?" said Cornelia.

"Quite so, for my name is Count Sergius Narkine. I am a political outlaw!"

And Mr. Sergius briefly related his history.

Count Sergius Narkine belonged to an opulent family in the Government of Perm. As he had stated previously, he had quite a passion for geographical sciences and discoveries, and he had spent his youth in travels and voyages in every part of the world.

Unfortunately, he had not confined himself to those bold undertakings where he might have acquired great celebrity. He had mixed himself up with politics, and, in 1857, had been compromised in a secret society which he had been led to join. In short, the members of this society were arrested, tried with all the severity peculiar to the Russian government, and, for the most part, sentenced to transportation for life in Siberia.

Count Sergius Narkine was among the majority. He had to start for Iakoutsk, the locality assigned to him, and part with his only surviving relative, his father. Prince Wassili Narkine, now an octogenarian, who resided on his estate at Walska, near Perm.

127

After spending five years at Iakoutsk, the prisoner had succeeded in making his escape to Okhotsk on the coast of the sea of that name. There he had been able to take passage on board a ship sailing for one of the Californian ports; and it was thus that, for seven years past, Count Sergius Narkine had lived either in the United States or in New England, always endeavoring to get nearer to Alaska and to enter it as soon as it should become American. Yes! his heart's fond hope was to return to Europe by way of Siberia,—the very thing projected, and now being carried out, by Cascabel. His feelings may be imagined, the first time he heard that the people to whom he owed his life were on their way to Behring Strait for the very purpose of passing into Asia.

Naturally he would have wished for nothing more than to accompany them. But, could he expose them to the reprisals of the Russian government? If it became known that they had "aided and abetted" the return of a political exile to the Muscovite empire, what would happen? And yet, his poor old father! how glad he would be to see him once more!

"Well then, come, Mr. Sergius, come along with us!" exclaimed Cornelia.

"Your liberty, my friends, your lives perhaps, will be at stake, if it is known that—"

"And what matter, Mr. Sergius?" said Cascabel. "We all have an account open, there above, haven't we? Well, let us try to get as many good actions as we can on the credit side! They'll balance the bad ones!"

"Do bear in mind, my dear Cascabel—"

"Besides, you'll never be known, Mr. Sergius! We know a trick or two, we do; and hang me if we aren't a match for all the agents of the Russian police."

"Still—" continued the Count.

"And then, why—if needs be—you might dress like ourselves; unless you were ashamed."

"Oh! my friend!"

"And who would ever get it into his head that Count Narkine was a member of the Cascabel troupe?"

"Well, I accept, my friends! Yes! I accept! And I thank you."

"That will do,—that will do," said the showman. "Do you think we haven't as many thanks to offer you, ourselves! And so then. Count Narkine—"

"Do not call me Count Narkine. I must continue to be simpy Mr. Sergius for everybody, even for your children."

"You are right. It is needless they should know. That's a settled thing! You come with us, Mr. Sergius. And I, Cæser Cascabel, undertake to bring you to

Perm, or—may I lose my name!—which would be an irretrievable loss for art, you will confess."

As to the welcome accorded to Mr. Sergius on his return to the *Fair Rambler* when John, Kayette, Sander, Napoleona, and Clovy heard that he would accompany them to Europe, it will be readily imagined without any need of description.

CHAPTER XVI - FAREWELL TO THE NEW CONTINENT

AND now, the only thing was to carry out the prearranged journey toward Europe.

All being well considered, the plan showed fair chances of success. Since the checkered course of their gypsy lives brought the Cascabels through Russia, nay more, through the very Government of Perm, the best thing Count Sergius Narkine could really do was to join them for the rest of the journey. How could it be suspected that the political prisoner who had made his escape from Siberia was among the artists of a showman's caravan? If no indiscretion was committed, success was sure; and, once in Perm, after he had seen Prince Wassili Narkine, the Count would shape his course to the best of his interests. Having crossed Asia without leaving behind him any clue that the police might get hold of, he would make up his mind according to circumstances.

On the other hand, it is true, if he were recognized along the road, unlikely as it seemed, it might have terrible consequences for him, and for the Cascabels too. But neither Mr. Cascabel nor his wife would take that danger into account, and, had they consulted their children on the subject, the latter would have approved of their conduct. Still Count Narkine's secret should be strictly kept; their traveling companion would continue to be Mr. Sergius.

Later on, Count Narkine would be in a position to acknowledge the devotion of these good French people, although Mr. Cascabel would hear of no other reward than the pleasure of obliging him, while, at the same time, outwitting the Russian police.

Unfortunately,—an event which neither of them could anticipate,—their plans were about being seriously compromised, at the very start.

At their landing on the opposite shore, they would straight away be exposed to the greatest dangers, and, doubtless, arrested by the Russian agents in Siberia.

Sure enough, the very day after the conclusion of this new arrangement, two men were talking, up and down one end of the harbor, where no one could hear their conversation.

They were the two agents we have already named, and who had been surprised and puzzled by the presence of Mr. Sergius among the occupants of the *Fair Rambler*.

Residing at Sitka for several years past, and intrusted with the political surveillance of the province, it was their duty (it has been said) to spy the doings of the refugees in the neighborhood of the Columbian frontier, to report them to the Governor of Alaska, and to arrest any of them who should attempt to cross the border.

Now a serious matter it was, that, if they had no personal knowledge of Count Narkine, they had been given his description at the time of his escape from the Iakoutsk citadel. On the arrival of the Cascabel family at Port Clarence, they were astonished at the sight of this Russian, who had neither the gait nor the manners of an itinerant artist. How did he happen to be among these show people, who, coming from Sacramento, followed so strange a route to return to Europe?

Their suspicions once aroused, they had made inquiries, had taken observations, cleverly enough not to excite attention, and after comparison of Mr. Sergius with the description they had in hand of Count Narkine, their doubts had given place to a feeling of certainty.

"Yes, this is indeed Count Narkine!" said one of the agents. "No doubt he was roaming about the frontiers of Alaska until the province would be annexed, when he fell in with those gypsies, who came to his help, and now he is preparing to cross over to Siberia with them!"

Nothing more accurate; and if, at first, Mr. Sergius had had no thought of venturing beyond Port Clarence, the two agents felt no surprise whatever when they heard that he had resolved to follow the *Fair Rambler* beyond the strait.

"That is a good windfall for us!" answered the second agent. "Had the Count remained here, on American soil, we dared not have arrested him,"

"While, now, as soon as he sets his foot on the other side of the strait," continued the former, "he will be on Russian territory, and he cannot escape us if we be there to receive him in our arms!"

"That's an arrest that will be to our greater glory—and profit! what a master-stroke for our coming home! But how shall we go about it?"

"It's very simple! The Cascabels will start off presently; and as they will take the shortest cut, there is no doubt but they will make for the port of Numana. Well, if we get there before, or even at the same time as Count Narkine, we shall have nothing to do but collar him!"

"Quite so, but I would rather be at Numana before him, so as to warn the coast police, who might lend us a hand in case of need!"

"That's what we shall do, if possible. These showmen will be obliged to wait until the ice is strong enough to bear their wagon, and we can easily get ahead of them. Let us stay here then, in the meantime, and keep our eye on Count Narkine without letting him know. Even though he must mistrust Russian officials on their way home from Alaska, he cannot possibly guess that we have recognized him. And so, he will surely make a start; we shall arrest him at Numana, and then conduct him, under safe escort, to Petropaulovski or to Iakoutsk."

"And if his acrobats wanted to defend him."

"Well, they will pay dearly for having helped a political exile to return to Russia!"

So simple a plan was fated to succeed, since the Count was utterly unaware of his having been recognized, since the Cascabels had no idea that they were the object of special surveillance. And so the journey, so auspiciously commenced, ran the risk of having a sad termination for Mr. Sergius and his companions.

And, while this plot was being devised, they were all enjoying the prospective happiness of remaining together, of starting together for Russia. What joy it was for John and Kayette especially!

Needless to say that the two police agents had kept to themselves the secret they were going to work out. And no one at Port Clarence could have imagined that so important a personage as Count Sergius Narkine was under the roof of the *Fair Rambler*.

Meanwhile, it had not been found possible, yet, to fix a day for the departure. They watched with the greatest impatience every change in the temperature,—a truly anomalous temperature,—and never in his life had Mr. Cascabel so ardently wished for such a frost "as the rocks themselves could not stand."

Still, it was of importance that they should be on the other side of the strait ere winter had taken complete possession of those regions. As it would attain its greatest severity only during the first weeks of November, the *Fair Rambler* would have time to reach the southern regions of Siberia. There, in some village or other, they would wait for the favorable season to push on to the Ural mountains.

Under these conditions, Vermont and Gladiator could traverse the steppes without too much fatigue. The Cascabel family would reach Perm just in time for the fair, that is, by the month of July of the following year.

And those icebergs kept on forever drifting north, carried on by the warm current of the Pacific! That ever restless flotilla of ice kept on shifting about in the strait instead of the long-looked-for compact and steady mass!

On the 13th of October, however, the drifting seemed to slacken. To the north, to all appearance, a blockade stopped the way. And sure enough, far away in the horizon, you could see a continuous line of white peaks, a sure sign that the Arctic Sea was now wholly frozen. The white glare reflected by the ice filled the sky; the entire solidification could not tarry long.

Now and again Mr. Sergius and John would consult the fishermen at Port Clarence. Several times already both had thought that the crossing might be attempted; but the seamen, who "knew every inch of the strait," had advised them to wait.

"Don't be in a hurry," they would say. "Let the frost do its work! It hasn't been hard enough yet! And then, even if the water was all frozen on this side of the strait, there is nothing to show that it is so on the other, especially in the neighborhood of the Isle of Diomede."

And the advice was a wise one.

"Winter is not very forward, this year!" said Mr. Sergius to a fisherman, one day.

"No," the man replied, "it is rather late. And that's another reason why you should not hurry before you are sure that you can get across. And then again, your wagon is heavier than a man on foot; it needs greater strength under it. Wait till a good fall of snow brings all the icebergs to a level, and then you can fire away, the same as on a highroad! Besides, you'll soon make up for lost time, and you won't have run the risk of remaining in distress, fair in the middle of the strait!"

Such reasoning should needs be heeded, coming as it did from practical men. And so, Mr. Sergius did his utmost to calm his friend Cascabel, who proved the most impatient of the party. The chief point was to endanger, by no imprudent act, either the success of the journey or the safety of the travelers.

"Come," he would say to him, "be calm and reasonable! your *Fair Rambler* is not a boat, and if it got caught between two ill-joined blocks of ice, it would not be long going to the bottom. The Cascabel family has no need of increasing its celebrity by seeking a watery grave in the strait of Behring!"

"And would it be increased thereby?" replied the vain César, with a smile.

In any case Cornelia intervened and distinctly stated she would allow no imprudence to be committed.

"Why, it's on your account, Mr. Sergius, that we are in such a hurry!" exclaimed Mr. Cascabel.

"Well, I, my friend, am in no hurry concerning you!" Count Narkine replied.

In spite of the general feeling of impatience, John and Kayette did not feel the time weigh heavily on their hands.

He continued to be her teacher. Already she was beginning to talk and understand French fairly well. Between them there was now no difficulty to understand one another. And then Kayette was so happy in this home, so happy near John, who was all attention to her! In very truth, Mr. and Mrs. Cascabel should have been blind not to see what kind of a feeling she had awakened in their son. Indeed they were growing uneasy about it. They knew what Mr. Sergius was, and what Kayette would be one day. She was no longer the poor Indian girl, on her way to beg a situation as a servant at Sitka; she was the adopted daughter of Count Narkine. And John was preparing a world of bitter disappointment for himself in the future.

"After all," Mr. Cascabel would say, "Mr. Sergius has eyes to see with; he is very well aware of what is going on! Well, Cornelia, if he says nothing, we have nothing to say, either!"

One day, John asked the young girl:

"Are you pleased, little Kayette, to be going to Europe?"

"To Europe? Yes!" replied she. "But I should be better pleased still to be going to France!"

"You are right. A fine country, and a good country is ours! If ever it could become yours, you would like it."

"I would like any country where your people would be, John, and my greatest desire is to leave you no more!"

"Dear little Kayette!"

"It is very far to France?"

"Any country is far away, Kayette, when you long to be there? But we shall arrive—too soon perhaps—"

"Why so, John?"

"Because you shall stay in Russia with Mr. Sergius! If we do not part here, we shall have to part there! Mr. Sergius will keep you, little Kayette! He will make a fine young lady of you; and we shall never see you again!"

"Why talk like that, John? Mr. Sergius is good and grateful. It was not I that saved his life, it was you, yes, it was you! If you had not been there, what could I have done for him? If he is alive now, it is to your mother, it is to you all that he owes it! Do you think Mr. Sergius can forget it? If we do part, John, why do you say it will be for ever?"

"I do not say so, little Kayette!" answered John, who could no longer contain his emotion. "But,—I fear so! Never see you again, Kayette! If you knew how unhappy I should be! And then, it is not merely to see you I should have wished. Look, since you are alone in the world, why cannot our home be enough for you! My father and mother love you so."

"Not more than I love them, John!"

"'And my brother and sister too! I had cherished the hope that they would have been a sister and a brother for you!"

"So they will always be. And you, John?"

"I—I should be—a brother too, little Kayette,—but more devoted—more loving!"

And John went no farther. He had seized Kayette's hand, he pressed it in his. Then he went away, unwilling to say more. Kayette, full of emotion, felt her heart throbbing violently, and a tear dropped from her eye.

On the 15th of October, the seamen about Port Clarence informed Mr. Sergius that he might get ready to go. The cold had become more intense for the last few days. The mean temperature did not now rise to ten degrees Centigrade below zero. The ice-field appeared absolutely motionless. They no longer could hear even those significant crackling sounds that can be noticed before the blocks of ice are completely cemented together.

It was probable they would presently witness the arrival of some of those natives of Asia, who cross the strait during the winter and carry on a certain amount of trading between Numana and Port Clarence. This roadway indeed, is rather largely frequented at times. It is no unusual thing for sleighs, drawn by dogs or by reindeer, to go from one continent to the other, covering in two or three days the sixty miles that separate the two nearest points of the respective shores. This spot affords, then, a natural thoroughfare, opened at the beginning and closed at the end of winter, say, practically, for over six months. But care must be taken not to start either too soon or too late, so as to avoid the frightful catastrophes that would result from a breaking up of the ice.

In view of the journey through Siberia until the day when the *Fair Rambler* would halt to take up its winter quarters, Mr. Sergius had purchased, at Port Clarence, various articles of absolute necessity on a journey accomplished in such climes, among others several pair of those snow-shoes which the Indians put on like skates, and which enable them to skim swiftly over a vast extent of frozen ground. Itinerant "artists" needed no very long apprenticeship to become familiar with them. Within a few days, John and Sander had become expert "snow-racers" by practicing on the frozen creeks along the shore.

Mr. Sergius had also completed the stock of furs bought at Fort Yukon. It was not sufficient for the travelers to wrap themselves up in those warm furs to preserve themselves against the cold, they should likewise pad the compartments of the *Fair Rambler* with them, cover the beds, the partitions, and the floor with them, so as to keep up the heat generated by the kitchen stove. Besides,—too great emphasis could not be laid on it,—the strait once traveled over, Mr. Cascabel's intention was to spend the hardest months of winter in one of the villages that are to be found in the southern districts of lower Siberia.

At last, the departure was fixed for the 21st of October. For forty-eight hours a misty sky had been melting into snow. An immense white sheet gave the vast ice-field a uniform surface. The fishermen affirmed their belief that the strait was one mass of ice from shore to shore.

Indeed evident proofs of the fact were soon forthcoming. Several traders arrived from Numana port, and their journey across had been effected without obstacles or dangers.

Moreover, on the 19th, Mr. Sergius was told that two of the Russian agents who were at Port Clarence would not wait any longer to go to the Siberian shore, and had started that very morning, intending to halt at the Isle of Diomede and pursue their journey the following day.

Which led to this remark of Cascabel's:

"Here are two fellows who were in a greater hurry than we are! Why, they might, surely, have waited for us! We'd have kept each other company on the road!"

Then he said to himself, that, very likely, the officials had been afraid to be delayed, if they kept on with the *Fair Rambler*, for she could not sail many knots an hour on that layer of snow.

As a matter of fact, although Vermont and Gladiator had been rough-shod, it would take the wagon several days to reach the opposite shore, taking into account the rest at the central island.

In reality, if the agents had preferred to start before Count Narkine, it was, of course, to be able to take all the necessary measures for his arrest.

It had been decided they would start at sunrise. The few hours of light that the sun still gave should be availed of. In six weeks' time, about the time of the solstice of the 21st of December, continual night would spread over the countries crossed by the polar circle.

On the eve of the departure, a "tea," offered by Mr. and Mrs. Cascabel, gathered together, under a shed appropriated to the occasion, the notables of Port Clarence, both officials and fishermen, as well as several Eskimo chiefs who had shown some interest in the travelers. The meeting passed off merrily, and Clovy "obliged" with the funniest songs in his repertory. Cornelia had brewed a bowl of burning punch in which, if she had spared the sugar, she had not spared the brandy. This beverage was all the more appreciated by the guests, as, on their way home, they were going to be exposed to a biting cold,

—one of those freezing chills which, during certain winter-nights, seem to come from the utmost ends of the star-spangled sky.

The Americans drank to France, the French people drank to America. Then the guests parted after any number of shake-hands with the Cascabels.

Next day, the two horses were harnessed at eight o'clock in the morning. The ape, John Bull, had ensconced himself in the awning, his nose barely visible through an opening in his fur covering, whilst Wagram and Marengo gamboled around the *Fair Rambler*. Inside, Cornelia, Napoleona, and Kayette had shut themselves up hermetically to look after their daily work: the "house" to be cleaned up, the stove to be seen to, the meals to be prepared. Mr. Sergius, and Mr. Cascabel, John, Sander, and Clovy, some at the horses' heads, others going ahead as scouts, were to see to the safety of the wagon, by avoiding the bad places on the "road."

At length the signal was given for the start, and simultaneously the hurrahs of the population of Port Clarence broke forth.

The next moment, the wheels of the *Fair Rambler* made the crispy surface of the ice-field crackle.

Mr. Sergius and the Cascabel family had finally left the land of America.

PART TWO

CHAPTER I - BEHRING STRAIT

A SOMEWHAT narrow pass is this Behring Strait, through which the sea of the same name communicates with the Arctic Ocean. It recalls the Strait of Dover between the British Channel and the North Sea; it lies in the same direction, but is three times as wide. Whereas it is only about twenty miles from Cape Gris-Nez on the French coast to South Foreland on the English side, a distance of sixty miles separates Numana from Port Clarence.

It was, therefore, toward the port of Numana, the nearest point on the Asiatic coast, that the *Fair Rambler* directed its course on leaving its last halting place in America.

Naturally, by cutting obliquely across Behring Sea, Cæser Cascabel would have traveled on a lower parallel and one considerably below the polar circle. In that case, his course would have brought him southwest, toward the island of St. Lawrence, a rather important island, inhabited by numerous tribes of Eskimos, no less hospitable than the natives of Port Clarence; then, on the other side of the Gulf of Anadyr, the little troupe would have landed at Cape Navare and thence plunged into the territories of Southern Siberia. But this would have been lengthening the sea portion, or rather the ice-field portion of the journey, and therefore exposing the party for a longer period to the dangers of those fields of ice. It may be surmised that the Cascabels longed to be on land again; it would have been inopportune, therefore, to alter in any way their first intention of going straight toward Numana, barely halting in the middle of the strait at the isle of Diomede, a spot as firm on its rocky foundations as any part of the continent.

If Mr. Sergius had been in charge of a vessel, with the little caravan and its material aboard, he would have adopted quite another tack. On leaving Port Clarence, he would have sailed more to the south of Behring Island, which is greatly frequented for winter-quartering by seals and other sea mammifers; thence he would have reached one of the ports of Kamtchatka, perhaps even Petropaulovski, the capital of this government. But, for want of a ship, the best thing to do was to take the shortest cut, the sooner to set foot on the Asiatic continent.

The Strait of Behring is of no very great depth. As a consequence of the rising of the sea bottom, which has been observed since the ice period, it might even come to pass in the distant future that Asia and America should become surface-joined in this spot. This would be the bridge of Mr. Cascabel's dreams, or, more correctly, a causeway available for travelers. But, however useful to the latter, it would be a great bane to seafaring people, and especially to whalers, as it would shut them out of the Arctic Seas. Some future De Lesseps would then have to come and cut through this isthmus and re-establish things in the original condition. It will be for the descendants of our great- grandchildren to think about such an eventuality.

The soundings of hydrographers in various portions of the strait have brought out the fact that the deepest chan- nel is that which runs along the coast of Asia, near the Tchuktchi peninsula. There does the cold current from the north flow, whilst the warm current goes up the shallower half of the strait, next to the American coast.

To the north of this peninsula, near the island of Koliutchin in the bay of that name, Nordenskjold's ship, La Vega, was to be ice-bound, twelve years later, for a space of nine months (September 26, 1878, to July 15, 1879), after he had discovered the northeast passage.

Well, then, the Cascabels had started on the 21st of October, under fair conditions. It was cold and dry. The snowstorm had calmed down, the wind had slacked and shifted slightly to the north. The sky bore one uniform gray tint. Hardly could the sun be felt from behind that veil of mist which its rays, weakened by their obliquity, could not succeed in piercing. At noon, when at its maximum height, it barely rose a few degrees above the horizon in the south.

A very wise measure had been unanimously agreed on before leaving Port Clarence: they should not journey when it was dark. Here and there the ice-field presented large crevices, and, as it was impossible to avoid them in the darkness, a catastrophe might have been the result. It was therefore resolved that as soon as they could see no farther than a hundred paces ahead, the *Fair Rambler* would halt. Better spend a fortnight covering the sixty miles than grope along blindly when daylight would no longer be sufficient.

The snow had not ceased falling for twenty-four hours, and had formed a pretty thick carpet, which had become quite crystallized by the cold. This layer rendered locomotion less difficult on the surface of the ice-field. Should they have no more snow while they crossed the strait, they would be all right. However, it was to be feared that where the cold and the warm currents met, flowing in opposite directions, the bergs thus disturbed in their drifting course might have got heaped up on each other, and our travelers might see their road lengthened by various detours.

We have already said that Cornelia, Kayette, and Napoleona had taken their places inside the wagon. In order to lighten the load as much as possible, the men were to go on foot.

In accordance with the prearranged marching order, John scouted, ahead of the party, to reconnoiter the state of the ice-field; he might be relied upon. He had a compass with him, and although very accurate landmarks were a matter of considerable difficulty, he made for the west with sufficient precision.

At the head of the horses stood Clovy, ready to hold up or to pick up Vermont and Gladiator in the event of their stumbling; but they were rough-shod and steady on their legs. Besides, the surface was so level that there was noth- ing they could stumble against.

Close to the wagon Mr. Sergius and César Cascabel, with their wooden winkers before their eyes, and fur-clad from head to foot like all their companions, walked and chatted along.

As to young Sander, it would have been hard to assign any one place to him, or at least to keep him there. He went and came, and ran and gamboled like the two dogs, and now and again indulged in a good old slide. Still there was something wanting to his happiness: his father would not give him leave to put on his racket-shoes.

"With those skates on," he would say, "I should run across the strait in a few hours!"

"And what would be the use of that?" Mr. Cascabel would reply, "since our horses don't know how to skate!"

"I must teach them, some day!" answered the youngster, accompanying his remark with a somersault.

Meanwhile, Cornelia, Kayette, and Napoleona were busy in the kitchen, and a tiny streak of smoke, of good omen, came out of the little chimney-pot. Although they did not suffer from the cold, hermetically closed as were their apartments, they should think of those who were outside. And they did so; for they kept always in readiness for them a few cups of warm tea, strengthened with a little of that Russian "water of life," that vodka, which would bring a dead man back to life again.

As to the horses, they had sufficient food to bring them to the other side of the strait, thanks to the bundles of dried grass supplied by the Eskimos of Port Clarence.

Wagram and Marengo seemed quite pleased with the flesh of the elk, and of that they could have plenty.

Besides, the ice-field was not so bare of game as might be thought. In their running hither and thither, the two dogs raised thousands of ptarmigans, guillemots, and other birds peculiar to the polar regions. These birds, dressed with care, and rid of their oily taste, are very acceptable eating. But as nothing could have been more useless than shooting them, since Cornelia's pantry was amply supplied, it was agreed that the two sportsmen's guns should lie quiet during the journey from Port Clarence to Numana.

Of amphibious animals, seals, and other mammifers so numerous in these seas, not one was seen during the first twenty-four hours of the journey.

Bright and cheerful as the first start had been, it was not long ere Mr. Cascabel and his companions began to feel that undefinable impression of sadness which seems begotten by those interminable plains, those endless tracts of whiteness where the weary eye seeks in vain for the horizon.

By eleven o'clock they were already unable to see the highest rocks of Port Clarence; even the lofty head of Cape Prince of Wales was lost in the gray of the distant mist. No object was visible more than a mile and a half away, and, as a consequence, it would be long ere they could perceive the summit of East Cape on the Choukotsky peninsula. Still, this height would have been an excellent landmark for them and would have enabled them to direct their course accurately.

The Isle of Diomede, lying about midway across the strait, is marked by no rocky uprisings. As its mass is hardly raised above the level of the sea, our travelers would not recognize it until the wheels would crackle by crushing the layer of snow on its stony soil.

On the whole, with his compass in his hand, John guided the *Fair Rambler* without too much trouble, and they proceeded, if not swiftly, at least safely.

While going along, Mr. Sergius and César Cascabel would talk of their present situation. This crossing of the strait, which before starting had seemed so simple a thing and would appear simpler still when accomplished, forcibly struck them as very dangerous, now that they had set about it.

"All the same, it's a hard job we have attempted!" Mr. Cascabel would say.

"No doubt," answered Mr. Sergius. "Crossing Behring Strait with a heavy wagon is an idea that would not have struck everybody!"

"I believe you, Mr. Sergius. Well, what can be done? When a man has got it into his head to go home, nothing can stop him! Ah, if it was only a question of going a few hundred miles through the Far West or through Siberia, I would not cast a second thought on it. There you walk on firm ground! There is no chance of the soil gaping under your feet. While sixty miles on a frozen sea, with a wagon and horses, a good load and all the rest of it!—My word! I wish we were the other side! The hardest part, or at least the most dangerous part of our journey would be over!"

"Quite so, my dear Cascabel, especially if the *Fair Rambler*, on the other side of the strait, can get quickly to the south of Siberia. An attempt to follow the coast line, in the heart of winter, would be too imprudent. So, as soon as we reach Numana, we must cut toward the southwest and pick out a good little village for our winter-quarter."

"So we shall. You must be acquainted with the country, Mr. Sergius?"

"Only with that part of it between Yakoutsk and Okhotsk, which I crossed after my escape. As to the road leading from Europe to Yakoutsk, all I remember is the horrible sufferings undergone day and night by the prisoners on their journey. What sufferings!—I would not wish them to my deadliest enemy!"

"Mr. Sergius, have you given up all hope of returning to your country, I mean as a free man? Will your government never allow you to return?"

"Not unless the Czar proclaimed an amnesty applying to Count Narkine and all the patriots sentenced along with him. Will political circumstances occur that would render such an eventuality possible? Who knows, my dear Cascabel?"

"Well, it must be a sad thing, living in exile! Just as if a man had been turned out of his own house!"

"Yes, far from all the loved ones!—And my father, now so old, that I would love to see again—"

"You shall see him again, Mr. Sergius! Take the word of an old showman who has often foretold events when telling people their fortunes. You will make your entry into Perm along with us! Aren't you one of the Cascabel artists? By the way, I must teach you a legerdemain trick or two; it might be useful some day; not to speak of the trick we shall play the Russian police, the day we enter the country under their very noses!"

And César Cascabel could not keep from bursting with laughter. Only fancy! Count Narkine, a great Russian nobleman, lifting weights, juggling with bottles, giving the answers to clowns, and taking in coppers for it!

About three in the afternoon, the *Fair Rambler* had to stop. Although night had not come yet, a thick mist considerably shortened the distance that the eye could reach. John returned from his scouting and suggested a halt. Directing one's self under these conditions was a matter of great uncertainty.

Besides, as had been foreseen by Mr. Sergius, in this part of the strait, furrowed by the channel of the eastern current, the unevenness of the ice-field, the unequal levels of the iceblocks were felt through the snow. The wagon jolted violently; the horses stumbled almost at every step; half a day's journey had been sufficient to wear them out with fatigue.

Six miles, at very most, had our party been able to cover during this first stage of theirs.

As soon as the horses had come to a stand-still, Cornelia and Napoleona had alighted, carefully wrapped up from head to foot on account of the sudden transition from an indoor temperature of ten degrees above zero to an open-air temperature of ten degrees below. As to Kayette, accustomed to the severity of the Alaskan winter, she little thought of putting her warm furs on.

"You must cover yourself warmer than that, Kayette," said John to her; "you run a chance of catching cold."

"Oh," said she, "I am not afraid of cold! We know all about it in the valley of the Yukon."

"No matter, Kayette."

"John is quite right," said Mr. Cascabel, intervening. "Run in, and put on something warm, my little Kayette. Besides, I warn you that if you catch cold, it is I will doctor you up, and that will be terrible. I'll go the length, if necessary, of cutting your head off to make you stop sneezing!"

In the face of such a threat, there was nothing for the young girl to do but obey, and she did so.

Then all set about organizing the camping. In truth, it was very simple this time. No wood to cut in the forest for want of a forest; no fire to light, for want of fuel; no grass even to gather for the horses' food. The *Fair Rambler* stood there, offering to its guests its usual comfort, its good temperature, its little couches ready prepared, its table ready laid, its never-failing hospitality.

All that was required was to provide for Vermont's and Gladiator's meal with a portion of the grass brought from Port Clarence. This done, the two horses were wrapped up in thick blankets, and could now enjoy a long rest till the following day.

Nor did they forget the parrot in his cage, the ape in his nest, or the two dogs, who seemed so fond of their dried meat and ate it voraciously.

"Well now, well now!" exclaimed Cascabel, "this may be the first time that Frenchmen sat down to such a nice supper, in the middle of Behring Strait!"

"That's probable," answered Mr. Sergius. "But, before three or four days, I hope we shall sit at our meals on firm ground."

"At Numana?" inquired Cornelia.

"Not yet; on Diomede Island, where we shall make a stay of a day or two. We get on so slowly, it will take us a week, at least, to reach the coast of Asia."

When meal was over, although it was only five o'clock in the evening, nobody declined to retire to rest. A whole night of a stretch on one's back, under warm covering, and on a soft mattress, was not to be despised after the hardships of a tramp on an ice-field. Mr. Cascabel did not even think it necessary to see to the security of the little camp. There were no awkward encounters to be dreaded in such a desert. Besides, the dogs would be a reliable watch, and would announce the approach of the rovers, should there be any, who would come near the *Fair Rambler*.

None the less, Mr. Sergius got up two or three times to observe the state of the ice-field; a sudden change in the temperature might modify it at any moment; this was, perhaps, his greatest anxiety.

There was no change, however, in the appearance of the weather, and a little northeasterly breeze glided on the surface of the strait.

The next day, the journey proceeded under the same conditions; no difficulties to overcome, properly speaking, but any amount of fatigue to undergo. Six miles had been traveled over when they halted and made the same arrangements for the night as on the preceding evening.

The following day, October 25[1], it was not possible to start before nine in the morning, and, even at that hour, it was barely daylight.

Mr. Sergius noticed that the cold was less piercing. Clouds were gathering in disorderly masses on the horizon, toward the southeast. The thermometer showed a tendency to rise; weaker atmospherical pressures were beginning to be felt.

"This is what I don't care for, John!" said Mr. Sergius. "So long as we are on the ice-field, we must not complain if the cold becomes more intense. Unfortunately, the barometer is going down and the wind is shifting to the west. The worst thing we have to dread is a rise in the temperature. Watch the condition of the ice-field carefully, John; do not overlook the slightest sign, and come back immediately to put us on our guard."

"Rely on me, Mr. Sergius."

Of course, from and after the following month on to the middle of April, the changes of which Mr. Sergius was afraid could not take place; the winter would then be permanently set in. But as the season had been late this year, its first period was marked by alternate fits of frost and of thaw which might cause a partial dislocation of the icefield. Better would it have been to undergo a temperature of twenty-five to thirty degrees below zero the whole length of the journey across the strait.

They started, then, with a kind of half daylight. The weak rays of the sun were unable to pierce the thick layer of mist, in their oblique projection. Moreover, the sky was beginning to get streaked with low and long clouds that the wind drove swiftly toward the north.

John, right ahead of the party, watched carefully the layer of snow, which had grown softer since the day before, and gave way at every step under the feet of the horses. Still, they were able to cover six miles more in this stage, and the night passed off without any incident.

The next morning, the 24th,[2] starting time was ten o'clock. Great was Mr. Sergius's anxiety when he found a further rise in the temperature,—quite an anomalous phenomenon at this time of the year and under this latitude.

It being less cold, Cornelia, Napoleona, and Kayette wished to follow on foot, and with their Eskimo boots they tramped along with comparative ease. All had their eyes protected with the Indian spectacles already mentioned, and were getting accustomed to look through the narrow slit. These winkers always excited Sander's mirth: he, young rascal, little thought of the fatigue and skipped about like a kid in a meadow.

Truly, the wagon made but slow progress. Its wheels sank into the snow and made it heavier still for the horses to draw; and when their felly knocked against an accidental protrusion or the rough crest of an ice-block, severe shocks, which it was impossible to avoid, were the consequences. At times also, huge blocks, heaped up on each other, absolutely barred the way, and circuitous detours had to be made to get round them. This was. after all, only a lengthening of the road, and it was preferable it should be intercepted with mounds rather than with fissures. Thus, at least, the solidification of the ice-field was not compromised.

Meanwhile the thermometer kept on rising and the barometer falling, slowly but steadily. Mr. Sergius felt more and more anxious.

A little before noon the women had to return indoors. The snow began to fall abundantly, in tiny, transparent flakes that looked as if they would resolve into water. You would have thought it was a shower of light white featherlets that thousands of birds might have shaken off throughout the space.

César Cascabel suggested that Mr. Sergius should seek shelter in the *Fair Rambler*; the latter declined; could he not put up with what his companions endured?

As a matter of fact, this fall of snow alarmed him to the greatest extent; melting as it did, it would eventually unsolder the ice-field. It was a necessity to seek a refuge as fast as possible on the unshakable foundations of Diomede Island.

And yet, prudence made it imperative to proceed with the utmost caution. So, Mr. Sergius determined to scout ahead with John, whilst Mr. Cascabel and Clovy walked by the horses' heads; the poor brutes missed their footing every moment, and, should an accident happen to the wagon, there would be no alternative but to abandon it in the middle of the frozen sea,—which would have been an irretrievable loss.

While plodding onward with John, Mr. Sergius did his utmost with his glass to pierce the western horizon rendered a still more confused mass by the snow-storm. The eye could reach but a very short distance; their guiding was now mere guess-work, and Mr. Sergius would certainly have ordered a halt if the solidity of the field had not seemed to him very seriously endangered.

"At any cost," said he, "we must reach Diomede Isle this day, even though we had to stop there till the cold sets in again."

"How far do you think we are still?" asked John.

"Four or five miles, John. As we have another couple of hours' daylight, or at least that kind of half-light which enables us to see where we are going, let us do all we can to arrive before it is quite dark."

"Mr. Sergius, would you like me to go on ahead and reconnoiter the situation of the island?"

"No, John, by no means! You would run the chance of losing your way in the storm, and that would be quite another complication! Let us try to go by the compass, for, should we pass above or below the island, I know not what would become of us."

"Hark, sir, do you hear?" cried John, who had been stooping.

Mr. Sergius did the same and was able to observe that indistinct crackling sounds, like those of glass which is being chipped, were running through the ice-field. Was this the sign of at least a partial disintegration, if not of the complete breaking up of the ice? As yet no crevice starred the surface as far as the eye could see.

The situation had become extremely dangerous. Spending the night in these conditions, our travelers might be the victims of a catastrophe. Diomede Island was the only refuge held out to them, and they should reach it at any price.

How Mr. Sergius must have regretted he had not waited a few days longer, patiently, at Port Clarence!

John and he came back to the wagon, and Mr. Cascabel was acquainted with the state of things. There was no occasion to tell the women about it; they would have been needlessly frightened. It was therefore agreed they should be left inside the vehicle, and the men began to tug at the wheels to help the broken-down horses; they scarce could stand on their lamed feet; their coats reeked with sweat under the frozen breeze.

About two o'clock, the downpour of snow lessened sensibly, and was shortly reduced to a few scattered flakes that the wind whirled about in the air. It then became less difficult to keep in the right direction. The horses were urged on vigorously, determined as Mr. Sergius was that there should be no halting until the *Fair Rambler* stood on the rocks of Diomede Island.

From his calculations, it should now be no farther than a mile or two away, and by making one last effort they might get there perhaps within an hour's time.

Unfortunately, the light, already so uncertain, soon grew weaker and weaker, and became at last nothing more than a faint reverberation. Were they on the right track or on the wrong? Might they go on in the same direction? How could they tell?

Just then the two dogs barked loudly. Was this the approach of a danger? Had the dogs scented a band of Eskimos or of Tchuktchis on the tramp across the strait? Should it be so, Mr. Sergius would not hesitate to ask their aid, or, at least, he would try to ascertain from them the exact position of the island.

Meanwhile, one of the little windows of the wagon had been opened, and Cornelia was heard inquiring why Wagram and Marengo were barking in that manner.

She was told that they did not know yet, but that there was no cause for alarm.

"Must we get out?" she added.

"No, Cornelia," answered Mr. Cascabel. "You and the lassies are comfortable where you are. Stay there!"

"But if the dogs have scented some animal or another, a bear for instance, —"

"Well, they will let us know! As to that, have the guns ready. But meanwhile, no getting out without leave!"

"Close your window, Mrs. Cascabel," said Mr. Sergius. "We have not one minute to lose. We are off again this very moment."

And the horses, that had been stopped at the first barking of the dogs, resumed their laborious toiling onward.

For half an hour the *Fair Rambler* was able to move somewhat quicker, the surface of the ice-field being less rough. The worn-out steeds, with downcast heads and trembling legs, still pulled away with noble spirit. But this was evidently a supreme effort on their part, and they would surely break down if it had to be kept up much longer.

It was almost night. The remnant of light diffused through space seemed to come rather from the surface of the field than from the brightness of the upper zones.

And the two dogs still kept on their barking, running forward, standing still with their noses up in the air and every muscle in their bodies stiffened, then returning to their masters.

"There is surely something extraordinary!" observed Mr. Cascabel.

"There is the Isle of Diomede!" exclaimed John.

And so saying, he pointed to a heap of rocks, the round back of which could be seen confusedly a few hundred paces away to the west.

What gave some likelihood to John's guess was that the rocky mass seemed marked with black spots, the color of which came out in relief on the whiteness of the ice.

"Yes, it must be the island," said Mr, Sergius.

"Why! don't I see those black spots moving?" cried Mr. Cascabel.

"Moving?"

"Of course."

"That must be just a few thousand seals that have sought a refuge on the island—"

"A few thousand seals!" repeated Cascabel.

"Goodness gracious, boss!" exclaimed Clovy, "if we could only catch them and show them at the fair!"

"And if they could all say papa!" added Sander.

Was not this the heart's cry of a young showman!

CHAPTER II - BETWEEN TWO CURRENTS

AT last the *Fair Rambler* was on firm ground; no breaking up of the ice-field need longer be apprehended under its wheels; it is easy to surmise how much this boon was appreciated by the Cascabels.

It was quite dark by this time. The same arrangements were made as the preceding night for the camping, a few hundred paces inside the island; then both the "intellectual people and the others," as Cæser Cascabel used to say, were duly looked after.

Indeed, relatively speaking, it was not cold. The thermometer recorded no more than four degrees below zero. It little mattered, besides. As long as they remained here they had nothing to fear from a rise in the temperature. Should it occur, they would wait until a more considerable fall had thoroughly set the ice-field. Winter in all its severity could not be far off.

There being no light, Mr. Sergius put off to the following day the exploration he wished to make of the island. The chief object they first gave their best attention to was the night encampment of the horses, who needed a good supper and a good rest, for they were literally worn out. Then, when the table was laid, the meal was hastily dispatched, eager as each one was to seek the comfort of his couch after such a hard day's toil.

The consequence was that the *Fair Rambler* was soon buried in sleep, and, that night, Cornelia dreamed neither of a sudden thaw nor yet of yawning gulfs swallowing up her home on wheels.

The next morning, the 25th of October, as soon as daylight was sufficient, Mr. Sergius, César Cascabel. and his two sons went and reconnoitered the state of the island.

What surprised them from the first was the incredible number of otaries that had taken refuge on it.

As a matter of fact, it is in this portion of Behring Sea, bounded to the south by the fiftieth degree of northerly latitude, that these animals are found in largest quantities.

On examining the map one cannot but be struck with the outline presented by the coast of America and by that of Asia, and especially with the resemblance they bear each other. On both sides the same figure is pretty clearly defined: Cape Prince of Wales is the counterpart of the Tchutchki peninsula, Norton Bay corresponds to the gulf of Anadyr, the extremity of the Alaskan peninsula is curved in the same way as the peninsula of Kamtchatka, and the whole is inclosed by the chainlet of the Aleutian Islands. It cannot, however, be concluded therefrom that America was abruptly severed from Asia, and Behring Strait opened by some terrestrial convulsion in prehistoric times, for the salient angles of one coast do not correspond with the internal angles of the other.

Numerous islands, too, in these parts: the Isle of St. Lawrence, already named; Nunivak Island, on the American coast; Karaghinski, on the Asiatic side; Behring Island with Copper Isle by its side, and, within a short distance of the Alaskan shore, Pribylov Islands. The resemblance of the coasts is then increased by the identical arrangement of the archipelago.

Now, these Pribylov Islands and Behring Island are in a special manner the favorite residences of the colonies of seals that frequent these seas. They could be reckoned by millions here; and, naturally, it is here that professional hunters come, not only for the otaries but for the sea loutra so common less than fifty years ago and now made scarce by wholesale destruction.

As to the otaries,—a generic name comprising the sealions, the sea-cows, the sea-bears,—they collect here in numberless flocks, and their race seems inexhaustible.

And still what a relentless hunt is carried on after them as long as the warm seasons last! Without respite, without mercy, the fishermen pursue them into their very "rookeries," kinds of parks where the families gather together. It is the full-grown otaries especially that are pitilessly tracked, and these animals would eventually disappear, were it not for their extraordinary fecundity.

As a fact, from the year 1867 to the year 1880, 388,982 otaries were destroyed in the reserved parks of Behring Island alone. On Pribylov Islands, in the course of a century, no fewer than 3,500,000 skins have been got together by the Alaskan fishermen, and at the present time they do not supply less than a hundred thousand a year to the trade.

And how many there are on the other islands of Behring Sea, Mr. Sergius and his companions were in a position to estimate from what they saw on Diomede Island. The soil disappeared from view under a swarm of seals packed together in close groups, and nothing could be seen of the carpet of snow on which they lay so securely.

Meanwhile, if they were the object of a curious survey, they, too, examined the visitors of the island. Without stirring, but apparently uneasy, annoyed, perhaps, at this taking of possession of their domain, they made no attempt at running away, and sometimes uttered a kind of prolonged bellowing in which a note of anger was clearly discernible. Then standing erect, they would give their paws, or rather their fins, spread out like so many fans, a violent shaking to and fro.

Ah! if these thousands of seals had been endowed with the gift of speech, according to young Sander's wish, what a thunder of "papas" would have come out of their mouths!

Needless to say that neither Mr. Sergius nor John thought of firing on this legion of animals. Yet, there was a fortune of "peltry on foot" there before them, as Cascabel put it. But it would have been a useless, as well as a dangerous slaughter. Formidable as they were by their number alone, the seals might have greatly endangered the position of the *Fair Rambler*; hence Mr. Sergius recommended the greatest caution.

And now, was not the presence of these seals on Diomede Island a sign which it was right not to neglect? Were it not prudent to consider why they had thus sought a refuge on this heap of rocks, which offered them no resources?

This was the subject of a very serious discussion, in which Mr. Sergius, César Cascabel, and his eldest son took part. They had walked on toward the central part of the island, while the women looked after household matters, and Clovy and Sander were busy with the "animal element" of the troupe.

Mr. Sergius was the first to broach the question:

"My friends," said he, "we must consider whether it would not be better to leave Diomede Island, as soon as the horses are rested, than to prolong our stay."

"Mr. Sergius," eagerly replied Cascabel, "I am of opinion we should not tarry here, playing the 'Swiss Robinson family' on this rock! I confess it, I am longing to feel a bit of the Siberian coast under my heel."

"I understand that, father," answered John, "and yet, it would not be right to go and expose ourselves again as we did when we so impatiently started across the strait. But for this island, what would have become of us? Numana is still some thirty miles away from us—"

"Well, John, with a good pull and a strong pull, we might cover that distance in two or three stages, perhaps."

"It would be hard to do so, even if the state of the icefield permitted it."

"I think John is right," observed Mr. Sergius. "That we should be in a hurry to be on the other side of the strait is but natural. But seeing how much milder the temperature has become, it seems to me it would hardly be prudent to leave terra firma. We left Port Clarence too soon; let us try and not leave this island too hastily. What we may be sure of is that the strait is not completely frozen over its whole surface."

"Where do those crackling sounds come from, which I heard even as late as yesterday?" added John. "Evidently they are due to the insufficient cohesion of the iceblocks."

"That is one proof," rejoined Mr. Sergius; "and there is one other."

"Which?" inquired John.

"One which seems to me of equal importance: it is the presence of these thousands of seals that have instinctively invaded this island. No doubt, after leaving the upper regions of the sea, these animals were making their way toward Behring Island or the Aleutian Islands, when they foresaw some imminent atmospheric disturbance, and felt they should not remain on the ice-field. Are we on the eve of a breaking up of the ice-field under the influence of the temperature or through some submarine phenomenon? I know not. But, if we are in a hurry to reach the Siberian coast, these creatures are not less anxious to reach their rookeries on Behring Island or Pribylov Islands, and as they halted here, they must have had very good reasons for doing so."

"Well then, what do you advise, Mr. Sergius?" asked Mr. Cascabel.

"My advice is that we should stay here until the seals show us, by starting off themselves, that we may resume our journey without danger."

"That's awkward, and no mistake!"

"It is not as bad as it might be, father," said John; "may we never have worse to put up with!"

"Besides, this cannot last very long," continued Mr. Sergius. "Let the winter be ever so late this year, here is the end of October coming on, and although the thermometer, at this very moment, is only at zero, it may fall some twenty degrees from one day to another. If the wind happens to shift to the north, the ice-field will be as solid as a continent. I propose then, after due consideration, that we wait, if nothing compels us to go."

This was prudent, to say the least. And so it was agreed that the *Fair Rambler* should stay on Diomede Island, as long as the safety of her journey across would not be assured by an intense frost.

Throughout this day, Mr. Sergius and John partly surveyed the granite rock that offered them such security. The islet measured less than three miles in circumference. Even in summer it must have been literally barren. A heap of rocks, nothing more. None the less, it would have been able to support the pier of the famous Behring bridge, wished for by Mrs. Cascabel, in the event of the Russian and American engineers ever thinking of joining two continents,—contrary to what Mr. Lesseps is so fond of doing.

In the course of their ramble, the visitors took good care not to frighten the seals. And still, it was evident that the presence of human beings kept these animals in a singular state of excitement. There were huge males, whose hoarse cries sounded like an alarm for the members of their families, and in a moment one sire would be seen surrounded by forty or fifty of his full-grown offspring.

154

These unfriendly dispositions could not but cause some anxiety to Mr. Sergius, especially when he noticed a certain tendency on the part of the seals to move nearer and nearer toward the encampment. Taken individually they were not formidable, of course; but it would be difficulty, nay impossible, to resist such enormous masses if they ever resolved on driving off the intruders, who did not leave them the sole and exclusive possession of Diomede Island. John, too, was greatly struck with this peculiarity, and both Mr. Sergius and he came home somewhat alarmed.

The day passed off without incidents, save that the breeze, which blew from the southeast, turned to squalls. Evidently some big storm was brewing, one of those Arctic tempests, perhaps, which last for several days; an extraordinary fall of the barometer left no doubt on this point; it had gone down seventy-two centimeters.

The approach of the night was full of ill-omens therefore. And, to add further to them, as soon as the travelers had taken their places inside the *Fair Rambler*, howls, on the nature of which there was no mistake to make, increased the roar of the elements. The seals had shuffled their way close to the vehicle; presently it would be overborne by them. The horses neighed with fright, dreading an attack from this unknown foe, against which Wagram and Marengo barked in vain. The men had to get out of bed, rush out and bring Vermont and Gladiator nearer to the wagon, to watch over them. The revolvers and the guns were loaded. However, Mr. Sergius recommended that they should not be used till the very last extremity.

The night was dark. As nothing could be distinguished in the intense obscurity, torches had to be lit. Their fitful rays enabled them to see thousands of seals arrayed around the *Fair Rambler* and doubtless only waiting for daylight to attack it.

"If they attack us, resistance will be a matter of impossibility," said Mr. Sergius, "and we should run the risk of being overwhelmed!"

"What are we to do then?" asked John.

"We must start off!"

"When?" inquired Cascabel.

"This very moment!"

Was Mr. Sergius right in his resolve to leave the island, great though the danger was which gloomed ahead? Surely, it was the only thing to be done. Very probably the only object the seals had in view was to drive away the intruders who had invaded their domain, and they would not trouble to pursue them beyond its limits on to the field of ice. As to scattering these animals by force, an attempt would have been more than imprudent. What could guns and revolvers do against their thousands?

The horses were put to, the women re-entered their apartments, the men, ready on the defensive, stood by each side of the wagon, and the journey westward was resumed.

So foggy was the night that the torches cast their light scarcely twenty paces ahead. At the same time the storm broke out with greater fury. It did not snow; the flakes fluttering in the air were those that the wind lashed off the surface of the ice-field.

With all this, had the solidification but been complete! Unfortunately, it was far from it. You could feel the blocks getting severed from each other with long, crackling sounds. Now and again fissures would gape and send up sheaves of sea water.

Mr. Sergius and his companions went on thus for an hour, afraid every moment to see the ice-field breaking up under their feet. Keeping in one direction became impracticable, and yet John endeavored to guide himself somehow on the needle of the compass. Luckily, this tramp toward the west differed from their journeying toward Diomede Island, which they might easily have passed by, either too far south or too far north, without recognizing it; the Siberian coast lay for a distance of some thirty miles on three-fourths of the horizon, and they could not miss it.

But they should manage to get there first, and the chief condition of their doing so was that the *Fair Rambler* should not go to the bottom of Behring Sea.

Meanwhile, if this danger was the most formidable, it was not the only one. At every moment, caught on the flank by the southeasterly wind, the wagon ran the risk of being upset. By way of precaution, Cornelia, Napoleona, and Kayette had been made to alight, and it required all the efforts of Mr. Sergius, Cascabel, John, Sander, and Clovy, tugging at the wheels, to keep the *Fair Rambler* erect against the blast. Needless to tell what little headway was made by the horses under these conditions, when they felt the ground continually yielding under their feet.

About half-past five o'clock in the morning,—the 26th of October,—in the midst of the very deepest obscurity, the vehicle was compelled to stop; the horses could not go a step further. The surface of the field, upheaved by the swell driven by the squall from the lower regions of Behring Sea, now presented a series of various levels.

"What are we to do?" said John.

"We must go back to the island!" exclaimed Cornelia, who was unable to appease Napoleona's terror.

"That's out of the question now!" replied Mr. Sergius.

"Why so?" inquired Mr. Cascabel. "Of the two I would still rather fight seals than—"

"I tell you again we must not think of returning to the island!" repeated Mr. Sergius. "We should have to go against the squall, and the wagon could not stand it. It would be smashed to pieces, if, indeed, it did not run away before the wind."

"So long as we are not obliged to abandon it!" sighed John.

"Abandon it!" cried Cascabel. "And what would become of us without our *Fair Rambler?*"

"We shall do our very utmost not to be reduced in that extremity," answered Mr. Sergius; "we shall! That wagon is our plank of salvation, and we shall endeavor to keep it at any price."

"So, it is not possible to go back?" urged Cascabel.

"It is absolutely impossible; and we must keep on going ahead!" was the reply. "Let us be brave-hearted, keep a cool head, and surely we shall reach Numana!"

These words seemed to brace up the travelers. It was but too evident that the wind forbade their returning to Diomede Island. It blew from the southeast with such violence that neither cattle nor men could have walked against it. The *Fair Rambler* itself could no longer remain stationary. The merest attempt to make it resist the displacement of the air would have toppled it over.

About ten o'clock, daylight became half apparent,—a pale, misty light. The clouds, low and ragged, seemed to drag shreds of vapor after them and madly lash them about, across the strait. In the whirlwind of snow, small chips of ice, dashed off the field by the blast, flew by like a veritable volley of small shot. In such circumstances, one hour and a half was spent in covering little more than a mile, for they had, in addition, to avoid the pools of water and turn round the mounds of ice heaped upon their way. Underneath, the swell from the high sea caused sudden oscillations and a kind of billowy motion, accompanied by continuous crackling noises.

Suddenly, about a quarter to one o'clock, a violent shock was felt. A network of fissures radiated over the field around the vehicle. A crevice, measuring thirty feet in diameter, had just yawned beneath the feet of the horses.

At a shout from Mr. Sergius, his companions stopped short within a few paces of the abyss.

"Our horses! Our horses!" cried John. "Father, let us save the horses!"

It was too late. The ice had given way. The two unfortunate steeds had just disappeared. Had not the traces snapped, the *Fair Rambler* too would have been drawn into the depths of the sea.

"Our poor horses!" cried Cascabel, in despair.

Alas! those old friends of the showman's, who had gone the world over with him, those faithful companions, who had so long shared his roaming life, were buried in the deep. Big tears burst from the eyes of Mr. Cascabel, his wife, and his children.

"Back! Quick, back with it!" Mr. Sergius called out.

And by dint of pushing and striving, they succeeded, not without trouble, in moving the wagon away from the crevice, which was getting wider as the oscillations of the ice-field increased; and they let it stand some twenty feet inside the circle of dislocation.

The situation was none the less greatly compromised. What were they to do now? Abandon the *Fair Rambler* in the middle of the strait, then come back and fetch it with a team of reindeer from Numana? It seemed as though there was no other course to follow.

Suddenly John cried out:

"Mr. Sergius! Mr. Sergius! Look, sir!—We are drifting!—"

"Drifting?"

It was but too true! Not a doubt of it now; a general breaking up had just set all the ice in motion between the two banks of the strait.

The repeated shocks of the storm, added to the rise in the temperature, had split up the field insufficiently cemented in its middle part. Wide gaps had been opened in the north by the displacing of the blocks, some of which had slid up on the ice-field and others underneath it. This enabled the floating ice-island which bore the vehicle to drift at the will of the hurricane. A few bergs had remained stationary, and Mr. Sergius, using them as landmarks, was able to make out the direction of the drift.

The reader sees how alarming the situation now was, jeopardized as it had already been by the loss of the horses. There was now no possibility of reaching Numana, even after abandoning the wagon. They would now be confronted no longer by crevices that they might avoid by a detour, but by numerous gaps, which there was no means of getting over, and the direction of which shifted about according to the caprice of the swell. And as to the block that conveyed the *Fair Rambler*, and whose course could not possibly be controlled, how long would it withstand the shock of the billows that dashed against its sides?

No! There was nothing to be done! To dream of directing the floating berg, so as to bring it on to the Siberian coast, were above the power of man. Move about thus it would until some obstacle would stop it; and who knows if that obstacle would not be the frozen shore of the polar sea!

About two o'clock in the afternoon, thanks to the increased darkness caused by the spreading fog, the eye was already unable to pierce beyond a very short radius.

Sheltered as best they could, and turned toward the north, Mr. Sergius and his companions stood in mournful silence. What could they have said, since there was nothing to be even attempted? Cornelia, Kayette, and Napoleona, wrapped in blankets, kept closely pressed against each other. Young Sander, more surprised than alarmed. whistled a tune. Clovy busied himself tidying up the various things that had been knocked out of place in the wagon by the shock it had received.

If Mr. Sergius and John had kept cool-headed, the same could not be said of Mr. Cascabel, who blamed himself for having brought all his people into this frightful adventure.

However, it was of importance, first of all, to have a right idea of the situation.

It has not been forgotten that two currents cross each other in Behring Strait. One comes down to the south, the other flows up toward the north. The former is the Kamtchatka current, the latter the Behring. If the berg loaded with the staff and the material of the *Fair Rambler* got into the first current, it would of necessity retrace its course, and there were chances of its landing on the Siberian coast. If, on the contrary, it was drawn into the second, it would float in the direction of the Ice Sea, where no continent or group of islands could stop it.

Unfortunately, as the hurricane grew wilder, it shifted nearer and nearer to the south. Into the depths of that funnel formed by the strait the air was engulfed with a violence which can hardly be imagined, and little by little the wind altered its first direction.

This Mr. Sergius and John had been able to ascertain, and they saw they were losing all chance of being caught by the Kamtchatka current. Checked with the compass, the drift was found to incline toward the north. Might they hope that the berg would be carried to the peninsula of the Prince of Wales on the Alaskan coast, in sight of Port Clarence? This would have been a truly providential termination of the eventualities of this helpless drift. But the strait widens at so great an angle between East Cape and Cape Prince of Wales that no prudent man would have indulged such a hope.

Meanwhile, the state of things on the surface of the iceberg was becoming almost unbearable; no one could keep on his feet, so wildly did the storm rage. John would fain go and examine the sea from the fore part of the block, and was thrown down; indeed, but for Mr. Sergius, he would have been hurled into the waves.

What a night was spent by these ill-fated people,—these shipwrecked wanderers, we may say, for there they were, like the survivors of a wreck. What continual anguish! Huge icebergs would come sometimes and knock against their floating islet with such crashes and shocks as to threaten its smashing to pieces. Then heavy seas would roll over its surface and submerge it as though it were doomed to be swallowed up in the abyss. They were all soaked with those cold douches which the wind pulverized over their heads. The only way to avoid them would have been to get back into the wagon; but it shook so under the blast that neither Mr. Sergius nor Cascabel dared advise their companions to shelter themselves in it.

Endless hours passed by thus. The gaps became wider and wider, the drifting was more free, the shocks were less frequent. Had the block got into the narrow portion of the strait that opens out, several miles farther, into the ice sea? Had it reached the regions lying above the polar circle? Had the Behring current finally overcome the Kamtchatka current? In that case, if the American coast did not stop the berg, was there no cause to fear that it would be carried on and on, to the Arctic ice-field?

How slow was the daylight in coming!—that light which would enable them to ascertain their position. The poor women prayed. Their deliverance could now come but from God.

Daylight appeared at last; it was the 27th of October. No sign of a calm in the atmospherical disturbances; the fury of the storm seemed even to increase with the rising of the sun.

Mr. Sergius and John, compass in hand, searched the horizon. In vain did they endeavor to descry some high land toward the east and the west.

It was but too evident, their iceberg was following a northerly course under the impulse of the Behring current.

As may be imagined, this storm had caused the greatest anxiety to the inhabitants of Port Clarence concerning the fate of the Cascabels. But how could they have brought help to them, since the breaking up of the ice stopped all communication between the two shores of the strait?

There was anxiety, too, at Numana, where the two Russian agents had announced the departure of the *Fair Rambler*, although the feelings they experienced for its occupants did not spring from sympathy. They had been awaiting Count Narkine on the Siberian coast, as we have said, in the well-grounded hope of capturing him; and now there was every appearance of his having perished in this disaster, along with the whole Cascabel family.

There was no doubt left in their minds about this when, three days later, the corpses of two horses were washed ashore by the current, in a little creek on the coast. They were those of Vermont and Gladiator, the only horses possessed by the show people.

"'Pon my word," said one of the agents, "it was a good thing we came across before our friends!"

"Yes," replied the other, "but the sad part of it is to have missed such a splendid job!"

CHAPTER III - ADRIFT

THE reader now knows what the position of our shipwrecked party was on the date of the 27th of October. Could they have deluded themselves respecting their fate or preserved the faintest hope? Adrift through Behring Strait, their last chance had been to get into the southern current and be brought to the Asiatic coast; and it was the northern stream that was bearing them away to the open.

When shifting about in the Polar Sea, what would become of their berg, on the supposition that it would not dissolve, that it would resist all the shocks it would receive? Would it get aground on some Arctic land? Driven for a few hundred leagues by the east winds that were then predominant, would it not be cast on the shores of Spitzberg or Nova Zembla? In this case, even though at the price of untold fatigues, would the wanderers succeed in reaching the continent?

Mr. Sergius was weighing the consequences of this last hypothesis, and talked about it with Mr. Cascabel and John while scanning the fog-shrouded horizon.

"My friends," he said, "we are evidently in a great peril, since this berg may break up at any moment; and on the other hand there is no possibility of our leaving it."

"Is that the greatest danger we are threatened with?" asked Mr. Cascabel.

"For the time being, it is. But when the weather gets cold again, this danger will diminish and eventually disappear, even. Now, at this time of the year and in this latitude, the present rise in the temperature cannot possibly last beyond a few days."

"You are right, Mr. Sergius." said John. "But in the event of this ice-block keeping intact, where will it go?"

"In my opinion, it cannot go very far, and it will soon adhere to some icefield. Then, as soon as the sea is thoroughly frozen over, we shall try to get back to the continent and resume our old itinerary."

"And what shall we do, now that our horses are gone?" exclaimed Mr. Cascabel. "Ah, my poor horses! my poor horses!—Mr. Sergius, those noble things! they were like two of our own selves! and it is all through my fault!"

Cascabel could not be consoled. His heart overflowed. He blamed himself for being the cause of this catastrophe. Horses crossing a sea on foot! Who had ever heard of such an idea?—And he thought more of the old steeds than of the inconvenience their loss would entail.

"Yes, in the conditions we are in, owing to this thaw, that is an irretrievable misfortune," said Mr. Sergius. "That we men should put up with the privations and the fatigues resulting from this loss, goes for nothing. But what will Mrs. Cascabel do, what will Kayette and Napoleona do, who are but children yet, when we have abandoned the *Fair Rambler*—"

"Abandon it!" exclaimed Cascabel.

"We shall have to do so, father!"

"Verily," exclaimed Mr. Cascabel, threatening himself with his own fist, "it was tempting Providence to undertake such a journey!—Following such a road to return to Europe!"

"Do not break down in such a way, my friend," replied Mr. Sergius. "Let us face danger without flinching. It is the surest way to overcome it!"

"Come, father," John added, "what is done cannot be undone, and we all agreed that it should be done. Do not blame yourself alone, then, for lack of caution, and recover your old pluck!"

But despite all these encouragements Mr. Cascabel felt crushed; his self-reliance, his innate philosophy, had received a severe blow.

Meanwhile Mr. Sergius used all the means at his disposal, his mariner's compass, certain landmarks he fancied he had fixed, and what not, so as to ascertain the direction of the current. Indeed it was at these observations that he spent the few hours during which daylight somewhat brightens up the horizon in this latitude. Nor was it an easy task when the landmarks were forever changing.

Beyond the strait the sea seemed to be free for a considerable distance. Evidently, with this anomalous temperature, the Arctic ice-field had never been completely formed. If it had appeared to be so for a few days, it is because the blocks of ice traveling north or south under the influence of the two currents had met together in this narrow portion of the sea between the two continents.

As the result of his manifold calculations, Mr. Sergius thought himself justified in stating that the course they were following was sensibly northwest. This was doubtless due to the fact that the Behring current, hugging the Siberian coast after having repelled the Kamtchatka current, was describing, as it got out of Behring Strait, a wide curve, subtended by the parallel of the polar circle.

At the same time, Mr. Sergius was able to ascertain that the wind, still very violent, blew straight from the southeast. Just for a moment it had veered to the south; that was due to the lay of the coasts on each side; now in the open sea, it had resumed its former direction.

As soon as this state of things had been discovered, Mr. Sergius returned to Cæser Cascabel and straightway told him that under the circumstances nothing more fortunate could have happened. This good item of news restored a little peace of mind to the head of the family.

"Yes," he said, "it is a lucky thing we are going in the very direction we wanted to go!—But, what a round we shall have made! Gracious goodness, what a round!"

Thereupon our friends set about making the best possible arrangements, as if their stay on the drifting islet was to be of long duration. First of all, it was decided they should continue to dwell inside the *Fair Rambler*, less exposed as it now was to be thrown on its side, since they were traveling with the wind.

Cornelia, Kayette, and Napoleona could now return to their household work, and see to the cuisine, which had been absolutely neglected for the past twenty-four hours. The meal was soon prepared, they sat to table, and if this dinner was not seasoned with the gay conversation of former days, it at least revived the guests who had been so sorely tried since their departure from Diomede Island.

The day closed in these conditions. The squalls kept up with unabated violence. The air now swarmed with birds, petrels, ptarmigans, and others, so justly named the harbingers of storms.

The next day and the subsequent days, the 28th, 29th, 30th, and 31st of October, brought no change in the situation. The wind, keeping steadily in the east, did not modify the state of the atmosphere.

Mr. Sergius had carefully taken the shape and dimensions of the iceberg. It was a sort of irregular trapezium, from three hundred and fifty to four hundred feet long and about a hundred wide. This trapezium, a good half-fathom above the water at its borders, swelled up slightly toward its center. No fissure was visible on its surface, although dull, crackling sounds sometimes ran through its mass. It seemed, therefore, as if, until now at least, the billows and the blast had been powerless against it.

Not without great efforts, the *Fair Rambler* had been drawn to the center. There the ropes and poles belonging to the tent used for the performances held it down so tight that there was no chance of its being knocked over.

What was most alarming was the shocks they received every time they knocked against enormous icebergs, which moved about at unequal speed, according as they obeyed the impulse of the currents or turned round on their own axes in the middle of whirlpools. Some of them, measuring at times fifteen or twenty feet in height, came straight toward them as though going to board an enemy's ship.

They were perceived from a distance, they were seen drawing near—but how could their assault be possibly avoided? There were some that tipped over with a loud clash when the displacing of their center of gravity disturbed their equilibrium; but when collisions took place they were terrible indeed. The shock was often such that, but for timely precautions, everything would have been smashed inside the wagon. They were continually threatened with a possible and sudden dislocation. Hence as soon as the approach of a large block was announced, Mr. Sergius and his companions gathered around the *Fair Rambler* and clung to each other. John always tried to get near Kayette. Of all dangers, the most frightful for them would have been to be carried away separately on different broken pieces of the berg; and naturally they were safer on its central part, where it was thickest, than along its borders.

At night, Mr. Sergius and Cascabel, John and Clow, mounted guard in turns, and strained every nerve to watch over their wreck in the midst of that profound darkness, haunted by huge white figures that glided about like gigantic specters.

Although the air was still full of the mist that was swept about by the never-relenting gale, the moon, which was very low in the horizon, permeated it with its pale rays, and the icebergs could be perceived at a certain distance. On the first cry of whoever was on guard, everybody was on foot, and awaited the result of the meeting. Frequently the direction of the approaching enemy would change and it would float clear away; but sometimes a clash would occur, and the shock snapped the ropes and pulled up the stakes that held the *Fair Rambler*. It looked as though everything should come to pieces; surviving the collision was something to be thankful for.

Meanwhile, the temperature kept on contrary to all records. This sea, not frozen yet in the first week of November. These regions still navigable a few degrees above the polar circles! All this, surely, was extraordinary ill-luck! With all this, if some belated whaler had passed by within sight, they would have made signals to him, they would have attracted his attention by firing a few shots. After picking up the shipwrecked party, he might have brought them to some port on the American coast, to Victoria, San Francisco, San Diego, or on the Siberian coast, to Petropaulovski or Okhotsk. But no, not a sail! Nothing but floating icebergs! Nothing but the immense, solitary sea, bounded to the north by an impassable barrier of ice! Very fortunately, unless in the event of a most unlikely continuance of this anomalous condition of the temperature, there was no anxiety to be felt concerning the question of food, even though they kept adrift for several weeks. In view of a lengthy journey through Asiatic regions, where it would not be easy to procure victuals, they had made ample provisions of preserves, flour, rice, grease, etc. They had no longer, either, to trouble themselves about food for the horses, alas!

165

In truth, if Vermont and Gladiator had been spared until now, how would it be possible to provide for them?

On the 2d, 3d, 4th, 5th, and 6th of November, nothing new happened save that the wind showed a tendency to fall, and shifted somewhat to the north. Scarcely did daylight last for a couple of hours,—which added still to the horror of the situation.

In spite of Mr. Sergius's incessant observations, it became very difficult to judge of the course of the drift; and, unable as they were to dot it on the map, they no longer knew where they were. However, on the 7th, a landmark was discovered, recognized, and fixed with a certain amount of accuracy.

On that day, about eleven o'clock, just as the vague rays of dawn whitened the space, Mr, Sergius and John, accompanied by Kayette, had just gone to the fore part of the iceberg. There happened to be, in the showman's material, a pretty good telescope with which Clovy used to show country people the equator,—represented by a thread stretched across the object-glass,—and the inhabitants of the moon, personified by insects which he had previously introduced inside the tube. Having carefully cleaned this telescope, John had taken it with him, and endeavored with its help to discover some land away in the open.

For a few moments he had been examining the horizon very carefully, when Kayette, pointing toward the north, said:

"I fancy, Mr. Sergius, that I perceive something yonder!—Why, isn't it a mountain I see?"

"A mountain?" replied John. "No, it is probably nothing more than an iceberg!"

And he turned his telescope in the direction shown by the young girl.

"Kayette is right!" he said, almost immediately.

And he gave the instrument to Mr. Sergius, who pointed it, in his turn, in the same direction.

"Quite right," said he, "it is even a pretty high mountain. Kayette was not mistaken."

On further observation, it was found that there should be land to the northward, at a distance of some sixteen or eighteen miles.

That was a fact of the utmost importance.

"To be o'ertopped by so great an elevation, a piece of land must be of considerable extent," remarked John.

"It must, John," answered Mr. Sergius; "and when we go back to the *Fair Rambler*, we must try and find it out on the map. That will enable us to ascertain our own situation."

"John, it seems to me as if there was smoke coming out of the mountain," suggested Kayette.

"It would be a volcano then!" said Mr. Sergius.

"It is so, quite so," added John, who was again peering through his glass. "The smoke can be seen distinctly."

But daylight was already dying away, and even with the magnifying power of the instrument, they were soon unable to perceive the outline of the mountain.

One hour later, however, when it was almost quite dark, vivid flashes of light appeared in the direction which had been recorded by means of a line traced on the surface of the berg.

"Now let us go and consult the map," said Mr. Sergius.

And all three returned to the encampment.

John looked in the atlas for the general map of the boreal regions beyond Behring Strait, and this is what was calculated.

As Mr. Sergius had already ascertained, on one hand, that the current, after flowing north, curved toward the northwest about one hundred and fifty miles outside the strait, and, on the other hand, that their ice-raft had been following that direction for several days, what they had to find out was whether there were lands ahead to the northwest.

And sure enough, at a distance of some twenty leagues from the continent, the map showed a large island to which geographers have given the name of Wrangell, and the outline of which, on its northern side, is but vaguely defined. It was very probable, indeed, that the iceberg would not come in contact with it, if the current continued to carry it through the wide arm of the sea which separates the island from the coast of Siberia.

Mr. Sergius felt no doubt on the identity of Wrangell Island. Between the two capes on its southern coast. Cape Hawan and Cape Thomas, it is surmounted by a live volcano, which is marked on the recent maps. This could be no other than the volcano that Kayette had discovered, and the glare of which had been distinctly perceived at the fall of day.

Now it was an easy matter to make out the course followed by the berg since it had come out of Behring Strait. After having turned round with the coast, it had doubled Cape Serdze-Kamen, Koliutchin Bay, Wankarem

Promontory, Cape North, then it had entered Long Strait, which separates Wrangell Island from the coast of the Tchutki province.

To what regions would the iceberg be borne away when it had cleared Long Strait, it was impossible to foresee. What was of a nature to alarm Mr. Sergius the more was, that, to the northward, the map showed no other land; ice alone spread over that immense space, the center of which is the pole itself.

The only hope to which they could cling now was that the sea might get entirely frozen up under the action of a more intense cold,—an eventuality which could not be delayed much longer; one which should have come to pass several weeks since. Our rovers should then get stranded on to the ice-field, and by directing their steps toward the south, they might try to reach the Siberian continent. True, they would be under the necessity of abandoning the *Fair Rambler* for want of a team; and what would they do, if they had a long distance to cover?

Meanwhile the wind kept blowing violently from the east, though no longer in the hurricane fashion of the preceding days. Such are these horrible seas, huge waves would unfurl with a loud roar and come dashing against the crest of the floating block; then rebounding off, they would sweep right over its surface, and give it such shocks that it trembled to its very center, as though it would burst open.

Besides, those giant waves, hurled on as far as the wagon, threatened to wash away any one who was not inside it. Hence measures of precaution were taken, on the advice of Mr. Sergius.

As there had been an abundant fall of snow during the first week in November, it was easy to construct a kind of rampart, aft of the iceberg, to protect it against the waves, which, most frequently struck it from behind. Everybody set to work; and when the snow, duly trodden and beaten, had been heaped to a height and thickness of four or five feet, and had become quite hard, it presented an obstacle to the fury of the billows, the spray alone oversprinkling its summit. It was like a sort of barricade erected astern of a disabled vessel.

While this work was going on, Sander and Napoleona could not refrain from throwing an occasional snow-ball at each other, and aiming not a few at Clovy's back. And although the present was not exactly the time for play, Mr. Cascabel did not scold too severely, except on one occasion when a ball, missing its aim, fell full on Mr. Sergius's hat.

"Who is the good-for-nothing—?" He had not time to finish.

"It was I, father," cried little Napoleona, quite confused.

"You good-for-nothing child!" exclaimed Cascabel. "You will excuse her, will you, Mr. Sergius?"

"Leave the child alone, friend Cascabel," replied the latter. "Let her come and give me a kiss; and it will be all over."

And it was done accordingly.

Not only was a bank erected on the back part of the iceberg, but soon the *Fair Rambler* itself was surrounded with a kind of rampart of ice, so as to protect it more efficiently still, whilst its wheels, being packed up with ice, right up to the axle, made the wagon absolutely steady. Inside this rampart, which went up to the height of the gallery, a narrow space had been left which permitted to circulate all around the vehicle. You might have fancied it was a ship wintering in the midst of icebergs, with its hull protected by a cuirass of snow against the cold and the squalls. If the block itself did not give way, our shipwrecked party had nothing more to apprehend from the billows, and, in these conditions, they might perhaps find it possible to wait until the Arctic winter had taken entire possession of these hyperborean regions.

But then, when that time had come, they would have to start off for the continent! They would have to leave the home on wheels that had conveyed them through the length and breadth of the New World, and in which they had found so comfortable and so safe a shelter! Abandoned among the bergs of the Polar Sea, the *Fair Rambler* would disappear at the breaking up of the ice when the warm weather came.

And when Cascabel thought over all that, he who was always so ready to look at things on their bright side, he raised his hands to heaven, he cursed his ill luck, and blamed himself for all these disasters, forgetting that they were due to the ruffians who had robbed him in the gorges of the Sierra Nevada, and who were entirely responsible for the present state of things.

In vain did good Cornelia endeavor to drive his gloomy thoughts away, at first by gentle words and afterwards by stinging reproaches. In vain did his children and Clovy himself claim their share in the consequences of the fatal resolutions that had been adopted. In vain did they assert over and over again that this route had been unanimously agreed upon by the family. In vain did Mr. Sergius and "little Kayette" try to console the inconsolable Cæser. He would heed nothing.

"You are no longer a man, then, aren't you?" said Cornelia to him one day, giving him a good shaking.

"Not so much as you are, wifey!" he replied, as he tried to recover his equilibrium, that had been slightly disturbed by his wife's muscular admonition.

In reality, Mrs. Cascabel was full of anxiety for the future. And still, she felt the necessity of reacting against the dejection of her husband, hitherto so unyielding to the blows of evil fortune.

And now the question of food was beginning to trouble Mr. Sergius. It was of the greatest importance that the provisions should last, not only till such time as they would set out on the ice-field, but right up to the day when they would reach Siberia. Needless to rely on their guns at a time of the year when sea-birds would be seen but seldom flying across the mist. Prudence, therefore, made it obligatory to cut down the rations in view of a journey that might last a long time.

It was under these conditions that the iceberg, irresistibly drawn along by the currents, reached the latitude of the Aion Islands, situated to the north of the Asiatic coast.

CHAPTER IV - FROM THE 16TH OF NOVEMBER TO THE 2ND OF DECEMBER

IT was with the help of a great deal of guessing that Mr. Sergius came to believe he had recognized this group of islands. As far as possible, when he took down his observations, he had made allowance for the drift, which he calculated at an average of some forty-five miles in twenty-four hours.

This archipelago, which indeed he was unable to see, lies, according to the maps, in long. 150 and lat. 75, say about three hundred miles from the continent.

Mr. Sergius was right: by the 16th of November the iceberg was to the south of this group of islands. But at what distance? Even by using the instruments habitually employed by navigators, that distance could not have been estimated in an approximate way. As the disk of the sun showed itself but for a few minutes through the mist of the horizon, the observation would have given no result. They had definitely entered the long night of the polar regions.

By this time the weather was horrible, although it had a tendency to get colder. The thermometer wavered a little below zero, centigrade. Now this temperature was not low enough yet to bring about the cohesion of the icebergs scattered on the surface of the Arctic basin; in consequence no obstacle could hinder the drifting of the floe.

Meanwhile, in the indentations along its margin could be noticed the formation of what polar navigators in winter quarters call bay-ice, when it occurs inside the narrow creeks of a coast. Mr. Sergius and John attentively watched these formations, which would, ere long, spread over the whole sea. The ice season would then be "full on," and the situation of the wanderers would be changed for the better,—at least they hoped so.

During the first fortnight in November the snow did not cease falling in extraordinary abundance. Swept along horizontally by the blast, it accumulated in thick masses against the rampart erected around the *Fair Rambler*, and in a short time made it considerably higher.

On the whole, this accumulation of snow presented no danger; nay, it was an advantage in this way, that the Cascabels would be the better protected against the cold. Cornelia would thus be able to spare the paraffine oil and use it exclusively for kitchen purposes,—a question to be taken into serious consideration, for, when this oil became exhausted, how would they replace it?

Fortunately, besides, the temperature remained bearable inside the apartments,—three or four degrees above zero. It even went up when the *Fair*

Rambler was buried in the snow; and now, it was not the heat that was likely to run short, but rather the air, to which all access was closed.

It then became necessary to remove the snow, and every one had his share in this toilsome task.

And first of all, Mr. Sergius had the little corridor cleared out that had been contrived inside the rampart. Then a passage was cut through, so as to make sure of a free exit, and due care was taken, of course, that this passage should face the west. Without this precaution, it would have been obstructed by the snow that the wind drove from the east.

All danger was not warded off, however, as will be seen presently.

Needless to say that they left their rooms neither night nor day. There they found a safe shelter against the storm as well as against the cold, which was increasing, as shown by the slow and steady fall of the thermometer. None the less, Mr. Sergius and John did not fail to make their daily observations whilst a vague glimmer of light tinted yonder horizon, beneath which the sun would continue to decline until the solstice of the 21st of December. And day by day they were disappointed in that faint hope of perceiving some whaler wintering in the vicinity, or endeavoring to make his way to some port on Behring Strait; always and ever disappointed in the hope of finding the block adhering to some ice-field adjacent, perchance, to the Siberian coast! Then both, returning to the encampment, would try to reproduce on the map the supposed course of the drift.

It has been mentioned already that fresh game had ceased to put in an appearance in the kitchen of the *Fair Rambler* since its departure from Port Clarence. As a fact, what could Cornelia have done with those sea-birds which it is so hard to rid of their oily taste? In spite of her culinary talents, ptarmigans, and petrels would have been ill-received by her guests. So John refrained from wasting his powder and shot on these birds of too Arctic an origin.

However, whenever he was on guard outside, he never went without his gun, and one afternoon, the 26th of November, he had an opportunity to make use of it.

Suddenly a shot was heard, and immediately after John called loudly for help.

The feeling of surprise caused by the unusual occurrence was not unmingled with a certain amount of anxiety. Out rushed Mr. Sergius, Cascabel, Sander, and Clovy, followed by the two dogs.

"Come here! Come here!" John cried.

And so saying, he ran backward and forward, as though he tried to cut off the retreat of some animal.

"What is it?" inquired Mr. Cascabel.

"I have wounded a seal, and it will escape us if we let it reach the sea."

It was a fine animal. It had been wounded in the chest, and a streak of blood reddened the snow; still it would have managed to escape, had not Mr. Sergius and his companions come to the spot.

With a first blow of its tail, it knocked young Sander to the ground, but Clovy threw himself bravely on it, kept it down not without difficulty, and John finished it with a shot in the head.

If this was not a very dainty bit of venison for Cornelia's daily boarders, it was no trifling stock of meat for Wagram and Marengo. No doubt, had they been able to speak, they would have thanked John heartily for this lucky windfall.

"And, by the way, why don't animals talk?" said Mr. Cascabel, when they were all seated in front of the stove in the kitchen.

"For the very simple reason that they are not intelligent enough to talk," replied Mr. Sergius.

"Are you of opinion, then," asked John, "that the absence of speech is due to a lack of intelligence?"

"Most assuredly, my dear John, at least among the superior animals. Thus, the larynx of the dog is identical with that of man. A dog could talk, then; and if it does not do so, it is because its intelligence is not sufficiently developed to enable it to communicate its impressions by speech."

This theory was, to say the least, open to discussion, but modern physiologists admit it.

It is worth nothing that a change was gradually taking place in Mr. Cascabel's mind. Although he still continued to hold himself responsible for the present situation, his philosophy was reassuming its former sway. With his life-long habit of weathering all storms, he could not believe that his good star had set. No, its light had been clouded; that was all. Hitherto, indeed, the family had not been too severely tried with physical suffering. True, if dangers increased, as there was reason to fear they would, the moral power of endurance of the troupe might be severely taxed.

Hence, with an eye to the future, Mr. Sergius did not cease encouraging all the little world around him. During the long idle hours, seated at the table by the light of the lamp, he would chat with them, would tell them the various adventures of his travels through Europe and America. John and Kayette, sitting near each other, listened to him with great profit, and to their questions he always gave some instructive reply. Then, availing himself of his experience, he ended by saying:

"Do you see, my friends, there is no reason to despair. The block we are on is sound and hard, and now that the cold weather is set, it will not come to pieces. Notice, moreover, that it is drifting in the very direction we wished to go, and that we are going on without fatigue, as if we were on a ship. A little patience and we shall get into port safe and sound."

"And which of us is despairing, if you please?" said Mr. Cascabel to him, one day. "Who takes the liberty to despair, Mr. Sergius? Whoever despairs without my permission shall be put on bread and water!"

"There is no bread!" cried young Sander, with a grin.

"Well then, on dry biscuit, and he shall be kept indoors!"

"We can't go outside!" remarked Clovy.

"That's enough!.... Those are my orders!"

During the last week in November, the snowfall took extraordinary proportions. The flakes fell so thick that they had to give up all thought of walking one step out of doors, and a veritable catastrophe well-nigh ensued.

On the 30th, at break of day, as he awoke, Clovy was surprised at the difficulty he experienced in breathing, as though the air hindered the proper action of the lungs.

The others were sleeping still in their "apartments" with a heavy, painful sleep that gave one the idea that they were undergoing gradual asphyxia.

Clovy tried to open the door in the forepart of the wagon, to renew the air. He was unable to do so.

"Hallo, boss!" he called out in so powerful a tone of voice that he awoke all the guests of the *Fair Rambler*.

Mr. Sergius, Cascabel, and his two sons were up in a moment, and John exclaimed:

"Why, we are smothering here! We must open the door!"

"Just what I can't do!" replied Clovy:

"The windows, then?"

But as the windows opened outward, it was found equally impossible to open them.

In a few minutes the door was unscrewed down, and they understood why they had not been able to slide it as usual.

The corridor, left inside the rampart all round the vehicle, was filled up with a quantity of snow driven into it by the squall, nor was the corridor alone thus crammed up, but likewise the passage outward through the ice wall.

"Could the wind have changed?" suggested Mr. Cascabel.

"That is not likely," answered Mr. Sergius. "So much snow would not have fallen if the wind had shifted westward."

"Our iceberg must have turned round on itself," observed John.

"Yes, that must be so," replied Mr. Sergius. "But, let us see, first, to what is most urgent. We must not let ourselves be stifled for want of breathable air."

And immediately, John and Clovy, with pickaxe and shovel, set about clearing the corridor. A laborious task in truth; the hardened snow filled it to its highest, and there was reason to believe it even covered up the wagon.

To get on the quicker, they had to relieve each other in turn. Naturally it was impossible to shovel the snow out; so they had to throw it into the first compartment of the wagon, where, under the action of the internal temperature it resolved itself into water almost immediately, and flowed out.

At the end of one hour, the pickaxe had not yet pierced its way through the compact mass jammed in the corridor. It was impossible to get out, impossible to renew the air inside the *Fair Rambler*, and respiration became more and more difficult through lack of oxygen and excess of carbonic acid.

All were panting, and sought in vain for a little pure air in this vitiated atmosphere. Kayette and Napoleona experienced a sensation of choking. There was no concealing the fact that Mrs. Cascabel was most affected by this state of things. Kayette, overcoming her own sufferings, endeavored to give her some relief. What would have been needed was to open the windows so as to renew the air, and we have seen that they were externally blocked up with the snow, as the door had been.

"Let's work with a will!" Mr. Sergius would go on repeating. "Here we have dug six feet through this block. It cannot be much thicker now!"

No, it should not be much thicker, if the snow had ceased falling. But perhaps it was falling still, even now.

John, at this time, hit on the idea of making a hole through the layer of snow that formed the roof of the corridor,—a layer that should be thinner than the rest presumably, and probably less hard.

Sure enough, this task was performed successfully and under more favorable conditions; and half an hour later,—it was not one minute too soon, —the hole gave access to the outer air.

175

This proved an immediate relief for all the occupants of the *Fair Rambler*.

"Oh, how good that is!" exclaimed little Napoleona, opening her mouth wide, the better to fill her lungs.

"Fine!" added Sander, as he passed his tongue over his lips. "I'd rather have it than jam, just now."

It was some time before Cornelia quite recovered from that fit of incipient asphyxia, under which she had become almost unconscious.

The hole having now been made wider, the men hoisted themselves up to the crest of the ice rampart. Everything was white to the utmost limits that the eye could reach. The wagon had entirely disappeared under an accumulation of snow which formed a huge mound in the center of the floating block.

By consulting the compass, Mr. Sergius was able to ascertain that the wind still blew from the east, and that the iceberg had wheeled round half a turn on itself,—which had made its aspect exactly the reverse of what it originally was,—and by turning the opening of the passage to the windward had caused the latter to be blocked up with snow.

In the open air, the thermometer recorded only six degrees below zero, and the sea was free, so far as could be judged in the midst of almost complete darkness. It must be observed, moreover, that in spite of the rotatory movement which the berg had made upon itself,—owing, no doubt, to its being temporarily caught in some whirlpool,—it had none the less continued to drift toward the west.

With a view to anticipate the recurrence of a similar accident, which might be attended with such deplorable consequences, Mr, Sergius thought it wise to take an additional measure of precaution. On his recommendation they dug through the rampart a second passage opposite to the first; and now, whatever might be the aspect of the berg, they would always be sure of some means of communication with the outside. Henceforth, no more fear of a deficiency of pure air inside the wagon.

"All the same," said Mr. Cascabel, "for a God-forsaken spot, this is a God-forsaken spot, and no mistake! I am not quite sure that it is good enough for seals, and it's nothing to the climate of old Normandy!"

"I quite agree with you," replied Mr. Sergius. "Still, we must take it as it is."

"Don't I take it? by Jove! Of course I take it, Mr. Sergius,—in abomination, I do!"

No, good Cascabel, this is not the climate of Normandy, not even that of Sweden, Norway, or Finland during their winter season! It is the climate of the North pole, with its four months of darkness, its roaring squalls, its continual fall of dust-like snow, and the thick veil of mist which does away with the possibility of what we Southerners call a horizon.

And what a gloomy mental perspective loomed in the distance! When this helpless drifting had come to an end, when the berg lay stranded and still, and the sea was no longer but an immense ice-field, what course would they adopt? Abandoning the wagon, journeying without it, a distance of several hundred leagues to the coast of Siberia,—the mere thought of it was truly frightful. Hence, Mr. Sergius would ask himself whether it might not be best to winter at the very spot where the floating berg would stop and to enjoy, until the fine season returned, the hospitality of that *Fair Rambler* whose rambles were all over, no doubt! Yes, at the worst, spending the period of intense cold in these conditions would not have been an impossibility. But, before the temperature would rise, before the Arctic Sea would break up, they should have left their winter-quarters and crossed the ice-field, which would dissolve very quickly when it once began to do so.

As to that, the wanderers were in no hurry yet, and it would be time enough to consider this question when winter was over. They should then have to take into account the distance; that would separate them from the continent of Asia, always under the supposition of their having some means of calculating it. Mr. Sergius was in hopes that the distance would not be considerable, seeing that the iceberg had been floating uniformly toward the west after doubling Capes Kekournoi, Chelagskoi, and Baranov, and cleared Long Strait and Kolima Bay.

Why had it not stopped at the mouth of this latter bay? From there, it would have been relatively easy to reach the province of the Ioukaghirs, in which Kabatchkova, Nijneikolymsk, and other villages, would have offered them safe winter quarters. A team of reindeer might have been sent to the ice-field for the *Fair Rambler* and would have brought it on to the continent. But Mr. Sergius felt convinced that this bay must have been left behind, as well as the mouths of the Tchukotski and Alazeia rivers, being given the speed of the drift. To check this drift, nothing now appeared on the map, save the line of those archipelagoes known by the names of Anjou Islands, Liakhov, and Long Islands, and on these islands, uninhabited for the most part, how would they find the resources necessary to the home-journey of the staff and material? Still, even this would be better than a helpless, aimless drifting about the furthest limits of the polar regions!

The month of November had just ended. Thirty-nine days had come and gone since the Cascabels had left Port Clarence to venture across Behring Strait. But for the loosening of the ice-field, they would have landed at Numana quite five weeks ago; and now, having pushed their way to the southern provinces of Siberia and settled down in some village, they would have nothing more to dread from the Arctic winter.

Now, the drift could not keep on much longer. The cold was gradually increasing and the thermometer steadily falling. On examining his ice island, Mr. Sergius found that its area was enlarging daily, owing to the various blocks it "annexed," as it shifted its way among them; indeed, it had grown, superficially, one-third larger than it was at first.

During the night from the 30th of November to the 1st of December, an enormous block came and adhered to the aft portion of the float; and, as the base of this block went down rather deep into the water and it was thereby drawn with greater speed by the current, it soon whirled the islet half a turn round and dragged it on ahead just like a steam tug towing a barge along.

At the same time, as the cold had grown more intense and drier, the sky had quite brightened up again. The wind now blew from the northeast,—a fortunate circumstance, since it bore to the Siberian coast. The sparkling Stars of the Arctic firmament lit up the long polar nights, and frequently an aurora borealis would flood the space with its luminous jets, springing up from the horizon like the leaflets of a fan. Away, away the eye could travel, until, yonder on the very utmost limits of its range, it discerned the first bank of the polar ice. On the background of the now clearer horizon, this chain of eternal icebergs came out in relief with its sharp crests, its rounded-off ridges, its forest of peaks and offshoots. It was a marvelous sight, and our friends would temporarily forget their sad situation, gazing in admiration at those cosmic phenomena, peculiar to hyperborean regions.

The speed of the drift had slackened since the wind had changed, the current being now the sole cause of it. It was therefore probable that the iceberg would not be carried much farther westward, for the sea was beginning to freeze in the interstices between the slowly gliding blocks. Up to the present, it is true, this "young ice," as whalers call it, yielded to the least shock. The blocks, scattered about on the open, being separated but by narrow channels, the iceberg would sometimes knock against considerable masses; it would remain still for a few hours, and eventually would resume its course. Nevertheless, there was every reason to look forward to an imminent halt, and this time it would be for the whole duration of winter.

On the 3d of December, about noon, Mr. Sergius and John had gone right to the bow of their disabled ship. Kayette, Napoleona, and Sander had followed them, well wrapped up in furs, for it was bitter cold. Away to the south, the faintest glimmer of light showed that the sun was crossing the meridian. The doubtful whiteness that pervaded the space was doubtless due to some distant aurora borealis.

All their attention was drawn to the various motions of the icebergs, their strange shapes, the shocks they gave each other, the "somersaults" executed by those whose equilibrium would happen to be displaced by the wearing out or the breaking off of their submerged base.

Suddenly, the block that had towed the raft for the past few days seemed to shiver all over, toppled into the sea, and in its fall broke off the edge of the iceberg, a huge wave flooding the latter at the same time.

All rushed back with all possible speed, but almost immediately cries were heard:

"Help! Help! John!"

It was Kayette's voice. The portion of the berg on which she stood had been snapped off by the shock and was drifting away with her.

"Kayette!" cried John. "Kayette!"

But, caught by a side current, the broken block was being carried away from the berg, which then happened to be held back by a whirlpool. Yet a little while, and Kayette would have disappeared in the middle of the drifting ice.

"Kayette! Kayette!" John called.

"John! John!" repeated the young girl, one last time.

On hearing the cries, Mr. Cascabel and Cornelia had come running to the spot. There they stood, horror-stricken, near Mr. Sergius, who was at utter loss to know what to do to save the unfortunate child.

Just then, the broken block having come within five or six feet of where they were, John sprang off with one bound before they could hold him back and fell by the side of Kayette.

"My son! My son!" sobbed Mrs. Cascabel.

Saving them was now out of the question. By the impulse of his fall, John had pushed the block far away. Both were soon out of sight among the icebergs, and even their cries, lost through the space, ceased to be heard.

After two hours' anxious watching, night came: Mr. Sergius, Cascabel, Cornelia, all were compelled to return to the encampment.

What a night the poor people spent pacing to and fro around the *Fair Rambler* amid the piteous howlings of the dogs! John and Kayette carried away! Without shelter, without food,—lost! Cornelia wept; Sander and Napoleona mingled their tears with hers. Cascabel, utterly crushed by this new blow, no longer uttered but incoherent words, the general purport of which was that all the misfortunes that had befallen his home were his own doing. As to Mr. Sergius, what consolation could he have offered them, when he, himself, was inconsolable?

The next day, the 4th of December, about eight o'clock in the morning, the iceberg had begun to move forward again, having at last cleared the whirlpool by which it had been detained all night. Its course was the same as that followed by John and Kayette, but as they were eighteen hours ahead, all hope of overtaking them or finding them again should be given up. They were beset by too many dangers, besides, to escape them safe and sound, what with the cold, which was becoming excessively keen, with the pangs of hunger that they would be unable to appease, and the incessant collisions with icebergs, the smallest of which could have crushed them on its way!

Better not attempt to depict the grief of the Cascabels! In spite of the fall in the temperature, not one of them would consent to go indoors, and they kept on calling John, calling Kayette, neither of whom could hear their heart-rending cries.

The day wore itself out, and the situation was still unchanged. Night came, and Mr. Sergius ordered father mother, and children, to seek the shelter of the *Fair Rambler*, although nobody could sleep for one single moment.

Suddenly, about three in the morning, a frightful shock was felt, and so violent was it that the wagon was well-nigh upset. Whence came this shock? Had some enormous iceberg collided with the raft, and perchance broken it?

Out rushed Mr. Sergius.

An aurora borealis cast its reflection through the space; it was possible to discern objects within a radius of half a league around the encampment.

Mr. Sergius's first thought was to cast his searching eye in every direction.

No sign of John or Kayette.

As to the shock, it had been caused by the knocking of the berg against the ice-field. Thanks to a further fall in the temperature,—which had gone down to twenty degrees below zero, centigrade,—the surface of the sea was now completely solidified. There, where all was unrest yesterday, everything was now still and steady. All drifting was permanently at an end.

Mr. Sergius hastened back and announced to his friends the final halt of their floating berg.

"So, the sea is all set ahead of us?" inquired the bereaved father.

"Ahead of us, and behind, and all around us," replied Mr. Sergius.

"Well, let us go look for John and Kayette! There is not one minute to lose."

"Let us be off!"

Cornelia and Napoleona would not remain with the *Fair Rambler*; it was accordingly left in Clovy's charge and all started off, the two dogs scouting ahead, and scenting all over the ice-field as they went.

They walked at a good speed on the ice, which was as hard as granite, and naturally they made for the west, where, if Wagram and Marengo ever fell on the track of their young master, they would soon recognize it. At the end of half an hour, however, they had found nothing yet, and they had to halt, for one quickly got out of breath with a temperature so low that the air seemed frozen.

The ice-field, which spread out of sight, north, south and east, seemed bounded on the west by certain heights which did not present the usual appearance of icebergs. They might be the outline of a continent or of an island.

Just at this moment, the dogs, with loud barks, made a rush for a whitish mound on which a certain number of black specks could be perceived.

They at once resumed their tramp onward, and presently Sander remarked that two of those black specks were making signs to them.

"John!—Kayette!" he cried, rushing on ahead after Wagram and Marengo.

They were, indeed, Kayette and John, safe and sound.

But they were not alone. A group of natives surrounded them; and these were the inhabitants of Liakhov Islands.

CHAPTER V - LIAKHOV ISLANDS

THERE are, in this part of the Arctic Sea, three archipelagos, designated under the general name of New Siberia, and conaprising Long Islands, Anjou Islands, and Liakhov Islands. The latter, the nearest to the continent of Asia, consist of a group of islands lying between the 73d and the 75th degrees of latitude north, and the 35th and 140th of longitude east, on a surface of some forty thousand square miles. Among the principal ones may be named the isles of Kotelnoi, Blinoi, Maloi, and Belkov.

Barren lands these are; no trees, no product out of the soil; barely some signs of a rudimentary kind of vegetation during the few weeks of summer; nothing but bones of cetacea and of mammoths, accumulated here ever since the period of geological formation; fossil wood in very large quantities; such are the archipelagos of New Siberia.

Liakhov Islands were discovered in the early years of the eighteenth century.

It was on Kotelnoi, the most important and the most southerly of the group, some three hundred miles from the continent, that the staff of the *Fair Rambler* had landed, after a drift of forty days over a space of six or seven hundred leagues. To the southwest, on the coast of Siberia, lies the vast bay of the Lena, a wide opening through which the river of that name, one of the most important in northern Asia, pours out its waters into the Arctic Sea.

Evidently then, this Liakhov archipelago is the ultima thule of the polar regions in this longitude. Beyond it, right on to the insurmountable barrier of the polar ice, no land has been descried by navigators. Fifteen degrees higher is the North pole.

Our wanderers had therefore been cast ashore at the very world's end, although at a lower latitude than the latitude of Spitzbergen or that of the northern parts of America.

On the whole, granting that the Cascabels had journeyed farther north than they had originally intended to do, still they had constantly drawn nearer and nearer to Russia in Europe. The hundreds of leagues they had covered since leaving Port Clarence had caused them less fatigue than exposure to danger. Drifting away, under these conditions, was so much land journey saved through countries that are almost untravelable during winter. And there would have been, perhaps, no reason for complaining, if, by a last stroke of ill luck, Mr. Sergius and his companions had not fallen into the hands of the natives of Liakhov. Would they obtain their liberty or could they ever recover it by flight? It seemed doubtful. In any case, they would know all about it ere long; and when they were fixed on that point, it would be time enough to adopt a line of action, according to circumstances.

Kotelnoi Island is inhabited by a Finnish tribe, reckoning from three hundred and fifty to four hundred souls, men, women, and children. These repulsive-looking natives are among the least civilized of those who inhabit these parts, be they Tchuktchis, Ioukaghirs, or Samoyedes. Their idolatry is beyond belief, despite the noble efforts of the Moravian Brothers, who have never been able to conquer the superstitious spirit of these Neo-Siberians or their innate thieving and pillaging propensities.

The principal industry of the Liakhov archipelago consists in the catching of cetacea, great numbers of which frequent this part of the Arctic Sea, and likewise in seal hunting, these animals being as plentiful here as in Behring Island during the warm season.

Winter is very severe in this latitude of New Siberia. The natives live, or rather earth themselves, in the depths of dark holes, dug under heaps of snow. These holes are sometimes divided into rooms, where it is not difficult to maintain a pretty high temperature. What they burn is that fossil wood, not unlike peat, of which (as was already said) these islands contain considerable strata, not to mention the bones of cetacea, which are also used as fuel.

An opening, made by these Northern Troglodytes in the ceiling of their caves, supplies a means of exit for the smoke of their very primitive hearths. Hence, at first sight, the soil seems to emit vapors similar to those which come out of sulphur mines.

As to their food, the flesh of the reindeer constitutes its chief basis. These ruminants are parked on the islets and islands of the archipelago in large flocks. Their "table" is, moreover, provisioned with the flesh of the elk and with dried fish, large quantities of which are stored up before winter. It follows therefrom that the Neo-Siberians need have no fears on the score of famine.

One chief was at this time reigning over the Liakhov group. His name was Tchou-Tchouk, and he wielded an uncontested authority over his subjects. In their abject submission to the regime of absolute monarchy, these natives are the very antithesis of the Eskimos of Russian America, who live in a kind of republican equality. And with respect to social well-being, they differ even more from them, thanks to their savage manners and inhospitable ways, which are the source of frequent complaints on the part of whalers. Alas for the good-hearted natives of Port Clarence! How they would be regretted, ere long!

Certain it is that the Cascabels could not have fared worse! After the catastrophe in Behring Strait, coming to land just on the Liakhov archipelago, and falling among such unsociable creatures, was indeed outstripping all the bounds of ill luck.

Nor did Mr. Cascabel conceal his disappointment when he saw himself surrounded with some hundred natives, howling, gesticulating, and threatening the castaways whom the vicissitudes of this luckless journey had thrown into their power.

"Well, well, who are these apes after?" he exclaimed, after pushing away those who were closing too near him.

"After us, father!" said John.

"A funny way they have of bidding visitors welcome! Are they thinking of eating us up?"

"No, but very probably they intend keeping us prisoners on their island!"

"Prisoners?—"

"Yes, as they have done already with two sailors who arrived here before us."

John had no opportunity to give more complete details. The new-comers had just been seized by a dozen natives, and, whether they willed it or not, they had of necessity to follow their captors to Tourkef village, the capital of the archipelago.

Meanwhile, a score of other savages started in the direction of the "*Fair Rambler*", which could be perceived away in the east, thanks to the little streak of smoke issuing from its funnel.

A quarter of an hour later the prisoners had reached Tourkef, and were led into a pretty large cave dug under the snow.

"This is the jail of the locality, no doubt!" remarked Mr. Cascabel, as soon as they were left alone around a fire, lighted in the center of the hovel.

But first of all John and Kayette had to tell the tale of their adventures.

The block of ice on which they were had followed a westerly course after it had been lost to sight behind the drifting bergs. John held the young girl in his arms lest she should be knocked off by the continual shocks they received. They had no provisions; they were fated to be without a shelter for long hours to come; but at least they were together. Keeping close against each other, they would not feel hungry or cold, perhaps.

Night came on. Even though they could not see, they could hear each other. The hours passed on in the midst of continual anguish and with the never-ceasing dread of being thrown into the abyss beneath them. At last the pale rays of dawn appeared, and just then their float was locked to the ice-field.

Away John and Kayette ventured over the immense waste; they walked on and on, and at last reached Kotelnoi Island, where they naturally fell into the hands of the natives.

"And you say, John, that there are other shipwrecked prisoners?" inquired Mr. Sergius.

"There are, sir."

"You have seen them?"

"Mr. Sergius," said Kayette, "I have been able to understand these people, for they talk Russian; and they spoke of two sailors who are kept prisoners in the village."

As a matter of fact, the language of the northern tribes of Siberia closely resembles Russian, and Mr. Sergius would be in a position to explain himself with the inhabitants of these isles. But what was there to expect from these plunderers who, driven away from the more populous provinces near the mouths of the rivers, have sought in the far away archipelagos of New Siberia a den of safety, where they have nothing to fear from the Russian authorities.

However, Mr. Cascabel's ill temper knew no bounds since he had been denied the liberty of going and coming where he willed. He repeated to himself, and not without good grounds, that the *Fair Rambler* would be descried, pillaged, destroyed, perhaps, by these ruffians. In truth, it was not worth while having escaped out of the cataclysm in the Strait of Behring, to come headlong into the claws of this "polar vermin."

"Come, César," Cornelia would say to him, "compose yourself. What use is there in flying into a passion! After all, much worse than all this might have befallen us!"

"Worse, Cornelia?"

"Why, of course, César! What would you say if we had not found John and Kayette? Well, there they are, both of them, and we are alive, all of us! Just think of the dangers we have run, and escaped! Why, it is nothing short of a miracle, and my opinion is that instead of raving like a madman, you ought to be thanking Providence—"

"So I do, Cornelia, thank Providence from the bottom of my heart. All the same, surely it's no harm if I curse the devil for having pitchforked us into the clutches of those monsters! Why, they are more like brutes than like human creatures!"

And Cascabel was right, but Cornelia was not wrong. Not one of the guests of the *Fair Rambler* was missing. Such as they had left Port Clarence, such they had met together again in this Tourkef village.

"Yes, we are all together again, inside a mole-hill, or a polecat's hole, if you choose," grumbled Cascabel; "a den that an ill-licked bear would not consent to lie in!"

"By Jove!—What about Clovy?" exclaimed Sander.

And, forsooth, what had become of the poor fellow who had been left in charge of the wagon? Had he, at the risk of his life, attempted to defend his master's property? Was he now in the power of the savages?

And now that Sander had recalled Clovy to the members of the family then present:

"And what about Jako!" said Cornelia.

"And John Bull!" said Napoleona.

"And our dogs!" added John.

Needless to say that all the sympathy was for Clovy, The ape, the parrot, Wagram and Marengo were, of course, a question of very secondary consideration.

At this moment a loud noise was heard outside. There was a veritable storm of indignant recriminations, and to the general confusion was superadded the barking of the two dogs. Almost immediately, the orifice used to gain access to the den was flung open; in bounded Wagram and Marengo, and after them appeared Clovy.

"Here I am, boss!" cried the poor fellow, "unless, maybe, it's not myself! For I really don't know what's become of me!"

"That's exactly how we feel, too!" replied the boss, as he stretched out his hand to him.

"And our *Fair Rambler*?" inquired Cornelia tremblingly.

"The *Fair Rambler*?" answered Clovy. "Why, those gentlemen outside ferreted it out under the snow; they yoked themselves to it like so many heads of cattle and brought it here to this village."

"And Jako?" said Cornelia.

"And Jako, too."

"And John Bull?" added Napoleona.

"And John Bull, likewise."

Everything considered, since the Cascabels were detained at Tourkef, it was better their wagon should be there too. although running the risk of being ransacked.

Meanwhile hunger began to make itself felt, and there was no visible sign of the natives concerning themselves about the feeding of their prisoners. Very fortunately, the prudent Clovy had taken the precaution of cramming his pockets, and out of their depths he drew several tins of preserves, which would be sufficient for the first meals. Then, all wrapped themselves up in their furs and slept as well as they could in an atmosphere rendered almost unbreathable by the smoke from the peat fire.

Next morning, the 4th of December, Mr. Sergius and his companions were led out of their hovel; and with unspeakable relief they slowly inhaled the outer air, although the cold was intense and keen.

They were brought to the presence of Tchou-Tchouk.

This cunning-faced personage, whose general appearance was the reverse of attractive, occupied a sort of subterraneous dwelling, larger and more comfortable than the dens of his subjects. It had been dug at the foot of a huge, gloomy, snow-capped rock, the summit of which was not unlike the head of a bear.

Tchou-Tchouk might have been fifty years of age. His smooth face, lit with a pair of small eyes which glistened like live coals, was animalized, if I may apply the word to the facial aspect of the lower animals, by the sharp tusks that came out between his lips. Seated on a heap of furs, clad in reindeer skins, his legs buried in sealskin bouts and his "upper end" duly protected by a fur hood, he lazily nodded his head backward and forward.

"What an astute old scoundrel he looks!" murmured Mr. Cascabel.

By his side stood two or three notables of the tribe. Outside lounged a half hundred natives, clad much in the same way as their chief; whether men or women the prisoners could not tell, Neo-Siberian fashion in dress being no "respecter" of sexes.

And first of all, Tchou-Tchouk, addressing Mr, Sergius, whose nationality he doubtless had guessed, said to him in very intelligible Russian:

"Who are you?"

"A subject of the Czar!" replied Mr. Sergius, thinking that the imperial title might perchance awe this petty sovereign of an archipelago.

"And those?" continued Tchou-Tchouk, pointing to the members of the Cascabel family.

"French people."

"French?" repeated the chief.

187

And it seemed as though he had never heard of a people or a tribe of that name.

"Why, of course, French!—French people from France, you old wretch!" exclaimed Mr. Cascabel.

But this was said in the most vernacular French, and with all the freedom of speech of a man who feels sure and certain that he will not be understood.

"And she?" inquired the monarch, turning to Kayette; for it had not escaped his notice that the young girl should be of a different race.

"An Indian," answered Mr. Sergius.

Whereupon a somewhat lively conversation ensued between him and Tchou-Tchouk, the principal passages of which he translated for his friends.

The outcome of the whole discussion was that the party should consider themselves prisoners, and that they should remain on Kotelnoi Island so long as they would not have paid down, in good Russian money, a ransom of 3000 roubles.

"And where does this son of Ursa Major think we shall get them?" cried Cascabel. "No doubt, by this time his ruffians have stolen what remained of your money, Mr. Sergius!"

The king made a sign, and the prisoners were shown out. They were allowed to go about in the village on condition that they would not leave it; and, from the very first day, they could notice they were closely watched. At this season, indeed, in the heart of winter, it would have been impossible for them to run away with a view to reach the continent.

Straightway the whole troupe had made for the *Fair Rambler*. A great number of natives had crowded around it, in ecstasy before John Bull, who gratified them with his choicest grimaces. They had never seen an ape before, and imagined, very probably, that this red-haired quadruman belonged to the human species.

"Why, they belong to it themselves!" remarked Cornelia.

"They do, but they are a disgrace to it," added her husband.

Then, on second thought:

"And, my word!" said he, "I made a big mistake in calling those savages 'apes'! They are not up to them in any respect, and I offer you my best apologies for what I said, my little John Bull!"

And by way of answering, John Bull turned heels over head. But, one of the natives having tried to get hold of his hand, he bit his finger so deep as to make the blood flow.

"That's it, John Bull! Bite them! Bite them hard!" called Sander.

This, however, might have ended unpleasantly for the little ape, and he might have paid a dear price for his bite, if the attention of the natives had not been drawn away by the apparition of Jako; his cage had just been opened, and he was coming out for a walk with the leisurely strut of an Eastern potentate.

Parrots were not known any more than monkeys in these archipelagos of New Siberia. No one had ever seen a bird of this kind, with such bright colors on its feathers, with two round eyes that looked like the glasses of a pair of specticles, and a beak curved round like a hook.

But who will describe the sensation Jako created when out of its beak came forth clearly articulated words! One followed another until the whole repertory of the loquacious bird had been poured out, to the utter amazement of the natives. A bird that spoke! And the superstitious creatures would throw themselves on the ground as if words had been uttered by the mouths of their divinities. Nor did Mr. Cascabel fail to excite his parrot the more:

"Go on, Jako!" he would say, teasing him the while. "Go on! Say all you like to them! Tell the fools to go to Jericho!"

And Jako would bid them "Go to Jericho," one of his favorite expressions. And the bidding came out with such trumpet-like sound that the natives took to their heels, with all the outward signs of the greatest terror.

And, in spite of all their anxiety, the ill-fated troupe enjoyed "a hearty old chuckle," as their illustrious head would have put it.

"Well, well," he said, as he recovered a little of his old good temper, "it will be the very devil, surely, if we can't manage to get the better of this flock of two-footed cattle!"

The prisoners were left to themselves; and as it appeared that Tchou-Tchouk allowed the *Fair Rambler* to remain at their disposal, they had nothing better to do than re-enter their old home. No doubt the Neo-Siberians thought it inferior to their holes under the snow.

Truth to say, the wagon had been stripped only of a few unimportant articles, but what remained of Mr. Sergius's money had been taken away. This, however, César Cascabel had quite made up his mind that he would not leave behind, not even as a ransom.

Meanwhile, it was a stroke of good fortune that they should be once more in their little parlor, their dining-room, the little compartments inside the *Fair Rambler*, rather than live in the loathsome dens of Tourkef. There was scarcely anything missing. The bedding, the utensils, the tins of preserves had apparently failed to "tickle the fancy of the ladies and gentlemen of the locality." And so, if they had to wait for months, watching their opportunity to escape from Kotelnoi Island,—well, they would winter where they were.

In the mean time, since they were left quite free to come and go as they chose, Mr. Sergius and his companions resolved to put themselves in communication with the two sailors who,—it was probable,—had been shipwrecked and cast on this island. They might, perhaps, act in concert with them and devise some plan to cheat Tchou-Tchouk's watchfulness and make their escape when circumstances would be favorable.

The remainder of the day was spent setting things in order inside the little home. No light task was it, either! And how Cornelia grumbled, she who was so very careful in her household work. It kept Kayette, Napoleona, and Clovy as busy as bees right away till bedtime.

It should be recorded, by the way, that from the time he had determined to play some huge trick on His Majesty Tchou-Tchouk, Mr. Cascabel seemed to have recovered from the recent blows he had received. "Richard was himself again."

The following day Mr. Sergius and he went in search of the two sailors, who were very likely to enjoy the same liberty as they did. Sure enough, they were not kept in a prison; the meeting took place at the door of the den which they occupied at the other end of the village, and no objection whatever was made on the part of the native warders.

These sailors were of Russian origin; one was thirty-five years of age, the other forty. Cold, want, and hunger had furrowed their long-drawn cheeks; their sailors' clothes were covered with rags of fur; under their thick head of hair and their overgrown beard, their features could scarce be distinguished. They were the very picture of misery. Still, they were strongly built, muscular fellows, who would be well able to give a helping hand, should an opportunity present itself. For all that, it did not seem as though they were very desirous of getting intimate with these strangers, whose arrival on the island had already been announced to them.

The identity of their position, a common desire to get out of it by aiding each other, ought surely to have drawn the two parties together.

Mr. Sergius questioned the two men in Russian. The elder gave his name as Ortik, the younger as Kirschef; and, not without a certain amount of hesitation, they consented to tell their history.

"We are sailors belonging to the port of Riga," said Ortik. "A year ago we embarked on board the whaler Seraski, for a season in the Arctic Sea. When it was over, we were unlucky enough not to reach Behring Strait in time; our boat was caught between icebergs, north of the Liakhov Islands, and was crushed to pieces. All the crew perished except Kirschef and myself. We set out together in a small boat; a storm drove us on to these islands, and we fell into the hands of the natives."

"When was that?" asked Mr. Sergius.

"Two months ago."

"How did they receive you here?"

"Like yourselves, most likely," replied Ortik. "We are Tchou-Tchouk's prisoners; and let us off he won't, except for a ransom."

"Where shall we get it?" interrupted Kirschef.

"Unless," continued the other, in a blurting sort of a way, "unless, may be, you have money for yourselves and for us; for we are countrymen, I think—"

"We are," answered Mr. Sergius; "but the money we possessed has been stolen by the natives, and we are quite as destitute as you can possibly be yourselves."

"Worse luck!" growled Ortik.

Both, then, gave a few details on the way they lived. It was that narrow, dark cave they used for a dwelling-place; and, while watching them continually, their captors allowed them a certain degree of liberty. Their clothes were in rags, they had nothing to eat but the usual food of the natives, and that in barely sufficient quantity. They thought, moreover, that when the fine season drew near, they would be more closely guarded, and all attempt at an evasion would become impossible.

"Seeing that all we'd have to do would be to get hold of a fishing canoe, to get across to the continent, you may be sure that the natives will look after us, and perhaps shut us up!"

"But the mild season will not return for four or five months," said Mr. Sergius, "and, remaining prisoners until then—"

"Why, you have a way to get off, then?" asked Ortik, interrupting him.

"We have not, at present. Meanwhile, it is quite natural that we should try and help each other mutually. You seem to have suffered a great deal, my friends, and if we can be of any assistance to you—"

The two sailors thanked Mr. Sergius, but there was a visible lack of candor in their thanks. If, from time to time, he would procure them some better food than what they had, they would feel grateful to him. That is all they cared for, unless he could, perhaps, oblige them with some covering. As to living together, they would rather not. They preferred staying in their hole, but promised to call on their visitors.

Mr. Sergius and Cascabel, the latter of whom had understood a few words of this conversation, took leave of the two sailors.

Although these men's appearance was all but sympathetic, this was no reason for refusing to help them. Shipwrecked people owe aid and assistance to each other. They would come to the relief of the sailors, therefore, within the limits of their means; and, should a chance of escaping offer itself, Mr. Sergius would not forget them. They were countrymen of his, after all; and they were men like him.

A fortnight elapsed, and they gradually fell in with the shortcomings of their new situation. Each morning they were compelled to appear before the native sovereign and to listen to his pressing demands about their ransom. He flew into fits of passion, would use threats and swear by his idols! It was not for himself, it was for them he claimed the tribute of deliverance.

"You old swindler!" Mr. Cascabel would say. "Commence by giving us back our money! We shall see afterwards!"

On the whole, future prospects were anything but bright with hopes. There was cause to fear that from one day to another Tchou-Tchouk might carry his threats into effect.

And day after day, Cascabel puzzled his brains to find out some means of playing "Cheek-cheek" a trick worthy of him. It was all to no purpose; and the poor artist began to wonder if his bag of tricks was not empty, and by his bag of tricks he meant his brain-box. Indeed, the man who had indulged that grand idea,—as bold as it was now to be regretted,—of returning from America to Europe by way of Asia, seemed but too fully justified in saying to himself that he was nothing more than a "regular fool."

"No, César, you are not a fool!" Cornelia would say. "You will hit upon something choice in the end! It will strike you when you think of it least!"

"You think so, wifey?"

"I am sure of it!"

Was it not touching to see Cornelia's unshakable confidence in the genius of her husband, in spite of the unlucky plan he had conceived with regard to this journey?

Of course Mr. Sergius was ever there, ready to encourage everybody. And yet, the efforts he made to induce Tchou-Tchouk to give up his claims were absolutely fruitless. And even though the savage chief had consented to restore them their liberty, the Cascabels could not have left Kotelnoi Island in the middle of winter, with a temperature wavering between thirty and forty degrees below zero.

The 25th of December being at hand, Cornelia decided that Christmas should be celebrated with some éclat. The said éclat would simply consist in offering her guests a more carefully prepared dinner, one more plentiful than usual, although its various courses would be composed exclusively of preserves. Moreover as there was no lack of flour, rice, and sugar, the good housewife displayed all her skill in the making of a gigantic cake, the success of which was, beforehand, a certainty.

The two Russian sailors were invited to this meal, and accepted the invitation. It was the first time they had ever come inside the *Fair Rambler*.

No sooner had one of them,—the younger, called Kirschef,—opened is lips than the sound of his voice struck Kayette. She seemed to think that voice was not unknown to her; but where she could have heard it, she was unable to guess.

In truth, neither Cornelia, her little daughter, or even Clovy, felt any sympathetic attraction toward these two men, who seemed ill at ease in the presence of their own fellow-creatures.

As the banquet was drawing to an end, Mr. Sergius, at Ortik's request, was led to relate the adventures of the Cascabels in the province of Alaska. He added how he had been picked up half dead by them, after an attempt at murder committed on his person by some of Karkof's men.

Had their faces been fully in the light, these two men might have been seen exchanging a singular glance when the crime came to be mentioned. But this passed off unnoticed, and after taking their good share of the cake, which had been liberally soaked with vodka, Ortik and Kirschef left the *Fair Rambler*.

They were scarce outside when one of them said:

"There is a meeting that wasn't on the card! Why, that's the Russian we attacked just at the frontier; and that Indian is the cursed girl that prevented us finishing him off!"

"And clearing out his belt!" added the other.

"Yes! Those thousands of roubles would not be in Tchou-Tchouk's clutches now!"

And so, these two would-be sailors were really outlaws belonging to that Karkof gang, whose deeds had spread terror over western America. After their unsuccessful assault on Mr. Sergius, whose features they had been unable to notice in the darkness, they had succeeded in making their way to Port Clarence. There, a few days later, they had stolen a boat and had endeavored to cross Behring Strait; but, dragged away by the currents and a hundred times well-nigh hurled into the jaws of death, they had ultimately been cast on the chief island of the Liakhov Archipelago, where they had been made prisoners by the natives.

CHAPTER VI - IN WINTER QUARTERS

SUCH was the situation of Mr. Sergius and his companions on January the 1st, 1868.

Alarming as it was already, through their being prisoners of the Neo-Siberians of the Liakhov Islands, it was now complicated by the presence of Ortik and Kirschef. Who knows if the two scoundrels would not endeavor to turn so unexpected a meeting to profit? Luckily, they were ignorant of the fact that the traveler attacked by them on the Alaskan frontier was Count Narkine, a political prisoner escaped from the Iakoutsk fortress, seeking to re-enter Russia by joining an itinerant showman's troupe.

Had they known it, they surely would have felt no hesitation in making use of the secret, levying blackmail on the Count, or in handing him over to the Russian authorities, in exchange for a reprieve or a pecuniary reward for themselves.

But was there not a possible danger of a mere accident betraying the secret to them, although Cascabel and his wife alone were now acquainted with it?

Meanwhile, Ortik and Kirschef continued to live apart from the troupe, determined though they were to join them, whenever an opportunity to regain their liberty should present itself.

For the present, indeed, and so long as the wintry period of the polar year would last, it was but too evident there was nothing to be attempted. The cold had become so excessive that the damp air exhaled by the lungs turned into snow. Sometimes the thermometer went down as low as forty degrees below zero, centigrade. Even in calm weather it would have been impossible to bear such a temperature. Cornelia and Napoleona never dared venture out of the *Fair Rambler*; indeed, they would have been prevented if they had. How endless they thought those sunless days, or rather those nights, of almost twenty-four hours' duration!

Kayette alone, accustomed to North American winters, was bold enough to face the cold out of doors; and in this she was imitated by the native women. They were seen going about their daily work, clad in reindeer-skin dresses, two hides thick, wrapped up in fur palsks, their feet incased in sealskin boots, and their heads covered with a cap of dogskin. Not even the tips of their noses could be seen,—which was not much to be regretted, it seems.

Mr. Sergius, Cascabel, his two sons, and Clovy, carefully protected by their furs, paid their obligatory visit to Tchou-Tchouk every day; and so did the two Russian sailors, who had been supplied with warm covering.

As to the male population of New Siberia, they boldly sally forth in any weather. They go hunting on the surface of their wide plains, hardened with frost; they quench their thirst with snow, and feed on the flesh of the animals they kill on the way. Their sleds are very light; they are made with the bones, ribs, and jaws of whales, and are set up on sliders on which they get a coating of ice by simply watering them just before starting off. To draw them along they use the reindeer, an animal which is of the greatest service to them in many ways. Their dogs are the Samoyede breed, closely resembling the wolf species, and quite as ferocious as the latter, with long legs and a thick coat of hair, dotted black and white or yellow and brown.

When the Neo-Siberians travel on foot, they put on their long snow-shoes, "or skis," as they call them, and with these they swiftly skim over considerable distances, along the straits which separate the various islands of the archipelago, "tracking it" on the tundras or strips of alluvial soil usually formed on the edge of Arctic shores.

The natives of the Liakhov group are very inferior to the Eskimos of Northern America in the art of manufacturing weapons. Bows and arrows alone constitute their whole offensive and defensive arsenal. As to fishing implements, they have harpoons with which they attack the whale, and nets which they spread under the grundis, a kind of bottom ice on which seals may be caught.

They likewise use lances and knives when they attack the seals, a mode of warfare attended with no little danger, for these animals are formidable.

But the wild animal which they most dread to meet, or to be attacked by, is the white bear, which the intense-cold of winter and the necessity of getting some kind of food after long days of enforced fasting sometimes drive into the very villages of the archipelago. It must be acknowledged that the savages display real pluck on such occasions; they are never known to run away before the powerful brute, maddened as it is by hunger; they throw themselves upon him, knife in hand, and most of the time they come off victorious.

On several occasions, the Cascabels witnessed encounters of this kind, in which the polar bear, after grievously wounding several men, had to yield to the numerical strength of his foes. The whole tribe then came forth and the village kept a merry holiday. And what a windfall was this stock of bear's meat, so relished, it would seem, by Siberian stomachs! The best joints naturally found their way to Tchou-Tchouk's table and into his wooden bowl. As to his very humble subjects, each of them had a small share of what he condescended to leave them. Thence an opportunity to indulge in copious libations and eventually the general intoxication of the villagers,—"on what?" you will say: well, on a liquor made with the young shoots of the salix and the rhodiola, and the juice of the red whortleberry and the yellow marsh berries, a large supply of which they gather during the few weeks that the mild season lasts.

On the whole, not only is bear-hunting dangerous sport under such circumstances, but the game is scarce; the reindeer's flesh is the mainstay of the native cuisine, and with its blood a soup is made which, it must be confessed, never excited but loathing on the part of our artists.

Should it now be asked how the reindeer manage to live during the winter, it will be sufficient to say that these animals are at no trouble to find vegetable food, even under the thick layer of snow which covers the ground. Besides, enormous provisions of fodder are stored up before the cold sets in, and this alone would be enough for the feeding of the thousands of ruminants contained in the territories of New Siberia.

"Thousands!.... And to think that just a score of them would be such a boon to us!" Mr. Cascabel would go on repeating to himself, and he wondered how he would ever replace his lost team.

It seems now opportune to emphasize the fact that the inhabitants of the Liakhov archipelago are not idolatrous only, but extremely superstitious; that they attribute everything to the divinities they have wrought with their own hands, and obey them with the blindest servility. This idolatry is beyond all belief, and the mighty chief Tchou-Tchouk practised his religion with a fanaticism which had no equal but that of his subjects.

Each and every day, Tchou-Tchouk repaired to a sort of temple, or rather sacred place, named the Vorspük, which means the "prayer-grotto." The divinities, represented by simple wooden posts, gaudily painted over, stood in a row in the inmost recess of a rocky cavern, and before them the natives came and knelt, one after the other. No spirit of intolerance ever prompted them to close the Vorspük to their foreign prisoners; on the contrary, the latter were invited to it; and thus it was that Mr. Sergius and his companions could satisfy their curiosity and examine the gods of these forsaken regions.

On the summit of each post was stuck up the head of some hideous bird, with round, red eyes, formidable, wide-open beaks, and bony crests curved round like horns. The faithful prostrated themselves at the feet of these posts, applied their ears against them, muttered their prayers, and although the gods had never vouched an answer, they retired, fully convinced they had heard the reply from above,—a reply generally in accordance with the secret wish of the petitioner.

When Tchou-Tchouk thought of laying some new tax on his subjects, the cunning chieftain never failed to obtain the celestial approbation; and where was the man among his subjects who would have dared deny what the gods willed?

One day in each week there was a religious ceremony more important than the others,—in this way, that the natives displayed more than ordinary pomp.

Let the cold be never so intense, let snow-drifts whiz along the surface of the ground like so many sweeps of a mower's scythe, no one would stay indoors when Tchou-Tchouk headed the procession to the Vorspük. And will anybody guess how both men and women accoutered themselves for these grand solemnities since the capture of the new prisoners? Why, with the gala dresses of the troupe, of course. The many-colored tights so nobly worn by Mr. Cascabel; Cornelia's robes, which had once been new; the children's stage dresses; Clovy's helmet, with its gorgeous plume; all these were donned by the Siberian worshipers outside their ordinary wearing apparel. Nor had they forgotten the French horn, into which one of them blew as though it were for dear life; the trombone, out of which another drew impossible noises; nor yet the drum or the tambourine; in fact, all the musical apparatus of the showman's stock added its deafening din to the éclat of the ceremony.

It was then Mr. Cascabel thundered against the thieves, the ruffians, who took such liberties with his property, to the great danger of breaking the springs of his trombone, straining his horn, or bursting his drum.

"The wretches!—The wretches!" he would say; and Mr. Sergius himself was powerless to calm him down.

After all, it must be owned, the situation was of a nature to sour one's temper, so slowly, so wearily did the days and the weeks draw along. And then, what would be the end of this adventure, if it did come to an end?

Still, the time that could not now be devoted to rehearsals,—and heaven knows if Mr. Cascabel expected his artists would be rusty when they reached Perm,—that time was not permitted to slip by unemployed and profitless.

With a view to cause a reaction against low spirits, Mr. Sergius continually strove to interest his friends with his tales or his lessons. As a return, Cascabel had undertaken to teach him a few tricks of legerdemain, "for his own pleasure," he said; but, in reality, a little proficiency in that way might be of use to Mr. Sergius if he ever had to play the showman's part in actual practice, the better to deceive the Russian police. As for John, he was busy completing the young Indian's course of instruction; and she, on her part, strained every nerve to learn to read and write under the guidance of her teacher.

Let them not be charged with egotism, if both accepted the situation without too much grumbling, absorbed as they were in a feeling which leaves room for no other. Mr. Sergius was not an unobservant witness of the intimacy which grew between John and his adopted daughter. Kayette had such a bright intelligence, and John displayed such zeal in developing it. Had fate decreed, then, that this honest fellow, so fond of study, so highly gifted by nature, should never be aught but an itinerant showman, should never rise above the sphere in which he was born? That was the secret of the future; and what future dared they now look forward to, prisoners as they were in the hands of a savage tribe on the utmost confines of the known world?

No sign was there of any change in Tchou-Tchouk's intentions; a ransom he should have ere he released his captives; and there seemed no likelihood of relief from the outside world. As to the money demanded by the greedy chief, how could they ever manage to get it?

True, the Cascabels possessed a treasure, unknown to themselves. It was young Sander's nugget, his famous nugget, a priceless treasure in its finder's eyes. When there was nobody by, he would draw it out of its hiding-place; and how he would gaze on it, and rub it and polish it! Willingly, of course, he would have parted with it to buy off the troupe out of Tchou-Tchouk's hands, but the latter would never have accepted as ready money a lump of gold under the shape and form of a stone. So, Sander kept to his first idea of waiting till they reached Europe, feeling sure that there he would have no trouble in converting his stone into coin, and compensate his father for the two thousand dollars that had been stolen from him in America!

Nothing could be better, if the journey to Europe could only be accomplished! Unfortunately, even a start was, for the present, out of the question. And this preyed also on the minds of the two miscreants whom ill-luck had thrown in the way of the Cascabels.

One day,—the 23d of January,—Ortik went to the *Fair Rambler* for the very purpose of having "a talk on the matter" with the wagon people, and, above all, ascertaining what they intended doing, in the event of Tchou-Tchouk permitting them to leave Kotelnoi Island.

"Mr. Sergius," he began, "when you left Port Clarence, your intention was to pass the winter in Siberia?"

"Yes," replied Mr. Sergius, "it was agreed we should try to reach some good village and stay there till spring-time. Why do you ask that question, Ortik?"

"Because I should like to know if you still think of taking up the same track, supposing, of course, these cursed savages let us go."

"Not at all; that would be lengthening needlessly a journey which is long enough of itself. It would be better, I think, to make straight for the Russian frontier, and find out one of the passes in the Ural mountains."

"In the northern part of the chain then?"

"Quite so, it being the nearest to where we are now."

"And the wagon," continued Ortik; "would you leave it here?"

Mr. Cascabel had evidently understood that part of the conversation.

"Leave the *Fair Rambler* here!" he exclaimed. "Not a bit of it, if I only can get a team! And I trust, before long—"

"What, you have an idea?" inquired Mr. Sergius.

"Not the shadow of one, yet! But Cornelia keeps telling me I'll hit on one, and Cornelia's word was never belied. An A 1 woman she is, sir, and she knows me, I tell you!"

Cascabel was his own old self again, brimful of trust in his lucky star, and refusing to believe that four Frenchmen and three Russians could not manage to get the better of a Tchou-Tchouk.

Mr. Cascabel's intention with regard to the *Fair Rambler* was communicated to Ortik.

"But, to take your wagon with you," said the sailor, who showed great concern on this point, "you must have a set of reindeer."

"We must."

"And do you think Tchou-Tchouk will supply you with them?"

"What I think is that Mr. Cascabel will find some plan to make him do so."

"Then, you will try to make your way to the coast of Siberia across the ice-field?"

"Just so."

"Well, in that case, sir, you must be away before the ice begins to break, that is, before three months' time."

"I am aware of that."

"But, can you do it?"

"Perhaps the natives will consent, in the long run, to let us off."

"I don't believe they will, Mr. Sergius, so long as you have no ransom to give them."

"Unless the fools are compelled to do so!" exclaimed Mr. Cascabel, to whom this conversation had just been translated.

"Compelled! By whom?" inquired John.

"By circumstances!"

"Circumstances, father?"

"Yes, circumstances," replied the veteran showman; "circumstances, you see, that's everything!"

And he scratched his head, and almost tore his hair off, but "not a shadow of an idea," to use his own words, came out of his skull.

"Come, my friends," said Mr. Sergius, "it is essential we should prepare for the event of the natives refusing to restore our liberty. Should we not make an effort to do without their consent, if they will not give it?"

"We shall, sir," answered John. "But then, we must leave the *Fair Rambler* behind."

"Don't talk like that!" sobbed Cascabel. "Don't talk like that! You break my heart!"

"Just think, father!"

"No, I won't! The *Fair Rambler* is our home! It is the roof under which you might have been born, John! And you would have me leave it at the mercy of those amphibious creatures, those walruses!"

"My dear Cascabel," said Mr. Sergius, "we shall do all that can be done to induce the natives to set us free. But, as there seems to be every probability of their refusal, running away is our only resource; and if ever we succeed in eluding the watchfulness of our guardians, we can do so only at the loss of—"

"The home of the Cascabel family!" cried Cascabel. And if those words had contained as many a's as they had consonants, they could not have passed with greater forte through his trembling lips.

"Father," suggested John, "there might be one other way, perhaps—"

"What is it?"

"Why might not one of us try to make his escape to the continent, and tell the Russian authorities? I am willing to start right away, Mr. Sergius."

"No such thing," interrupted Cascabel.

"No, don't do that!" added Ortik, in a hesitating way, when he was told John's proposal.

Mr. Cascabel and the sailor happened to agree on this point; but if the former thought of nothing but the danger Count Narkine would run, should he have any dealings with the Russian police, it was for his own sake the latter was desirous not to find himself in the presence of the authorities.

As to Mr. Sergius, he took another view of John's suggestion and sad:

"Well do I recognize you by your acts, my brave-hearted fellow, and I thank you for thus offering to devote yourself for us, but your devotion would be fruitless. At the present time, in the middle of this Arctic winter, venturing across the ice-field to cover the three hundred miles which separate this island from the continent would be folly! You would inevitably perish in the attempt, my poor John! No, my friends, let us not part from each other; and if, in some way or another, we manage to get away from the Liakhovs, let us go all together!"

"That's what I call sensible advice!" added Cascabel; "and John must promise me to do nothing in that way without my permission."

"I promise you, father."

"And when I say we shall go all together," continued Mr. Sergius, turning to Ortik, "I mean that Kirschef and you will both follow us. We shall not leave you in the hands of the natives."

"I thank you, sir," answered Ortik. "Kirschef and I will be of some use to you during the journey through Siberia. If, for the present, there is nothing to be done, we must make sure and be ready before the ice breaks up, as soon as the great cold ceases."

This last reminder having been given, Ortik withdrew.

"Yes," Mr. Sergius continued, "we must be ready—"

"Be ready we shall," interrupted Cascabel; "but how? May the wolf gobble me up if I know!"

And, sure enough, how to take leave of Tchou-Tchouk, with or without his consent, that was the all-absorbing question on the order of the day. Eluding the vigilance of the natives seemed, to say the least, very difficult. Coaxing the chief to better terms could hardly be thought of. There was then but one alternative: duping him. César Cascabel said so twenty times a day; not a moment did he cease puzzling his brain in that direction; he would often "take his head to pieces," as he said, and examine every nook and corner of it; and still, the end of January came and his search had yielded nothing yet.

CHAPTER VII - A GOOD TRICK OF MR. CASCABEL'S

TERRIBLE indeed was the beginning of February, a month when the mercury frequently freezes in the thermometer. Of course, it was nothing yet like the temperature of the interstellar space, like those two hundred and seventy-three degrees below zero, which immobilize the molecules of bodies and constitute the absolute solid state.

Still, one might readily have imagined that the molecules in the air no longer glided over each other, that the atmosphere was solidified: the air they breathed burnt like fire. The fall of the thermometrical column was such that the occupants of the *Fair Rambler* were compelled to remain indoors permanently. The sky was spotless; so bright and clear the constellations shone, it seemed as though the eye pierced through the farthest depths of the celestial canopy. As to the light of day, about noon-time it was but a palish mingling of the morning and the evening twilight.

This notwithstanding, the natives still braved the weather in the open air. But what precautions they took to save their feet, their hands, their noses, from sudden freezing! They were veritable perambulating bundles of furs. And what necessity drove them out of their dens under such climatic conditions? The will of their sovereign. Was it not imperative to see that the prisoners, who could not now pay him their daily visit, did not leave his domain?

To any ordinary creature this would have seemed altogether superfluous in such weather.

"Good-evening to you, you amphibious brutes!" Mr. Cascabel would say to them, as he looked at them through his little panes of glass, after removing the icicles from their internal surface. Then he would add: "Really, those things must have walrus blood in their veins!.... Why, there they come and go where respectable people would be frozen stark and stiff in five minutes!"

Within the *Fair Rambler*, which was hermetically closed, the temperature was maintained at a bearable degree. The heat from the kitchen stove,—in which they burnt fossil wood, so as to spare their stock of paraffine oil— permeated all the little rooms. These, indeed, had to be ventilated from time to time. But scarcely was the front door opened when every liquid substance inside the wagon froze instantaneously. There was not less than forty degrees' difference between the inside and the outside temperature,—a fact that Mr. Sergius could have ascertained, had not the thermometers been stolen by the natives.

By the end of the second week in February the temperature showed a slight tendency to rise. The wind having turned to the south, the snow again began to drift over this part of New Siberia with unequaled fury. Had not the *Fair*

Rambler been sheltered by high mounds, it could not have withstood the squall; buried, however, as it was, deeper than the height of its wheels in the snow, it was now in perfect safety.

True, there were a few fitful returns of cold, which caused sudden changes in the state of the atmosphere; still, about the middle of the month the average thermometric record had gone up to some twenty degrees below zero centigrade.

Mr. Sergius, Mr. Cascabel, John, Sander and Clovy ventured accordingly to take a little outing, while using the utmost caution to anticipate the evil effects of too abrupt a transition. From the hygienic point of view, this was the greatest danger they were exposed to.

All the surroundings of the encampment had entirely disappeared under one uniform white carpet, and it was impossible to recognize any of the inequalities of the ground; nor was this for want of light, for, during two hours, the southern horizon was brightened up with a kind of pale light which was, henceforth, going to increase as the spring solstice would draw nearer. It then became possible to enjoy a few walks, and from the very first, by special command of Tchou-Tchouk, a visit had to be paid him.

There was no change in the intentions of the stubborn native. On the contrary, the prisoners were now warned that they should procure a ransom of three thousand roubles within the shortest possible delay, or Tchou-Tchouk would see what was best to be done.

"You abominable wretch!" said Cascabel to him in that pure French vernacular that his majesty did not understand. "You treble brute!—You king of fools!"

All these epithets, however applicable to the sovereign of the Liakhovs, did not improve the state of things. And a very serious feature in the case was that Tchou-Tchouk now threatened vigorous measures.

It was at this time that, under the sway of pent-up rage, Mr. Cascabel was struck with a truly splendid idea.

"By all the walruses of the Liakhovs!" he exclaimed, one fine morning, "if that trick, that jolly old trick, could only succeed!—and why wouldn't it?—with such fools!"

But although these words had escaped his lips, Mr. Cascabel deemed it advisable to keep his secret to himself. Not a word of it did he tell anybody, not even Mr. Sergius, not even Cornelia.

It appears, however, that one of the conditions essential to the success of his project was his being able to speak distinctly the Russian dialect used by the tribes of northern Siberia. So that, while Kayette was improving her acquaintance with French under the teaching of her friend John, Mr. Cascabel suddenly undertook to improve his smattering of Russian under the direction of his friend Sergius. And where could he have found a more devoted teacher?

And so, on the 16th of February, whilst taking an airing round the *Fair Rambler*, he acquainted the latter with his desire to learn the language more thoroughly.

"You see," he said, "as we are going to Russia, it may be very useful to me to speak Russian; and I shall feel quite at home while we stay at Perm and Nijni."

"Quite so, my dear Cascabel," replied Mr. Sergius. "Still, with what you already know of our language, you could almost get along, even now."

"No, Mr. Sergius, not at all. If I manage to make out what is said to me at present, I am utterly unable to make myself understood, and that is just what I should like to get at."

"As you like."

"And, besides, Mr. Sergius, it will kill time for you."

On the whole, there was nothing to wonder at in Cascabel's proposal, and no one did wonder at it.

And behold him plowing away at his Russian with Mr. Sergius, keeping at it several hours a day, less, it would seem, with regard to the grammar of the language than its pronunciation. This was apparently what he specially aimed at.

Now, if Russians learn to speak French with great ease, and without keeping any of their own accent, it is much harder for French people to speak the Russian language. Hence it were difficult to realize all the care Mr. Cascabel bestowed on his study, all the efforts of articulation he made, and the powerful utterances with which he made the *Fair Rambler* resound, in order to acquire a perfect pronunciation of every word he learnt.

And really, thanks to his natural aptitude for languages, he made such remarkable progress as to astonish even his staff.

When the lesson was over, away he went on the beach, and there, where he was sure not to be heard by anybody, he practised a certain number of sentences in a stentorian tone of voice, uttering them on different keys, and rolling his r's after Russian style. And God knows if, in the course of his nomadic career, he had got into the habit of this full-mouthed oratory.

Sometimes he would meet Ortik and Kirschef, and as neither of them knew a word of French, he conversed with them in their own tongue, thus ascertaining that he was beginning to make himself understood.

These men now came to the *Fair Rambler* more frequently; and Kayette, who was always startled by the sound of Kirschef's voice, sought in vain to recollect on what occasion she could have heard it.

Between Ortik and Mr. Sergius the conversation, which Cascabel was now able to join, turned invariably on the possibility of leaving the island, and nothing practical could be devised.

"There may be one opportunity that we have not thought of yet, and that may present itself," said Ortik one day.

"What is it?" inquired Mr. Sergius.

"When the polar sea opens again," said the sailor, "it sometimes happens that whalers pass within sight of the Liakhov archipelago. If such luck happened us, might we not make signals to them and induce them to come along shore?"

"That would be exposing the crew to become Tchou-Tchouk's prisoners, like ourselves, and would not in any way help us to escape," answered Mr. Sergius; "for the crew would not be numerous enough and would certainly fall a prey to the natives."

"Besides," added Cascabel, "the sea will not be free for three or four months more, and I'll never have patience till then!"

Then he added, after a moment's thought:

"And again, if ever we could get on board a whaler, even with that good old Tchou-Tchouk's consent, we should leave the *Fair Rambler* behind."

"That is a parting we shall probably find it difficult to avoid," observed Mr. Sergius.

"Probably?" said Cascabel. "Nonsense!"

"Could it be you have found something?"

"Well, well—"

And Mr. Cascabel said no more. But what a smile wandered on his lips! What a flash of light brightened up his countenance!

Cornelia no sooner heard of her husband's enigmatic reply than she said:

"César has undoubtedly made out something. What it is I don't know. But I am sure he has. After all, from such a man, it is no wonder!"

"Father has got more brains than Mr. Tchou-Tchouk!" added little Napoleona.

"Did you notice," observed Sander, "that father has lately got into the habit of calling him 'good old fellow'? Quite a little pet name—"

"Unless it be just the opposite!" suggested Clovy.

And in the mean time, Mr. Cascabel—like Demosthenes haranguing the Grecian billows—trained his vocal organs against the roar of the elements on the shore of the frozen sea.

During the second fortnight in February the temperature continued to rise uniformly; the wind kept in the south; the currents spreading through the atmosphere were sensibly less cold. There was therefore no time to be lost.

After having to battle with the breaking up of the Behring ice-field, thanks to the late coming of winter, it would be incredible ill-luck to be now exposed to similar dangers through the early advent of spring.

In a word, if Cascabel had made a hit, if he did induce Tchou-Tchouk to let him go with his staff and material, this should take place while the ice-field was still one solid mass between the archipelago and the coast of Siberia. The ice-field being crossed, the *Fair Rambler* could then, with a good team of reindeer, cover the first part of her journey with comparative ease, and no possible breaking up of frozen seas would now trouble the travelers.

"Say, my dear Cascabel," Mr. Sergius asked, one day. "you really do hope that your old rascally Tchou-Tchouk will supply you with the reindeer you need to draw the wagon to the continent?"

"Mr. Sergius," said Cascabel with a very serious look, "Tchou-Tchouk is not an old rascal! He is, in truth, a good fellow, an excellent fellow. Now, if he allows us to depart, he will permit us to take the *Fair Rambler* with us, and if he shows us such kindness, he cannot do less than offering us a score of reindeer, fifty, a hundred, a thousand reindeer, if I demand them!"

"You have a hold of him, then?"

"Have I?—Just as if I held the tip of his nose between my fingers, Mr. Sergius! And when I catch hold, I catch hold, I do!"

Cæser's attitude was that of a man who is sure of himself, his smile that of self-satisfaction. On this occasion, he even went so far as placing the tip of his right hand to his lips and sending a flying kiss in the direction of Tchou-Tchouk's residence. But, feeling that he wished to keep his own counsels in this matter, Mr. Sergius had sufficient tact and good taste not to inquire further.

And now, owing to the return of a milder temperature, Tchou-Tchouk's subjects were resuming their habitual occupations, their bird catching and seal hunting. At the same time, the religious ceremonies, momentarily suspended during the period of intense cold, brought back the faithful to the grotto of the idols.

It was on the Friday in each week that the tribe assembled in largest number and with greatest pomp. Friday, it seems, is the Neo-Siberian Sunday. Now, on this Friday, the 29th,—1868 was leap-year,—a general procession of all the natives was to take place.

The previous evening, at bed-time, Mr. Cascabel simply said:

"To-morrow, let everybody be ready for the Vorspük ceremony; we shall all accompany our friend Tchou-Tchouk."

"What, César," said Cornelia, "you want us to—"

"I do!"

What could be the meaning of so imperative a recommendation? Did Cascabel hope to win the good graces of the sovereign of these isles by taking part in his superstitious worship? No doubt Tchou-Tchouk would have been pleased to see his prisoners paying their homage to the divinities of the country. But adoring them, embracing the religion of the natives, was quite another thing, and it was most unlikely that Mr. Cascabel would go the length of apostacy for the sake of alluring His Neo-Siberian Majesty. Fie on the very thought!

Be that as it might, next morning at break of day the whole tribe was on foot. Glorious weather; a temperature marking barely ten degrees below zero; and as much as four to five hours' daylight in perspective, with a little foretaste of sunlight peeping yonder over the horizon.

The inhabitants had come out of their mole-hills. Men, women, children, old people had put on their Friday-best sealskin cloaks and reindeer palsks. They presented an unequaled show of white and black furs, of hats embroidered with imitation pearls, of variegated breastplates, of leather strips fastened tight around their heads, ear-rings, bracelets, walrus-bone jewels hanging from their noses, etc.

Nor had all this appeared sufficient for so solemn an occasion. For some of the notables of the tribe had thought fit to adorn themselves with greater splendor still, i.e. with the various objects stolen out of the *Fair Rambler*.

And, sure enough, not to speak of the showman's tinsel trumpery that they had decked themselves with, of the clown's hats and the dime-museum helmets they had put on their heads, some wore on a string slung over their shoulders the steel rings used for juggling exercises, others had hung on their belts a row of wooden balls and dumb-bells, finally the great chief Tchou-Tchouk displayed a barometer on his chest as though it were the insignia of a new order, created by the sovereigns of New Siberia.

Needless to say the full orchestra of the troupe was there, the horn vying with the trombone, the tambourine endeavoring to drown the big drum, all mingling in frightful discord.

Cornelia was no less enraged than her children at the deafening concert of these artists, to whom "walruses could have given points," as Clovy said.

Well, incredible as it may seem, Mr. Cascabel positively smiled at the barbarians; he complimented them, hurrahed and clapped his hands, shouted "Bravo! bravo!" and would keep on repeating:

"Really, these people surprise me! They are particularly gifted for music! If they'll only accept engagements in my troupe I guarantee them enormous success at the Perm fair and at St. Cloud afterwards."

Meanwhile, in the middle of this tumult, the procession was going through the village on its way to the sacred place, where the idols awaited the homage of their faithful ones. Tchou-Tchouk walked at their head. Immediately behind him came Mr. Sergius and Mr. Cascabel, then the latter's family and the two Russian sailors, escorted by the whole population of Tourkef.

The cortege soon stopped before the rocky den in which stood the gods, wrapped up in gorgeous furs and adorned with paintings that had been newly "touched up" for the occasion.

Then Tchou-Tchouk entered the Vorspük, his hands raised heavenward, and after bowing his head three times, he squatted on a carpet of reindeer skins, spread on the ground. Such was the way to kneel down in that country.

Mr. Sergius and his companions hastened to imitate the sovereign, and the whole crowd fell to the ground behind them.

After all had become silent, Tchou-Tchouk drawled out a few words half chanted, half spoken, to the three idols.

Suddenly a voice is heard in answer to his invocation, a distinct, powerful voice, coming from the inner part of the cavern.

Wonder of wonders! The voice comes out of the beak of one of the divinities, and this is what it says in Russian:

"Ani sviati, êti innostrantzi, katori ote zapada prichli! Zatchéme ti ikhe podirjaïche?"

Which means:

209

"These strangers, who have come from the West, are sacred! Why do you detain them?"

At these words, distinctly heard by all the worshipers, there was general stupefaction.

It was the first time that the gods of New Siberia condescended to speak to their faithful.

Then, a second voice, in a tone of command, issues from the beak of the idol on the left, and thunders out:

"Ja tibié prikajou élote arrestantof otpoustite. Tvoïe narode doljne dlia ikhe same balchoïe vajestvo imiète i nime addate vcié vieschtchi katori ou ikhe bouili vziati. Ja tibié prikajou ou siberskoïé beregou ikhe lioksché vosvratitcia."

Three sentences addressed to Tchou-Tchouk, and which may be translated:

"You are commanded to set these prisoners free! Your subjects are commanded to show them every kindness and to restore to them all the objects that have been stolen from them. All are ordered to help them to reach the coast of Siberia!"

This time the stupefaction of the audience turned to terror. Tchou-Tchouk had half-risen on his trembling knees, his eyes gazing fixedly before him, his mouth gaping, the fingers of his hands stretched widely apart, in a paroxysm of fright. The natives, who had also assumed a semi-standing position, hesitated between kissing mother earth once more and taking to their heels.

At last, the third divinity, who stood in the middle, begins to speak in its turn. But lo, how terrible, how wrathful and threatening is its voice!

Its words also are aimed directly at His Neo-Siberian Majesty:

"Jesle ti take niè sdièlèle élote toje same diène, kakda èti sviati tchéloviéki boudoute jelaïte tchorte s'tvoié oblacte!"

That is to say:

"If this be not done on the day when these sacred people will desire it, let your tribe be vowed to celestial wrath!"

By this time, both the king and his subjects were panting with affright, and lay almost motionless on the soil, while Mr. Cascabel, raising his two arms toward the idols in token of gratitude, thanked them loudly for their divine intervention on his behalf.

And meanwhile his companions made all possible efforts to refrain from bursting out with laughter.

A simple trick of ventriloquism was the means devised by our genius, our truly unsurpassed artist, to bring his "good, honest fellow" Tchou-Tchouk, to reason.

What more was needed to dupe the superstitious natives?

"The strangers who have come from the West,"—(what a happy expression Mr. Cascabel had hit upon),—"the strangers who have come from the West are sacred! Why does Tchou-Tchouk detain them?"

He surely would do so no longer! He would let them go as soon as they liked, and the natives would show all sorts of kindness to travelers so visibly protected by heaven!

And while Ortik and Kirschef, who knew nothing of Mr. Cascabel's talents as a ventriloquist, did not conceal their real bewilderment, Clovy repeated:

"What a genius my boss is! What brains he has got! What a man, unless—"

"Unless he be a god!" exclaimed Cornelia, bowing low before her husband.

The trick had been played, and it proved a thorough success, thanks to the unheard-of credulity of the Neo-Siberian tribes. This credulity had been judiciously observed by Cascabel, and that was what had suggested to him the thought of turning his ventriloquial powers to profit for the general cause.

It is useless to add that his companions and he were all led back to their encampment with all the honors due to "sacred" men. Tchou-Tchouk, half through fear, half through respect, was at a loss to know what salutations to make to them, what compliments to pay them. The Cascabels and the Kotelnoi idols were well-nigh being merged into one in his mind.

And, in truth, how could these Tourkef people, sunk in such ignorance as they were, have imagined they were the dupes of a juggler? Not a doubt of it, it was the divinities in the Vorspük that had sent forth those dreadful utterances.

It was out of their beaks, hitherto silent, that those injunctions in very plain Russian had come. And, besides, had there not been a precedent? Had not Jako, the parrot, spoken too? Had not the natives heard in amazement the words that escaped from his beak? Well, what a bird had done, why might not bird-headed gods do it also?

From this day forward, Mr. Sergius, César Cascabel, and his family, not to forget the two sailors who were claimed as countrymen, could consider themselves as free. The winter season was now far advanced and the temperature was gradually becoming bearable. It was therefore resolved that no time should be lost in leaving the Liakhov Islands. Not that there was any reason to fear a change in the intentions of the natives. They were too thoroughly "bewitched" for that.

Mr. Cascabel was now on the best terms with his "friend Chicky-Chicky," who would willingly have blacked his boots for him, if he had been asked. Of course "the good honest fellow" had seen to the immediate restitution of all the things stolen out of the *Fair Rambler*. He himself, on bended knees, had returned to César Cascabel the barometer he wore around his neck, and the "sacred man" had vouched to hold his hand for the religious kiss that Tchou-Tchouk deposited on it. Did he not consider that hand capable of hurling forth thunder and lightning and letting loose the billows and the winds?

In short, by the 8th of March, the preparations for the departure of the whilom prisoners were completed. Mr. Cascabel having asked for twenty reindeer, Tchou-Tchouk had straightway offered him a hundred, which his new friend declined with thanks, while adhering to his first request. All he asked for, in addition, was a stock of fodder sufficient for his team until they had crossed the ice-field.

Early on that day, the "sacred people" took leave of the natives of Tourkef. The whole tribe had collected to be present at their departure and wish them a safe journey.

"Dear Chicky-Chicky" was there, in the foremost rank, trembling with genuine excitement. Mr. Cascabel advanced toward him and giving him a gentle tap on his chest, simply said to him in French:

"Ta-ta, old brute!"

That familiar tap was destined to raise His Majesty still higher in the estimation of his subjects.

Ten days later, on the 18th of March, after journeying without danger or fatigue over the ice-field which joined Liakhov Archipelago to the Siberian coast, the occupants of the *Fair Rambler* reached the continent, at the mouth of the Lena.

After so many incidents and accidents, so many dangers and adventures since their departure from Port Clarence, Mr. Sergius and his friends had at last set foot on the mainland of Asia.

CHAPTER VIII - THE COUNTRY OF THE IAKOUTS

THE original itinerary, such as it was to be followed from the Behring Strait to the European frontier, had been necessarily modified by the long drift and the subsequent landing at the archipelago of New Siberia.

Crossing Asiatic Russia in its southern part was now out of the question. Besides, the fine season would presently improve the condition of the climate, and there would be no need for the projected winter quarters in a Siberian village. Indeed, it may be said that the issue of the recent events had been as favorable as wonderful.

Now the problem to be studied was the direction to be taken, so as to reach the Ural frontier between Russia in Europe and Russia in Asia, in the shortest possible time. And that question Mr. Sergius had determined to solve before leaving the encampment they had just made on the coast.

The weather was cahn and clear. Now that the solistitial period was at its full, daylight lasted for more than eleven hours, and was, in a kind of way, still further prolonged by the twilight, which keeps on for a considerable time in the seventieth parallel.

The little caravan was now composed of ten persons. Kirschef and Ortik having joined it, as has been remarked. Although there was no very intimate sympathy between them and their companions, the two Russian sailors were among the proteges of the *Fair Rambler*; they had their place around the common table; it was even agreed they should sleep inside the wagon so long as the temperature would not permit them to sleep in the open air.

For the mean temperature still kept within a few degrees below zero,—a fact it was easy to ascertain since the "amiable Chicky-Chicky" had restored the thermometer to its legitimate owner. The ground, as far as the eye could reach, was entirely buried under an immense winding-sheet, and would remain so until the April sun would shine upon it. On this hardened snow, as well as on the grassy plains of the steppes, the team of reindeer would be well able to draw the heavy wagon along.

Thus far the provision of fodder so graciously supplied by the Kotelnoi natives had been amply sufficient for the cattle; henceforth, what with the moss that they root out from under the snow, what with the leaves of the shrubs scattered here and there on the soil of Siberia, they would provide their own food themselves. Nor should we omit to put it on record, that during the trip across the ice-field. the new team had shown great docility, and Clovy had experienced no difficulty in driving them.

The travelers' food was equally assured, thanks to the stock of preserves, flour, grease, rice, tea, biscuits, and brandy, which was still safe in the *Fair Rambler*. Cornelia had, moreover, at her disposal, a certain quantity of native-made butter, packed in small boxes of birch-wood, which friend Chicky-Chicky had presented to friend Cascabel; all they needed to renew was their provision of paraffine oil, and that could be done at the first village they came to. Besides, fresh game would soon rise on their track, and many a time would Mr. Sergius and John have an opportunity to utilize their skill, to the profit of the kitchen.

The help of the two Russian sailors was also to be taken into account. They had stated that the northern regions of Siberia were partly familiar to them, and there was every appearance of their proving useful guides.

This, indeed, was the subject of the conversation which was held in the encampment at the above date.

"As you have gone through this country before," said Mr. Sergius to Ortik, "you are going to direct us—"

"It is the least I might do," hastily replied Ortik; "seeing that it is thanks to Mr. Cascabel we are free men again."

"Thanks to me?" exclaimed Cascabel. "Not a bit, but thanks to nature enabling my vocal apparatus to take excursion trips up and down my internal organization."

"Ortik," continued Mr. Sergius, "what direction do you advise us to take when we leave the bay of the Lena?"

"The shortest cut, if you please, Mr. Sergius. If it is a disadvantage to give a wide berth to the large towns in the more southerly districts, we shall feel at least that we are making straight for the Ural chain. Besides, there are any number of villages on the way in which you can renew your provisions, or even make a stay, if that is necessary."

"What would be the use of that?" asked Cascabel. "We have no business stopping in villages. The great point is to lose no time and push on ahead as fast as we can. The country is not a dangerous one to go through, I guess?"

"Not at all," answered Ortik.

" Besides, we are in sufficient force, and woe betide the wretches who would attack our *Fair Rambler*! They would have cause to be sorry for it!"

"Be easy about that, Mr. Cascabel," remarked Kirschef. "There is nothing to be feared."

It may have been noticed that this Kirschef spoke but seldom. An unsociable fellow, sullen and taciturn, he usually let his companion "do the talking business." Ortik was evidently gifted with more intelligence than he, indeed with more real intelligence, as Mr. Sergius had remarked on several occasions.

On the whole, the itinerary proposed by Ortik was such as to suit everybody. Avoiding the important towns, where they might fall in with military posts, was a suggestion which recommended itself to Count Narkine, at the same time as it was particularly agreeable to the two would-be sailors.

The general plan once adopted in principle, they had only to examine the various provinces through which they should strike obliquely, between the Lena and the Urals.

John, therefore, produced the map of Northern Siberia; Mr. Sergius made a careful study of those parts where the Siberian rivers are rather an obstacle than a help to travelers westward; and this is what was agreed upon:

To cross the Iakout district, where villages are few and far between, in a southwesterly direction.

To pass thus from the basin of the Lena to that of the Anabara, and thence to those of the Khatanga, the Ienisei, and the Obi, say a distance of some two thousand two hundred miles.

To journey on through the basin of the Obi to the Ural Mountains, the natural frontier of Russia in Europe, a shorter trip of less than four hundred miles.

Lastly, to continue southwest for another three hundred miles, and thus reach Perm.

This meant, in round numbers, three thousand miles.

Should they experience no delay along the road, should there be no obligatory stay in any of the villages, this distance could be covered under four months. From twenty to twenty-five miles a day was not too much to expect from the team, and under such conditions, the *Fair Rambler* would be at Perm, and afterwards at Nijni, by the middle of July, just at the time when the famous fair would be at its highest.

"Will you come with us right up to Perm?" asked Mr. Sergius, turning to Ortik.

"It is not likely," answered the sailor. "After crossing the frontier, my idea would be to strike out for St. Petersburg, and from there make my way to Riga."

"That's all right," remarked Mr. Cascabel. "But let us get to the frontier first."

It had been previously resolved that they would halt for "a good twenty-four hours," as soon as they set foot on the continent. Such a halt was fully justified by their rapid transit across the ice-field, and so the whole of that day was given to rest.

The Lena throws itself into the gulf of that name through a zig-zag network of mouths, separated by a multitude of channels and creeks.

The waters poured into the Arctic Sea by this beautiful river have been gathered from a number of tributaries over a distance of 4500 miles. Its basin is considered as measuring no less than a hundred and five millions of hectares.

The map having been thoroughly examined, Mr. Sergius deemed it best that they should follow, at first, the coast line of the bay, so as to avoid the many channel-mouths of the Lena. Alihough the waters were still frozen, it would have been unwise to venture in such a maze. A chaos of huge blocks had been accumulated there by winter, and picturesque as were the veritable icebergs with which they were overtopped, they would have been none the less difficult to journey through.

Beyond the bay, on the contrary, lay the boundless steppe, hardly relieved here and there by the merest rise on its surface; here, the journey would be accomplished with ease.

No doubt of it, Ortik and Kirschef must have been frequently through these countries before. Their companions had remarked it more than once since they had left their prison quarters. These two sailors were quite expert hands at organizing an encampment, and at constructing a good ice-hut in case of need. They knew, as well as the native fishermen along the coast, how to cause the absorption of the dampness contained in their clothing by burying them under the snow; they were never at loss to distinguish between the blocks produced by the freezing of salt water and those due to the congealing of soft water; in fine, they seemed to have on their fingers' ends all those "tips and points" familiar to Arctic travelers.

That evening, after supper, the conversation, bearing not unnaturally on the geography of the north of Siberia, led Ortik to relate how himself and Kirschef had come through these parts.

"How is it," asked Mr. Sergius, "that you sailors should have tramped through this country?"

"Mr. Sergius," he replied, "two years ago, Kirschef. half a score of sailors, and myself, were at Arkhangel, waiting to get aboard some whaler, when we were hired to go to the relief of a ship that was in distress among the icebergs, north of the mouth of the Lena. Well, it is on our way from Arkhangel to this bay that we followed the northern coast of Siberia. When we reached the Seraski, we managed to set her afloat again, and we remained aboard for the fishing season. But, as I told you, she was wrecked that same season, and out of the whole crew, Kirschef and I were the only survivors. It was then we were driven by the storm on to the Liakhov Islands, where you found us."

216

"And you were never in the Alaskan provinces?" inquired Kayette, who, it will be remembered, spoke and understood Russian.

"Alaska?" said Ortik. "That's a country in America, isn't it?"

"Yes," said Mr. Sergius. "It lies in the northwest of the New World, it is Kayette's native country. Did your fishing excursions ever take you in that direction?"

"Don't know that part at all," replied Ortik, in the most natural tone of voice.

"We never went beyond the Strait of Behring," added Kirschef.

Once again the latter's voice produced its usual effect on the young woman, though she was utterly unable to recollect where she could have heard it. In any case, it could only have been in Alaska, since she had never been out of the country before.

However, after so explicit a reply from Ortik and Kirschef, Kayette, with that reserve natural to those of her race, asked no other question. But none the less, a prejudice—nay, an instinctive mistrust, toward the two sailors— remained fixed in her mind.

During this twenty-four hours' halt, the reindeer had been able to take all the rest they needed. Fettered though they were, they could go about, in the neighborhood of the encampment, and had been busy nibbling the shrubs and unearthing the mosses.

On the 20th of March, the little caravan set out at eight o'clock in the morning. The weather was bright and clear, the wind blowing from the northeast. The reindeer had been yoked four abreast, by means of a well-devised system of traces. They thus proceeded in four rows, guided on one side by Ortik and on the other by Clovy.

For six days they journeyed on without any occurrence worthy of mention. The most of the time, Mr. Sergius and Cascabel, John and Sander, went on foot throughout the whole day, and, now and then, Cornelia, Napoleona, and Kayette joined them, when no home duty kept them indoors.

Each forenoon, the *Fair Rambler* covered a koes, a Siberian measure of distance equivalent to twenty versts, say about eight miles. In the afternoon, its record was about the same, which made up five good leagues per day.

The 29th, after crossing on the ice the little river Olenck, Mr. Sergius and his companions reached the village of Maksimova, forty-two leagues southwest of the gulf of Lena.

There was no harm in Mr. Sergius stopping in this village, away in the extreme corner of the northern steppe. There was no Captain-Governor, no military post occupied by Cossacks; no cause of fear for Count Narkine's safety.

They were in the heart of the Iakout country, and the Cascabel party met with a kindly welcome at the hands of the inhabitants of Maksimova.

This country, hilly and wooded in the east and south. offers in the north nothing but vast level plains, enlivened here and there by a few clumps of trees, whose green foliage would soon be developed by the warm season. The plains produce an enormous quantity of hay, this being due to the fact that, while winter is very cold in hyperborean Siberia, the temperature is excessive during the summer months.

Here thrives a population of a hundred thousand Iakouts, who keep up the practices of the Russian rite. A religious, hospitable, moral people, they are grateful to Providence for the gifts they receive from her, and full of resignation when her hand weighs heavy upon them.

Along the road from Lena Bay to this village, a certain number of Siberian nomads had been met. They were strongly built men, of average height, flat-faced, dark-eyed, with thick heads of hair and no beard. The same types were found at Maksimova; their intelligence, their peaceful, sociable habits, and their industry, struck the visitors.

Those of the Iakouts who lead a nomadic life, always on horseback and always fully armed, are the owners of the numerous flocks scattered over the steppe. Those who live in the sedentary homes of the hamlets and villages are particularly given to fishing, and "make a living" out of the well-stocked waters of the thousand streams that the big river absorbs on its way to the sea.

However, gifted though they be with so many public and private virtues, they are too ready, it must be confessed, to make an excessive use of tobacco, and—what is of more consequence—of brandy and other spirituous liquors.

"To a certain extent they are excusable," observed John. "For three whole months they have nothing but water to drink, and the bark of the pine tree to eat."

While the nomads inhabit "yourts," a kind of cone-shaped tent, made of some white woven stuff, the sedentary tribes occupy wooden houses, constructed according to the taste and the requirements of each one. These houses are kept with care; the slope of the roofs is very steep, and thus aids the melting of the snow under the rays of the April sun.

Hence, this village of Maksimova has quite a smiling appearance. The men are of a pleasant type; their countenance is open, they look straight in one's eyes, and their physiognomy is not devoid of a certain air of pride. The women seem graceful and rather pretty, though tattooed. Very reserved in their ways and habits, they would never let themselves be seen bareheaded or barefooted.

The party was cordially received by the Iakout chiefs, the kinoes, as they are styled, and by the elders, or starsynas, that is, the notables of the place. Each of them would fain have given the newcomers free board and lodging; but, while thanking them for their kindness, Cornelia would hear of no other than money transactions, and among other things she gladly purchased a provision of oil, her stock of which was no longer equal to the possible demands of her culinary department.

On this occasion, of course, as on every other, the *Fair Rambler* had produced its usual effect. Never had a showman's wagon been seen in this country. Many were the visits paid to it by natives of both sexes, and there was no cause to regret having granted them the privilege. In this province, indeed, thieving is very uncommon, even from strangers. And should it occur, immediate punishment overtakes the offender. As soon as convicted, he is scourged before the public; then after the physical chastisement comes the moral punishment; branded for the remainder of his life with the stain of his guilt, the culprit is deprived of all civil rights and can never again recover the title of "honest man."

On the 3rd of April, our travelers stood on the banks of the Oden, a small river which throws itself into the Gulf of Anabara after a course of a hundred and fifty miles.

The weather, hitherto very favorable, began to show signs of a change. Presently, a heavy fall of rain occurred. The first effect of which was to begin the melting of the snow. It lasted for a whole week, during which the wagon had to sludge its way through mire and dangerous swamps whenever it had to pass through marshy localities. Thus did spring herald itself in this high latitude, with a temperature averaging two or three degrees above zero.

This stage occasioned great fatigue to our wayfarers. But they had every reason to congratulate themselves on the co-operation of the two Russian sailors, who proved as devoted as truly useful.

On the 8th following, the *Fair Rambler* had reached the right bank of the river Anabara, some forty leagues from Maksimova.

They were still in time to cross the stream on the ice, although the field had commenced to break lower down. They could even from this place hear the noise of the blocks rumbling away toward the gulf; one week later, they would have had to seek a practicable ford,—which would have been no easy task, for the waters rise very rapidly with the melting of the snows.

Already the steppe, grown green once more, was getting carpeted with a crop of fresh grass very welcome to the team. The shrubs were budding.

Before three weeks, the first leaflets would have burst out of their little cradles, along the stems. Nature was restoring new life, too, to the poor skeletons of the trees, that had been reduced to the state of dried wood by the cold of winter. Here and there, a few groves of birches and larch trees bowed their heads more readily under the softened breath of the breeze. All this hyperborean vegetation was reviving in the heat of the sun.

The provinces of Siberia in Asia are all the less desert, according as they are farther removed from the coast. Sometimes our troupe would meet a collector, on his way to gather the tax from village to village. They would stop and exchange a few words with the itinerant government official. He generally was not slow to accept the glass of vodka that was offered him; and then, with a hearty "safe home!" each party would go on its way.

One particular day the *Fair Rambler* fell in with a "convoy" of prisoners. The unfortunate wretches, sentenced to the salt-boiling establishments, were being led to the eastern confines of Siberia, and their Cossack escort spared them no evil treatment. Needless to say that Mr. Sergius's presence gave rise to no comment on the part of the commander of the escort; but Kayette, always suspicious of the Russian sailors, thought she noticed that they were anxious not to attract the attention of the Cossacks.

On the 19th of April, the wagon halted on the right bank of the Khatanga, which throws itself into the gulf of the same name. No more ice-bridge this time, no means of walking dry-footed to the opposite shore. A few drifting blocks were the last remnants of the breaking up of the ice. A fordable spot should needs be found, and a considerable delay might have ensued, had not Ortik discovered one about half a verst up stream. Nor was the river crossed without difficulty, the wagon being sunk into the water up to the axle-trees; this done, however, another stage of some seventy-five miles brought the *Fair Rambler* to the Lake Iege.

What a contrast, here, with the monotonous aspect of the steppe! It looked like an oasis in the middle of the sands of Sahara. Let a sheet of limpid water be imagined, with a girdle of evergreen trees, of pines and fir trees, clumps of shrubs in all the brightness of their fresh verdure, purple whortleberries, black "camarines," red currant trees, and briers just crowned by spring with budding flowers.

Under the cover of the thickish underwood, clustering yonder on the east and west of the lake, Wagrani and Marengo will surely be at no loss to raise some game, be it a quadruped or a fowl, if Mr. Cascabel will only let them ferret about for a couple of hours.

And besides, on the surface of the lake, geese, ducks, and swans are swimming in numerous bands. Overhead, couples of cranes and storks swoop through the air, on their way from the central parts of Asia. The beholder would well-nigh clap his hands with delight, at a sight so full of charms.

On the proposal of Mr. Sergius, it was agreed they should make a two days' halt amid this landscape. The encampment was pitched at the head of the lake, under shelter of some tall pine-trees, the tops of which arched over the water's edge.

Then the sportsmen of the troupe, followed by Wagram, "took their guns and away," after promising not to go too far. A quarter of an hour had scarce elapsed when their gun-shots commenced to be heard.

In the mean time, Mr. Cascabel and Sander, Ortik and Kirschef, resolved to try what a little fishing would bring along the bank of the lake. Their implements consisted merely of a few lines supplied with hooks, which they had bought from the natives at Port Clarence; but what more was required by fishermen worthy of the great art, and endowed with sufficient intelligence to cope with the cunning of a fish, and with patience enough to wait until he condescends to bite at their bait.

In reality, this last accomplishment was hardly necessary on the day in question; scarcely had the hooks reached a suitable depth when the floats at once began to bob at the surface of the water. So abundant was the fish that enough could have been caught in half a day to replace the meat on one's table from one end of Lent to the other. Young Sander was beside himself with delight; so much so, indeed, that when Napoleona came over and asked him to let her have the rod in her turn, he would not grant her request. This led to an argument and subsequently to the intervention of Cornelia. The latter, considering the fishing pastime had lasted long enough, ordered both the children and their father to gather up their tackle, and when Cornelia gave an order no time should be lost in complying with it.

Two hours later, Mr. Sergius and his friend John returned with their dog, who seemed to cast a wistful look of regret behind him at the half-explored thickets.

The sportsmen had not been less fortunate than the fishermen. For several days to come, the bill of fare would be as varied as excellent, what with the fish of Lake Iege and especially the splendid game indigenous to those territories of upper Siberia.

Among others, the sportsmen had brought home a number of those "karallys," which move about in companies, and a few couples of those silly little birds called "dikoutas," that are smaller than the wood-hen, but whose flesh is exquisite.

It is easy to imagine what a sumptuous dinner was prepared that day. The table had been laid under the trees, but none of the guests noticed that it was somewhat cool to banquet in the open air. Cornelia had surpassed herself with her grilled fish and roasted game. And as the supply of flour had been renewed at the last village, as well as the provision of Iakout butter, no wonder if the cake of former days, with its golden brown crust, made its appearance at dessert-time. Each one had a few good sips of brandy-wine, thanks to certain flasks that the villagers of Maksimova had consented to part with, and the day came to a close without any cloud darkening its restful peace.

One would readily have believed that the period of trials was over, and that the famous journey would be accomplished to the greater honor and profit of the Cascabel family!

Next day was another day of rest, which the reindeer most religiously observed by incessant feeding.

On the 24th of April, at six in the morning. the *Fair Rambler* was under way again, and four days after, the western confines of the Iakout district had been reached.

CHAPTER IX - RIGHT ON TO THE OBI

IT is useful to revert to the situation of the two Russians that some evil genius had thrown in the path of the Cascabel family.

It might be thought that, grateful for the welcome they had met with, Ortik and Kirschef had returned to better sentiments. No such thing had come to pass. After the many crimes they had already committed under Karnof, the wretches thought of nothing but fresh atrocities.

Their immediate aim was to get possession of the *Fair Rambler* and of the money restored by Tchou-Tchouk; then, having re-entered Russian soil under the disguise of showmen, they would resume their horrible life.

Now to carry out these plans, they should first "get rid" of their traveling companions, of the kind-hearted people to whom they were indebted for their liberty; this they would feel no hesitation about. But they would be unable to execute their designs without help; this is why they were making directly for one of the Ural passes frequented by the former accomplices of their evil deeds; there they would find as many lawless recruits as they needed to overpower the entire staff of the *Fair Rambler*.

Meanwhile, who could have suspected them of harboring such abominable intentions? They showed the utmost readiness to make themselves useful, and not a word of complaint had ever been uttered against them. While inspiring no sympathy, they aroused at least no feeling of mistrust,—save in the mind of Kayette, who could not overcome the first impression they had made upon her. Just for a moment the thought had flashed across her brain that it was on the night when Mr. Sergius had been assaulted on the Alaskan frontier that she had heard Kirschef's voice. But how could she believe that the murderers were the very two sailors they had afterwards found, nearly four thousand miles away from the spot, on one of the islands of the Liakhov Archipelago? So, while watching them closely, Kayette took good care to communicate her suspicions, in appearance so unlikely, to no one.

And now it is not amiss to mention, likewise, that if Ortik and Kirschef were suspicious in the eyes of the young girl, they, too, had their mischief-brooding instincts of curiosity aroused by Mr. Sergius's presence in the caravan. That a traveler, dangerously wounded on the frontier of Alaska, should have been picked up, nursed, and conveyed to Sitka by the Cascabels, was very natural. But, after his recovery, why had he not remained at Sitka? Why had he followed the showman's troupe to Port Clarence? Why was he even now accompanying them right across Siberia? The presence of a Russian in the ranks of itinerant artists was, to say the least, a strange occurrence.

And, one day, Ortik had whispered to Kirschef:

"Say, might not this fellow, Sergius, be trying to get back to Russia unknown to anybody? What do you say? May be there'd be something to be got out of that! I vote we keep our weather eye open on him."

And without suspecting it. Count Narkine was being spied by Ortik with a view to find his secret out.

On the 23d of April, the travelers left the Iakout district and entered the territory of the Ostiaks. A miserable, half-civilized tribe these are, though this part of Siberia contains several rich tracts,—among others that of Berezov. As they passed through the villages of this region, they could perceive how different they were from the attractive picturesqueness of the Iakout hamlets. Repulsive dens, hardly fit for cattle, where it were scarce possible to breathe, —and what an atmosphere!

Where else, indeed, could more loathsome beings be found than these natives, the following description of whom was read by John out of his "General Geography":

"The Ostiaks of upper Siberia wear a double garment to preserve themselves against the cold: it consists of a thick layer of greasy dirt on their skin and the hide of a reindeer over it."

As to their food, it is composed almost exclusively of half-raw fish and of meat which never undergoes any cooking process whatever.

Fortunately, the habits of the nomads—whose flocks are, here, also, scattered about over the steppe—do not exist in the same degree among the inhabitants of the chief villages. Thus at Starokhantaskii, our party found a population that was somewhat more presentable, though inhospitable and ill-disposed toward strangers.

The women, tattooed with bluish designs, wore the vakocham, a kind of red veil with blue stripes, a gaudily colored skirt, a lighter-shaded corset, whose defective make deforms their figure, and beneath it a wide belt, ornamented with round bells, which jingle at every movement they make, like the bells on the harness of a Spanish mule.

As to the men, during the winter season—and some of them still wore the winter fashions—they positively look like wild beasts, entirely wrapped up as they are in hides, the hair of which is turned outward. Their heads are covered over with the hood of the maltza and the parka, in which mere slits have been made for the eyes, the mouth, and the ears. Impossible to see one feature of their faces, however easily one might bear the privation.

Several times, along the road, our party met some of those sleds locally styled narkes, and usually drawn by three reindeer which, unencumbered by any other bar than a simple leather trace, which is passed under their chest, and a single rein fastened to their horns, can run on for twenty or twenty-five miles without taking breath.

Such performances were not to be expected from the team of the *Fair Rambler*; and in truth there was no cause to complain of their services, which were really valuable.

Commenting upon them, Mr. Sergius happened to remark, one day, that it might be prudent, perhaps, to substitute horses for them, as soon as they could get them:

"What, put horses in their place!" answered Mr. Cascabel. "Why so? Do you not think these animals will be able to bring us all the way to Russia?"

"If we were going to the north of Russia," replied Mr. Sergius, "I should feel no anxiety; but central Russia is very different. These reindeer support heat with great difficulty; it seems to overwhelm them and to render them unfit for any labor. And, as a proof, about the end of April, you see numerous flocks of them making their way toward the northern territories, and more especially the upper plateaux of the Ural, which are always covered with snow."

"Well, we shall see when we reach the frontier. My word, it will cost me something to part with them! Just imagine the effect, if I entered the Perm fair with twenty reindeer yoked to the chariot of the Cascabel family! What an impression it would create! What a glowing advertisement!"

"Evidently, it would be splendid," said Mr. Sergius with a smile.

"Triumphal, sir! Triumphal is the word! and, while we are on the subject, it is quite understood, of course, that Count Narkine is a member of my troupe, and that, an opportunity offering, he will have no objection to perform before the public?"

"That's understood."

"Then you must not neglect your legerdemain lessons, Mr. Sergius. As you are supposed to be practising for your own pleasure, neither my children nor the two sailors can feel surprised at it. And, do you know, you are getting on wonderfully quick!"

"How could I help it with such a teacher as I have, friend Cascabel?"

"I beg your pardon, Mr. Sergius, but I give you my word you possess very remarkable natural dispositions for the art. With a little practice, you would become a first-class juggler, and make money at it, too!"

On May the 6th, the Ienisei was sighted, some three hundred miles from lake Iege.

The Ienisei is one of the chief rivers of the Siberian continent, and throws itself into the Arctic Sea on the gulf of the same name, under the seventieth parallel.

By this time, not one iceberg was left on the surface of the wide river. A large ferry, for the use of vehicles as well as passengers, from one bank to the other, enabled the little caravan to cross the stream with its full complement of men and cattle, but at the cost of a rather heavy toll.

On the other side, the steppe again with its endless horizons. Not unfrequently, groups of Ostiaks might be seen performing their religious duties. Although most of them have been baptized, the Christian religion seems to have no very strong hold on them, and they still continue to kneel before the heathenish idols of the Shaitans. These are human-faced idols, hewn in large blocks of wood, a small model of which, ornamented with a brass cross, is to be found in every house, nay, in every cabin.

It would appear that the Ostiak priests, the Schamans, as they are called, derive a good living out of this double-sided religion, not to speak of the great influence they wield over these fanatics, at the same time Christians and idolaters. None but an eye-witness could believe the earnestness with which these unfortunates wriggle and struggle, like people in epileptic fits, in the presence of their idols.

The first time young Sander saw a half-dozen of those possessed beings, he of course proceeded at once to imitate them, walking on his hands, disjointing his hips, bending backward, capering heels over head like a clown, and winding up his performance with a series of frog-leaps.

"I see, my child," said the father, who had instantly turned his critical eye on the exercises, "that you have lost none of your suppleness. That's right, that's right! We must not get rusty! Think of the Perm fair! The honor of the Cascabel family is at stake!"

On the whole, the journey had proceeded without too much fatigue since the *Fair Rambler* had left the mouth of the Lena. Sometimes a detour had to be made round thick forests of pines and birch trees, which varied the monotony of the plains, but through which there was no beaten track.

Indeed, the country was almost desert. Miles of ground were traversed without meeting a hamlet or even a farm. The population is extremely scarce, and the Berezov district, which is the richest, does not contain more than 15,000 inhabitants on an area of 3000 kilometers. By way of compensation, and probably for that very reason, the region swarms with game.

Mr. Sergius and John could, therefore, indulge their sporting tastes to their hearts' content, at the same time as they stocked up Mrs. Cascabel's larder. Most part of the time they were accompanied by Ortik, who gave proofs of remarkable skill. It is by thousands that the hares scour the plains, not to mention the feathered tribe, the numbers of which are countless. Elks, too, there were, and deer and wild reindeer, and even huge-sized boars, formidable brutes, which our gunmen prudently abstained from disturbing.

As to birds, there were ducks and plungeons, geese, thrushes, heath-hens and hazel-hens, storks, and white partridges. Quite a variety, as may be seen! Hence, whenever a shot had been wasted on a slightly inferior game, Cornelia did not hesitate to throw it to the dogs, who gladly received their mistress's gift.

This abundance of fresh game naturally resulted in good living; such good living indeed that Mr. Cascabel was inclined to preach sobriety to his artists.

"Children, take care you don't get fat," he would repeat to them. "Fat is the ruin of your joints. It is the bane of the acrobat! You eat too much! Come, moderate your appetite! Sander, I do believe you are getting stout! Stout at your age, for shame!"

"Father, I assure you!"

"None of your protestations. I have a great mind to measure you around the body every evening, and if I find any sign of embonpoint, I'll take the fat out of you!—It's just like that fellow Clovy! A blind man would see the fat accumulating on him!"

"On me, boss?"

"Yes, on you! And a clown has no business to get fat, especially when he rejoices in the name of Clovy! Why, in no time you'll be as round as a beer-barrel!"

"Unless, in my old days, I turn to a plantation pole!" replied Clovy, as he tightened his belt one hole higher.

The *Fair Rambler* had soon to get over the Taz, which pours out its waters into the gulf of Ienisei, just about the point where our itinerary cut the Arctic polar circle to enter the temperate zone. It may be seen thereby how obliquely it had leaned to the southwest since the Liakhov Islands had been left behind.

In this connection, Mr. Sergius, who always found an appreciative audience, thought it right to explain what this polar circle was, beyond which, during summer, the sun never rises more than twenty-three degrees above the horizon.

John, who already possessed certain notions of cosmography, understood the explanation. But despite all the efforts of his intellectual powers, Mr. Cascabel was unable to get that polar circle into his brain.

"In the way of circles," he said, "those I know best are the hoops that the riders jump through, round the ring! After all, that is no reason why we should not drink the very good health of this one!"

And accordingly, the toast of the polar circle was honored with a good bottle of brandy-wine, just as the line is feted when ships cross from one hemisphere to the other.

The Taz was not crossed without some difficulty. No ferry plied across this little river and a fordable spot had to be found,—which required several hours. Again did the two Russians display the greatest zeal; and on several occasions, the wheels of the wagon having sunk into the soft bed of the stream, they readily set to work, with water up to their waist.

Less trouble was experienced, on the 16th of May, to get to the other bank of the Pour, a narrow river with a shallow bed and a slow current.

By the beginning of June the heat had become excessive, a fact which always seems anomalous in countries belonging to so high a latitude. During the last fortnight of the month, the thermometer marked from twenty-five to thirty degrees. As there was no shade whatever along the steppe. Mr. Sergius and his companions were severely taxed by this temperature. Even the night did not temper the sultriness of the day, for, at that period, the sun hardly disappeared beneath the horizon of these immense plains. After a slight dip to the north, its disk, like a ball of iron at white heat, at once rises again to resume its daily course.

"That nasty sun!" Cornelia went on repeating, as she wiped the perspiration from her face. "What an oven we are in! If we only could have had this in winter!"

"Then, winter would have been summer," remarked Mr. Sergius.

"Just so!" said Cascabel. "But what strikes me as bad management is, that we have not one single lump of ice to cool ourselves with, after having had considerably more than we needed, for whole months together."

"Come, friend Cascabel, if we had ice, it would be a sign that the weather was cold, and if it was cold—"

"It would not be hot! You are always right, Mr. Sergius!"

"Unless it was half and half!" Clovy deemed it right to add.

"That would be better still!" continued Mr. Cascabel "All the same, it's powerfully hot!"

It must not be supposed that the sportsmen had laid up their guns, for all that. The only difference was that they started very early in the morning, and a capital plan they found it. Indeed, they were rewarded, one day, with a splendid capture, all the honor of which fell to John. So large was this game that they had some trouble to fetch it home. Its coat was short; in the front part of the body, the hair was reddish and looked as if it had been gray during the winter months; along its back ran a yellow streak; its long horns curved gracefully over its head.

"What a beautiful reindeer!" exclaimed Sander.

"Oh, John!" said Napoleona, with a tinge of reproach in her voice, "why did you kill a reindeer?"

"To eat it, my little pet."

"And I am so fond of them."

"Why," rejoined Sander, "since you are so fond of them you can eat as much of this one as you like; there will be enough for everybody!"

"Don't fret about it, my darling," said Mr. Sergius. "That animal is not a reindeer!"

"What is it, then?" asked the child.

"It is an argali."

Mr. Sergius spoke true. These animals, which inhabit the mountains during winter and the plains in summer, are, strictly speaking, overgrown sheep.

"Very well," observed Mr. Cascabel, "since it is a sheep, Cornelia, we shall have mutton chops on the gridiron, if you please."

And it was done accordingly. And as the flesh of the argali is extremely savory, it is probable that the manager of the troupe may have acquired, on that day, a little more embonpoint than was in accordance with the exigencies of his profession.

From this point forward, the track of the *Fair Rambler* toward the Obi lay through an almost barren country. The Ostiak villages became scarcer and scarcer; seldom did they meet, here and there, a few groups of nomads migrating toward the Eastern provinces. Nor was it without good reasons that Mr. Sergius sought in preference the least populated parts of this district; and it was important to avoid the large town of Berezov, situated a little beyond the Obi. Incased within a magnificent forest of cedars spread out in terrace fashion on the flank of a steep hill, surmounted by the steeple of its two churches, watered by the Sosva, on which incessantly ply the numerous vessels of the trading community, this city, with its two hundred houses, is the center of a largely frequented market, to which are conveyed the products of northern Siberia.

It was evident that the arrival of the *Fair Rambler* at Berezov would of necessity attract the curiosity of the public, and the police would not have failed to scrutinize rather closely the individual members of the Cascabel family. Better keep away from Berezov and even from the district of that name. Policemen are policemen; and, especially when they are Cossacks, it is more prudent to have no dealings with them.

This disinclination, however, on the part of Mr. Sergius, to pass by Berezov did not escape the notice of Ortik and Kirschef, and confirmed their suspicions that he was a Russian trying to re-enter Russia secretly.

The first week of the month of June had gone by when a slight modification was made in the itinerary, in order to cut to the north of Berezov. It was, at most, a detour of some thirty miles; and, on the 16th of the month, after having for some time followed the stream of a large river, the little caravan encamped on its right bank.

This river was the Obi.

The *Fair Rambler* had covered close on five hundred and fifty miles since it had left the basin of the Pour. A distance of barely three hundred miles now separated it from the European frontier. The chain of the Urals, the partition line between these two parts of the world, would soon terminate the horizon.

CHAPTER X - FROM THE OBI TO THE URAL MOUNTAINS

THE Obi, fed by the waters of the Ural on the west, and by numerous tributaries on the east, spreads over a distance of 4500 kilometers, and its basin does not contain less than 330,000,000 hectares.

Geographically speaking, this river might have served as a natural boundary line between Asia and Europe, if the Urals had not stood a little to the west of its course. From the sixtieth degree of latitude the river and the mountain run almost parallel. And whilst the Obi goes and throws itself into the vast gulf of that name, the extreme ramifications of the Ural are sunk deep beneath the Sea of Kara.

Mr. Sergius and his companions, standing on its right bank, contemplated the course of the river and the many willow-tufted islets with which it is dotted. Close to the river bank, aquatic plants waved to and fro their sharp-edged blades, now bright with fresh blooms. Up and down the stream, numbers of vessels glided along the cool and limpid waters, purified by their passage through the filter of the mountains, where they have their springs.

The boat service was regularly organized on this important artery, and, in consequence, the *Fair Rambler* was able to reach Mouji village, on the opposite bank, easily.

It is, in truth, but a small village, and as such was safe for Count Narkine, not being used as a military post. It was, however, becoming urgent to obtain duly legalized documents; for, the foot of the mountains was now within short distance, and the Russian authorities insisted on seeing the papers of every traveler who presented himself at the frontier. Mr. Cascabel, accordingly, resolved to get his papers duly "regularized" by the Mayor of Mouji: This formality having been fulfilled, Mr. Sergius, being comprised among the artists of the troupe, would succeed in entering the territory of the Russian empire without arousing the suspicions of the police.

Why should a deplorable misadventure have compromised a plan that seemed so easy of execution? Why were Ortik and Kirschef there, determined to mar its success? Why were they on the eve of bringing the *Fair Rambler* through one of the most dangerous passes of the Ural, where they would surely fall in with whole bands of malefactors?

And, meanwhile, Mr. Cascabel, who little dreamt of such a denouement, and could not therefore do anything to prevent it, congratulated himself on the successful prospects of his bold undertaking. After making his way through Western America and the whole of Northern Asia, here he was within 300 miles of the European frontier! His wife and his children, in perfect health, showed no signs of the fatigues of so long a journey. True, he had felt his courage fail at the time of the catastrophe in Behring Strait and during the drift on the Polar Sea; but he had proved himself more than a match for the "fools" on Liakhov Islands, and had made them enable the *Fair Rambler* to continue its journey through the continent.

"Verily, God does well what he does!" he would often say to himself.

A stay of twenty-four hours in this village of Mouji had been agreed upon. The inhabitants gave a cordial greeting to the new-comers, and Mr. Cascabel received, in its time, the visit of the gorodintschy, or mayor of the locality.

This official personage, somewhat distrustful of strangers, deemed it his duty to ask a few questions of the head of the family. The latter at once produced his "census paper," on which Mr. Sergius was entered as one of the troupe.

The worthy mayor was not without a little feeling of surprise at seeing a countryman of his among French performers; for he had not failed to remark that Mr. Sergius was a Russian, and he drew Cascabel's attention to the fact.

The latter begged of him to observe that if there was a Russian among them, there was likewise an American in the person of Clovy, and an Indian in the person of Kayette. He was never concerned with the nationality of his artists; the all-important question with him was their talents. And he immediately added that the said artists would be but too happy if His Worship the Mayor,—this sounded better on Cæser Cascabel's lips than gorodintschy, —His Worship the Mayor would kindly permit them to perform in his presence!

His Worship was highly gratified by the proposal, which he straightway accepted, and promised to sign the papers after the performance.

As to Ortik and Kirschef, as they were entered on the list as shipwrecked Russian sailors on their way home, no difficulty was made about them.

Accordingly, in the course of the same evening, the whole troupe repaired to the residence of the gorodintschy.

It was a pretty large house, with a fine coat of yellow paint, in remembrance of Alexander I, who was particularly fond of that color. On the wall of the drawing-room hung an image of the Virgin Mary, accompanied by the portraits of some Russian saints, looking their best in their silvered frames. Benches and stools had been placed in readiness for the mayor, his wife, and his three daughters. Half a dozen notables of the locality had been invited to share the enjoyment of this soiree, while the simple ratepayers of Mouji, huddled around the house, had the privilege of peeping in through the windows.

The Cascabel family was greeted with much sympathy. The exercises were commenced, and no one would have thought that the performers had neglected their rehearsals for several weeks. Young Sander's dislocations were highly appreciated, as was Napoleona's gracefulness; she had no tight rope at her disposal, and executed a step de circonstance, to the delight of the spectators. With his bottle juggling, his plates, his rings, and his balls, John astonished the beholders. After which, Mr. Cascabel's exhibition of muscular power proved him the worthy husband of Cornelia, who, on this occasion, carried two of the Mouji notables on her outstretched arms.

As to Mr. Sergius, he very cleverly went through several legerdemain tricks which his eminent professor had taught him,—not uselessly, as it now appeared. No doubt could now exist in His Worship's mind regarding the genuineness of this Russian's engagement in the itinerant troupe.

Jams, currant cakes, and excellent tea were then served all round. Then, the soirée having come to an end, the mayor signed without hesitation all the papers that Cascabel presented to him. The *Fair Rambler* was now legally in a position to face the Russian authorities.

It is worthy of notice, moreover, that the good mayor, a man in easy circumstances, felt bound to offer Mr. Cascabel a score of roubles in return for his performance.

Mr. Cascabel felt inclined, at first, to decline any renumeration; but, on the part of an itinerant showman, this might have seemed a strange proceeding.

"After all," he said to himself, "twenty roubles is twenty roubles!"

And with a "world of thanks" he pocketed the sum.

The following day was devoted to rest. There were a few purchases to make, of flour, rice, butter, and various drinks, which Cornelia was able to obtain at reasonable prices. She would not think of renewing her stock of preserves in this poor village; but game was likely to be plentiful between the Obi and the European frontier.

By twelve o'clock, all the "shopping" had been done. Dinner-time came, and around the festive board there were two very sad hearts. Did not John and Kayette see the time draw near when they should part?

What would Mr. Sergius do when he had seen his father, Prince Narkine? It being impossible for him to remain in Russia, would he set out again for America, or would he stay in Europe? All this, it may be surmised, gave Cascabel great food for reflection. He would fain have his mind fixed on the subject, and accordingly, that same day after dinner, he asked Mr. Sergius if he would care to "come out for a stroll."

The latter, feeling that his friend wished to have a private talk with him, readily acceded to the proposal.

Just then the two sailors were bidding good-by to the family, intending, they said, to wind up the day at some tavern or another in the village.

And so, Mr. Sergius and Mr. Cascabel left the *Fair Rambler*, walked a few hundred paces out of the village and sat down by the edge of a small wood.

"Mr. Sergius," said Cæser, "if I have asked you to take a little ramble, it is because I would like to have a few words with you, by ourselves, concerning your situation—"

"My situation, my friend!"

"Or rather what your situation will compel you to do when you are in Russia."

"In Russia?"

"Well, I am not wrong,—am I?—in reckoning that we shall be on the other side of the Urals in about ten days, and that we shall reach Perm in a week's time after that."

"That's very probable, if there is no obstacle in the way."

"Obstacles! Not one obstacle will there be!" replied Cascabel. "You will cross the frontier without the shadow of a difficulty! Our papers are in due form, you belong to my troupe, and who would ever dream that Count Narkine is one of my artists?"

"Nobody, of course, since the secret has been told to no living soul but Mrs. Cascabel and yourself, and that it has been kept—"

"As sacred as if she and I had carried it to our graves," interrupted the showman, with much genuine dignity. "And now, Mr. Sergius, would it be an indiscretion on my part to ask you what you propose doing when the *Fair Rambler* halts in the streets of Perm?"

"I shall make all haste to the chateau of Walska, to see my father!" burst from the lips of Mr. Sergius. "It will be a great joy for him, a very unexpected joy, for it is now thirteen months since he has heard from me; thirteen long months since I had my last opportunity of writing to him! What must be his thoughts!"

"Do you intend making a pretty long stay with Prince Narkine?"

"That depends on circumstances that I cannot foresee. If my presence at home is suspected, I may see myself compelled to leave my father!—And still,—at his age—"

"Mr. Sergius, it is not for me to give you any advice. Better than any one else, you know how you should act. But, let me beg of you to observe that you will be exposed to very great dangers if you remain in Russia! Should you ever be discovered, your very life would be at stake!"

"I know that, friend, just as I know the dangers that would threaten you and yours if ever the police came to know that you have aided my return on Russian soil!"

"As to that, my folks and myself are out of consideration in this matter."

"Not at all, my dear Cascabel, and I shall never forget what all of you have done for me!"

"That is all right and square, Mr. Sergius; we did not come here to exchange protestations of friendship. Come! We must have an understanding about what you mean to do at Perm."

"Nothing simpler! Since I am one of your troupe, I shall stay with you so as to arouse no suspicion."

"But Prince Narkine—?"

"Walska is but six versts out of town, and each evening, when the performance is over, I can easily make my way there, without being noticed. Our servants would let themselves be killed before they would betray or compromise their master. Thus I can spend a few hours with my father and return to Perm before daybreak."

"That's settled, Mr. Sergius, and so long as we stay in Perm things will get on smoothly, I hope. But when the fair comes to a close, and when the *Fair Rambler* will depart for Nijni, and then for France—"

That, evidently, was the knotty point. What would Count Narkine determine to do after the Cascabels had left Perm? Would he remain concealed at the chateau of Walska? Would he still keep on Russian territory, at the risk of being discovered? Mr. Cascabel's inquiry was definite.

"My dear friend," replied Mr. Sergius to him, "many a time and oft have I asked myself that question: 'What shall I do?' and to this day I am utterly unable to answer it; that is all I can say to you. My conduct will be dictated by circumstances."

"Well then," continued Mr. Cascabel, "suppose you were obliged to leave Walska, suppose you could not remain in Russia, where your liberty, your very life would be in danger, do let me ask you, Mr. Sergius, if you would think of returning to America."

"I have formed no plan whatever in that direction," was the count's reply.

"Pray, Mr. Sergius, excuse me if I insist. Why might you not come to France with us? By continuing in my troupe, you could pass the western frontier without danger. Would not this be the safest plan? And then, in that way. we would have you a little longer with us, and our dear little Kayette, too!—Not that I would take her from you. the poor child! She is, and she will be, your adopted daughter, sir; and that is rather better than being a sister to John, Sander, and Napoleona, the children of a showman!"

"My friend," replied Mr. Sergius, "let us not speak of what the future may have in store for us. Who knows if it will not grant to each of us the wish of his own heart? Let us now see to the present, that is the essential point! What I can say to you with certainty—but pray breathe not a word of it to any one— is, that in the event of my being compelled to leave Russia, I should be very happy to retire to France, and there wait until some political event might, perchance, alter my position. And then, as it is home you are now going—"

"That's it! That's it! You'll come home with me!" burst out César Cascabel, and he had clutched the exile's hand, and hugged it, and pressed it, as though he would fain rivet it to his own.

At length they returned to the encampment, where the two sailors did not put in an appearance till the next day.

Off went the team at early morn and struck for the west.

For the several days that followed, the heat was very great. Already the first undulations of the Ural chain began to be felt, and the gradual rising of the ground told severely on the reindeer, already oppressed by the temperature.

On the 28th of June, over two hundred miles from the Obi, the *Fair Rambler* entered the little village of Verniky. Here a peremptory demand for the papers was followed by their immediate production, to the complete satisfaction of the authorities. Then the wagon resumed its course toward the chain of the Ural, two peaks of which, the Telpoes and the Nintchour, rose over yonder horizon to a height of from four to five thousand feet.

No great speed was made; yet there was no time to be lost, so as to be in Perm for the best part of the fair.

In view, indeed, of the performances to be given there, Mr. Cascabel now insisted on everybody rehearsing his exercises. It was their duty to keep intact the fame of French acrobats, artists, gymnasts, equilibrists, and clowns in general and the reputation of the Cascabel family in particular. And hence, the artists had now to get into training during the evening halts. Mr. Sergius himself toiled and moiled toward perfection in those card-tricks and sleights of hand for which his teacher had discovered in him such a wonderful natural aptitude.

"What an artist you would have made!" he would continually say to him.

On the 3d of July, the troupe encamped in a clearing encircled with birch trees, pines, and larch trees, overtopped by the alpine-like crests of the Ural.

It was on the following day that they were to venture into one of the passes of the chain under the guidance of Ortik and Kirschef, and they foresaw if not serious fatigues at least very uphill work, in more senses than one, until the highest level of the gorge had been attained.

As this part of the frontier, usually frequented by smugglers and deserters, was not very safe, they would do well to keep continually on the defensive; and certain measures were adopted with an eye thereto.

In the course of the evening the conversation fell on the difficulties that might have to be encountered during the crossing of the mountain. Ortik loudly stated that the pass he had indicated, a pass named the Petchora, was one of the most practicable along the whole chain. He knew it for having gone through it when Kirschef and he were on their way from Arkhangel to the Baltic Sea, going to the relief of the Seraski.

While Mr. Sergius and Ortik were engaged on this subject, Cornelia, Napoleona, and Kayette were busy with the supper. An appetizing quarter of a deer was roasting before a fire that had been lit under the trees, and a rice pudding was acquiring its due golden-brown tint in a tin laid on a heap of live coals.

"I do hope there will be no complaints about the bill of fare to-night!" said the good housewife.

"Unless the roast and the pudding get burnt!" Clovy felt bound to suggest.

"And why should they get burnt, Mr. Clovy?" asked Cornelia, "if you only take care to keep on turning the spit of the one and stirring the tin of the other!"

Clovy took the hint, and began mounting his guard. Wagram and Marengo kept him company by the fire, and John Bull, too, squatted hard by, licking his lips in anticipation of his share of the banquet.

In due time supper was laid and gave rise to a veritable concert of praise, which Cornelia and her help received with genuine satisfaction.

When bedtime came, as the temperature had risen still higher, Mr. Sergius, César Cascabel and his two sons, Clovy and the two sailors said they would sleep out in the clearing under shelter of the trees. It would, besides, be easier for them to watch over the *Fair Rambler*.

Cornelia, Kayette, and Napoleona alone sought the comfort of their little couches indoors.

six
With a July twilight, the duration of which seems indefinite in this seventieth parallel, it was after eleven o'clock when the night had about fallen, —a moonless night, besprinkled with stars, drowned, so to say, in the mists of the upper zones.

Stretched on the grass, and wrapped up in blankets, Mr. Sergius and his companions felt their eyelids close in their first sleep when the two dogs began to give various tokens of agitation. They would sniff the air repeatedly, and would growl in that peculiar way so expressive of extreme uneasiness.

John stood up first and cast a look around the clearing.

The fire was dying away and profound darkness reigned under the thick canopy of the trees. John made a closer survey and thought he saw luminous dots moving about, like so many red coals, in the dark. Wagram and Marengo were now barking loudly.

"Danger!" cried out John. "Danger!"

In a moment the sleepers were on their feet.

"What is it?" asked his father.

"Look there, father!" said John, pointing to the shining spots, now still and motionless in the dark background of the thicket.

"What can those be?"

"Wolves' eyes!"

"Yes, they are wolves!" said Ortik.

"And a whole band of them!" added Mr. Sergius.

"By Jove!" exclaimed Mr. Cascabel.

"By Jove!" was an inadequate expression to convey the full gravity of the situation. There might be hundreds of wolves all around the clearing; and these animals are truly formidable when they are in large numbers.

Just then Cornelia, Kayette, and Napoleona appeared at the door of the *Fair Rambler*.

"Well, father?" inquired the little girl.

"It's nothing, only wolves having a little stroll by moonlight! Stay where you are, and just hand us our guns to keep them at a safe distance."

Immediately guns and revolvers were cocked.

"Call back the dogs!" said Mr. Sergius.

Wagram and Marengo, who had ventured toward the edge of the wood, came back at John's bidding, a prey tea terror which it was hard to control.

238

A general volley was fired in the direction of the luminous points, and frightful howls showed that most of the shots had hit their marks.

But the number of wolves must have been considerable, for the circle seemed to close around, and a half hundred of them invaded the clearing.

"Quick! Back to the wagon!" exclaimed Mr. Sergius.

"They are coming down upon us! There alone can we defend ourselves!"

"What about the reindeer?" remarked John.

"We can do nothing to save them!"

And sure enough, it was now too late. Already some of the animals, had been devoured, whilst the others had broken their fetters and run away into the depths of the wood.

On Mr. Sergius's order, all retired inside the *Fair Rambler* with the two dogs, and the front door was closed.

It was high time! In the glimmer of the twilight the wolves could be seen bounding against the vehicle and leaping up to the height of the windows.

"What will become of us now, without a team?" Cornelia could not help saying.

"Let us get rid of this legion, first!" replied Mr. Sergius.

"Surely we'll manage to do that, somehow; come!" exclaimed her husband.

"Yes, if there are not too many of them," remarked Ortik.

"And suppose we don't run short of powder," added Kirschef.

"In the mean time, fire!" ordered Mr. Sergius.

And a murderous discharge flew through the half-opened windows. By the light of the shots fired from the two sides and the back of the wagon, they saw a score of wolves lying on the ground, either mortally or grievously wounded. But nothing seemed to check the rage of the brutes; their number appeared in no way lessened, and several hundreds of them by this time crowded the clearing, now alive with their restless silhouettes.

Some had crept under the wagon and endeavored to claw the panels out. Others had leaped on the front platform and would have burst the door open, had it not been barricaded from the inside just in time. Others again had even climbed on to the roof, leaned over the ledge down to the windows, struck at them with their paws, and persisted in their mad attempt until a bullet brought them to the ground.

Napoleona, greatly frightened, could not be kept from crying aloud. The fear of the wolf, so intense among children, was, in her case, but too fully justified in the present instance. Kayette, who was cool and composed, in vain endeavored to calm her little friend. Nor did Mrs. Cascabel herself, it must be confessed, feel very sanguine on the issue of this veritable battle.

As a matter of fact, should the assault continue much longer, the situation would become more and more dangerous. How could the *Fair Rambler* withstand the efforts of these numberless wolves? And, should it ever be upset, would not the horrible mangling of all its occupants be the inevitable consequence? Now the "engagement" had lasted for about half an hour when Kirschef suddenly growled:

"There'll be no more ammunition, presently!"

Some twenty cartridges were all that remained for the supply of the rifles and the revolvers.

"We must not fire, now," said Mr. Cascabel, "except when we are sure of our mark."

Sure of their mark?.... Did not every shot hit its mark in this mass of assailants? Unfortunately the wolves were far more numerous than the bullets; their numbers kept on increasing while the firearms would soon be reduced to silence. What would be done then? Wait for daylight? And what if the light of day did not put the wolves to flight?

It was then that Mr. Cascabel, brandishing his revolver, so soon fated to be useless, cried out:

"I have an idea!"

"An idea?" inquired Mr. Sergius.

"Yes, and a good one! The only thing is to capture one or two of those devils."

"How will you do that?" asked Cornelia.

"We shall just half-open the door with great caution and seize on the first two that will try to force their way in."

"Do you really mean it, Cascabel?"

"What risk do we run, Mr. Sergius? A few bites? Well, I'd rather be bitten than torn to pieces."

"Very well; then let it be done quickly!" said Mr. Sergius, though he did not exactly know what Cascabel was about.

The latter, with Ortik, Clovy and Kirschef behind him, posted himself in the first compartment while John and Sander kept back the dogs in the innermost one, where the women had been ordered to stay.

The articles of furniture, used to bar the door, were removed, and Mr. Cascabel opened it in such a way as to be able to shut it again quickly.

At that very moment a dozen wolves, crowding the platform and hanging on to the steps, were positively storming the forepart of the wagon.

No sooner was the door ajar than one of them rushed in headlong. Kirschef closed it again immediately.

In a trice Mr. Cascabel had overpowered the animal, with Ortik's help, and thrown over his head a piece of cloth he had provided himself with, and which he fastened tightly round its neck.

The door was opened a second time; and a second wolf underwent the same treatment as the first.

It needed the united efforts of Clovy, Ortik, and Kirschef to keep the raging brutes under control.

"Above all, don't kill them," Mr. Cascabel would say to them; "and hold them tight!"

Not kill them?.... What on earth did he mean to do with them? Give them an engagement in his troupe for the Perm fair?

What he meant to do, what he did do with them, his companions were not long to know.

The next moment a flame of fire lit up the compartment, which was filled, at the same time, with frantic howls of pain; one of the windows was thrown wide open, and away the two wolves were hurled through the air.

The effect produced by their appearance among the besiegers could be seen all the better as the clearing now gradually filled with moving torches.

Cascabel had thoroughly soaked the two wolves with paraffine and then set them ablaze; and it was in that state they had joined their companions.

Well, that idea of Mr. Cascabel's had been a grand idea, like all those that came out of his wonderful head. The wolves, maddened with terror, were all taking to flight. away from the two burning animals. And what yells they uttered now, far more terrible than those which had been heard at the beginning of the attack! In vain did the two paraffined brutes struggle to extinguish their blazing fur, blinded as they were by the hood tied over their heads. In vain they rolled themselves on the ground and leaped about in the middle of the band; the fire was unquenchable.

At last, the whole panic-stricken legion quitted the encampment, rushed out of the clearing, and disappeared in the depths of the wood.

The howls became fewer, and finally silence reigned all round the *Fair Rambler*.

By way of precaution, Mr. Sergius recommended his friends to wait till daylight before venturing forth to reconnoiter. But, in reality, no new attack was to be dreaded. The enemy had dispersed, and was fleeing as fast as their legs could run.

"Ah, César!" sobbed Cornelia, as she threw herself in her husband's arms.

"Ah, my friend!" said Mr. Sergius.

"Ah, father!" exclaimed the children.

"Ah, boss!" blubbered Clovy.

"Well, well, what's it all about?" quietly replied Cascabel. "If a man had no more brains than wolves, what would be the use of being a man?"

CHAPTER XI - THE URAL MOUNTAINS

THE chain of the Ural is deserving of the tourist's visit, quite as much, at least, as are the Pyrenees and the Alps. In the language of the Tartars, the word "Ural" signifies "belt," and here we have, in very truth, a belt stretching from the Caspian to the Arctic Sea over a distance of 2900 kilometers,—a belt ornamented with precious stones, enriched with fine metals, gold, silver and platinum,—a belt girt around the loins of the old continent, between Asia and Europe. A vast orographic system, it pours its waters through the beds of the Ural River, the Kara, the Petchora, the Kama, and a number of tributaries fed by the melting of the snows. A superb barrier of granite and quartz, it shoots up its needles and peaks to an average height of 2300 yards above the level of the ocean.

To our travelers, the Urals were suggestive of other thoughts besides.

And, first of all, while crossing the chain they would find it difficult to avoid those villages, those zavodys, those numerous hamlets, the population of which owes its origin to the former workmen employed in the mines. On the other hand, on its way through these grand defiles, Mr. Cascabel's troupe need have no fear of military posts, since their papers were duly legalized. And even though they had struck the range in its central part, they would have had no hesitation to follow the beautiful Ekaterinburg road, one of the most frequented in that region, so as to emerge from the mountain on the territory of the government of that name. But, since Ortik's itinerary had brought them farther north, it was better to enter the pass of the Petchora, and go down, afterwards, as far as Perm.

That is what they proposed doing on the very next morning.

When daylight came, they were able to ascertain how considerable the number of their assailants had been. Should they have succeeded in forcing their way into the *Fair Rambler*, not one of its occupants would have survived the carnage.

Two or three scores of wolves lay dead on the ground,—of those large-sized wolves, so formidable to the wayfarers across the steppe. The main body had fled as if the devil was after them; and even he could hardly have "made it hotter" for them. As to the two paraffined animals, their charred remains were discovered a few hundred paces away from the clearing.

And now, one question had to be solved: at this end of the Petchora pass, the *Fair Rambler* was at a considerable distance from the nearest zavody, for there are few of them on the eastern side of the Ural.

"How shall we manage?" asked John. "Our reindeer have run away—"

"If they had only run away," answered Mr. Cascabel, "we might perhaps get them back again; but it is very probable the poor things were devoured last night!"

"Yes, the poor things!" repeated Napoleona. "I was so fond of them; just as fond as I was of Vermont and Gladiator."

"And they would have been food for the wolves, if they had not drowned," said Sander.

"Just what would have happened them!" added Cæser Cascabel, heaving a deep sigh. "But how are we to replace our deer?"

"I shall start off at once to the nearest village," said Mr. Sergius, "and get horses at any price. If Ortik can show me the way—"

"Ready to go when you like, sir," replied Ortik.

"Evidently," added Cascabel, "that is the only thing to be done!"

And it would have been done, that same morning, if, to the astonishment of all, two of the reindeer had not been seen coming back across the clearing about eight o'clock.

Sander was the first to perceive them.

"Father!" he cried, "father! Here they are! They are coming home!"

"What, alive?"

"Well, these two don't look as if they had been entirely devoured, since they walk—"

"Unless the wolves had left them their legs!" suggested Clovy.

"Oh, the good creatures!" exclaimed Napoleona. "I must go and give them a kiss!"

And running to her two lost pets, she threw her arms around their necks and embraced them heartily.

But, alas, two of them could not have drawn the *Fair Rambler*. Luckily, several others presently began to appear by the edge of the wood, and, within an hour, fourteen had mustered back out of the twenty that had come from Tourkeff.

"Hurrah for the reindeer!" shouted young Sander. "Only, it's a pity they don't know what I'm crying out!"

The six animals, now missing, had been devoured by the wolves ere they had time to snap their fetters off, and their carcasses were afterwards found in the vicinity. The fourteen others had run away, on the approach of the wild beasts, and instinct now brought them back to the camp.

No need to tell how the good creatures were welcomed home. With them, the wagon could now resume its journey on through the defile of the Ural. Every one would put his shoulder to the wheel in the more difficult passes, and Mr. Cascabel would be able to make his triumphal entry into Perm.

What troubled him, however, was that the *Fair Rambler* had lost something of its splendor of former days, with its sides belabored with the teeth of the wolves, its panels scratched and clawed. Even before this recent siege, the billows and the squalls had played havoc with the harmony of its coats of paint and the relief of its gilt borders. The snow-drifts had half slashed away the escutcheon of the Cascabels. What time and skill it would now take the artist to restore its ancient luster! For, in truth, the combined efforts of Cornelia and Clovy were now powerless.

By ten o'clock the reindeer were harnessed, and a start was made, the men going on foot, as the ground was rising sensibly.

The weather was fine and the heat bearable in this upper region of the chain. But how often they had to help the willing team, and clear out the wheels of the wagon from the ruts into which they would sink axle-deep. At every sharp angle of the pass it became necessary to lay all hands on the *Fair Rambler*, lest it should knock, fore or aft, against the edges of the rocks.

These defiles in the Urals are not the work of man. Nature alone has wrought a passage for the outpourings of the chains through these meanderous clifts. A small river, an affluent of the Sosva, came down, right here, toward the west. Sometimes its bed became so wide as to leave the wayfarer barely a narrow zigzag path. Here, its banks, standing almost perpendicular, were covered with the merest layer of moss and rocky plants. There, their gentle slope bristled with trees, with firs and pines, birches and larch-trees and other indigenous growths of Northern Europe. And far away, lost in the clouds, were the profiles of the snow-capped crests that fed the torrents of this orographic system.

During this first day's march, the little troupe met not a soul along this evidently unfrequented pass. Ortik and Kirschef seemed pretty well acquainted with it. Two or three times, however, they appeared to hesitate, in places where several tracks presented themselves. They would then stop, and converse together in a low tone,—which could surprise nobody, since there was no motive for suspecting their good faith.

Still Kayette never ceased to watch them, unknown to them. Those secret conversations, the glances they exchanged, excited her distrust more and more. They, on their part, were far from dreaming that the young woman felt the least misgiving toward them.

At the fall of day, Mr. Sergius selected a halting place by the bank of the little river, and when supper was over, Mr. Cascabel, Kirschef, and Clovy undertook the task of mounting guard as a measure of precaution, one after the other. It must be confessed, they deserved no little credit, either, for not falling asleep at their post, after the fatigues of the day and their want of sleep during the preceding night.

Next day, another stage up the defile, which was becoming narrower as it ascended higher,—a stage as laborious as the previous one, and at the end of which an advance of five or six miles had been made in twenty-four hours. This, however, had been foreseen, and reckoned among the delays of the journey.

More than once Mr, Sergius and his friend John were greatly tempted to pursue some fine head of game through the wooded gorges, right and left of their track. In the occasional clearings, whole flocks of elks, deer, and hares were seen to scamper. And Cornelia would gladly have accepted a little fresh venison. But, if game was plentiful, the ammunition, it will be remembered, had been quite exhausted during the engagement with the wolves, and it could not now be renewed before the next village had been reached. And so the guns hung useless on the rack, and Wagram would often stare at his master and positively looked as if he uttered the words:

"Say, boss, you've given up shooting altogether, have you?"

Still one circumstance there was, in which the intervention of firearms would have been fully justified.

It was three o'clock in the afternoon; the *Fair Rambler* was coming along a rocky bank, when a bear, whose presence had been announced by the barking of the dogs, appeared on the other side of the stream.

It was an enormous brute; and there he sat on his hind quarters, swinging his huge head to and fro, and shaking his thick brown fur, as the little caravan was advancing toward him.

Did he think of pouncing upon them? Was it a look of curiosity or one of envy he cast on the team and their drivers?

John had silenced Wagram, wisely deeming it useless to excite this formidable animal, as they were unarmed. Why run the risk of changing his may-be friendly or careless humor into hostile disposition, when it was quite possible for him to simply cross from one bank of the little river to the other?

And that is why it came to pass that both parties stood looking at each other quietly, like two travelers crossing each other on the highway, while Mr. Cascabel muttered; "What a pity we can't capture this magnificent Bruin!—A

246

genuine Bruin from the Ural mountains, ladies and gentlemen!—What a sensation he would make!"

It would have been hard, however, to induce him to join the troupe; he evidently preferred the wilds of his forest home to the glories of the showman's career, for he presently raised himself lazily on all fours, gave a last swing to his big head, and half-trotted himself out of sight.

A return of civilities being always de rigiieur, the bear's parting nod was acknowledged by the polite raising of Sander's hat. John would much rather have raised his gun for him to the level of his shoulder; but what could he do?

At six in the evening, another halt in very analogous conditions to those of the previous evening. Next morning another start at five o'clock and another day's painful progress. Always plenty of toiling, but thus far no accident.

And now the worst of the journey was over, since the *Fair Rambler* had now reached the culminating point of the pass, the very apex of the defile. There was nothing left now but to go down the western slopes of the mountain toward Europe.

That evening, the 6th of July, the worn-out team stopped at the entrance into a sinuous gorge, flanked on the right by a thick wood.

The heat had been stifling all the day. To the east, heavy clouds stood out in bold relief against the pale vapors of the horizon, thanks to the long well-marked streak that formed their basis.

"There is a storm coming on," said John.

"Worse luck!" replied Ortik. "In the Urals, storms are terrible sometimes!"

"Well, we shall get under shelter," rejoined Mr. Cascabel. "I'd rather have the storms than the wolves!"

"Kayette," said Napoleona to the young Indian girl, "are you afraid of thunder?"

"Not at all, my pet," replied Kayette.

"You are quite right too, little Kayette," remarked John "You must not be afraid!"

"That's all very fine!" answered his sister. "But when you can't help yourself!"

"Oh, the little coward!" cried Sander. "Why, you silly girl, thunder is only a game of skittles with very big bowls."

"Yes, bowls of fire that come down on your head, sometimes!" retorted the little girl, just as a sudden flash of lightning made her close her eyelids.

They hastened to organize the encampment so that every one might get under cover before the storm came on. Then, after supper, it was arranged that the men would keep watch as during the preceding nights.

Mr. Sergius was going to offer his services when Ortik anticipated him, saying:

"Would you like Kirschef and me to take the first watch to-night?"

"As you like," answered Mr. Sergius. "At midnight, John and I will come and relieve you."

"That's settled, Mr. Sergius!" said Ortik.

Natural as this proposal was, it drew Kayette's attention, and vaguely, almost without a thought, she felt a presentiment of something wrong being in contemplation.

Just now, the storm burst out with great violence. Flashes of lightning cast their fitful rays through the summits of the trees and the roll of the thunder traversing the space was over and over re-echoed through the mountains.

Napoleona, the better to shut her eyes and her ears, had covered herself up in her little bed. She soon had imitators. though not through the same cause, and by nine o'clock, all inside the *Fair Rambler* were fast asleep despite the roar of thunder and the hissing of the gale.

Kayette alone was not sleeping. She had not undressed, and though almost exhausted with fatigue, she could not rest for a moment. She shuddered with anguish when she thought that the safety of all those dear ones was intrusted to the keeping of the two Russian sailors. And so, after a long hour had passed, she should ascertain what they were doing: she raised the curtain of the little window above her couch, and peeped out.

Ortik and Kirschef had just interrupted the conversation they were having together, and were moving toward the opening of the gorge, where a man had suddenly appeared.

Ortik immediately beckoned to the latter not to come nearer for fear of the dogs; indeed, under ordinary circumstances, Wagram and Marengo would already have announced his approach, but, owing to the stifling temperature, they had sought a shelter under the *Fair Rambler*.

Ortik and Kirschef went over to the man, a few words were exchanged, and by the light of a flash, Kayette saw that the sailors followed him under the trees.

Who was he, why had the sailors communicated with him, were things that should be found out at once.

Slowly, softly, Kayette slipped out without disturbing a single one of her companions. As she passed by John, she heard him pronouncing her name—

Had he seen her?

No! John was dreaming, dreaming of her!

Noiselessly she opened the door and slid it back again, and when she found herself outside:

"Now!" she whispered to herself.

No fear, no hesitation even, was there in the young woman's breast. Still, it was her life she risked if ever she was discovered.

Kayette plunged into the forest, the underwood of which flared up as if with the glare of a huge conflagration whenever a flash of lightning rent the clouds above. Creeping along the thicket, in the middle of tall grass, she reached the trunk of an enormous larch tree. A whisper she heard some twenty paces beyond, caused her to stop where she was.

Seven men were there; Ortik and Kirschef had joined them; they were all under a tree, and this is what Kayette overheard of the conversation, carried on in Russian.

"Devilish lucky," said Ortik, "that I took the Petchora pass! A fellow is always sure to meet old chums this way! Am I right, Rostof?"

Rostof was the man that Ortik and Kirschef had perceived by the edge of the wood.

"We have been following that wagon these two days," said he; "on the quiet, of course. As we had recognized your two faces in there, we thought there might be a good job on, perhaps."

"A good job, or may-be two," answered Ortik.

"But where do you come from?" inquired Rostof.

"Right away from America, where we had joined the Karnof fellows."

"And these people you are with, what are they?"

"French show people, of the name of Cascabel, coming home to Europe. We have a long tale of traveling adventures to tell you some other time. Let me come to the chief thing—"

"Ortik," interrupted one of the men, "is there any coin in that wagon?"

"A remnant of two or three thousand roubles."

"And you have not taken French leave of those French people yet?" asked Rostof with a sneer.

"No, there is a bigger haul to make than a paltry thing like that; and we wanted more hands."

"What is it?"

"Well, listen here. If Kirschef and I have managed to come all the way through Siberia, without any risk and cross the frontier, it's thanks to these Cascabels. But what we have done, there is another man that has done it, too, in the hope that no one would go ferret him out among a lot of acrobats. He is a Russian, who has no more right than we have to set his foot in Russia, although the charges against him aren't the same color as ours. He is a political convict, a man of what they call noble birth, and as much fortune as you like. Now, his secret is known to nobody but the said Cascabel and his wife—"

"How did you come to know it?"

"By a conversation we overheard the other day at Mouji between the showman and his Russian friend."

"And his name is—?"

"For the world at large, his name is Sergius; but in reality it is Count Narkine; and it's as much as his life is worth, if ever he is caught on Russian ground."

"Wait till I think," said Rostof. "Count Narkine—Isn't that the son of Prince Narkine, the same that was transported to Siberia, and they made such fuss about him when he escaped out of it, a few years ago?"

"That's the man!" answered Ortik. "Well, Count Narkine has millions of roubles, and I reckon he won't fight shy of giving us one,—if we threaten to give him up to the police!"

"That's a mighty good idea, Ortik! But what's the use of us in that concern?"

"Because it must not look as if Kirschef and me had anything to do with this first job, so that if it turned out no good, we might fall back on the other. For this card to turn up trump, we two must remain for the present as we are, the two shipwrecked Russian mariners, saved and brought home by the Cascabels. By and by, when we have got rid of them, we can roam over the whole country, and the police will never dream of suspecting us when we've got our tights on."

"Say, Ortik, shall we attack you to-night, and pounce on Count Narkine, and let him know our price for keeping mum?"

"Not yet, not yet!" said the sailor. "As the count means to push on as far as Perm to see his old father, better let him go all the way. When he is there, one fine morning, he'll get a note requesting him to come to a certain rendezvous —for a very urgent affair—and then you can have the pleasure of making his acquaintance."

"Just now, there is nothing to be done, then?"

"Nothing at all, but try and get on ahead of us, and be in Perm a little before our caravan."

"Right you are!" answered Rostof.

And the wretches parted, without the least suspicion of having been watched.

Ortik and Kirschef returned to the encampment a few moments after Kayette, and concluded from the general stillness that their absence had passed off unnoticed.

And now Kayette was in possession of the plan of these monsters. She had learnt, moreover, that Mr. Sergius was Count Narkine, and that his very life was threatened, as well as that of her French friends. The secret that had hitherto sheltered him was going to be betrayed, if he did not consent to part with a portion of his fortune!

Terrified at her discovery, she felt for a few moments crushed under its blow, but her resolute determination to foil Ortik's designs soon overcame all other feelings, and she strove to think out the means of doing so. What a night she spent! What anxious hours she lay there thinking, and thinking.

Might not all this have been a horrible dream?

No, it was indeed a reality.

And poor Kayette could entertain no doubt about it, when, next morning, she heard Ortik say to her good Mr. Cascabel:

"You know we intended, Kirschef and myself, to leave you when we got over the mountain, and make our way to Riga. Well, we have been thinking we had better go with you to Perm and ask the governor, there, to send us home. Would it be the same to you to let us go on with you?"

"Why, of course, my friends!" answered Cascabel. "When people have come such a distance together, they should keep together to the last. Parting always comes too soon."

CHAPTER XII - A JOURNEY'S END WHICH IS NOT THE END

SUCH was, then, the abominable plot now in course of execution against Count Narkine and the Cascabel family! And that, at the very moment when, after so much toil and so many dangers, the journey was drawing so near to a successful termination! Two or three days more, the chain of the Ural would be left behind, and 300 miles to the southwest would bring them to Perm.

It will be remembered that César Cascabel had made up his mind to sojourn for some time in that town, so that Mr. Sergius might have every facility to repair to Walska every night, and without exposing himself. After which, according to circumstances, the count would remain in his ancestral home, or would come with him to Nijni,—perhaps to France even!

Quite so! But in the event of Mr. Sergius not leaving Perm, they should have to part with Kayette, who would, of course, remain with him!

That is what John went on repeating to himself, what unmanned him, what broke his heart. And John's grief, so true, so deep, was shared by his father and his mother, his brother and his little sister. None of them could resign themselves to the thought of seeing Kayette no more!

That morning, John, more sad at heart than ever, came to the young girl and observed her pale, drawn features, her eyes red for want of sleep:

"Little Kayette," said he, "what is wrong?"

"Nothing wrong with me, John!"

"Yes, there is! You are ill! You did not sleep. Why, you really look as if you had cried!"

"It is last night's storm! I could not close my eyes all the night."

"That long journey has told greatly on you, has it not?"

"Not in the least, John. I am strong. Have I not been used to all sorts of hardships? I shall soon get over that."

"Then, what is wrong with you, Kayette? Do tell me, I beseech you!"

"Indeed, I am all right, John."

And John insisted no further.

Seeing the poor fellow so unhappy, Kayette had been well-nigh telling him everything. It pained her to have a secret from him! But knowing his strength of feeling, she said to herself he might not contain himself perhaps in the presence of Kirschef and Ortik. His indignation might get the better of him—

the least act of imprudence might cost Count Narkine his life; and Kayette had kept silent.

After long consideration, she determined to communicate all she had heard to Mr. Cascabel. But she should have an opportunity of being alone with him, and during the crossing of the Ural this would be a difficult matter, for it was important that the two sailors should suspect nothing.

As to that, there was plenty of time yet, since the miscreants were to make no move till the troupe reached Perm.

So long as Mr. Cascabel and his people would continue to be the same as they now were toward the sailors, the suspicions of the latter would not be aroused; and it may be mentioned, in this connection, that, on hearing that Ortik and Kirschef intended remaining with the troupe as far as Perm, Mr. Sergius had readily expressed his satisfaction thereat.

At six in the morning on the 7th of July, the *Fair Rambler* resumed its journey. One hour later, they were at the first springs of the River Petchora, after which the pass is named. Beyond the mountain range, this river becomes one of the most important in northern Russia, and after a course of 1350 kilometers throws itself into the Arctic Sea.

At this elevation in the pass, the Petchora was yet but a torrent, rushing through a ravined and sinuous bed, at the foot of tall groves of firs and pine trees. Its left bank would prove a safe track right on to the mouth of the pass, and, with some caution in the steeper parts, the descent would be accomplished rapidly.

Throughout this day Kayette could not find an opportune moment for her private talk with Mr. Cascabel. Nor did she fail to observe that there were now no private whisperings between the two Russians, either; no more lurking away on their part at halting time,—what could have been their motive for such maneuvering now? Their accomplices had gone ahead, for a certainty, and not before reaching Perm did the sailors expect to meet them again.

The following day yielded a good day's work. The defile, now wider, afforded a better road for the wagon. They could hear the Petchora, deeply incased between its banks, rumbling over its rocky bed. As the pass assumed a less wild aspect, it also became more frequented. Traders were now met, with a bundle on their shoulders and an iron-tipped stick in their hand, tramping their way from Europe to Asia. Bands of miners, on their journey to or from the mines, exchanged a word or two with our party. On coming out of the gorges, a few farms or small villages would now greet the sight. Away to the south, the Denejkin and the Kontchakov overtopped this part of the Urals.

After a night's rest, the little caravan reached the extremity of the Petchora pass, about twelve o'clock. It had at last crossed the entire width of the chain and had set foot on European soil.

Another stage of 350 versts, and Perm would reckon "one more house and one more family within its walls," as Mr. Cascabel used to put it.

"Well, my word!" he would add. "A nice old ramble we have had, my friends!.... Say, was I not right!.... There are more ways to get home than one! Instead of coming into Russia by one side, we came by the other! Well, what's the difference, so long as France is over there?"

And, had he been urged on, ever so little, the good man would have stated his belief that he already recognized the air of Normandy, wafted eastward across the whole of Europe, and that he could swear to it by the little sniff of sea breeze that was in it.

Just outside the defile was a zavody, consisting of some fifty houses and a few hundred inhabitants.

It was decided that they would halt here till the following day to renew certain provisions, and among others, the stock of flour, tea, and sugar.

At the same time Mr. Sergius and John were able to get powder and shot and replenish their exhausted ammunition stores.

They had no sooner returned than Mr. Sergius called out:

"And now, come along, friend John! Shoulder your gun, and we shall not return with an empty bag."

"As you like, sir," replied John, more through courtesy than for his own pleasure.

Poor fellow! The thought of the now imminent parting made him careless of everything.

"Will you come with us, Ortik?" asked Mr. Sergius.

"With pleasure, sir."

"Try to bring me home some choice game," recommended Mrs. Cascabel, "and I promise you a good supper."

As it was only two in the afternoon, the sportsmen had ample time to search the woods in the neighborhood, even if the thickets had not swarmed with game as they did.

Mr. Sergius, John, and Ortik started off accordingly, while Kirschef and Clovy looked after the reindeer, and prepared a park for them under the trees in the corner of a meadow, where they could graze and ruminate at ease.

Meanwhile, Cornelia was returning to the *Fair Rambler*, where there was plenty of work to be done:

"Now then, Napoleona!"

"Here I am, mother!"

"And Kayette?"

"Going at once, madame!"

But this was the very opportunity Kayette had watched for, so anxiously, to be alone with the head of the family.

"Mr. Cascabel," she said, going over to him.

"Well, my pet?"

"I should like to speak to you."

"To speak to me?"

"Yes, privately."

"Privately?"

Then, mentally, he asked himself:

"What can my little Kayette want to see me for?—Might it be about my poor John?"

And both walked a short distance away, to the left of the zavody.

"Well, my dear child," asked Cascabel, after a while, "what is your wish? What is this private talk about?"

"Mr, Cascabel, these three days I have been longing to speak to you, without anybody hearing us or even seeing us."

"Why, it must be a, very serious matter, my darling."

"Mr. Cascabel, I know that Mr. Sergius is Count Narkine?"

"Eh?—Count Narkine?" stammered Cascabel. "You know?—And how did you come to know that?"

"Through those who were listening to you while you spoke with Mr. Sergius, the other evening at Mouji."

"Can that be?"

"And, in my turn, I overheard them conversing about Count Narkine and about you, unknown to them."

"Who are they?"

255

"Ortik and Kirschef."

"What!—They know?"

"Yes, sir, and they know, besides, that Mr. Sergius is a political convict who is returning to Russia to see his father, Prince Narkine."

Cæser Cascabel, stupefied at what he had heard, stood for a moment, dazed, his arms hanging helplessly, his mouth gaping. Then, collecting his ideas:

"I am sorry," he said, "that Ortik and Kirschef should know the secret; but since, by an unfortunate accident, they have come to hear of it, I am sure they won't betray it!"

"It is not by accident, and they will betray it."

"What, honest sailors as they are!"

"Mr. Cascabel, listen: Count Narkine runs the greatest danger."

"Eh?"

"Ortik and Kirschef are two criminals who belonged to Karnof's band. They are the men who attacked Count Narkine on the Alaskan frontier. After embarking at Port Clarence to get across to Siberia, they were cast on the Liakhov Islands, where we found them. As they know that the Count's life is in danger if he is recognized on Russian territory, they will demand a large portion of his fortune from him, and if he refuses, they will denounce him to the police,—And then, Mr. Sergius is done for, and so are you, perhaps!"

While Gascabel, crushed by this revelation, listened in silence, Kayette explained to him how the two sailors had always excited her suspicions. It was but too true that she had heard Kirschef's voice before. Now, she fully remembered it! It was on that frightful night when the two ruffians had attacked Count Narkine. And now, a few nights ago, while they were on guard together, she had seen them going away from the encampment with a man who had come for them; she had followed them, and she had been the unsuspected witness, of a conversation between them and seven or eight of their old accomplices—All Ortik's plans were now unveiled. After bringing the *"Fair Rambler"* round by the Petchora pass, where he was sure to meet numbers of malefactors, he had at first thought of murdering Mr. Sergius and the whole of the little caravan; but, hearing that Mr. Sergius was Count Narkine, he had said to himself that it was better to extort an enormous sum of money from him under threat of being handed over to the Russian authorities.... They would wait till all had reached Perm. Neither of the two sailors would appear in this business, in order to keep their position with the troupe, in the event of a failure. It was their associates who would communicate with Mr. Sergius by a letter, asking him for an interview, etc., etc.

It was with the utmost difficulty Cascabel could control his rage while Kayette told her tale of horrors. Such monsters! To whom he had rendered so many services, whom he had delivered from prison, whom he had fed and brought back to their country!—Well, a nice present, a precious restitution he was making to the empire of the Czar! The fiends! The—

"And now, Mr. Cascabel," asked Kayette, "what are you going to do?"

"What am I going to do, pet? Why, it's very simple; I am going to denounce Ortik and Kirschef to the very first post of Cossacks we meet, and they'll swing for it!"

"Think, sir," replied the young girl, "you can't do that."

"Why not?"

"Because the first thing the two men will do will be to betray Count Narkine, and, along with him, those who have been the means of his returning to Russia."

"Devil may care for what concerns me!" exclaimed Cascabel. "If I was the only one in question—But Mr. Sergius is another thing! You are right, Kayette; I must think it over."

So saying, he moved on a few paces, a prey to the wildest agitation, striking his head with his fist as though in the hope of knocking an idea out of it. Then, retracing his steps toward the young girl:

"You tell me distinctly," he asked, "that it is Ortik's intention to wait till we reach Perm before setting his accomplices to work?"

"Yes, Mr. Cascabel; and he recommended them, above all, to make no move whatever until then. So, I should think we must have patience and continue the journey to the end."

"That's hard!" interrupted Cascabel, "very hard!—Keep them with us, bring them along with us to Perm. shaking hands with them at night, showing them a friendly face—By the blood of my fathers, I don't know what keeps me from going at them this minute, and wringing their necks like so—just like—so—"

And in a paroxysm of rage, Cæser Cascabel worked the muscles of his sinewy hands as if he had been in reality making Ortik and Kirschef pay the penalty of their many crimes.

"You know you must control yourself, Mr. Cascabel," said Kayette. "You are supposed to know nothing—"

"You are quite right, my child."

"I'll only ask you if you would think well of warning Mr. Sergius?"

"No—the more I think of it—no! It seems to me wiser not to tell him. What could he do?—Nothing—I am there to watch over him—and I will! Besides I know him well! Rather than expose us to any danger, he might give a good tug to the left while we'd be pulling to the right. No—for a certainty, no! I'll say nothing to him."

"And will you say nothing to John?"

"To John, little Kayette? Not a word! He is a passionate youth! He could not keep quiet in the face of those abominable creatures! He can't control himself like his father! I know he would burst out! No, not a word to John any more than to Mr. Sergius!"

"And Madame Cascabel, won't you tell her?"

"Ah, Madame Cascabel—that's another question. She is a superior woman, you know, able to give an advice—and a helping hand, too! I never had a secret from her, and beside she knows all about Count Narkine—yes, I will tell her! That woman, you could give her State secrets to keep—rather than betray them she'd let her tongue be cut out; what more could you expect from a woman?—Yes, I will tell her!"

"Now, ought we not go back to the *Fair Rambler*?" suggested the young girl; "for our absence must not be remarked."

"You are right, little Kayette, always right."

"Above all, control yourself, won't you, Mr. Cascabel, when you see those two men before you?"

"It will be hard, my child, but never fear, I'll have a smile for them—the wretches! To think that we soiled ourselves with their contact. And that's the reason, is it?—why they told me they would not go directly to Riga! They would honor us with their company right in to Perm! The scoundrels! The ruffians! The devils!"

And Mr. Cascabel exhausted on them all the most formidable epithets in his vocabulary.

"If that is the way you are going to contain yourself—"

"No, little Kayette, never fear! I am relieved now! You see it was choking me, strangling me! I'll be cool now. I am so, already! Let us go back to the *Fair Rambler*. What fiends!"

And both returned toward the zavody. Neither of them spoke now. They were absorbed in their thoughts. So marvelous a trip, but yesterday on the eve of completion, and now on the brink of so fatal an issue through this odious plot!

As they neared home, Mr. Cascabel stopped:

"Little Kayette?" he said.

"Well, sir?"

"On the whole, I have made up my mind not to say anything to Cornelia!"

"Why so?"

"Because, you see—generally speaking I have noticed that a woman keeps a secret all the better as she knows nothing about it. That's why this secret in particular shall remain with both of us!"

One moment later Kayette had returned to her household duties; and as he passed by him. Mr. Cascabel had made a friendly gesture to that "honest Kirschef," while he muttered between his teeth:

"Hasn't he the face of a devil!"

And two hours after, when the sportsmen came home. Ortik was warmly congratulated by the boss on the magnificent deer he brought on his shoulders. On their part, Mr. Sergius and John had shot two hares and a few brace of partridges, so that Cornelia was able to offer her famished guests a sumptuous supper, of which Mr. Cascabel took a large share. Truly, our actor was "splendid"! Not a trace of his anxious thoughts could be detected on his countenance. No one could have supposed that the man was aware there were two murderers at his table, whose ultimate designs were nothing short of the slaughter of himself and family. He was literally in a charming mood, full of fun and communicative mirth, and when Clovy had fetched out one of the "good bottles," he drank to their return to Europe, their return to Russia, their return to France!

The next day, July the 10th, the team struck directly for Perm. The defile being now cleared, the journey was likely to be accomplished without difficulty, nay, without any incident. The *Fair Rambler* was following the right bank of the Vichera, which skirts the foot of the Ural. Small towns, villages, and farms now dotted the road; hospitable country people, abundant game, and a warm greeting everywhere. The weather, though very hot, was cooled by a little northeast breeze. The reindeer journeyed bravely on, and shook their pretty heads as they went along. Mr. Sergius had gratified them with the help of two horses, which he had bought at the last zavody, and they could now cover up to thirty miles a day.

Truly, this was a glorious début for the little troupe on the soil of old Europe! And their manager would have been a happy man indeed, if he had not cause to continually repeat to himself that he had two scoundrels among them:

"And to say that their band has been tracking us like a pack of jackals scenting a caravan! Come, César Cascabel, you must think of some trick to play those gallows-birds!"

How unlucky that a grand scheme, so skilfully combined, should be disturbed by this fiendish complication. The papers of the Cascabels fulfilled all the necessary formalities; the Russian authorities let Mr. Sergius pass freely as a member of the troupe; and when they arrived at Perm, he could have gone to and fro on his daily visits to Walska, with all possible ease. After seeing his father and staying for some time with him, he could have traversed Russia under his disguise as an "artist" and made his way to France, where he would be in complete safety. And then, no more parting!—Kayette and he would both be of the family!—And later on, who knows if that poor John—really, really, the gallows was not enough for those demons. And Mr. Cascabel, in spite of himself, would burst out into sudden and apparently groundless fits of passion.

And when Cornelia would inquire:

"César, what can be the matter with you?"

"With me? Nothing!" he would answer.

"Then why do you rage so?"

"I rage, Cornelia, because if I did not rage I should go mad!"

And the good woman was at a loss to find the clue of the enigmatic reply.

Four days passed by in these conditions. Then, some sixty leagues southwest of the Urals, the *Fair Rambler* reached the little town of Solikamsk.

No doubt Ortik's associates could not be far ahead now; but, as a measure of prudence, neither Kirschef nor he made any effort to ascertain the point.

As a matter of fact, Rostof and his companions were there, and would start, that same night, for Perm, just a hundred and fifty miles away to the west. Nothing could now hinder their abominable project.

Next morning, at daybreak, under date of the 17th of July, the Koswa was crossed in a ferry. Three or four days more, and the famous series of performances "by the artists of the Cascabel family, on their way to the Nijni fair," would be commenced at Perm. Such, at least, was the program of the tour.

As to Mr. Sergius, he would at once make the necessary plans for his nightly calls at Walska.

Let his feeling of impatience be imagined, if possible, as well as the anxiety he betrayed when conversing about all this with his friend Cascabel. Ever since he had made his escape, and during the thirteen months of this extraordinary trip from the Alaskan frontier to Europe, he had been without a word from Prince Narkine. Considering the age his father was, even then— was he quite sure he would find him at the chateau still?

"Nonsense, nonsense, Mr. Sergius!" Cæser Cascabel would say. "The prince is in as good health as you or I, and even better! You know I was born for a fortune-teller, and I read the future as easily as the past. Well, I tell you Prince Narkine is now waiting for you, hale and strong, and you shall see him in a few days!"

And Cascabel would have had no hesitation to swear to his prophecy were it not for that cursed Ortik.

"I am not bad-hearted, not I," he would mutter to himself; "but, if I could gnaw his neck off with my teeth, I would—yes, I would, and think he got off cheap!"

Kayette, meanwhile, grew more and more alarmed as they approached nearer to Perm. What decision would Mr. Cascabel take? How would he defeat Ortik's plans without compromising Mr. Sergius's safety? It seemed to her almost impossible. And so she found it very hard to conceal her anxiety, and John, ignorant of the cause, suffered cruel tortures, seeing her so uneasy, so downcast at times.

In the forenoon of the 20th of July, the Kama was crossed, and, about five in the evening Mr. Sergius and his companions were already engaged in making their preparations, on the chief square of Perm, for a stay of several days.

One hour had not elapsed before Ortik had communicated with his accomplices, and Rostof was penning a note, which was to reach Mr. Sergius the same day, and in which a rendezvous was given him in one of the taverns of the town, for very urgent business. Should he fail to come, they would see about securing his person, should they even capture him at night on the road to Walska.

At nightfall, when this note was brought by Rostof, Mr. Sergius had already set out for his father's chateau. Mr. Cascabel, who was by himself just then, gave every token of great surprise on being handed this message. He took it, however, undertaking to deliver it safely, and meanwhile said nothing about it to anybody.

Mr. Sergius's absence annoyed Ortik. He would rather the attempt at blackmail had been made before the interview between the prince and the count. He concealed his vexed feelings, however, and remarked, as he sat to supper, in the most unconcerned fashion:

"Mr. Sergius is not with us this evening?"

"No," answered Mr. Cascabel. "He is gone out. Those formalities with the authorities in this country are such a plague!"

"When will he be back?"

"Some time in the evening, I guess."

CHAPTER XIII - AN ENDLESS DAY

THE government of Perm looks as if astride on the back of the Ural, one foot in Asia, the other in Europe. Its boundaries are: the government of Vologdia to the north-west, that of Tobolsk to the east, Viatka to the west, and Orenburg to the south. And accordingly, thanks to this dual situation, its population is a strange mixture of Asiatic and of European types.

Perm, its capital, is a town of 6000 inhabitants, situated on the Kama, and an important center for the metal trade. Previous to the eighteenth century, it was merely a village. But, having been enriched by the discovery of a copper mine in 1723, the village was declared a town in 1781.

Is the latter denomination justified even now? Scarcely, in truth! Monuments, there are none; the streets are for the most part narrow and dirty, the houses destitute of comfort, and the hotels such that no traveler has ever yet taken it into his head to say a word in their favor.

Of course, the Cascabels were but little concerned with the town architect's business. Did they not prefer their own "home on wheels" to any other? Would they have exchanged it for the New York "St. Nicholas" or the "Grand Hotel" in Paris?

"Just think, will you?" repeated its proud owner. "The *Fair Rambler* has come from Sacramento to Perm!—Only that little trip, that's all!—Just show me one of your hotels in Paris, London, Vienna, or New York that has ever done as much!"

What answers could be given to arguments of this kind?

On that day, then, Perm had been increased by one house, standing in the very middle of its principal "square," with the authorization of the civil governor of the place. Nor had the slightest contraction of the official's brow accompanied his perusal of the artists' papers.

Immediately on the arrival of the *Fair Rambler*, public curiosity had been on tiptoe: French showmen, just arrived from the depths of America, with a wagon drawn by a team of reindeer!—The profit to be derived from such a bait none knew so well as the eminent manager of the troupe.

As luck would have it, the fair was at its full, and would last a few days longer; some good takings in perspective, therefore! At the same time, not a day was to be lost, for, Perm first, and Nijni after, should yield the wherewith to accomplish the remainder of the journey to France. Beyond that—well, they would trust to Providence, and thus far the Cascabels had not a little to be thankful for.

The consequence of all this was that all hands were at work at early morn. John, Sander, Clovy, and the two Russian sailors vied with each other in their eagerness to prepare all that was necessary for the performance. As to Mr. Sergius, he had not returned as he had promised,—a source of considerable vexation to Ortik, and of some uneasiness to Mr. Cascabel.

Meanwhile, at the earliest moment, a huge bill had been posted up, written in Russian, of course, and in large characters, under the dictation of their absent friend, before his departure.

It read as follows:

THE CASCABEL FAMILY.

French Troupe Returning from America.

Gymnastics, Juggling, Equilibrism, Displays of Muscle and Skill, Dances, Graceful Arts.

Mr. Cascabel, first Hercules in any and every style.

Mme. Cascabel, first wrestler in any and every style, champion of the Chicago International Matches.

Mr. John, first equilibrist in any and every style.

Mr. Sander, clown in any and every style.

Mlle. Napoleona, dancer in any and every style.

Mr. Clovy, pantaloon in any and every style.

Jako, parrot in any and every style.

John Bull, ape in any and every style.

Wagram and Marengo, dogs in any and every style.

GREAT ATTRACTION!

THE BRIGANDS OF THE BLACK FOREST.

A pantomime or dumb show, with a grand wedding and wonderful dénouement. Immense success through three thousand one hundred and seventy-seven performances in France and foreign parts.

N.B.—Needless to say that this being a speechless play and the spoken language being replaced by gestures of all kinds, this masterpiece of the dramatic art ca n be understood by all, even by those persons afflicted with that much-to-be-regrette d ailment, deafness.

For the convenience of the public, admission will be free. The seats will be paid for only when they have been occupied.

Price: 40 Kopecks, without any distinction.

Generally, Mr. Cascabel gave his unique performances in the open air, merely describing a circle in front of the *Fair Rambler* with stout posts and fastening canvas thereon; but the grand square in Perm happened to be possessed of a wooden circus for the exercises of the equestrian troupes who might pass that way; and dilapidated as it was, and proof against neither wind nor rain, it was still strong enough, and might accommodate two hundred or two hundred and fifty spectators.

In any case, even in its present state, the "circus" was better than Cascabel's canvas. He had asked the mayor's permission to make use of it during his stay in the town, and this personage had graciously given his consent.

Not to flatter them, these Russians were really good fellows,—although there were Ortiks and beings of that ilk among them. But in what country are they not to be found! As to the circus of the town of Perm, it would not be disgraced by the doings of the Cascabel troup! There was but one thing to be regretted: it was that His Majesty Czar Alexander II did not happen to be passing through this locality. As he was then at St. Petersburg, however, it would have been hard for him to be present at this inaugural performance.

One other trouble for César Cascabel, was the fear that his staff might have got somewhat rusty in the matter of somersaults, dances, and other practices. The rehearsals, which had been suspended as soon as the *Fair Rambler* had entered the pass of the Ural, had not been resumed during the remainder of the journey. Pshaw, genuine artists would always be ready to shine in the noble art!

As to the play, it was useless to rehearse it! It had been gone through so often, and without a prompter, that no uneasiness need be had on that score.

And now Ortik found it difficult not to betray the annoyance he felt at Mr. Sergius's prolonged absence. The projected interview not having taken place the night before, he had been obliged to send word to his accomplices that the affair was postponed for twenty-four hours. And meanwhile he kept wondering why Mr. Sergius had not returned, seeing that Mr. Cascabel was distinctly expecting him back in the course of the evening. Had he been detained at the chateau? It was likely; for, there was no doubt as to his having gone there. Ortik should therefore have been less impatient. But it was stronger than himself, and he could not refrain from asking Cascabel if he had heard from the absentee.

"Not a word!" the latter replied.

"I thought you expected him last night?"

"Quite so! Something unforeseen must have happened. It would be a great pity if he could not see our performance. It will be simply marvelous! Wait till you see, Ortik, my friend!"

And César Cascabel spoke in his jolliest tone of voice; but at heart he was now truly anxious.

The previous day, after promising to be back before day-break, Mr. Sergius had started for Walska. Six versts there, six versts back, a mere nothing. Now, as there was no sign of him, three suppositions presented themselves to the showman's mind: either he had been arrested before he reached Walska, or he had safely got home but was detained by his father's state of health, or again, he had been captured on his way back during the night. As to supposing that Ortik's companions had drawn him into some ambush, that was out of the question; and to Kayette's suggestion in that direction he unhesitatingly replied:

"No, Kayette, no! That ruffian Ortik would not be so uneasy as he has every appearance of being. He would hardly have inquired as he did after Mr. Sergius if his mates had held him in their clutches. The rascal! So long as I don't see him grinning at the end of a stout rope, there will be something wanting to my happiness here below, Kayette!"

Nor was it to Kayette alone Mr. Cascabel's anxiety was apparent. How often Cornelia would say to him:

"Come, César, try and be calm. You overexcite yourself! You should be reasonable!"

"Cornelia, 'reasonable' is all very fine! But a man must have grounds for being reasonable. Now, there is no denying the fact that our friend should have been here long since, and that we know absolutely nothing about him."

"Very good, César; but, since nobody can even suspect that he is Count Narkine."

"No, nobody, unless—"

"What do you mean? 'Unless—' Is Clovy's crank 'unless' your latest fad? What do you mean, I say? You and I are the only two who know Mr. Sergius's secret. Do you imagine, by any chance, that I have let it out?"

"You, Cornelia, fiddlesticks! Nor I, either!"

"Well, then?"

"Well, there are, here in Perm, people who have had dealings with Count Narkine, years ago, and who might very well recognize him. It must seem strange, at first sight, that we should have a Russian amongst us! Then again, Cornelia, it may be that I exaggerate things; but you know, I am so fond of that man, I can't help myself; I must stir about, I must!"

"César, be careful that you don't excite suspicions with your stirring about! And above all, don't go compromise yourself asking people questions just at the wrong moment. Like yourself, I think this delay very unfortunate, and I do wish Mr. Sergius were here! Still, I don't put the very worst aspect on things; and I am of opinion that he has simply been detained by his father at Walska. Now, during daylight, he is afraid to set out, that's easy to understand, but he will come back after nightfall. So, César, no nonsense! A little cold blood, if you please, and bear in mind that to-night you are to play Fracassar, one of the greatest successes of your professional career."

No sounder reasoning could have been poured into Cascabel's ear, and it may seem strange that he still kept the truth from his sensible wife. Still, after all, he may not have been wrong. Who knows if the impulsive Cornelia would not have broken loose the seal on her lips at the sight of Ortik and Kirschef, when she would know what they were and what they meant to do?

Mr. Cascabel, therefore, held his tongue, and soon left the wagon to go and superintend his installation at the circus. Cornelia, on her part, had not too much of Kayette's and Napoleona's help to examine all the costumes and wigs and accessories for the evening's performance.

The two Russians, too, were busy (so they said) with the many formalities to be fulfilled so as to obtain their being sent home as shipwrecked sailors,—which necessitated numerous calls, and solicitations, and runs hither and thither.

While Mr. Cascabel and Clovy plied the brush and the broom, cleaning the dusty seats of the amphitheater, sweeping the ring, etc., John and Sander brought out and arranged the various objects and utensils indispensable to the several items on the program. This done, they would have to see to what the impresario described as "those brand-new sceneries," in which his inimitable artists would play that beautiful pantomimic drama, "The Brigands of the Black Forest."

John was more sad at heart than ever. He, of course, was unaware that Mr. Sergius, in reality a political convict of the name of Count Narkine, could not remain in his country, even if he willed. In his eyes, Mr. Sergius was a wealthy, landed estate owner, returning to his domains, there to settle with his adopted daughter. What a relief to his sorrowing heart, if he had known that a residence in Russia was an impossibility for his respected friend, and that he would leave the country again as soon as he had seen his father; if he could have cherished even a hope that Mr. Sergius would seek a refuge in France, and that Kayette would come with him. In such a case, the parting would have been postponed for a few weeks. It would have been a few weeks more for them to live near each other.

"Yes," John sighed to himself. "Mr. Sergius is going to stay here, and Kayette will remain with him! In a few days we shall be off, and then—I shall see her no more. Dear little Kayette! She will be happy in Mr. Sergius's grand house—and still!"

And the poor fellow's heart sank within him as he thought over all these things.

It was now nine o'clock; Mr. Sergius had given no sign of life yet. What Cornelia had said was turning out true: he should not be expected now before night time, or at least before it was so late that he would not run the risk of being recognized on the road.

"If that be so," soliloquized Mr. Cascabel, "he will not even be in time for the performance. Well, so much the better! I won't be sorry for it! A pretty turnout it will be for the first appearance of the Cascabel family on the boards of the Perm circus! With all this worry, I shall be a complete failure in Fracassar, after the glorious figure I have cut, up to this, in that good man's skin. Cornelia, let her deny it as she will, will be on thorns and needles all the time. Then there is John, who'll think of nothing but his little Kayette. Sander and Napoleona are ready to blubber out even now at the thought of her going away—what a fiasco! Clovy, my old fellow, the honor of the Cascabels depends on you this night!"

And as the disheartened manager could not keep still in any one place, the idea struck him to go news-hunting. In a town like Perm, news travels fast! The Narkines were well known and equally loved. In the event of the Count having fallen into the hands of the police, the rumor of his arrest would have spread like wildfire; it would be the topic of every conversation; nay, the prisoner would already be awaiting his sentence under lock and key in the fortress of Perm, by this time.

So, Clovy was left to finish the preparations of the circus, and his "boss" set off on his ramble through the town, along the riverside, where the watermen and their kin mostly congregate, away in the upper town, down in the lower districts; nowhere did the population seem in any way disturbed from its daily humdrum life. He joined the groups of gossipers here and there; he listened without appearing to do so.—Nothing!—Not a word that could have a reference to Count Narkine.

Not satisfied even with this, he strolled away along the road to Walska, by which the police would have brought back Mr. Sergius if they had taken him prisoner. Whenever he saw a group of wayfarers at a distance, he imagined it was a platoon of Cossacks escorting his friend.

In the chaotic state of his brains, Mr. Cascabel had almost ceased to think of his wife, his children, or himself, terribly compromised though he would be in the event of Count Narkine's arrest. For it would have been the easiest thing for the authorities to ascertain by what means he had succeeded in re-entering the Russian Empire, and who the good people were who had aided and abetted him. And the Cascabels might have to pay a dear price for their kind-heartedness.

Of all this going and coming on the part of Mr. Cascabel, and of his long watching on the Walska road, the result was that he was not at the circus when a man called and asked to see him at about ten o'clock in the morning.

Clovy was the sole tenant of the place at the time, and was working away in the middle of a cloud of dust that rose from the circus track. Out of this cloud he emerged on perceiving the visitor, who turned out to be a simple moujik; and both stood facing each other. Clovy being just as ignorant of the language of the said moujik as the said moujik was unacquainted with Clovy's, the conversation presented insurmountable difficulties. Not a syllable did Clovy understand when the man told him he wished to see his master, and that he had come to look for him at the circus before going to the *Fair Rambler*. All this was Greek to poor Clovy, the which the moujik perceiving, he ended as he should have begun, and presented him a letter directed to Monsieur Cascabel.

This time Clovy was up to the emergency. A letter bearing the famous name of the Cascabels could only be for the head of the family—unless it were for Mrs. Cornelia, or Mr. John, or Master Sander, or Missie Napoleona.

Clovy took it, and, by means of those cosmopolitan gesticulations, intelligible, it would seem, to mankind at large, he gave the moujik to understand that it was O.K., and that the letter would reach its destination safely, thanks to himself; whereupon he showed him to the door with any amount of bowing and scraping, but without having been able to gather the smallest conception of where he came from or who had sent him.

A quarter of an hour later, Clovy was preparing to return to the wagon, when Mr. Cascabel, more broken-down, more careworn than ever, appeared at the entrance of the circus,

"Here you are, sir!" he called.

"Well?"

"I've a letter here!"

"A letter?"

"Yes, a letter that has just been brought."

"For me?"

"Yes, sir."

"By whom?"

"What they call a moujik here."

"A moujik?"

"Yes—unless it's something else!"

During this purportless preamble, Mr. Cascabel had seized the letter, and on recognizing Mr. Sergius's hand-writing, he had grown so pale that his faithful attendant startled:

"What's up now, boss?"

"Nothing."

Nothing, indeed! And yet our strong-nerved man was well-nigh fainting in Clovy's arms.

What did Mr. Sergius say in that letter? Why did he write to Mr. Cascabel? Evidently to explain the cause of his absence. Could it be that he was arrested?

Mr. Cascabel tore open the letter, rubbed his right eye, then his left eye, and then ran right through the contents.

What a cry he uttered!—some such cry as escapes out of a strangled throat! His face convulsed, his eyes colorless, his features paralyzed by a nervous contraction, he strove to speak, but could not articulate a single sound.

Clovy thought his boss was going to be choked out of existence, and set about undoing his neck-cloth.

Be it the dread lest Clovy should call for help, be it that even this terrific emotion had to yield to the iron will of our hero, he seemed suddenly to recover himself by a superhuman effort, and assuming a mysterious look:

"Clovy," he said, "you are a discreet fellow?"

"I guess I am, boss. Did I ever let the cat out of the bag, unless—"

"That's enough; listen! You see this letter?"

"The moujik's letter?"

"That very same! Well, should you ever tell anybody I have received it—"

"Yes!"

"Should you ever tell John, or Sander, or Napoleona—"

"Right you are!"

"Or above all, Cornelia, my wife, I swear I'll get you stuffed for a freak!"

"Alive?"

"Yes, alive, so that you may feel it, you fool!"

And before such an awful threat, Clovy trembled from head to foot.

Then, his master, taking him by the shoulder, whispered in his ear with an air of princely complacency:

"She is tremendously jealous—is Cornelia! You see, Clovy, my boy, a man is a good-looking fellow, or he is not! A lovely woman—a Russian princess! —you understand—This is a note from her to me. Now that'll never fall to your lot, with such a nose as that!"

"Never," re-echoed Clovy, "unless—"

But, what that restriction could mean in Clovy's mind was never ascertained!

CHAPTER XIV - A DENOUEMENT WARMLY APPLAUDED BY THE SPECTATORS

THE play, which bore the equally new and attractive title, "The Brigands of the Black Forest," was a remarkable work of art. Composed in strict accordance with the ancient precepts of dramaturgy, it was based on the unity of time, action, and place. Its introduction neatly defined the characters of the various personages, the plot worked them well into a powerful imbroglio, the dénouement cleverly disentangled the plot; and, though foreseen, the issue produced, none the less, a very great effect. Nor did it lack even the sensational scene so loudly insisted upon by our modern critics, and that scene was a success.

For the rest, the public should have been ill-advised to expect from the Cascabel family one of those modern-taste plays, where all the details of private life are laid in the nude on the stage; where, if crime does not actually triumph, virtue is at times but sparingly rewarded. No, at the closing scene of the "Brigands of the Black Forest," innocence was acknowledged according to the rule, and wickedness met with due punishment under the most convenient form. The police suddenly appeared, just as all seemed hopelessly lost, and when they laid hand on the brigand, the hall broke out with loud cheers.

No doubt about it, the piece would have been written in a simple, powerful, personal style, respectful of grammar, and free from those pretentious neologisms, those documentary expressions and realistic terms of the new school,—if it had been written. But it was not written any more than spoken, and hence it could be played on all the stages, as on all the trestles, of the two worlds. An immense advantage this is for dumb shows, not to speak of the many errors of grammar and of orthoepy, which are entirely avoided in this kind of literature.

A remark has been made above anent the style of drama that should not be expected from the Cascabel family. The simple fact is that Cæser Cascabel himself was the composer of the particular masterpiece in question. "Masterpiece" is the word, since, adding up the old world with the new, it had been played three thousand one hundred and seventy-seven times! And he had so contrived it as to bring out in striking relief the special talents of the individual members of his troupe, talents so varied and so real that no such galaxy of artists had ever been presented to the public by the manager of any company, whether stationary or itinerant.

The masters of the contemporaneous drama have very justly laid down the principle: "On the stage you must always make your audience laugh or cry, or else they will yawn." Well, if all the dramatist's art is contained in that axiom, "The Brigands of the Black Forest" deserves to be styled a masterpiece a hundred times over. The spectators laugh even to tears, and weep—to tears likewise. There is not a scene, nor part of a scene, where the most heedless looker-on experiences the desire to open his mouth to yawn; and should that sensation, perchance, force itself upon him as the result of a dyspeptic affection, the incipient awn would surely be turned to a sob or a chuckle.

Like all well-planned dramas, this one was clear, rapid, simple in its evolution as in its conception. The facts followed each other in such logical succession as to suggest the probability of their having happened in the real world.

Let the reader judge of it by the following necessarily succinct account.

It was the story of two lovers who worshiped each other,—and for convenience sake, let it be stated, right here, that Napoleona was the fair loved one, and Sander was the young swain. But alas, Sander is poor, and Napoleona's mother, the haughty Cornelia, will not hear of the match!

The particularly new point in the plot is that "the course of true love" is, in addition, prevented from "running smooth" by the presence of a long, lanky suitor, Clovy, with pockets as full of gold as his skull is void of brain; and that the mother—here perhaps the author's inventive genius shines forth with more eclat still—the mother, who has an eye to the gold, does not ask better than to give him her daughter.

It would be really difficult to weave a plot more dexterously or to render it more interesting. Needless to say that silly Clovy never opens his lips, but the audience expects him to drop some absurd saying or another. He is ridiculous in his person, ridiculous in his disjointed gait, and has a habit of poking his overgrown nasal appendix everywhere. And when he stalks forward with his two wedding presents, John Bull, the ape, grinning from ear to ear, and Jako, the parrot (the only one of all the artists who speaks in this piece), the effect is side-splitting.

The boisterous laughter soon subsides, however, before the profound grief of the two young people, who can see each other only by stealth.

And now the fatal day has come for the sealing of the union, forced by Cornelia upon her daughter. Napoleona has been decked in the most charming style, but her tearful face is the picture of despair. And truly, it is a crime to give away the pretty little dove to that ugly-looking stork.

All this takes place on the village green in front of the church. The bell rings; the doors are thrown open; the bridal cortege has but to enter. Sander is there kneeling on the marble steps; they will have to trample him under foot. It is heartrending.

Suddenly, a young warrior appears, and the canvas walls tremble at his presence. It is John, the brother of the broken-hearted bride. He is returning from the wars, after conquering all his enemies,—whose names may vary according to the country in which the play is acted, Englishmen in America, Russians in Turkey, Frenchmen in Germany, and so on, ad infinitum.

The brave and affectionate John arrives in the nick of time, and will very quickly settle matters his own way. He has heard that Sander dotes on Napoleona, and that she is equally enamoured of him. Straightway, having spun Clovy around with a twist of his powerful arm, he challenges him to fight, and the half-witted fellow is seized with such a fright that he gladly gives up all claims to his bride.

This will be readily acknowledged to be a well-filled drama, and a lively succession of events. But the end has not come yet.

The repentant bridegroom turns toward Cornelia to release her of her promise. Cornelia has disappeared. There is a general rush in search of her— She is nowhere to be seen!

Presently cries are heard from the depths of the neighboring forest. Sander recognizes the voice of Cornelia, and although his future mother-in-law is in question, he does not hesitate—he flies to her help. Evidently, the proud lady has been kidnapped by Fracassar's band, perhaps by Fracassar himself, the famous brigand chief of the Black Forest.

As a matter of fact, that is precisely what has happened. While John keeps close to his sister to protect her in case of need, Clovy tugs at the church bell and alarms the villagers. A shot is heard—The public pants for breath. It would be hard for the stage to tax the fibers of the human heart farther.

It is at this moment that Mr. Cascabel, in the full Calabrian costume of the terrible Fracassar, appears on the scene at the head of his men, carrying off Cornelia in spite of her masculine resistance. But the heroic youth returns with a brigade of policemen, booted right up to the hip. His mother-in-law is delivered, the brigands are captured, and the happy Sander marries his beloved Napoleona.

It is but right to add that, owing to the small number of the performers, the main body of the brigands never appears on the scene, nor does the full platoon of policemen. On Clovy devolves the task of imitating their various cries and shouts behind the scenes, and he does it so perfectly as to deceive the hearers. As to the captain of the brigands, he has to put the handcuffs on his own hands for want of available supernumeraries. Withal, it could not be repeated too emphatically, the effect of this finale—thanks to its eloquent rendering—is extraordinary.

Such then was the offspring of Cæser Cascabel's mighty brain, which was about being played at the circus of Perm. Certain it was of its usual success, provided the interpreters should be up to the standard of the piece.

Generally speaking, they were so: Mr. Cascabel was as terrible as any bandit could look; Cornelia was infatuated with her noble birth and fortune; John, a true knight (old style), Sander very sympathetic, Napoleona such as would move the heart of a stone.

But, it must be confessed, the Cascabel family was not up to its habitual merry pitch on this occasion. Sad looks and sad hearts were the order of the day; and on the "histrionic boards," what would become of the necessary spirit? The play of the features would be uncertain, the gesture-replies would not be given with the required clearness. Perhaps the tearful episodes might be more life-like since everybody felt inclined to weep; but whenever fun and frolic held their court, the piece was likely to prove, as its author had said, a painful fiasco.

The noon-day meal was laid on the table. At the sight of the still vacant chair,—bitter foretaste of the approaching parting,—the general gloom became more intense, if possible. Nobody was hungry, nobody was thirsty. There was more than enough to exasperate the meekest of managers. Cascabel could not stand it, and he would not if he could. He had eaten as much as four navvies and drank in proportion. Why should others act differently?

"Now then!" he exclaimed. "Is this going to last much longer? I see nothing but faces as long as my arm, all around the table; to begin with you, Cornelia, and end with you, Napoleona. Why, Clovy is the only one whose face is about half admissible! Now I won't have that, I say I won't have it, at all! I must have cheerful people about me! To-night everybody must act his part with a smile on his face, and put plenty of 'go' into it, and bring down the house! I say everybody must—or, by the blood of my fathers—!"

This was the ne plus ultra of Cascabel's wrath, and whenever he uttered the fearful threat, the hearers knew there was nothing left them but to obey.

This terrific explosion, however, had in no way interfered with the bringing forth of a new idea in the fruitful brain of the said Cascabel, an event of habitual occurrence in all critical circumstances.

He had resolved on complementing his play, or rather in adding to the strength of his mise en schie; in what manner will be known forthwith.

It has been said that, hitherto, for lack of hands, the brigands and their pursuers were wisely kept out of sight. The brigand Fracassar-Cascabel was a host in himself. Still, he thought very judiciously that the piece would be more effective if there was a general muster of all the actors in the drama, in the final scene.

He should see to recruiting a few supers for this occasion. And, as good luck would have it, had he not Ortik and Kirschef just at hand? Why should these two "honest sailors" decline to play the part of highwaymen?

Before he left the stormy dinner-table, he explained the situation to the former, and added:

"How would you two like to take a part in the performance as robbers? You would render me a real service, friends!"

"Why, of course!" said Ortik. "I don't ask better, nor Kirschef, either; do you, mate?"

Kirschef assented at once, it being naturally the interest of the two ruffians to be on the best terms with their hosts.

"That's all right, then, my friends," continued Mr. Cascabel. "Besides, you will only have to come on with me when I appear on the scene, just at the winding up, and you'll have to do just like me: roll your eyes around, throw your arms and legs about, and roar with rage. You'll see: it's the easiest thing out! I'll bet a hundred to one you'll make a prodigious hit!"

Then, after a moment's thought:

"By the way, the two of you will only make two brigands. That's not enough. No, for Fracassar had a whole gang under his orders. If I could get five or six more men, the effect would be grander! Mightn't you find me, round about the town, a few 'disengaged gentlemen' who would not say 'no' to a good bottle of vodka and a half rouble?"

Ortik cast a furtive glance toward Kirschef.

"Most likely we might, Mr. Cascabel. Last night, at the tavern, we met half a dozen fellows."

"Bring them, Ortik; fetch them here this evening, and my dénouement is A 1!"

"That's a bargain, sir."

"Very good, my friends!—What a performance this is going to be! What a sensation for the public!"

And when the two sailors had got quite out of sight, Mr. Cascabel was seized with such a fit of irrepressible laughter that several of his vest-buttons were shot about in the little room.

Cornelia feared he might go into convulsions.

"César, you should really not laugh in that way so soon after eating!" she said to him.

"Cornelia, my dear—did your husband smile? Why, I am in no mood for doing any such thing!—If I did, it was unknown to myself. At heart I am truly grieved! Just think of it! Here it is, one o'clock! And our good Mr. Sergius is not back yet! And he won't be in time to make his début as the prestidigitateur of the troupe, either! Could anything be more unlucky!"

And while Cornelia returned to her dresses, he walked out, merely remarking he had some few indispensable errands to go on.

The performance was to commence at four o'clock,—a saving of artificial light, the apparatus for which was sadly deficient at the Perm circus! In any case, was not the bloom on Napoleona's cheeks fresh enough, and her mother's handsome features sufficiently well-preserved to make them boldly face the glare of broad noonday?

It would be difficult to realize the effect produced in the little town by César Cascabel's wonder-telling bill, not to speak of Clovy's big drum, which for a whole hour had filled the streets with its unearthly rattle. All the Russias of the Czar must have been roused from their slumber!

The result was that, at the aforesaid hour, quite a crowd besieged the circus: the governor of Perm, with his wife and children; a certain number of his subordinates, and several officers of the citadel could be seen waiting for the eventful moment, as well as a quantity of small traders, brought to town by the fair; in a word, an enormous concourse of people.

At the door the musical element of the troupe was in full force and vigor: Sander, Napoleona, and Clovy were there, with French horn, trombone and tambourine; and Cornelia, in flesh-color tights and pink skirt, presided at the drum. The discordant pandemonium was only fit for moujiks' ears!

Nor should César Cascabel's powerful voice be forgotten, calling out in good and intelligible Russian:

"Take your seats! Take your seats, ladies and gentlemen! It is forty kopecks per seat—without any distinction! Now is the time to go in!"

And as soon as the ladies and gentlemen had taken their seats on the benches of the circus, there was an eclipse of the orchestra, the members of which had now to take their several parts in the evening's program.

The first part was gone through without a hitch. Little Napoleona on the tight-rope, young Sander in his contortions, the clever dogs, the ape and the parrot in their drolleries, Mr. and Mrs. Cascabel in their displays of strength and of skill, obtained a real success. Of the warm applause bestowed on such deserving artists John also had his share. With his mind elsewhere, his hand may not perhaps have done full justice to his talent as an equilibrist. But this was detected by none but the master's eye, and the public never dreamt that the poor fellow was far from being heart and soul in his work.

As to the human pyramid, which preceded the interlude, it was unanimously encored.

In truth, Mr. Cascabel's verve and humor in presenting his artists, and looking around for the ever-ready applause they merited so well, had been astounding. Never had this superior man shown to a greater extent how far a determined nature can master its own self down. The honor of the Cascabel family was safe! Its name would be handed down among the Muscovites with every token of admiration and respect.

But, if the spectators had followed the first half of the program with interest, how impatiently they looked forward to the second! Nothing else was spoken of, the whole length of the entr'acte.

It lasted for ten minutes,—ample time to take a mouthful of fresh air out-of-doors,—then the crowd flowed in again, and not a vacant seat was left.

Ortik and Kirschef had returned, a full hour since, with a half dozen supers, who—the reader has guessed—were, of course, the former companions they had met in the Ural pass.

Mr. Cascabel made a careful survey of his new force.

"Good heads!" he remarked. "Good faces! Well built frames! Too candid a look, perhaps, for highwaymen! Well, with wigs à la hedgehog style and beards to match, I'll make something of them!"

And as he did not come forward till the very end of the piece, he had all the time necessary to do up his recruits, rig them up, dress their hair,—in a word, turn them out as presentable brigands.

And now, Clovy gave the three knocks.

At this moment, in a properly fitted theater, the curtain rises as the last note of the orchestra dies away. If it did not rise this time, it is because it is in the nature of circus rings not to have a curtain, even when they are transformed into stages.

At the same time, let it not be imagined that there were no "properties," at least in appearance. On the left, a large cupboard, with a cross painted on its door, represented the church, or if you like the chapel, the steeple of which was naturally somewhere behind the scenery! In the center lay the village green, portrayed to life by the sandy ring! To the right, a few shrubs in wooden boxes, skilfully displayed, gave a sufficient idea of the whereabouts of the Black Forest.

The piece opened amid the deepest silence. How pretty Napoleona looked, with her little striped skirt, slightly aged, her "love of a hat" laid just like a flower on her fair head of hair, and above all, her eye so innocent and soft. The first lover, Sander, in a tight-fitting orange-colored vest, considerably faded in the creases of the sleeves, told her his tale of love with such affectionate looks that no spoken language could have been more eloquent.

But, how to describe, in a fitting manner, the apparition of Clovy, with his absurd wig of fiery-red hair, stalking in, and pointing his legs like stilts, first one here and then the other there; his brainless though pretentious look; his nose foredoomed to carry goggles; and the grimacing ape and the loquacious parrot that followed in his wake!

And now comes Cornelia, a woman who will make a formidable mother-in-law! She pitilessly dismisses Sander, and yet it is easy to feel that under her faded costume there throbs a heart worthy of a matron of the olden days.

Great success for John, when he appears dressed as an Italian carabineer. He is very sad, poor fellow. He looks as if his thoughts were bent on other things beside his part. How much he would prefer to play Sander's, with Kayette for his lady-love, and to have nothing more to do than lead lier to the altar. And what a waste of time all this was, when they had so few hours to be together now!

However, so powerful was the dramatic situation, that it carried away the actor. How could it be otherwise, when we think on it! A brother returning from the wars, dressed as a carabineer, and taking the defense of his sister against the haughty prejudices of a mother and the ludicrous aspirations of a fool!

Superbly grand the scene between John and Clovy. The latter trembles with terror, and to such an extent that his teeth are heard to chatter, and his nose grows visibly longer and longer, until it suggests the idea of the point of a sword, that would have entered by the back of his head and would make its way out in the middle of his face.

Just then, cries, loud and repeated, are heard behind the scenes. Young Sander, carried away by his bravery, or perhaps bent on suicide,—for life is now a burden for him,—plunges into the thick of the forest of stage shrubs. The wild echoes of a violent struggle reach the audience, then the report of a gun.

And Fracassar, the leader of the brigands, bounds upon the scene. He is truly terrific, with his pink lights almost turned white, and his black beard well-nigh grown red. His fiendish gang follow in his footsteps. In their midst are Ortik and Kirschef, whom no one could know under their wigs and make-up. Cornelia is seized by the terrible chief. Sander rushes to defend her as usual,—and here it seems as though the customary dénouement will be spoilt on this occasion, for the situation has assumed a different aspect.

Hitherto, when Mr. Cascabel represented the whole band,—single-handed, —John, Sander, their mother, their sister, and Clovy himself, were in a position to keep him in check, waiting for the police, who were "pointed to" as coming in the distance behind the "properties." But, here was Fracassar, supported by eight real, flesh and bone, visible-to-the-naked-eye ruffians, whom it would be very hard to overpower. And there was every reason to ask how the whole thing would end, so as to keep within the limits of naturalness.

Suddenly, a platoon of Cossacks invade the circus ring. Who could have expected so providential an issue!

The truth was, that manager Cascabel had spared no trouble to give his performance the most extraordinary eclat, and the dramatis personae were all there to a man. Policemen or Cossacks were all one, as a matter of course. In the glance of an eye, Ortik, Kirschef, and all their companions are thrown to the ground and firmly pinioned,—this, the more easily, as it was their part to let themselves be captured after a mere show of resistance.

And now a voice is heard above the din:

"Not me, thank you, my brave Cossacks! These fellows, as long as you like; but I am not in that swim,—not I—only for fun!"

Whose voice is that? Why, it is that of Fracassar, or rather Mr. Cascabel, who now stands up, a free man, while his men, duly handcuffed, are in the power of the authorities.

And was this a reality?—It was; and this had been the latest of César Cascabel's grand ideas. After engaging Ortik and his associates in his troupe, he had communicated with the Perm police and had told them of a splendid haul to make. This explains the opportune appearance of the Cossacks, just as the dénouement of the piece required their presence; the masterly stroke had been a complete success; the whole band of malefactors were wriggling in vain in the net of their captors.

But presently Ortik was on his feet, and pointing Mr. Cascabel to the captain of the Cossacks:

"I denounce that man to you," he cried. "He has brought back a political convict to Russia! Ah, you have betrayed me, you cursed rope-dancer; well, I betray you in my turn!"

"Betray away, my friend!" quietly replied Cascabel, with a knowing wink.

"And the convict he brought back is a runaway from Iakoutsk fortress; his name is Count Narkine!"

"Quite true, Ortik!"

Cornelia, her children, and Kayette, who have gathered around, stand speechless with terror.

At this moment one of the spectators rises from his seat—it is Count Narkine.

"There he is!" yells Ortik.

"That is so! I am Count Narkine!" answers Mr. Sergius, unmoved.

"Yes, but Count Narkine amnestied and free!" exclaims Mr. Cascabel, with a heroic peal of laughter.

What an effect on the public! The strongest minds might well be unhinged by all this reality mingled with the fiction of the play! Indeed, a portion of the beholders may have gone home with a confused idea that the "Brigands of the Black Forest" had never wound up in any other way.

A few words will suffice to explain.

Since the time when Count Narkine had been picked up by the Cascabels on the Alaskan frontier, thirteen months had elapsed, during which he had had no news from Russia. How could it have reached him among the Yukon Indians or the natives of Liakhov? He was, therefore, unaware that six months ago a ukase of Czar Alexander II had amnestied all the political convicts in the same category as Count Narkine. The prince, his father, had written to him in America that he might now return home in safety; but the count had already left the country and the letter had been returned to the sender. The anxiety of Prince Narkine, when he ceased to hear from his son, can well be imagined. He lost all hope, thought him dead, perhaps, in exile. His health declined and he was in a critical state, when one night Mr. Sergius arrived at the chateau. What untold bliss it was for the prince to see his son again, and announce to him that he was a free man once more!

The count, naturally unwilling to leave his father after a few hours' interview, had sent a letter to Cascabel, telling him that everything was now all right, and that he would not fail to be at the circus for the second part, at least, of the performance.

It was then Mr. Cascabel had conceived the glorious idea that the reader knows, and had taken measures to "net" Ortik and his whole gang.

On hearing the explanation of the final scene, the spectators grew wild with delight. Vociferous hurrahs burst out on all sides, and a storm of indignant curses accompanied the brigands on their way out under the safe escort of their captors.

Mr. Sergius, too, needed to be told the secret of this capture: how Kayette had discovered the hideous plot against him and the Cascabels; how the young woman had risked her life in following the two sailors into the wood on the night of the 6th of July; how she had told all to Mr. Cascabel, and how the latter would not breathe a word of it to Count Narkine or to his own wife.

"A secret from me, César; a secret?" asked Cornelia, in a would-be reproachful tone.

"The first and the last, wifey!"

She, of course, had forgiven him already.

"You know I did not say it through selfishness. Excuse the word, won't you. Count Narkine?"

"Don't say 'Count Narkine.' Let me always be Mr. Sergius for you, my friends, always Mr. Sergius,—and for you too, my child," he added, clasping Kayette in his arms.

CHAPTER XV - CONCLUSION

CÆSER Cascabel's journey has at last come to an end! The *Fair Rambler* has now only to cross Russia and Germany to get on French soil, and the north of France, to be in Normandy. A pretty long trip, no doubt; but as compared with the ten or eleven thousand miles it has just covered, it is but a trifle, just "a ride you could have in a hackney coach," as Mr. Cascabel used to say.

Yes, it has come to an end, and a better end than might have been expected after so many adventures! Never was there a happier termination,—even in that admirable piece "The Brigands of the Black Forest," the issue of which gave the greatest satisfaction to all parties concerned, save Ortik and Kirschef, who were hanged a few weeks later; and save, likewise, their companions, who were sent off to Siberia for the remainder of their days.

The question of the separation now forced itself on all our friends with all the gloom of its hopeless perspective. How would it be solved?

Well, in a very simple manner.

The very night of the memorable performance, when all the artists had met together in the *Fair Rambler*, Count Narkine said:

"My friends, I am conscious of all that I owe you, and I should be an ungrateful being if I ever forgot it. What can I do for you? My heart bleeds at the thought of parting with you! Now, come, how would it suit you to remain in Russia, to settle and live here on my father's domain?"

Mr. Cascabel, who did not expect such a proposal, thought for an instant:

"Count Narkine—"

"Do call me Mr. Sergius, never any other name—to please me!"

"Well, Mr. Sergius, we are greatly touched. Your offer shows all your kindly feeling for myself and mine. We thank you from our hearts. But, you know, home is home."

"I understand you," interrupted the count. "Yes, I quite feel with you. Well, since you insist on returning to France, to your dear Normandy, I should be very happy to know that you are snug and comfortable in a nice little country house, with a farm, and a few acres of land around you. There you might rest after your long traveling."

"Don't imagine we are fatigued, Mr. Sergius!" exclaimed Cæser Cascabel.

"Come, my friend, speak to me openly. Do you care very much to keep to your profession?"

"Of course, since it is our bread-earner."

"You will not understand me," continued Count Narkine, "and you pain me thereby! Will you deny me the satisfaction of doing something for you?"

"Never forget us, Mr. Sergius," said Cornelia; "that is all we ask of you; for we, on our part, will never forget you,—nor Kayette!"

"Oh, mother!" cried the young woman.

"I can't be your mother, dear child!"

"Why not, Madame Cascabel?" asked Mr. Sergius.

"How could I, now?"

"By giving her to your son as a wife!"

All the effects produced by Manager Cascabel in the course of his glorious career were nothing to that produced by these words of Count Narkine.

John was beside himself with joy, and kissed over and over the hand of Mr. Sergius, who pressed Kayette against his breast. Yes, she should be John's wife, while continuing to be the count's adopted daughter! And John would stay with him as his private secretary. Could Mr. and Mrs. Cascabel ever have dreamt a better position for their son? As to accepting from Count Narkine anything more than the assurance of his continued friendship, they would not hear of it. They had a good trade, they would go on with it!

It is then that young Sander pushed his way to the front, and with faltering voice but beaming eyes, said:

"Why should you go on with it, father? We are rich! We don't want to work for our bread!"

And so saying, he drew out of his coat pocket the nugget he had picked up in the forests of Cariboo.

"Where did you make that out?" asked his father, seizing the precious stone between his fingers.

Sander related how he came by it.

"And you never told us about it?" exclaimed Cornelia. "You have been able to keep such a secret all this time!"

"Yes, mother, although it often teased me. I wished to give you a surprise, you see, and say nothing till we had got home!"

"You are a darling boy!" said Cascabel. "Well, Mr. Sergius, here's a windfall just at the right moment! Look at it, sir! It's a nugget! Real gold. Nothing to do but change it!"

Count Narkine examined the stone attentively, and weighed it up and down in his hand to estimate its value.

284

"Yes," he said, "it is real gold! It weighs at least ten pounds."

"And that's worth?" inquired Cascabel.

"It's worth twenty thousand roubles!"

"Twenty thousand roubles!"

"That's so! And as to changing it, it is the simplest thing in the world. You see, ladies and gentlemen, one, two, three!"

And, prestissimo! the worthy pupil of César Cascabel had substituted for the nugget a well-filled pocket-book, which passed into Sander's hand like a flash of lightning.

"That's splendidly done!" exclaimed the professor. "Had I not told you, sir, you had a wonderful natural aptitude for the art?"

"What is there in your portfolio?" asked Cornelia of the youngster.

"The value of the nugget," replied Mr. Sergius, "nothing more, nothing less!"

And, sure enough, it was found to contain a check for twenty thousand roubles on Rothschild Brothers of Paris.

What was the intrinsic value of the nugget? Was it a lump of gold or a vulgar stone that young Sander had so conscientiously brought home all the way from the Columbian Eldorado? This will never be known. The Cascabels were, of course, obliged to take Count Narkine's word for it, and trust to the friendship of Mr. Sergius, which, in their eyes, was a more precious treasure than the wealth of His Majesty the Czar.

The Cascabel family remained in Russia for one month longer. The Perm fair and the Nijni fair were now laid aside; but could father, mother, brother, and sister have taken their departure before witnessing the wedding ceremony of John and Kayette! It was celebrated in great pomp at the chateau of Walska, and never was a young couple united midst a concourse of happier people.

"Eh, Cæser? What, do you think?" said Cornelia, nudging her husband as they came out of the manorial chapel.

"Just what I said all through!" he replied.

A week later, both of them, with Sander, Napoleona, and Clovy,—who must not be forgotten, for he was really one of the family,—took leave of Count Narkine, and started for France with the *Fair Rambler*, but by rail this time, and by fast train, if you please!

Mr. Cascabel's return to Normandy was an event. Cornelia and he became big propriétaires in the neighborhood of Pontorson, and were known to have a nice lump sum laid up for Sander and Napoleona.

Count Narkine, John, his secretary, and Kayette, the happiest of wives, came to see them every year; and of their welcome it were idle to speak.

Such is the faithful tale of this journey, which might be reckoned one of the most surprising in the series of "Extraordinary Travels." Of course all "ends well" and "all is well." What else could have been expected when that good Cascabel family was in question?

The End

Printed in Great Britain
by Amazon.co.uk, Ltd.,
Marston Gate.